Praise for *The Perils of Pa...* from the inbox of Collette

MW00586456

"Dear Collette, I just finished your book and laughed myself silly ... no, sillier. I loved the character of Pauline with all of her strange, neurotic but totally believable behaviors. I saw just a little of myself in her—okay quite a bit actually. It made me realize I'm not that weird. P.S. When's that sequel coming out??? HURRY!"

Laurie J.

"We met at Ladies Night in Millbrook and were comparing the 'midlife crisis' of your character vs. myself. Pauline wins! I picked up the book on Friday and finished Monday and LOVED it. I can't wait to see what happens next to Pauline. Keep up the good work and I will be watching for each new publication."

Linda L.

"Pauline ... is hilarious! We have both finished experiencing her perils, laughed out loud, and loved the book. Well done! Nicholas still chuckles at the 'pet outsmartant.' I know I'll have to read your novel again to catch more of the quips. I particularly appreciated the contrast between the frenetic pace of Pauline's days/hours/minutes and the glowing atmosphere of peace when she finally makes her getaway a reality. Whew! Finally—the sigh of libidinous resolution. Thanks for sharing so much of yourself with us in Pauline."

Cathy M.

"I just finished your book—it was a scream—I laughed so hard— thank you! Wow, who knew you were so funny and could write so well! I think that you need to do a follow-up book with the same characters."

Annabelle M.

---

1. Previously published under title *The Queen of Cups*

"From the fabulous, striking cover, till the long overdue climax with Michael—thank God, what a release of tension, I enjoyed it thoroughly. Chick Lit is not my usual fare, though I did read the Bridget Jones books and enjoyed them thoroughly … Plus you are one funny lady. The book is absolutely hilarious."

Karen C.

"I was just talking to my friend Chris who borrowed your book. She loved it so much that she insisted on keeping the car light on so that she could read it coming home from Guelph the other night!"

Karen C.

"I loved the book and I am not sure if I can wait for the sequel. (Please hurry.)"

Donna L.

"Your book is delightful. Valerie and I have been reading it together—or, rather, Valerie has been reading it to me, and we have both been laughing out loud. It's hilarious and sharp."

Bruce P.

CHAPTER 1

Burn Notice

Burn Notice: An official statement by one intelligence agency to other agencies, domestic or foreign, that an individual or group is unreliable for any of a variety of reasons.—Department of Defense Dictionary of Military and Associated Terms

Stupid Friday meetings: two down, one to go. I peek at my watch and resist the urge to drum my fingertips on the table. The Employee Engagement meeting went way over, as usual, and overlapped the Supervisors Sharing the Vision session, so I've missed lunch again. The managers here love pointless events, committees, and meetings.

The Associate Director of Something or Other drones on and on. His only job around here, I'm pretty sure, is to make all meetings run longer. The second he shuts up, I gather my briefcase, my laptop, and a teetering stack of file folders into my arms, and rush to the elevator. Rushing is difficult while wearing a pencil skirt and heels, but today's Quarterly Update Meeting requires polish. Oh, and it began five minutes ago. I was up all night practicing for my presentation. This is going to be good. All my numbers are up this quarter. I even splurged from my own pocket to have the report professionally designed and bound.

I'm in luck: my assistant, Daria, is standing near the doors of the boardroom talking to a middle manager from human resources. I hurry over to her. "Could you please run these files up to my office and FedEx the orders?"

"Sure." Daria lifts the stack from my arms and turns away quickly.

"Wait up," I say, as I hold up my report. "Thanks again for a terrific job. You're the best."

Daria ducks her head, all modest, and wheels off to the elevators. Thank God for Daria. She's a fast learner, and the best second-in-command I've ever had. I slide into my seat in the boardroom as the Director of HR jogs in, all blinged out for the weekend, wearing the Wifi-Robes solar-powered Global Positioning Vest and the matching Wi-Fiber hiking shorts from our high-end summer lineup. He clears his throat loudly into the mic to get our attention. "Wifi-Robes needs to reduce duplication through the timely repurposing of resources. A challenging decision has been made to reposition the human inputs in this unit outside the structure."

We're being dumped. Jaws drop across the room as the pink slips are passed around. The DHR's assistant presses an envelope into my hands. Wait a minute. Rewind. This meeting was supposed to be a quarterly update. What about my presentation? I don't understand.

Gordo, a grey-haired guy from sales, removes his glasses and rubs his eyes, his face white. Next to me, Jen, from accounting, begins to sob out loud. She's pregnant. She and her husband just bought a house. What if they lose their home? How will they pay for the diapers? I lean over and give her a hug while glaring at the DHR. Someone passes around a box of tissues. I shove it along the table, and pause to straighten my neck, back and shoulders. This helps to force the lump in my throat to go back to where it came from: an old army trick Dad taught me a long time ago, two days after graduating from high school and just before I headed off for basic training. He said, *A good soldier displays tenacity and mental toughness during stressful situations.* When he died six months ago, he left me my final orders: *Eyes front, soldier. Close ranks, MARCH.*

When a grizzled old Master Sergeant barks an order, you do it without question. I've been a civilian for ten years now, but I can still muster up the right stuff when the going gets tough. Once a soldier, always a soldier.

Lump dispatched and shoulders squared, I open my envelope. There it is, a letter of termination, addressed to me. Lasered clearly in black ink is my name, *Parril, Pauline.* The notice is dated and signed by the DHR himself. There has to be a mistake. I'm the company materials consultant. All my former army training went into the design of that head gerbil's ridiculous hiking shorts. And the GPS vest—it actually repels mosquitoes electronically. Cutting edge stuff. Because of me, that rodent could go to battle in his swimming trunks if he wanted to.

The DHR outlines termination policy and procedures, but who can listen? Jen is texting away, probably to her husband. Gordo slumps, slack-jawed in his seat. I sit up straighter. *Eyes front, close ranks, MARCH.*

At last we are free to stumble back to our offices with glossy, four-color guides to the employment agency that will help us find new jobs. But there's nothing glossy about the skeletal severance package they handed us. We've been ordered to clear out our desks immediately. As I step from the elevator on my floor, I spy Daria coming out of my office.

She spots me and speed-walks away in the opposite direction, disappearing into the staff room at the far end of the hall. I clue in: Daria isn't rushing off to mourn me in the ladies' room. I'll bet my last paycheck she's running away from me because she gnawed off my job with Wifi-Robes's blessings. She'll be offered a tiny increase, and they'll get the equivalent of me for way less money.

My desk is buried under a sliding mountain of fabric samples, catalogs, reports, and file folders. Where to start? Dropping into my chair, I stare at the blinking light on my phone. One of my favorite clients is calling. I stare at the digital display until the light stops blinking and then I stare at the wall, the window, the floor, and the computer. Is this real life? I'm not sure. My head feels woozy. I attempt to sign in. My password no longer works. I try to phone Donald but the call goes straight to his voicemail. "Call me," I say.

I collect my personal stuff first: my *Team Player of the Year* plaque, a Pottery Barn coffee mug, and an outdated framed photo of Donald and the kids. Donald had more hair back then. He's taken to shaving his head lately, a style which makes him look fierce and athletic, like a Mohawk brave; he can boast of a native twig or two way back in his family tree, but mostly he's an English-Irish-Scottish Canadian, transplanted from the untamed wilds of Quebec to staid old Dingwall city, here in the well-trod Greater Boston area. I like that field and stream look, all rugged and dangerous with plenty of throw-down factor, (i.e., pick me up and throw me down on the bed). I would never tell him or his big head might billow, which would not be a useful bedroom look.

Inside the frame, the kids' innocent little faces smile at me. They're in for disappointment. The May long weekend is coming up, which means summer is right around the corner. Jack has been begging for a trampoline, and Olympia wants a bigger splash pool. No job, no new summer toys. No new anything.

As I open my desk drawer, a beefy security guard shuffles past my door. Wifi-Robes is making sure no one snakes off with the laptops, rolodexes, and other valuable consolation prizes.

I fill a stack of boxes with my personal files, binders and contacts, and haul them one by one out to the parking lot. Another security guard looks on from the shade of the building entrance, arms folded, as I stuff my bulging boxes into the Jeep. The late afternoon sun scorches the back of my neck. My blouse is drenched with sweat. Climbing in, I turn the key, roll down all the windows, and turn the fan on high. I try to take a deep breath, but my chest feels tight.

The dashboard clock reminds me that I'm running late. By now the kids are waiting for me at their After School Program, wondering where I am.

I better call to let the school know I will be later than usual. I'm in luck—I forgot to hand in my company phone, which is still lying amidst the crumbs at the bottom of my purse.

Of course the batteries are dead. I can hand it in and call the school from reception. I head back toward the entrance, arriving in time to see the guard turn his back on Gordo, who struggles to open the door, arms clutching a stack of boxes. I hurry to help carry Gordo's load to his car. I wish him well and head back to the building but my feet no longer obey me. I can't bring myself to step across the threshold one more time. I don't want to go back into the building. Ever. Again. I walk back to the car. In the glove compartment, I find the charger, plug in the phone and press the ON button; right away the phone emits a strangled whine and smoke begins to curl from the ports. I yank the plug out. Too late: the phone and the adaptor are fried leaving an acrid burnt-lead bad-for-the-lungs smell in the air.

Choking, I grab a file folder from one of my boxes, and try to fan the smoke out of the Jeep. The folder falls apart in my hands, and all its contents slip-slide onto the floor. I blink, hard. *A good soldier. Tenacity. Mental toughness.* I slam-shift through the gears and, as I accelerate through the parking lot, I tip the phone, still smoking, out the window beside the CEO row.

The highway is jammed with RVs and SUVs towing boats and trailers. The whole universe is going off to the beach or a cottage for the weekend to take advantage of this summery weather. I can't wait to get home and tell Donald my awful news. Maybe he'll make me one of his famous Triple Bloody Caesars in Olympia's beach pail. We could set up the old Adirondack chairs in the kids' sandbox and bury our toes together.

Dammit. The driveway is empty. Donald isn't home yet. The kids dash out of the car and run into the house while I unload my boxes of files into the garage. I'll stack them on the workbench for now, in front of Dad's big old Cadillac. A few weeks after he died, Mom handed me the keys, and said, "Daddy wants you to have it. It's way too big for me."

I love the smell of the leather seats, the baby blue paint-job and the shiny chrome fenders. Donald insists that I keep it even though it costs a small fortune to insure it and run it. I guess now I'll have to cancel the insurance, and keep it parked, at least until I find a new job. *A new job.* The thought sends a ripple of barely suppressed rage up and down my spine. I slam the box of files onto the workbench so hard it teeters and falls over. *Steady there soldier,* Dad whispers into my ear.

The space under the bench is stuffed with cans of old paint, plus an ancient desktop computer and printer. A decade's worth of defunct tools and electronics are heaped on shelves that rise high into the rafters. Why do we keep this trash? Maybe now that I'm jobless, I'll have time to tunnel through this K2 of clutter. Yes. That's what I'll do. Our garage will be the envy of the neighborhood. Maybe I should start a new business: I could call myself the Garage Whisperer. Might as well start right now.

I pull a box down from a shelf, and spy the hairy hind end of a fat grey spider scuttling into a crevice. Okay, maybe I'll whisper into the cobwebs another day. I shove the box back but something gets in the way. It's Donald's bag of fencing equipment. He used to be pretty good with a sword. On one of our very first dates, he taught me how to feint and dash, parry and lunge. Those dates with Donald were always fun. Back when we met, he was into everything: lacrosse, debating club, rowing on a team at the university.

Donald's lacrosse stick is abandoned in the corner of the garage along with his bike. Now all he does is obsess over work and, when he isn't working, he reads books with titles like *Sustainable Corporate Governance* and *Equity Leverage A to Z.* I shove Donald's stuff back into place to make more room for the box, and head into the house.

The kids are parked in front of the TV watching cartoons. Good. Let them. I feel way too scattered to take them to the park or help them find something better to do. I wander into the kitchen where I'm greeted by Donald's voice on the answering machine: "Hi, it's me. I tried to call you. My meeting's going over. Sorry. I'll try again later."

"Later" means 10 p.m. given the way things are going recently at Doubles Group Financial, Doubles being the key word. Donald's hours at the firm have doubled lately; he keeps saying things will ease up after the new Double-Double campaign winds down. Yeah, right. I try to call him back but all I get is his voicemail. Where is he? I'll microwave a few hot dogs for the kids. I'm not that hungry. Standing in front of the cupboard, I grab a handful of Ritz crackers and gobble them down. Who would blame me if I fix the kids up with a movie and popcorn, and nip across the road to Bibienne's house for a quick drink?

I step out my front door to find my next-door neighbor standing at the edge of his lawn, staring across at our yard, his lips compressed into a frown.

"Is everything okay, Lewis?"

"Your water sprinkler is too close to my property line."

"How so? It's on my lawn."

"When you water your lawn, my driveway is getting sprinkled."

I know better than to argue with Lewis. "Okay, no problem, I'll position the sprinkler further away."

I better not mention the sprinkler issue to Donald or he might freak out. Over the years, Lewis has complained about the height of our grass (too long), the color of our grass (yellow) and the condition of our grass (weedy). He also demands that we cut down our shady maple and repaint our porch.

The mature maples lining our street are the best feature of this old sprawling suburb with big front porches and quiet cul-de-sacs. Lewis chopped down all his trees last year, citing the aggravation of leaves choking his gutters.

Our grass is admittedly scruffy but that's because last month Donald spot-sprayed it with a home-brew of salt and vinegar to kill the crabgrass and clover, and ended up pickling the grass instead. He dug out the worst scorched areas and laid pieces of new sod, so now the lawn has bright green patches interspersed with the weedy yellow parts and the dead brown bits. Now all the neighborhood kids like to come over to play The Floor is Lava on our front lawn. The green bits are safe. Step outside them, you die.

I hurry down the sidewalk to Bibienne's where boring lawns go to die and reincarnate as boisterous perennial gardens full of day lilies, climbing honeysuckle, and chrysanthemums. Hummingbirds chase butterflies through pink and purple peonies as I go around the side to her garden doors only to find an abandoned wheelbarrow. Odd. Usually Bibienne is outside pruning her roses on a day like this.

One of the doors is ajar so I rap on the frame and step inside. I love Bibienne's roomy kitchen: an inspired mix of antique cabinets fitted with granite countertops. A cook's dream but nothing's cooking here. Beyond the kitchen, in the family room, I spy Bibienne reclined on the couch watching TV, legs stretched out and crossed at the ankles on the oversized ottoman in front of her. Without taking her eyes from the screen, she frowns at me while laying her palm on top of her head, as if to hold down her thick auburn hair, which is gathered away from her face in a hasty French twist. She raises a warning finger to her lips. Camilo Villegas and Adam Scott are playing so I know enough to remain silent until the next commercial break, when she turns her cool green eyes on me. I've interrupted men's tennis so this better be good.

"I've been fired. My assistant, Daria, stole my job."

"Oh. Okay." She gets up from the couch and pats my shoulder. "I'll make you a drink."

I nod and follow her to the kitchen. I'm safe. I can stick around and watch tennis with her as long as I don't make too much noise.

"I have ChocoLee chocolates, too." She drops ice cubes into tall glasses and fills them with red wine and lime soda. What luck. Bibienne always drinks Spanish wine cocktails and breaks out the chocolate when Villegas is winning.

Bibienne watches the end of the match with her lips parted and her hand across her heart. After the final point, she turns off the TV, fans her cheeks and sighs. "Él está bueno. Oh well, come see my new laptop. You can try it out while I top us off."

The connection is lightning fast. I wish I had ripped-speed access to the Internet. Bibienne sets my glass at my elbow and peers over my shoulder. "Career Search Australia?"

"Yeah. Look. They need a snake wrangler in Canberra. Wait a minute, there's an opening at the Bikini Car Wash."

I click around. There are a zillion postings for jobs all around the world, from San Francisco to Shanghai. Even Kalamazoo has a raft of listings. Here, in the greater suburbs of the Boston Commonwealth, not so much. Unless I want to commute all the way into the city, like Donald does when he isn't at the branch office here in town. Since Doubles got so busy, he has to go into the city more often than not these days.

Forget job searching for now. Bibi has a collection of fun apps on her desktop. I click on a Tarot icon. "Is this site any good?"

"Yes, it's one of the best," she says. "If you want a quick reading, try the Celtic Cross spread."

Bibienne knows a lot about tarot. She's so sharp and perceptive, her massage therapy clients are always asking her to read their cards for them.

I type in my question: What does the future hold for me?

The results show the Queen of Cups, seated in the auspicious Position One, which represents the "Questioner in Her Present Situation."

"The Queen of Cups is the good woman card," says Bibienne. "She's loving and kind. A bit of a dreamer, distracted. But see? She sits on a throne, which means she wields power and makes the rules. The suit of cups represents emotions. Overflowing emotions, hidden emotions, secrets maybe. Who knows what's in her cup?"

"Bra cups, cups of laundry detergent, cups of wine."

Bibienne points to my glass. "Your cup of wine is empty."

Position Two shows the Three of Swords: a lowly card suggestive of trickery and betrayal. "That would be Daria and WiFi-Robes," I say as Bibienne refills my glass and sits beside me.

"Could be." She examines the spread. "The Three of Swords usually represents sudden heartbreak or betrayal. But look over here. Your Three is countered by the Two of Swords, which means difficult decisions may need to be made. That's a double whammy.

See the blindfold on the woman in the picture? She can't see her way. She may not want to see, in fact, she may be in denial."

It all makes sense. I've been betrayed, lost my job, and now I have to make choices about what to do next, right? More curious though is the appearance of the powerful and authoritative Emperor standing in opposition to my Queen. Donald perhaps? But, if the Emperor is my husband, who is the Knight of Cups occupying the near future position? The Knight of Cups is a man of high romance, poetry, and passion. Here, Donald doesn't spring to mind. How intriguing: the card drawn for the position representing Final Outcomes turns out to be The Lovers. As I wander back home I can't help but note that two cups makes a couple.

In the kitchen, the answering machine is blinking. I press play: Donald is going out with some work buddies for drinks.

What? He's still in the city? Again? If this is anything like last time, he might as well have added, *don't wait up*. He better not miss his train this time.

My shoulders are sore this morning from falling asleep on the couch in front of the television. I woke up in the middle of the night and went up to bed to find Donald, naked and snoring on top of the covers with the lights on. Throwing a blanket over him, I snapped off the lights and climbed under the covers. Donald rolled away in the blanket, to his side of the bed.

"Why didn't you wake me when you came in last night?" I ask when he comes down for breakfast, still in his robe, rubbing his eyes. He's unshaven and his eyes are lined.

"It was late. You were sound asleep. I didn't want to bother you."

"It must've been pretty late. I stayed up past midnight." I pour water into the coffee maker. "I tried to call you a bunch of times. You forgot to turn on your cell."

"Did I?"

I turn to face him. The lump pops up in my throat again and I shove it down. "I wanted to tell you something. I got a pink slip yesterday."

"I knew it. Those idiots have been running in the red for a long time."

Tenacity. Mental toughness.

"I lose my job and that's all you can say?"

Donald leans back in his chair. "You were sick of that job anyway. Go find another one."

Donald has always had that Canadian stoicism that's comforting and infuriating at the same time.

"Just like that?"

"Sure."

"What about the budget?"

"Didn't you get a severance package?"

"Yes. But no one is hiring now, so close to summer."

"Take some time off then, do something with the kids."

Donald's right. I was fed up with that job. Now I have freedom to do whatever I want, right?

Donald says, "Why not take some time to think about what you want to do next? Maybe you could go into business for yourself?"

"What kind of business?"

Donald shrugs.

"But ... to start my own business, I'll need to do market research, put together funding proposals, write my business plan. In a few weeks, summer starts. How will I ever do all that with the kids underfoot?"

There's the snag: we can't afford day camp blessings on a slashed budget. The reality is that if I don't find something to do very soon, I'm about to be saddled with full-time responsibility for my little darlings.

Maybe Mom will agree to take Jack and Olympia for a week or two over the summer. She might like to have the kids' company; she's been awfully lonely since Dad died. Now all she does is watch golf on ESPN because she likes Phil Mickelson. She talks about Phil all the time. She's even visited his website to check out all the photos. "He's so handsome," she says, over and over. "He looks like your father did when he was younger."

Mom answers the phone, sounding breathless.

"Were you outside in the garden?"

"No."

I tell her I lost my job. There's a silence, and then I hear what sounds like muffled giggling.

"What's so funny? Mom, are you there?"

"Sorry, what did you say about your job?"

"I was let go. Downsized. I was hoping you might be able to help me out with the kids this summer while I look for a new job."

"I'd love to help out. But I'm going away. I've decided to do some traveling. Like that Julia Roberts girl in *Eat, Pray, Love.* But don't you worry, everything will be fine. You'll find a better job."

"Where are you going? Julia Roberts went to an ashram in India. Don't tell me you're going to an ashram in India?"

"Maybe. Sky's the limit, right? I can't talk now, Brian is here."

"Brian?"

"Brian from the golf club. We're partnering today, with another couple. A foursome."

"I'll call you tonight then."

"I won't be in till late. Call me tomorrow. You know, he kind of looks like Phil Mickelson."

Her voice trails off. I can hear sounds of more muffled giggling.

"Mom? Are you there?"

Then, a disgusting sucking, slurping, slobbery noise.

"Yes, well—later."

Moments after I hang up, the phone rings again.

It's a collect call from Serenity, my oldest daughter, who decided last week she hated her high school and wanted to go live with her Dad in Fort Drum. Reluctantly I gave her a bus ticket and helped her pack her suitcase thinking maybe my ex could take a turn at trying to propel her back to school again.

"Guess what, Mom? I got a ride all the way to Flushing."

"Flushing? You're supposed to be in Fort Drum. With your Dad. Where's your father? What kind of ride? What happened to your bus ticket?"

"We decided to save some scrilla and hitchhike. We're going to the Electric Daisy Carnival."

"We? What do you mean hitchhike? What are you thinking? Why aren't you calling from your cell?"

"I lost it. Don't worry. I'm still gonna stop in to see Dad."

Her father, my ex, is a Mountain Infantryman stationed in Fort Drum. He fights insurgents for a living. This is almost funny. No army base in the world can protect him from Serenity.

"But where are you staying?"

"We have a tent. Gotta go now, talk later."

She's gone. Hanging up the phone, I feel panicky at the thought of my 16-year-old daughter hitchhiking across the nation. Should I call the police? Try to track her down? There's nothing in Dr. Spock for this. Where are the useful references on raising extreme, no fear, generation Y-not teens?

Monday morning, Jack emerges from his bedroom, still wearing his pajama bottoms. He scowls. "I hate school. I'm not going."

"You're right," I say. "School can get pretty boring. You can stay home and help me wash windows." An empty threat, as I have no intention of wasting the holiest of holy opportunities, a kid-free day, doing housework.

Jack stomps back into his room. Where's Olympia? There she is, coming down the hall, wearing one of Jack's ratty old t-shirts.

Jack reappears, dressed in shorts. It's a damp overcast day so I hand him his rain jacket. "Sit nicely with your sister on the bus today. No spitting, yelling, kicking, or cussing. Got it?"

A scuffle breaks out in the hall: Jack, enraged at the sight of Olympia wearing his stuff, is attempting to strip her down. "Jack, leave your sister alone. Put your jacket on."

I pause in front of the hall mirror: a few unruly curls float around my head but I don't have time to tie them back. I'm wearing shorts and my favorite sandals, the cute strappy ones with the wedge heels, topped off with my hockey hoodie. Bibienne would say the outfit is a little on the hot mess side, but it'll have to do.

I hustle the kids out the door. There's just enough time to walk them to their bus, which pushes off in less than two minutes.

Halfway down the street, Jack stops pounding on Olympia long enough to say, "I forgot my lunch."

I race home to retrieve his backpack. But, of course, now we've missed the bus.

I pause in the driveway with Jack's backpack in my hand. I cancelled the insurance yesterday but the Caddy is still covered until the end of the month. Lifting the garage door, I beckon the kids. "We're taking Grandpa's car."

Jack and Olympia shout with glee. They love going for rides in Grandpa's big old shiny Cadillac. So do I. We're already singing *If You're Happy and You Know It* as we back out of the driveway. The engine hums in happy unison all the way to the school.

As I wheel out of the parking lot, the sun peeks from behind a bank of clouds. I flip the signal to turn left instead of right. Why not take the long way home? There's a pretty river road where I could take Dad's car for a good run, get the lead out and clear my head a bit. I roll the window down, turn the dial to a good station and prop my elbow out the window like Dad used to do.

The Caddy quits about ten miles into the middle of nowhere.

I'm stuck on the side of a deserted road while, of course, my phone is at home on the kitchen counter. Failed again. Stepping out of the car, I pop the hood and glower at the engine. I poke and prod at various greasy wires and belts while fighting an urge to hurl myself onto my knees to pound my fists into the gravel.

Turning my back on the engine, I lean against the bumper and fold my arms against the morning chill. The road is deserted. What feels like months go by on the muddy shoulder. A raincloud passes overhead. At last, a leather-jacketed motorcyclist pulls over, unbuckles his helmet, leans back on his seat and grins. "Need a hand?"

"Sure do."

The man hops off the bike and removes his helmet, revealing dark curls that graze his collar. He has dark eyes that meet mine in a forthright and open way. Like he somehow knows me. I suddenly feel safe and reassured. I draw in a quick sip of breath, and brush my windswept curls away from my eyes, and back behind my ears. He comes over to stand beside me in front of the open hood.

"Will it turn over?"

"Yes, but it won't kick in."

"*The Furies. All Out, All Game, All Season,*" he says, reading the slogan written under the crossed hockey sticks on the sleeve of my hoodie. "You play hockey?"

"I'm in a fun league with a bunch of my girlfriends. I play defense."

"Are you any good?"

"I can score goals."

"Hmm. I used to play hockey, back in college. Junior varsity. Then I wrecked my knee."

He turns to examine the engine, a good thing, as I'm sure my pupils just expanded three sizes. The man is as hot as a Latin cowboy with those dark romantic eyes, the Byronic kind that inspire lust-laced poetry in college girls. He's wearing tight blue jeans that show off a pair of lean legs, lovely long lean legs that could efficiently straddle a bawling calf and rope it tight. I feel a warning stanza coming on: Good girls don't make passes / at strangers with long lashes.

He leans in deeper to test a belt.

Or at strangers with sensational asses.

While he fiddles with the lucky little engine parts, I surreptitiously try to pick away the grease on my thumb. The man calls out from under the hood: "Are you sure there's gas in it?"

"Oh no." I say, suddenly remembering. "The gas gauge sticks sometimes. I've been meaning to get that fixed."

The man offers to go down the road for a can of gas. After kick-starting his bike—always so damn sexy to watch this maneuver—he points at a spare helmet lashed to the rear rack and says, "Want to come for the ride?"

The last rain-cloud vanishes as the sun floods the sky with brilliance. I'm astride the bike in a flash. Immediately, the regrets flood in: What do I do with my arms? Where do I hold on? Would it be improper to hug the driver, a stranger? As the bike leaps forward, I almost fall off. Losing all my inhibitions, I hold on tight, my nose pressed up against the soft hide of his jacket. The jacket and its owner smell wonderful: a mixture of sun-warmed leather, Ivory soap, and a lemony aftershave lotion.

What a thrill! I'm perched on the back of a magnificent motorcycle feeling the cool wind in my face. The bike is all shining chrome and soft leather seats, its dashing owner all mirrored sunglasses, clean denim, and polished leather boots.

At the gas station, I realize I've forgotten my bag on the seat of the Caddy. "Don't worry about it," the man says as he pays for the gas and lashes the container to the back of the bike.

The ride back out of town is even more glorious as I got the hang of leaning into the curves. In the straight parts the man lets out the throttle, turning the sun-dappled woods beside us into a green and gold blur. We slow down as we cross a bridge over the river, and he reaches back, taps me gently on the leg and points down the embankment. Standing motionless in the shallows at the edge of the water is a Great Blue Heron. He stops the bike on the shoulder and pulls out his camera to take a shot. We walk back onto the bridge and stand side by side together in a contented silence for a few minutes, leaning on the rail watching the river flow under us. For some reason this seems like a perfectly normal and natural thing to do with a stranger in the middle of nowhere.

Too soon, we have to move on and then the ride is over. Once gassed, the Caddy starts up with a healthy roar. The man pats the fender. "Nice wheels," he says whistling gently. He glances up at me. "Gorgeous."

I feel my cheeks grow warm.

"This was my Dad's car. He restored it himself. I helped with some of the body work." I run my hand across the hood. "My father died not long ago. A heart attack. He was here one minute, and then he was gone, just like that."

Why am I telling him this?

The man's brown eyes turn soft with sympathy. "I lost my Dad a couple years ago. I know what that feels like."

For a moment I'm lost in those deep brown pools.

"Wait," I say with a start, "I have to pay you back." I hurry to fetch my wallet from the car and count out the right amount of cash to cover my tab. He hesitates, and then accepts. Then he climbs back on his bike, leaning back a little to buckle his helmet while straddling the seat with those long lean legs.

There's nothing left to do but say, "Thank you." I suppose it's more appropriate than blurting out the thought he's inspired in me: *"Why don't we do it in the road?"*

"Any time," he says. He tips his helmet and rides away.

Home again, I walk in the door to find one of the cats, Bites-a-lot or Scratches, has experienced a hair-ball attack on the hall carpet. While I'm crouched down on my knees, scrubbing cat puke, I can't help but reflect on how my life has become a real whirlwind of excitement.

A few minutes later I catch sight of my rear end in the hall mirror. I twist and turn to try to assess the scope, limit and range of visible butt cleavage. It's been weeks since I hit the gym. I should sign up for that free Pilates class at work. Wait. The reality sinks in. It's Monday morning and I no longer have a job to go to. That means no Pilates. No paycheck. And I have no prospects.

CHAPTER 2

All Appropriate Action

All Appropriate Action: Action taken in self-defense that is reasonable in intensity, duration, and magnitude, based on all the facts known to the commander at the time.—Department of Defense Dictionary of Military and Associated Terms

The headhunter looks about ten years younger than me. He has a faux-hawk and bony hands. On his desk is a programmable power stapler. I've heard about them but have never seen one before. WiFi-Robes never splurged on high-end gadgetry. I should become an employment counselor.

He types my name into his computer.

"That's spelled P-a-u-l-i-n-e, not P-a-u-l-e-e-n."

He crosses out the e-e-n and changes it to i-e-n. "Now," he says, picking up my resume, "Says here you were in the army."

"Yes. Seven years."

"My wife's cousin was in the air force. His name was Allan. Al Anderson—do you know him?"

"No. Don't think so."

"No, wait, he was in the army."

"Well then…"

"He's a weird guy."

"Go army."

"It says here you're a sharpshooter."

"I can shoot an M16. I have specialized training in nuclear, biological and chemical warfare. And I'm a trained Unit Supply Specialist."

"Which means?"

"I know how to keep track of a large inventory. I spent a lot of time handing out foot powder and counting compasses and blankets. And filling requisitions and filing forms. And I can drive a forklift."

"Hmm. After the army, you worked at WiFi-Robes? What did you do there?"

"Ordering and consulting. I know a lot about making survival gear. I sourced out things like the rustproof grommets for stringing hats and jackets. I know where to buy the best kinds of string too."

"What do you see yourself doing next?"

"I don't know. That's kind of why I'm here."

"The first thing you need to know is the employment market has changed. These days, job hunting is super competitive. You have to find a way to stand out in the crowd." He hands me a tip sheet on resume writing and a sheaf of leaflets on structuring a targeted search. Then he ushers me out with a task: to request "information interviews" from prospective employers. That supposedly gets me in the door.

Last week's job search turned up zero leads. This week, already almost half over, is no better. This morning, like every morning, I checked the local online employment listings: all are disappointing. One ad requires me to be fluent in Tagalog and another wants me to pay for my own uniform before I get to bag the groceries. None of them say, "Travel and adventure. Top rates. Internet access. Programmable power staplers."

I've never been out of work in my life. My lip is twitching, signaling the onset of an attack of hives. Antihistamine bottle in hand, I slump on the couch to watch the bumps heaving up on my arms and chest. One hive is threatening to block the vision in my left eye. To calm down, I attempt some creative visualization: but picturing perky little Daria, Gone Grey and Sharper-in-Tooth, is an insufficient pick-me-up. My life has gone flat and stale. I'm 36 years old, out of work and reduced to wearing yoga pants without the yoga. Wednesday used to be hair, salt glow, or pedicure at lunchtime. If Dad were still alive, he'd say drop and give me 50. When I was a kid, he never stood for any sniveling. If I whined, he made me go down to the basement and polish his boots. He taught me how to stand at attention and snap off a crisp salute long before I laced up for basic training. The only time I ever saw my father, the rock-jawed Master Sergeant William Jackson Parril, come close to shedding a tear was the day I was sworn in.

My throat squeezes tight. His heart wasn't supposed to march off the parade square three months after his first pension check.

I would call Mom for advice but she's gone off to the Berkshires with her with her book club girlfriends. She would only tell me to buck up, anyway. Whatever that means. Bucking up sounds kind of raunchy. Now, there's a thought: maybe I could have a love affair.

My lip stops twitching. I'm beginning to warm to the idea. A love affair could be the play therapy I need.

I phone Bibienne to tell her about my self-help scheme.

"You're just bored."

"Maybe. But don't you think any woman worth her salt has at least one romantic affair during marriage?"

"No."

"But you take in stray animals. Why shouldn't I?"

"All my strays get neutered, first thing. And, besides, sex is overrated. I just took a workshop in LomiLomi Hawaiian Temple massage techniques. Excellent for stress release. The clinic will give you a decent discount."

"A massage isn't the same thing."

"I think you need to get away from it all for a bit." Bibi says. "My next client's here, gotta go."

Bibienne is the best massage therapist in town. I should book an appointment. And maybe Bibi's right: Donald and I could at least go away for the weekend—there isn't enough cash in the single income budget for a fancy vacation on Nantucket Island like last year, but we could afford a campout with the kids. A nice campground with all the facilities laid on should be a snap seeing as I aced the basic training on personal survival in the field. I've eaten boil-in-the-bag ham-steak with pineapple for breakfast, and dug my own latrines to capture the results; it's high time I teach the kids how to pee in the woods. I could show them how to set up a proper bivouac site, read a map and compass, and tie a clove hitch—all that good stuff Dad taught me.

No housework, just a few paper plates. After the kids are zipped into their sleeping bags, Donald and I could make out under the stars. We haven't camped or fooled around under the stars for ages. Come to think of it, it's been years since our last camping trip together.

Before Jack and Olympia came, just after we got married, Mom looked after Serenity while we backpacked a section of the Appalachian Trail for a week. We honeymooned those wonderful summer nights away in our little pup tent. Yes. The bush is calling me.

Donald greets my long weekend camping plan with a face that looks sad in a happy sort of way. "Impossible. I can't get away. The new Double-Double campaign launches next week."

"I know this is last minute but it's Memorial Day weekend. We have nothing planned."

"I do. My plan is to work."

"But we haven't done anything with the kids for ages."

"Maybe we can do something in July when school lets out."

I give him the face that looks sad in a mad sort of way.

"Fine then." Donald gives me the face that looks mad in a mad sort of way. He snatches up the phone. "I'll call my boss and quit my job then. We'll go camping."

"I didn't say quit your job. I thought it would be nice to have some family time. I'll take the kids camping myself. Don't worry about it."

Donald softens and comes over to hug me. "Thanks for handling this."

The kids are horror-struck with my camping plan even though I've promised them lakeside swimming and exhilarating hikes through the woods. Jack remains unconvinced: "Camping is lame. Why aren't we going to a real beach? Like Surfside?"

"Lakes have nice beaches too. Camping is fun," I insist.

"Will there be TV?"

"No."

"Playstation?"

"No."

"I'm not going."

I persevere with a wild promise: mouthwatering meals cooked over an open fire. Then I mention the possibilities of sighting small animals of the forest: raccoons, chipmunks, squirrels, etc. Jack runs off to find his slingshot while yelling something about hoping to meet up with bears. Olympia screams and clamps onto my leg: "I 'fraid of bears."

Recalling my own deep-seated fear of large carnivores, I remember a recent news item about a vicious bear attack upon a group of unlucky campers. "Bears are afraid of people," I say, while picturing Olympia being eaten. Cringing, I rush to lie down on my bed, in the throes of a sudden panic attack.

Now I'm horror-struck with my camping plan. The harsh reality hits me: I'm planning to spend the entire long weekend in bear country with two kids. Under canvas. What was I thinking? I'm sunk now. This morning, within minutes of hatching my camping plan, I went online. Now I'm all hooked up with prepaid reservations at a park in the Green Mountains. I also went out and bought a pile of brand new camping equipment, all financed with the severance money from my job. I have a red tent, a red lantern, a red cooler and three red sleeping bags. I've color-bombed our campsite in a rabble-rousing hue sure to fire up all the bears within forty miles of the park. I should've bought a crossbow and some camo.

After performing deep breathing exercises for ten minutes, I'm ready to lift my head from my pillow—until Donald pokes his head into the room to ask if I have any thoughts on dinner. I turn my pillow over to the cool side. Donald, with a cheerful wave of his hand, offers to go for takeout pizza; clearly he's pleased with my camping initiative and the prospect of having the house all to himself for a few days.

I feel bad for snapping at Donald last night over camping. He deserves a proper wifely good-bye before we set out tomorrow. At bedtime, while he's showering, I don my purple bra and panty set, and slather on a slab of my new body lotion that smells like warm toffee and is loaded with tempting slithery goodness. Donald comes into the bedroom and whistles. "Wow. Candles even."

"How many candles can you handle?" I say in my throatiest voice while locking the bedroom door.

He plants a quick kiss on my neck. "Hold on." He sits on the edge of the bed to use his towel to pat the skin dry between his toes. "Is that a new perfume or have you been eating caramels?"

"It's brown sugar body lotion."

"You might want to be careful around ants wearing that stuff," he says dropping the towel, pulling the front of my red silk panties out in a "V" and peeking in curiously while making sniffing noises.

"There're no ants down there. And you might not be going down there yourself if you don't stop snuffling at me like that."

Donald grins at me. "Hey, let's play anteater. You can be the anthill," he says pulling my panties down all the way.

Donald is soon back in the shower. A bit too soon. While he tackled my ants, he seemed distracted.

I toss and turn in the dark long after he falls asleep.

Packing for the camping trip takes most of the day. The kids flip out as I fling a mountain of toys out of the back seat of the Jeep. Both of them demand to take along items like hockey sticks, video games, stuffed animals, and a box of random toys they never touch at home.

"We need the space for the pillows, sleeping bags and our clothes," I say.

"Why do we have to go camping?," Jack yells as Olympia slumps down in the middle of the driveway, howling.

Donald rolls in from work, his face incredulous that we have yet to make it out of the driveway. He helps me carry the last few loads out to the Jeep and then retreats to the den to make a phone call. We push off. After twenty minutes of driving, I remember I've forgotten my wallet on the kitchen table. I race home, retrieve my wallet and pause for a moment to listen to Donald, talking on the phone in his den. His voice is bright, animated, and full of good cheer. When he kissed me goodbye less than 30 minutes ago, it was all poor me's, and shoot-me-nows.

Back in the car, Jack's screaming, "Limpy's putting her feet on me."

"Amn't."

"Get off. You stink."

"No, you get off, I hate you to death."

I rearrange the entire back seat so Olympia can hate Jack to death from behind a wall of pillows and sleeping bags piled between them.

Our estimated time of arrival now coincides with sundown. I hope I can erect the tenting equipment and, most importantly, locate the campground's comfort stations before darkness envelopes us.

We arrive at the park and join the long lineup of vehicles ahead. The sun sinks behind the trees while, all around us, massive SUVs grunt by hauling trailers equipped with TVs, microwave ovens and private plumbing. Pointing out an RV hauling a trailer full of Sea-Doos, I remark to Jack and Olympia: "These people are missing out on the authentic camping experience. Tenting is best."

"The kids in that RV are playing Nintendo." Jack folds his arms across his chest and glares at me.

The campsite is probably very picturesque but it's too dark to tell. The new flashlight won't work. I crash about in the pitch black with the tent poles and pegs, while the kids complain: we're starving and we want to eat right now. Forget the bid for a healthy meal cooked over a crackling open fire. The kids are ecstatic, their impressions of camping profoundly improved by access to unlimited marshmallows and a family-size bag of barbecue potato chips. I'm not sure if my precariously pitched tent, let alone my sagging self, can hold up through the night.

At dawn, with a flourish of tent unzipping, I release Jack and Olympia upon an unsuspecting campground. After tidying the tent, I set up the stove to make pancakes. Soon the aroma of fresh brewed coffee is wafting past my nose. Kicking off my sandals and digging my toes into the warm sand, I settle into my campchair with my steaming mug while the pancakes turn a golden brown in the frying pan. The site is a fabric of enchantment, embroidered with tall pines and thick clumps of yellow and purple wildflowers. A friendly chipmunk chatters at me for a handout from a nearby stump. I toss him a handful of peanuts and watch him stuff his cheeks.

The seams of the enchanted fabric rip apart with the sound of screaming. Olympia has fallen from a tree. I rescue her from the bushes, frantically pat her down for broken bones and apply first aid to her knee while hearing the first rumble of a thunderstorm on the horizon.

The torrent of rain swamps our campsite. I pass the day indoors, in the Visitors' Center, learning about Native American history, while Jack and Olympia swoop around the displays playing hide and seek.

As the tent is soaked through, we're forced to take refuge in the Jeep for the night. I'm tempted to abandon camp and go home but there's the problem of the rash bet I made with Donald: I have to tough out camping for the entire long weekend. The loser has to organize Olympia's next birthday party and the winner doesn't have to attend.

Finally, the monsoon is over. We slog down to the beach. I slather sunscreen on the kids and watch them frolic in the waves. Lying back in my beach chair, I read trampy pulp fiction. Periodically, I reapply sunscreen on the kids and turn a page. Nobody gets burned.

Later we roast hot dogs over the campfire and, again, nobody gets burned. The stars come out and I show the kids how to locate Cassiopeia, the Summer Triangle and the Northern Cross. At bedtime, we call home to say goodnight to Donald but he's out.

"Hey you guys," I say to the kids as they reach for the potato chips and the bag of marshmallows, "you might as well finish those up because we have to go home tomorrow."

Both Jack and Olympia burst into tears, and declare that camping is awesome, not lame at all, never was.

I drive home slowly, holding up traffic so as to time our arrival at exactly three days and not a minute less. Donald, with a glance at his watch, says, "I missed you." He looks tanned and rested.

I try not to display too much glee about winning the birthday party bet only because Olympia is in the room. It remains to be seen how Donald will try to scam his way out of delivering birthday party joys to a dozen six-year-olds.

Obviously Donald went all out yesterday to welcome his camp-worn wife home. There were no dishes in the sink or wet towels on the bathroom floor. He even put fresh linens on the bed. As I eat my breakfast, a wave of tenderness overwhelms me. What a good, dear man he is. While I acted as bear bait, Donald acted like a sensitive new-age guy keeping the hearth tidy and the home fires lit—although, looking around, I can see he didn't make it as far as dusting and vacuuming. The dustballs are piling up in the corners. I better find work soon so I can rehire the cleaning service.

After I get the kids off to school, I haul the vacuum upstairs to start in the master bedroom. The eviction of the bunnies from under the bed proceeds smoothly until a business card jams the vacuum nozzle. Dislodging the card, I toss it into the wastebasket.

Hold up a minute. I snatch it up again and scan the handwriting on the back:

Thanks for lunch! Let's do it again soon ~ L xo
Xo? Scrawled underneath the note is a phone number. The number is different than the one printed on the front of the card, under the name Lindsay Bambraugh, CFP, and the usual Doubles logo and company contact information.

Oh my God. My heart begins to pound. Hard.

Who is Lindsay Bambraugh?

And what is she doing xo'ing under my bed?

My legs feel hollow. I sit on the edge of the bed and turn the card over and over in my hands. Who is Lindsay Bambraugh? Suddenly I remember her, from last year's Doubles company picnic: Miss Leggy Bambraugh, of the grad gift nose job and huge Barbie boobs, waving around her designer purse studded with pink Swarovski crystals.

What's going on here? I need help. I send out an SOS text to Bibienne: *I think Donald's screwing around on me.*

Her text comes right back: *Meet me for lunch at the Greek place.*

I stumble into the restaurant and thrust the card into her hands. "Look what I found."

Bibienne says, "Calm down and let's see what we have here."

She studies the handwriting. "Circles over the 'i's. And look here—lying loops."

My blood boils over. How dare he consort with a woman who makes lying loops?

"What are lying loops?"

"Dishonesty. There's a stinger in the 'a' here too. Very dangerous."

"Do you think I should I confront him?"

"Na-ah. He'll never admit to anything, not unless you get some hard evidence. Who is Lindsay Bambraugh?"

"She's an advisor at Doubles, same as Donald. Definitely a lying loops type."

Bibienne nods her head slowly and says, "This means war."

I tuck the card into my pocket. I need time to think.

CHAPTER 3

Surveillance

Surveillance: The systematic observation of aerospace, surface, or subsurface areas, places, persons, or things, by visual, aural, electronic, photographic, or other means.—Department of Defense Dictionary of Military and Associated Terms

On the way home from lunch with Bibienne, my mind races. War means tactical planning. Do I want open warfare? Underground-style freedom fighting? Shock and awe? Extreme, no-rules warfare is appealing—I could begin with a bonfire of all Donald's belongings on the front lawn. But what if Donald is innocent of nothing but an unrequited lunch and a freak desire to launder sheets?

Even though my stalwart woman's heart knows the dirty, low-down, lying, cheating truth, concrete evidence is required prior to flaming his entire Conan Doyle collection.

However, maybe sleeping with the up and comers is Donald's way of speeding his career flag up the company pole? Maybe I should support Donald in his bid for advancement at Doubles? A promotion means a raise. Think of all the wonderful material benefits. Maybe tomorrow I should go out and buy that gorgeous Ms. Gina suit I've had my eye on? I need something respectable for my job hunt.

Not to mention that this clearly frees me up. So, where is my Knight of Cups? Nowhere in sight, that's where. I might as well forget about empty cosmic promises of dreamboats and concentrate on my nightmarish job search. I haven't landed a single interview and my severance payout is dwindling fast. Fortunately, I have a follow-up appointment with my headhunter this afternoon. He wants to check my progress on my resume.

As soon as I get home, I haul my briefcase from the closet, empty it on the kitchen table, and try to organize the papers into piles. I have at least 20 draft resumes, plus a stack of job listings and applications to fill out. Interspersed throughout are leaflets, notes and lists of addresses and phone numbers.

The counselor wants me to make a list of prospects: progressive companies that offer respectable wages, benefits and advancement opportunities. This part of the research could take forever.

Then, at any time in the process, things may break down. The employer may "resist" the "information interview." Or the company isn't hiring (it's more likely downsizing to the dimensions of a paper clip). If I score an information interview then I'm supposed to follow up with thoughtful thank-you notes to each person I met during the process, including the receptionist who hates my sucky guts by now.

Maybe the army'll take me back. They're desperate enough to take in any crazy broad who's prepared to wear Gortex and sleep in the mud. I'm sure I'm still a deadeye with a rifle and driving a tank's like riding a bike.

Back in the day, I was a first-class soldier. The army wasn't so bad. Basic training is brutal but it's like giving birth; you forget how hard it is. I toughed it out, ran obstacle courses, was gassed, and learned how to crawl around in the dirt—all a textbook preparation for motherhood.

I met Serenity's father during a weeklong war games exercise. Who can resist a man in a uniform? Not I—especially when I'm rubbing up against a burly one in the depths of a snug foxhole. Mistake. Never take off your thong in a foxhole unless you want to wear maternity combats.

But at least I got Serenity. I drag my mind back to the present where the thought of going back into uniform makes me want to throw up.

I stuff all the papers back into my briefcase and drive to the employment agency where the counselor beckons me into his office. I fidget in my chair trying to resist the urge to play with the programmable stapler while he looks over my updated resume.

Soon he shakes his head and leans over the desk to fix me with a serious gaze. "Your resume still needs a lot of work."

"Isn't resume preparation part of your services?"

"Your employer benefit doesn't cover resumes. There is an extra fee for the service depending on what you need." He hands me a glossy brochure. A professional resume costs a grand.

"Have you considered taking one of our employment courses?"

"A course? Like school?"

"We offer a four-week course on resume writing. Or the 12-week one on choosing your career is popular. You'll get a $200 discount if you take both."

"Wait a minute," I say. "What about taking some courses at the university? Maybe I could finish my degree in business administration? That might help pump up my resume."

"Aren't you on the GI Bill?" the counselor asks.

That's it. I'm going straight over to the university to reactivate as a full-time student. VA will pay for it. I'm a veteran, after all, and time is running out for me to use up my benefit.

I drive over to the university, park, and wander around looking for the registrar's office. It's been a long time since I've been on campus: there're not only two new bars, but convenient shopping, too. Dingwall University boasts a gleaming student center complete with banking machines, a variety of retail outlets and a fast food court. The classrooms and library are now tucked well out of the way of hungry student shoppers looking for a quick bite to eat.

Suddenly, I can't wait to begin my scholarly lifestyle: challenging my intellect with cutting-edge treatises, the thrill of classroom discussion and debate, the stimulus of mind meeting minds, the on-campus bars.

I am so last minute with registering for the summer semester, there isn't much left to choose from: the Registrar said I was lucky to snag my seats in Financial Management and Organizational Behavior. To fill up the rest of my slate I had to settle for Modern American Poetry, but at least it will be an easy A. And who could resist Feminist Interpretations of Drumming, and a seminar in Thigh Chi: Walking Meditation?

Donald rolls in from work and greets me in his usual way, a quick peck on the cheek, looking completely innocent, as if nothing has happened. Of course, I have no way of knowing if something has happened by looking at him. If I confront him, he is likely to deny any wrongdoing. Bibienne advised me to lay low and watch out for more clues. For now, the card is stashed in my lingerie drawer.

I don't have a shred of a chance to talk to him anyway: Olympia leaps at Donald as soon as he sets down his briefcase. "Daddy," she shrieks. "We have to plan my birthday party, remember?"

I sit back in my chair and fold my arms across my chest. After all, I won the camping bet fair and square; time for Donald to deliver. Besides, he's never organized a kid's birthday party before: it's high time he took his turn.

Donald opines that perhaps two little friends could pop by after dinner for a slice of birthday cake. "Half an hour is about right for these things, eh?" He looks at me for reassurance.

I look away quickly: it's critical to avoid eye contact in these situations; I wouldn't want pangs of sympathy to cloud my judgment and mess up the thrill of witnessing his final undoing.

Olympia is demanding a major theme party—say, pirates. With at least twenty-five friends. And lots of games. And feasting. And a sleepover. Like all the other kids' parties.

Donald is helpless in the face of birthday buccaneering. He's reduced to begging me for guidance. I want to say, "Did you know there's a dodgy note on a business card tucked under my trashy lace-up camisole at the back of my lingerie drawer?" Instead, I offer a hint to Donald that he could organize a backyard treasure hunt and perhaps Pin the Tail on the Donkey. Donald could be the donkey.

Then, I add, cruelly, "Oh—and don't forget to do the loot bags."
Donald gives me a blank stare. He's doomed. My evil twin pipes
up to suggest that he take Olympia to the mall to settle the selection
of party hats and invitations.

Olympia is requesting drums for a birthday gift. I'm thinking more
in the way of a quiet little watch. I'm diverted from thoughts of quiet
little watches by the sounds of a gunfight and explosives coming from
the driveway. Peering through the curtains, I see Serenity leaping from
the passenger seat of a rusty pickup truck. The front door bangs open
and in bounds my prodigal teenage daughter accompanied by a friend,
two filthy backpacks, and one enormous shaggy dog that appears to
be a cross between a Mastiff and a Cave Bear. The dog heads straight
to the cat food, devouring the contents of both bowls in seconds. Both
cats crabwalk from the room, and scurry upstairs to pee in my shoes as
punishment for this outrage.

Serenity has a pack of cigarettes rolled up in her t-shirt sleeve.
Before I can say anything, she waves her arm in the direction of her
friend: "This is Shae."

Shae sets down a case of beer and grins. Serenity's friend is clearly
in favor of piercings. She has a tattoo of what looks like a necklace of
power tools looping across her collarbones. In fact, her style might
best be described as chainsaw-positive.

I fold my arms at Serenity. "You weren't supposed to be running
around all of New York. I …"

"It was okay, she was safe with me," Shae says, tucking her hands
flat under her belt. Her biceps and triceps are populated with gangs
of sinewy muscles.

Serenity opens the fridge door, grabs four cans of soda and says,
over her shoulder, "Shae has nowhere to live. Her Dad kicked her out
when she came out as a lesbian. She can stay with us for now, right?"

Two pairs of bright imploring eyes blink at me.

"Um. All right. I guess."

Serenity hugs me and yells, "Thanks Mom." They sprint for the
stairs.

"Wait, what about the dog?"

"His name is George Bush," Shae calls back from the landing as George Bush lifts his leg to pee on the kitchen chair.

I shriek, "No, no, no—bad dog," at which George runs away across the kitchen, flops down beside the fridge and shoves his massive bony head between his huge paws with a look of "Sorry, gee whiz, you forget one lousy rule and look what happens."

"Don't look at me like that. You are so going to be living outside, Mister."

As Serenity's bedroom door thumps shut, I shout after them uselessly. "No smoking or drinking in the house, okay?"

A few minutes later Donald and Olympia arrive home hauling bags stuffed with party bling. Donald had so much fun at the mall, his neck muscles are twitching.

"Did you know there's a huge dog in the backyard digging a hole beside the fence? Does it belong to the rusty truck in the driveway?"

"Yes, that's George, Shae's dog. Shae is Serenity's girlfriend. Serenity asked if Shae could stay here for a while because she isn't getting along with her Dad."

"And you said?"

"What could I say? I felt bad for the kid. And if Shae goes, I'm pretty sure Serenity'll take off with her. Then she'll be back out on the streets again. I want her to stay home."

Donald snorts. "It's whatever Serenity wants then?"

"Please don't start on that again." I peek in the bags. "There's a lot of stuff here. How many kids are you letting Olympia invite?"

"I don't know. She made a list."

I hold up a couple of packages of party noisemakers, the blowout kind with the annoying whistles. "It's whatever Olympia wants then?"

I wish Serenity and Shae would go back on the road again. Every morning this week I've come down to dirty dishes piled in the sink— presumably an offering to the cleanup fairy. Today, abandoned beside the sink awaiting my magic cleanup wand is a jug of orange juice and an open peanut butter jar, a spatula jammed deep into the contents.

A swath of breadcrumbs garnishes the counter in front of the toaster. And George has raided the garbage can again. Hairy warts pop out on my nose and my teeth snaggle into sharp points. The fairy is running for her life: the witch is in the hovel. I grab George by the collar and shove him out into the back yard. Then I fly on my broomstick up the stairs to Serenity's room and rap on her door, three times, hard.

I hear the sound of giggling. "What?"

"May I come in?"

"Why? What do you want?"

"I want to talk to you."

Silence. Then, a click and a sigh.

I turn the handle and peek in. Serenity and Shae are still in bed, a laptop propped between them. I can't see what's on the screen as Serenity shoved the lid down as I came in. I can't see the floor either as it is strewn wall to wall with discarded articles of clothing. A pile of dirty dishes tilts on the night stand and there, propped in a bowl with a few stray popcorn kernels, is my cordless phone.

"Did you borrow money from my purse last night?"

"We ordered pizza. You were over at Bibienne's while we were babysitting, remember?"

"You could've asked me first."

"Sorry."

"I need you two to look after George. He's supposed to stay outside and I caught him on my bed. With muddy paws."

"Yeah. Okay."

It smells like smoke in here. Funny smoke. My eyes land on a massive bong perched on the dresser. I can feel my insides beginning to do a slow burn. "I thought I said no smoking in your room."

"We weren't. We were just cleaning out Shae's piece is all."

I cross my arms. "I mean it. Jack and Olympia …"

Serenity rolls her eyes. "You don't have to keep bugging us about it."

"Okay then."

I don't know what to do beyond stand here with my arms folded beaming death lasers from my eyes at them. Two pairs of eyes stare back at me, death laser shields fully activated. Serenity tosses her hands up in the air. "What?"

If I kick them out of the house for smoking, then I will have zero chance of getting Serenity back on track. "Don't be breaking the house rules. That's all."

I pick up my phone and, as I close the door behind me and walk away, I hear the door handle click, more giggling and a high-pitched, "Do that again." I can only assume they're having a sex-positive morning. I can't remember the last time I had a high-pitched giggle in the morning.

I go downstairs in time to catch Jack at the side door, inviting George back into the house.

I run to prevent George from reinstalling himself inside and, as I do, Olympia pipes up: "Mom, Serenity has a snake tattoo on her back. Can I have one, too?"

I lock the door and connect the chain too. "No, you can't have a tattoo." I refrain from adding that she'll have to wait until she's 18 or until she snags herself a fake ID like Serenity did way back when.

"Can I have a nipple ring then?"

"Serenity has a nipple ring?"

Before Olympia can answer me, the phone rings.

It's Mom, back from her road trip with her book club girls. I thought they were going to the Berkshire Theatre Festival like they do every year but I was wrong: Serenity ran into her at the Electric Daisy Carnival. Apparently, she was wearing a purple pantsuit and a headband that said YOLO.

"Serenity tells me she bumped into you at the Electric Daisy Carnival?"

"True story. It was great. You should go sometime."

Me, petulantly: "I would've except I only had to look for work and watch Olympia and Jack."

Mom is too busy planning her summer vacation to listen. Tuscany would be nice. Or Paris. I am standing at the kitchen sink looking out the window. From this vantage point, I can see George working on the landscaping. Today he is digging a series of ponds.

Mom interrupts my reverie. "You really should go on one of these boat cruises. Brian wants to see Greece in July but I say we save that for winter and do a river cruise in the south of France first."

Then, in a chirpy voice, she says she's planning a quick trip next week with Brian to the Midwest where Phil Mickelson is supposed to be touring: "I'll be walking all the courses with Phil!"

All day today the crusty old seadog, Donald, lived up to his end of the bargain and entertained Olympia and her friends in the backyard with so-called pirate pizza, cake, and games. Olympia's sixth birthday is upon me, the long awaited coming of age that heralds full day, every day, school attendance. This represents a huge developmental milestone. For me, that is. From now on, I can blame everything that Olympia says or does on her teachers.

Turning six also means Olympia's character is, according to the childrearing manuals, almost fully set. I'm terrified that this may be true. Last night at bedtime, Olympia announced firmly, "I don't believe in God." That's ten perfectly respectable commandments gone right out the window. I pity her teachers. They don't have a prayer.

CHAPTER 4

Chaff

Chaff: Radar confusion reflectors, consisting of thin, narrow metallic strips of various lengths and frequency responses, which are used to reflect echoes for confusion purposes. Causes enemy radar guided missiles to lock on to it instead of the real aircraft, ship, or other platform.—Department of Defense Dictionary of Military and Associated Terms

The alarm didn't go off. Now I have to leap around like a demented squirrel to get ready for my first day of school. I arrive downstairs as Jack howls, "You shut up, loser," and picks up a fork in an attempt to threaten Serenity.

"Don't cry, it only makes me stronger," she taunts, laughing, at which he stabs her in the forearm with the fork.

Serenity lunges for Jack while I throw my body between the two and yell, "What's going on here?"

Olympia pipes up from the sidelines: "Serenity and Shae ate all the Honeycomb in Serenity's room last night."

"What? The jumbo box I bought yesterday?" I'd like to jab Serenity with a fork myself.

I send Jack to his room while Serenity stomps off to find a bandage. Olympia is winding up to tears over the loss of sugary cereal. I make Olympia a plate of toast and hand it to her. So much for last year's course in handling sibling rivalry. I learned all about acknowledging their anger and describing the problem respectfully while Jack clobbered Olympia, Olympia bit Serenity, and Serenity creamed both of them.

I run down to the basement to search for a clean shirt. There are easily ten loads of laundry piled in front of the machine plus the contents of the hampers upstairs. I feel a strong urge to cut classes on my first day.

Jack appears beside me. "Where're my gym shoes?"

"Where's your father?"

"Dunno."

I ship Jack off with clean underwear and call upstairs to summon Donald. No answer. Where is he? We set a schedule and he promised; today was his turn to get the kids organized for school. He's a Certified Financial Planner with an MBA from Harvard. He can create a complex financial spreadsheet, but has no idea how to operate a household. It's time he learned some basic domestic management skills like how to fix the washing machine, which is suddenly refusing to start.

Remembering my race against the clock, I sort everything into piles for later and iron my blouse in record time. I run upstairs. Olympia is watching television in the family room, still wearing her pajamas. I yell for Donald again.

Serenity pops her head up from the couch. "Oh yeah. Donald left. He said to tell you he had an early meeting."

Arriving on campus, I stop to double-check my timetable: I have five minutes to get to the Administrative Studies Building for my first class, Organizational Behavior.

Congratulating myself for being exactly on time, I select a seat near the front of the lecture hall. I'm fully armed to take exceptional notes with my fine tipped roller ball pens and notebook, neatly dated and operationally ready on the desk before me.

Scanning the room, I can see that none of the students are prepared like me to take proper notes, and all of them look decades younger than me. A girl sitting in the next row is wearing silver knee high gladiator sandals. She has a matching silver bag. Worse, there's a woman standing near the door wearing bright yellow crocs and white capris. She looks like a kindergarten teacher. Thankfully, I'm wearing my favorite buckled slides, reliable yet saucy. They work anywhere. The woman with the bright yellow crocs walks over to the lectern and clears her throat into the microphone. She wants to know if everyone has downloaded a course outline. Everyone in the room has their own laptop on the desk in front of them. No one told me to download a course outline or bring a laptop to class. The prof is giving us instructions on how to link to a website for information on something called restriction enzymes. Then she wants us to go to a departmental webpage that has a set of links to the labs we need to download.

Labs? Wait a minute. There's something hinky going on here. Why does she keep talking about genomes and recombinant DNA technology? I take a peek at the laptop on the desk beside me. The heading on top of the screen says Course Outline: Cell and Molecular Biology.

I step on a few Crocs in my haste to exit.

As I enter the right lecture hall, in the next building, Professor Greshen looks up from his lectern. He glares at me with bulgy eyes, and pauses to remind the class that lateness is disrespectful and we should all try to be on time for lecture in the future.

All the seats are taken. Now I have to slouch at the back of the room and hang my head in shame with all the other rude latecomers.

At lunch, I review the course syllabus for my Modern American Poetry class. I'm required to attend one lecture plus one tutorial per week, and I have to read sixteen million poems, write two essays, and undergo one midterm and one final examination. Holy crap. The proposal for our first essay is due next week already.

According to my schedule, I'm assigned to a class led by a Prof. M. Fortune. Entering the lecture room, I spy a man sitting at the desk in front of the room, shuffling through papers. He looks familiar.

Where have I met him? I scrutinize Fortune as he closes the classroom door: neat denims, blue shirt and tie, leather jacket. Nice pouty lips. On the chair beside his desk, I spy a motorcycle helmet.

Help. It's the lean-legged Latin cowboy motorcycle guy. I hope he doesn't remember me stranded on the roadside in my scruffy hockey hoodie. Probably not, since today I'm superbly pulled together with glazed hair and wicked new colored jeans, unlike the windswept mess I was two weeks ago.

Fortune leans on the edge of his desk to deliver his opening lecture on the birth of modern American poetry. I like the way he cradles a small and tattered book of poetry in his large hands. He sets the book carefully on the desk and recites Whitman's *Leaves of Grass* from memory, and his voice sounds deep and soulful as if he means it. All the women in the class lean forward, sighing, captivated. Listening to Fortune recite is like a spa day for our parched womanly souls, complete with plush robes and scented steam.

At the end of class, Fortune stands beside the door, letting the students go out first. As I pass him, he grins at me and fakes a wrist shot, saying, "She shoots, she scores. And the crowd goes wild!"

Blushing, I step past quickly and hurry to the parking lot. My first day of school is finally over. Two long intro lectures plus hours of standing in lineups at the bookstore and traipsing from one end of the campus and back again several times with a heavy backpack means I'm going straight home, ordering takeout and spending the night curled up in a blanket on the couch. I better get to bed early as my first class in Financial Management starts at 8 a.m. tomorrow.

My phone beeps. It's a text from Bibienne: "Don't forget—we got ice time tonight."

I almost forgot. My tiredness vanishes: I'm signed up for the summer pick-up hockey league. Time to dig out my lucky dog tags. I'm so down with that: the crunch of bodies against the boards, passing the puck down the ice to victory, the beer celebration in the locker room. So what if my joints can't take it anymore? Even though Bibi and I are the most senior players on the bench, Bibi is still the best goalie in the league and I can still clean out the corners for them.

I glide around the ice, flexing my wrists and whipping pucks into the glass above the boards. In the corner, pitching pucks to us is our team captain, Mackie. As I skate by she yells, "Hey, Parril, get the lead out, we're taking out those pussies from Poughkeepsie tonight."

Good old Mackie's coming off her third tour of active duty. She and I go back a long way. She yanked me out of the mud in basic and re-upped after I left. One round was enough for me. Since then she's seen it all, from the Gulf to the scorching desert of Al Anbar and, to no one's surprise, always comes home without a scratch.

I pick up the pace. I've got my high sticking groove on now. Huh. That little left-winger over there thinks she knows how to play hockey? We'll show these kittens what it's all about.

CHAPTER 5

Hazard

Hazard: A condition with the potential to cause injury, illness, or death of personnel; damage to or loss of equipment or property; or mission degradation.—Department of Defense Dictionary of Military and Associated Terms

I hate being late. The parking lots are jammed so I have to park in the back of beyond and run for class through a cloudburst. As I arrive inside and hurtle around the corner, I spot Fortune ahead, also running late. He waits for me at the door, holding it open with a smile. The rain makes his hair curl up at the ends. I want to run my finger through one of the dark rings on his neck.

Fortune hands our essay proposals back. As I scan the pages, I can feel my mouth go all baggy: the top of the page is marked with a C+ and a scrawled comment: *A good start on a thorny topic, but not much more than a start. If you wish to try to improve your grade, you may take one week to rewrite and resubmit your work.*—M. Fortune

I'd like to stab a sharp stick through one of those scraggly curls. Rewrite my proposal? Fortune must have made a mistake. At the end of class, I wait behind to protest my mark.

Fortune glances over my paper for a minute, and says, "I can't increase your grade as things stand. In fact, I may have been too generous."

My face feels hot. "What do I need to do to improve it then?"

"I have time now to go over your proposal if you like, in my office. Or we could go to the Dingy Cup. I could use a coffee."

Dingwall's campus pub is packed but we manage to snag a tiny table at the back. Fortune begins: "Your ideas have potential but you need to think them through. Do you like to read?"

"Yes."

"Good. Who are you reading right now?"

I can't possibly tell him that waiting on my bed stand is the latest Stephenie Meyer novel. What have I read lately that isn't on the assigned reading list? What's underneath Meyer? "*Beloved!* Toni Morrison!" I say.

"Excellent," he says. "You need to read as widely as possible. Don't be afraid to read poetry as well as prose."

Taking a pen and paper, he jots down titles of books and papers that he wants me to read. Squeezed into the corner with Michael, shoulder-to-shoulder, poring over a growing list that contains names like Maya Angelou, Allen Ginsberg, and Robert Pinsky, I remember our motorcycle ride and the warm spring breeze in our faces. Now we're having iced coffees and talking rhyme, free verse, ballads, and couplets. I feel like I'm coming awake after a long and dreamless sleep.

What a boring way to spend a Saturday night: my butt is sore from sitting in front of the computer for hours, writing. I'll show that Michael Fortune how to revise an essay proposal.

The phone rings: it's Mom. She has a new boyfriend. "Ted's a stockbroker and he looked over my portfolio. He says Donald's a genius. I'm set for life."

Mom has been Donald's biggest fan ever since she and Dad went to Doubles for financial advice. They instantly fell for the down-to-earth style of their new fresh-faced young advisor from Montreal. Mom said, "He's smart as a whip," and added the information—so many times I wanted to scream—"He's so handsome. He won a scholarship to Harvard, you know. You have to meet him."

That was a dozen years ago. Now, a less than fresh-faced whip is snoring on the couch in the living room.

"Whatever happened to Brian? I thought you really liked him?"

"I do. We're still friends. I'm not about to make a commitment. Not after being tied down with one man for thirty-seven years. Good Lord. You have no idea how dull that can get."

In my head I multiply ten years by three and add seven. The result is a vision of Donald stretched out on the couch, still snoring, still clutching the remote. His hair is totally grey. Worse, we still have the same couch.

Where does the time go? I'm already three weeks into my courses and I have homework piled up to my ears.

The kids have taken turns being sick with colds for the past week, causing me to miss classes and get further behind in all my courses. Both Olympia and Jack are home from school today, sore throated and feverish, but still upright and combat ready. I spent the whole morning at the doctor's office and the drug store. Now the afternoon will be devoted to holding the line at home.

After constructing a giant fort with the entire household supply of cushions, pillows, and comforters in the middle of the living room, Jack teases Olympia by singing over and over, "Elmo's dead, Elmo's dead" until she screams and punches him. His nosebleed creates convincing evidence of a massacre in the fort. I'll clean up later. Right now I need a sandwich and a cup of tea. As I sit down at the kitchen table, Donald walks through the door, carrying a new golf bag.

The bag looks expensive and has the Doubles logo on it.

"All the advisors got one," says Donald who goes on to extol the virtues of the amazing Lindsay Bambraugh, who is currently donating her personal time to set up a Doubles charity golf tournament. The proceeds will go to the Boston Children's Hospital. According to Donald, Lindsay is "a big-hearted and generous woman," not to mention "a visionary who knows how to do business."

I can feel my toes curling up inside my shoes at the thought of Donald and Lindsay teeing off together at the golf tournement. I break into Donald's admiration fest. "I didn't know you were coming home for lunch today."

"I'm not home for lunch. I came home to get ready for the conference, pack my things."

"Conference?"

"The annual conference. That one I go to every year in June?"

"I thought you already had it? A couple of weekends ago? When you went to Chicago?"

"That was the divisional. This one is the main one, the national."

"You could've reminded me."

"It's on the calendar."

"Sorry. My bad. I forgot to check."

Google calendar is our main artery of planning and communication. I haven't checked it for weeks. Since losing my job, I've fallen right out of sync.

"How're the kids doing?" He peeks into the living room where Jack and Olympia are eating tuna sandwiches in their fort. "You're letting them eat in the living room? I thought we made a rule about that."

"They both have colds. I decided to let the living room rule slide for today. Since they're sick. They wanted to have a picnic. How am I? I'm exhausted, thank you for asking."

Donald glares at me and I glare back at him. "I was about to ask how you are. What's wrong?"

"The sitter called and she can't babysit tonight so there goes my hockey game."

"Can't you find anyone else?"

"Are you kidding? On a Friday night?"

"What about Serenity?"

"She and Shae have concert tickets. Forget about it. I probably wouldn't go anyway, with the kids sick."

An hour later Donald comes downstairs, carrying his bags and smelling of fresh aftershave. He stands in front of the hall mirror to adjust his tie.

"Can you do the park n' fly thing this time?"

"Don't worry. I've got it covered. I have a ride. Lindsay offered to pick me up."

"Oh. That's nice of her." His eyes flick sideways to meet mine ever so briefly, and then he bends down to poke around in his briefcase. I stare at the back of his head. Did he just gauge my reaction? Why the shifty eye contact? Was that shifty eye contact?

"Have a good weekend," I say with a half-smile, trying to keep the sarcastic tone out of my voice. Donald glances up at me. For a brief moment our eyes meet again in an all-in, Texas Hold-'em moment. Trouble is, I'm the big blind and I can't force his hand.

I sit down at the kitchen table and hoist my slippers up on the chair opposite me. Donald comes over to kiss the top of my forehead. "Thanks for handling everything."

Five minutes later, Lindsay pulls into the driveway and toots the horn. She waits behind the tinted windows of a sporty silver car with doublewide tires. Donald grabs his suitcase and, after running through the living room to peck the kids' cheeks, opens the door, then doubles back to collect his briefcase from the counter, kisses me on the cheek and rushes out.

I stare into my teacup, wondering if this is a fair game. If he's messing around on me, how do I find out for sure? He's always had a good poker face. Weeks have passed since the day I found the XO'd card and the troubling question remains: has Donald been letting the rules slide?

It takes hours but, at last, the kids are tucked into bed. I phone the convention center number to give Donald an update but there's no answer in his room. His cell goes straight to voicemail. It's 11 p.m. I send him a text to say goodnight. Nothing comes back. A few minutes later, while channel surfing from the comfort of the cleanest section of the kids' fort, I succumb to garrison mentality, and fortify my defenses with a substantial shot of brandy.

The explosions and screaming from a cartoon soundtrack at top volume began at dawn, and the kids are still coughing.

Today, I have to cram for my Organizational Behavior exam, work on my poetry essay and decipher an impossible chapter in my brutal finance textbook. Yesterday's shorts will have to do. I pour cereal into bowls. Then I sit at the desk in the den and open my textbook, which causes Jack to burst into the room: "I'm invited to play at Harold's house. Can I go?"

Harold's mother is barely speaking to me since she caught Jack downloading a list of cuss words onto Harold's laptop. As if Jack is responsible for expanding his bratty friend's vocabulary—three weeks ago I overheard Harold explaining to Olympia what WTF and CU Next Tuesday means.

If Harold catches Jack's cold, she'll never speak to me again, but the opportunity to offload Jack for the day is much too attractive. If the house is quiet, Olympia might even take a nap.

I hustle Olympia into her playclothes. Jack's swim trunks are still wet from yesterday. I roll them in a fresh towel and hand them over anyway. Releasing Jack onto Harold's doorstep, I wave to Harold's mother in a breezy fashion and then I drive away hurriedly. Speeding to the grocery store, I scour my memory to recall the items on my shopping list, still magnetized to the refrigerator door. Home again. I put away the groceries and head back to the books. Olympia, bored with TV, roller-skates through the den with my hockey stick, showing off her slashing and high-sticking skills. "Go play an away game in the hall," I say, at which she bonks into the doorframe, collapses on the floor and bursts into tears. Producing paper and markers, I say, "Here. Draw a picture for me."

My throat feels sore. No doubt I'm getting the kids' cold.

"Mommy, look." Olympia holds up a drawing of two kids with green ears watching an enormous purple TV. A big smiling yellow sun shines grandly over the scene. I'm relieved there's no blood, gore, flamethrowers, automatic weapons, etc. The drawing will make a creative—and easy—cover page for my poetry essay.

Olympia miraculously agrees to go for a nap. Back in the den, I'm bored to the bone with Organizational Behavior. But I press on. Maybe I'll find some tips in here on how to achieve order in the midst of milk spills, runny noses, and MIA husbands.

By evening, I'm felled by the kids' rotten cold. Bibienne suggests a scotch cure, her top remedy for colds, depression, broken bones, stubbed toes, chipped nail polish, etc. She says, "I'll bring you a slurp of Lagavulin—it's the best brand for sore throats."

The Lagavulin is soothing, my head clears, and my sense of smell returns. "See what a mess this place is? It stinks. My whole life stinks."

"You sound depressed."

"You think?"

"For starters, you lost your job recently. And your Dad died. Both of those are way up there on the Stink Scale."

"True. And there's Donald. All he thinks about is his job. He's hardly ever home. And who knows what he's doing on these conferences. It's like he's turned into my ex. The kids and house are all my department."

"Do you still think he's having an affair?"

"I don't know. We hardly ever have sex anymore. After the last time ... well, if I find out Leggy had a yeast infection recently ..."

"No way, a yeast infection? On top of everything else?"

I nod my head sadly.

Bibi lifts my chin gently and looks deep into my eyes: "Say, 'I hate my life.'"

"I hate my life."

"Now make a fist and pound on this cushion here as you say it. Get it out—say it again—louder."

"I hate my life, I hate my life, I hate my life." Pound, pound, pound.

"See, doesn't that feel better now? It's a healing mantra."

I drain my glass. Bibienne looks so beautiful. I could hug her.

"Marry me, Bib."

I love my life.

CHAPTER 6

Friendly

Friendly: A contact positively identified as friendly.—Department of Defense Dictionary of Military and Associated Terms

I've volunteered to help with the end-of-year school costume carnival. I'm dressing up as a non-traditional clown. Donald pops his head around the bathroom door to observe the installation of bright blue hair extensions and Lady Gaga-style fake eyelashes. He surveys my costume, borrowed from Bibienne: a purple striped bodysuit, red patent miniskirt and tarty little white boots. He glances at the glass of wine on the counter beside me and smirks: "Boozo the slut-clown. That's hot."

I tell him that, seeing as he's such a comedian, he can wear the clown costume and take Olympia and Jack to the Fun Fair himself.

Donald offers to drive us over to the school. Before entering the cafeteria, I beg Olympia to demonstrate self-control at the refreshment table.

"I threw up on a princess last year, didn't I?" recalls Olympia.

"Yes. Yes, you did."

She threw up on the pinkest, bitchiest princess ever. I nod with what I hope is an adequate measure of regret and disapproval to cover up my proud smirk.

Olympia and Jack disappear into the fray as I report to the volunteer booth. I am assigned to hand out drinks at the refreshments table. I step forward and somebody's brat dressed in a vampire costume and wearing roller blades runs over my foot. I wonder who brought this bloodsucking monster on wheels? They should teach their kid some manners.

The refreshments table is covered with orange cake crumbs and sticky purple punch spills and, soon enough, so am I. Removing my black bowler, I slump against the wall. This is going to be a long night.

"Hi there." A man dressed in a sheriff's costume salutes me with a tip of his wide-brimmed hat.

Who's this? Tall handsome lawman. Motorcycle. Dingwall. What's my poetry prof doing here?

"You don't know who I am, do you?"

"Of course I know who you are. Professor Fortune. Poetry class."

"That's okay. We're both just parents here. Call me Michael."

"Okay. Michael. I didn't know your kids go to this school."

"I just have one kid, a boy. He's over there, the one in the vampire costume."

"Oh … he's so cute!"

"These two are mine." I point at Olympia and Jack who are busy guzzling punch beside me.

"I can't believe you didn't recognize me."

"It took me a moment. You have a hat. And it's been awhile since I've seen you. I've missed a few of your classes."

"Quite a few, actually. I thought maybe you dropped the course."

"No. My kids were sick with colds, is all. I'll be there next week for sure."

"Careful," I say to Michael. "The purple punch is gross." I hold up my cup, wincing.

Michael says, "Hang on, I'll be right back." A few minutes later he returns carrying two opaque plastic cups and hands me one. It's filled with … beer!

"Cheers," I say, tipping my cup. "How are you managing this?"

"I'm a volunteer, on the organizing committee. A few of us Dads have a stash out back."

"Nice." I take a swig.

"Just between you and me, okay?" He zips his index finger across his mouth, sealing a pair of nicely formed lips. We lean against the wall and sip together in a quiet alliance.

After a few minutes, he straightens. "I better get back to work."

He moves away into the crowd. I watch him circle about the room, picking up empty cups, helping a lost child find a parent, and retying the laces of a green frog.

Michael comes back after awhile and points at my cup. "Another one?"

"Please."

He returns with a refill and heads back into the throng. As the crowd thins, he comes over and relaxes against the wall next to me. The wall shifts behind my back, and the room tilts a little.

Michael raises his cup to me with a grin. "Having fun?"

"Now I am."

"I still can't believe you didn't recognize me. I thought I might have made more of an impression. Especially after I rescued you from the roadside and all."

"No, really, I was very impressed with you. I mean, thanks for helping me."

"You're welcome."

"Not living it down, am I?"

Michael shakes his head. "Afraid not."

"I thought you had to work?"

"Nope." He leans against the wall so close to me that I can smell that lemony aftershave again. "I have everything under control." He smiles. "Now this outfit," he says, turning toward me, leaning in closer and pointing at my bodysuit, "is very, very nice."

"How many beers have you had? You realize you're flirting with a clown?"

Michael pulls back and draws a straight face. "No, I'm not."

"Admit it. You're into clowns."

Michael leans in toward me again, bumping against my hip with his holster. "Only the kind of clowns that wear short leather skirts."

I push him away using my index finger in the middle of the star on his chest. "Easy there, deputy. So what's in the holster? Can I see your gun?"

"Sure. Would you like to hold it?"

"Sure. Why not?"

"But if you start clowning around with it I'll have to cuff you."

Michael takes me by the wrist; Olympia tugs on my other arm: "Mommmmmm, I feel sick."

Time to go. I say goodbye, quickly, and turn away but not before catching a vibe from Michael that makes me feel kind of shiny, like I am the brightest star in the sky and he is making a wish on me.

Walking home along the sidewalk with Jack and Olympia, I can still feel Michael's fingers circling my wrist. But I am a married clown. Of course, Donald might be performing his own little circus act with Lindsay. I wish I knew for sure. I need a detective, not a tipsy professor wearing a tin star on his chest.

Beer joy turns to beer gloom as I recall that Donald is going away on a two-day business trip to New York City next week. Again. With Lindsay. Nothing much has changed and it's not funny anymore. I could use a good cry. I guess that's what they mean by a sad clown.

But I'm not a clown. I'm a soldier. And a good soldier never cries.

When I walked into class today, Michael barely glanced up from his desk where he was sorting papers. I said "Hi," and all I got was a distracted nod in return. He's probably embarrassed about drinking so much beer and flirting with me. He needn't worry; I'm a big girl. I know it meant nothing.

At the end of his lecture he reminded us about the essay submission deadline: we only have two more weeks before it's due. I have twenty-two pages of notes but no thesis. Hmmph. Suddenly, Michael Fortune's not as cute as when he wore a six gun and siphoned beer into me.

CHAPTER 7

Engage

Engage: In air defense, a fire control order used to direct or authorize units and/or weapon systems to fire on a designated target.—Department of Defense Dictionary of Military and Associated Terms

Since Donald, his mother, and I all have our birthdays in July, we usually celebrate together over the Fourth of July weekend. Donald's parents flew in last night from Montreal laden with toys for Jack and Olympia. Upon sight of his mother, Donald morphs into a Birthday Boy: he flops full length on the couch in front of the TV and falls asleep minutes after cramming his stomach with corn chips, jalapeno dip, and beer. Meanwhile, I'm trapped in the kitchen making my own birthday dinner. A battalion's worth of potatoes need peeling. Over the past week, I cleaned the house, laid in groceries, shopped for gifts for Donald and his mother, and wrapped them, all while I went to school and kept the kids entertained. Meanwhile, Donald worked overtime every night and played golf all last weekend in Lindsay's amazing charity tournament held, of course, at a five-star resort.

Bitter? Me?

Donald's mother offers to help, but while chopping garlic for the salad dressing, she manages to slice her thumb. Now she's bleeding on my diced shallots. Guess I can add making the dressing back on my list. The bitter gets the better of me. I trundle into the den and poke Donald's arm.

"I could use some help in the kitchen."

Donald's mother rushes in behind me, sucking her thumb, her free hand raised in a stop gesture toward Donald. "Don't get up. There's nothing to do."

"Maybe Donald could help with the stuffed peppers?" I clip my eyes at Donald, hold up a red pepper and add, "Like, stuff it."

Donald's mother says, "I don't mind. I can do it."

She hurries away to bandage her thumb. I trudge back to kitchen patrol. At least the kids aren't in my way. They're too busy smashing their new breakable toys with old unbreakable ones.

Back in the kitchen with a bandaged thumb, Donald's mother sits at the table to watch me heave a tray of marinated t-bone steaks out of the fridge. She wants to know how poor Donald is making out with his wife away at university all day.

"Same as always."

"Who gets the children off to school?"

"I do, usually. He goes in early most of the time."

"I suppose if he goes in so early he must be having to make his breakfast?" She obviously doubts my capacity to rise before noon.

Time for a little white lie, to avoid the sad hand-wringing over poor Donald's fate to cope with an indolent wife. "Of course not. Donald loves his bacon and eggs every morning."

Donald's mother frowns. "That's not heart smart."

I don't say that I suspect Donald goes in extra early to avoid the wild joys of organizing the children off to school. I also suppress the urge to remark that Donald is probably making out very well with the generous and big-hearted Lindsay Bambraugh on his frequent late nights at the office, probably pumping her pert bottom to a wet pulp on top of the file cabinets.

At dinner, Donald's mother tells us all about Donald's sister's children. Evan is reading at a grade ten level and he's only in grade 5. Jordana is studying four languages: French, Spanish, Mandarin, and Arabic. I think she also translated the Dead Sea Scrolls recently, but I stopped paying attention so I could focus on fluffing up my hips with extra potato salad. I won't mention that Serenity's standout talent is erotic lesbian spoken word poetry, Olympia is still working on two plus two, and Jack can do a rolling ollie on his skateboard now.

Donald and I bunk down in the spare room on the bed with the rock hard mattress. I slide under the covers, grateful for my pillow, exhausted. Donald slips his hand under my nightgown. What? Birthday sex on a slab with a gut full of steak and potato salad, and the in-laws in the next room? Donald, you're a fool.

After the in-laws head home to Montreal, we all pile into Donald's car to go across town to Mom's for a birthday lunch. Donald is grumbling. "Can't this wait? Our birthdays don't actually happen until next week."

I try to explain: "She wants to give us our birthday presents early since she's going away, plus she baked us a cake."

"We just had cake last night."

I roll my eyes. "Yes, I know. It really sucks to have to eat cake two days in a row."

Donald glares at me and then frowns when he sees George lunging into the back seat with the kids. Olympia has a lollipop in her mouth and Jack is busy munching his way through a bag of popcorn. Serenity and Shae borrowed my Jeep to go who knows where. Donald hates it when his unspoiled car gets spammed with dog hair and snack wrappers. He pauses in the driveway, saying, "I'm tired. Do you think you could drive?"

As soon as I back onto the road, Donald pulls out his Blackberry and checks his messages.

"I can imagine you must be totally worn out after two days of sitting out on the patio stuffing your face with steak sandwiches and chicken wings. I'd be weary too."

Donald glances up. "What do you mean?"

"I just spent two solid days in the kitchen with your mother. Chopping vegetables and making spinach dip."

"I tried to help. She wouldn't let me."

"That must've been terribly hard on you. Tell me, do you even remember what I bought to give to your mother for her birthday this year?"

Donald presses his mouth into a tight line. What did Donald give me for my birthday? A garage door opener.

"I bet you wouldn't buy Lindsay a garage door opener."

"What are you talking about?"

"You know what I'm talking about."

"No, I don't. Let's not do this now."

"When then? Can I make an appointment to talk to you? Sometime when you aren't working late or having sleepovers with Lindsay?"

Donald says nothing and stares out the passenger window.

"Who's Lindsay?" asks Olympia.

"Daddy's little friend at work."

Jack soon interrupts the stony silence portion of the quarrel to inquire if we will be getting a divorce and, if so, right on, since all the coolest kids come from broken homes plus they all get twice as much awesome stuff at Christmas and birthdays.

"You want your father and me to get a divorce?"

"No. I guess not. But Serenity always gets presents from her Dad and you guys and her Florida Nana too."

Olympia says, "The Florida Nana gave Serenity a purple cell phone."

We arrive in Mom's driveway and the kids race ahead to her door. Donald and I remain in the car a moment to compose ourselves. Turning to him, I twist the corners of my lips up, and hiss through clenched teeth: "Smile and pretend, okay?"

In the foyer, Donald maintains a wide bubble of space between us. I feel like popping him with a pointy stick. "Excuse me, honey," I say as I step past him into the living room, while tossing him an unhoneyed glance.

Mom's eyebrows rise. Somehow, we're already busted, but she says nothing.

We follow Mom outside to sit on her back deck and open our presents. Donald receives a silk tie. I'm excited about a large box tagged with my name. I tear off the wrapping with great expectations only to discover an electric grill that looks like a giant clam. Just what I wanted: a waffle iron for meat. It looks like the same one I gave Mom for Christmas last year.

How touching. My own mother has re-gifted me.

As usual Mom is armed with highly unsuitable gifts for the kids: for Olympia, a marionette with a million billion strings that tangle as soon as you look at them, and for Jack, a giant box of fireworks: Li'l Red Devils, screamers, rockets, Roman candles and giant Mexican sparklers. Jack is jumping up and down: "I can get $15 apiece for the screamers at school."

Olympia immediately shrieks, "If Jack gets to take his screamers to school, I wanna take some too."

Good thing school has let out for the summer. I warn both of them that under no circumstance are any fireworks to be taken to school or anyplace else for that matter, nor are they to be used without proper adult supervision. No one is to touch them until after dark tonight when we can have a backyard show.

I look over at Donald who steadfastly refuses to make eye contact with me. A little relaxed family fun and togetherness sure wouldn't hurt right now.

Mom wants to go over her itinerary: she's dividing her summer vacation between Brian and Ted. Brian will accompany her on her cruise through the Greek Islands and then she wants to play golf in Pebble Beach with Ted "because Phil might be there" and she "misses him."

She leans down to pet Jasper, her aging, cranky, and incontinent Schnauzer, who crouches under the table, growling and baring his teeth at Donald every time he shifts position.

"I was hoping you would take Jasper while I'm gone. I couldn't bear to place him in a kennel.

Donald's head snaps up. Now he wants to make eye contact. He looks me in the eye in a way that says he is not on board with taking the dog. I stare back at him in a way that says: *Nice, Donald. And here Mom is your big fan, too.* Donald says: *Seriously, no.* I glare back at him:

*Be supportive. Mom didn't want to do anything much after Dad died. Now
she's just trying to get out and enjoy herself.* Like Jasper, I want to lie
under the table and growl and bare my teeth at him, too. I smile at
Mom and say, "Sure. Of course."

Home at last. Jack and Olympia run ahead into the house with Jasper
and George. Donald's face goes all pissy when he surveys the state of
his car. Jasper is a big shedder. George likes to press his nose against
the windows. Olympia dribbled a trail of purple fruit punch clear
across the back seat. In a fit of temper, Donald flings the offending
juice box onto the front lawn.

"Who is supposed to pick that up?" I ask.

Donald ignores me and tosses Jasper's dog blanket on top of the
juice box.

"You're acting like the mess is somehow my fault."

"You gave Olympia the juice box."

"She was thirsty. How come your car is off limits? You don't mind
when my car gets trashed. You seem to think you are exempt from
all this parenting stuff."

"Give me a break."

"No, I'm sick of this. Give *me* a break. You conduct your life as if
you live in a hotel room with maid service. You come and go as you
please and, when family stuff intrudes and I'm not on it, boy, someone's head's got to roll."

"What do you want from me?"

Donald furiously scrubs at the juicebox stain with George's blanket.

"We could start communicating for a change."

"That's rich. Communicate? You didn't bother to ask me whether
I wanted to look after your mother's dog."

"I will take care of the dog, okay? Don't worry. You won't have to
lift a finger. It's not like you are around here to help much anyway."

Donald flings the dog blanket onto the ground and turns to me,
his jaw clenched with rage. "You want me to leave? Give me five
minutes, I'll pack my bags."

"Fine!" I shout. "Why don't you go move in with your big-hearted girlfriend?"

"What do you mean by that?"

"You know what I mean. Are you sleeping with her?"

"Who?"

"Lindsay."

"Don't be ridiculous." Donald turns his back to me and yanks Jack's box of fireworks from the trunk, setting them on the ground. "I'll go to a motel."

"That sounds like a fair and affordable plan. You walk away and leave me holding the bag. What about the kids? What do I tell them?"

"What do you want me to do?"

I snatch up Jasper's bag plus the box of fireworks and head into the house, pausing on the doorstep to watch Donald shake out George's dog blanket. I shout, "How about go sleep in the spare room?"

"You got it," Donald yells. Dropping George's blanket, he jumps behind the wheel of his car, and guns it out of the driveway. Is he going for a drive to cool off? His office? Lindsay's apartment? Who knows.

I go inside to stand in the foyer, and try to slow my breathing. I still have Jack's box of fireworks in my hands. There won't be any fun family fireworks party in the backyard tonight that's for sure. We just had our big show in the driveway. I stub my toes kicking the front door closed and shove the box into the back of the hall closet.

After days of silence, looks like Donald is making a bid to come out of the spare room tonight. He's offering to take me out to dinner at a classy restaurant in the city. No kids. He says he wants to talk. I accept his invitation, as I can't recall the last time we visited a dining establishment that doesn't boast a drive-thru window.

The waiter brings us a bottle of cold Chablis and a basket of warm rolls. Evidently, Donald knows a thing or two about fine wines and

Boston's coziest bistros. I wonder how he knows about this place? But who cares? I'm starving. There's no need for him to whisper herbed garlic nothings in my ear—all he needs is a pat of pesto butter and he'll have me licking his hand. Looking around, I realize that he's the tastiest-looking man in the room. Maybe a romantic night on the town is just what we needed.

Alas, between scarfing down all the rolls and digging into my Chef's Special Antipasto Platter, I can't remember the last time we made dinner table conversation without extensive interference from the kids. I wish Donald would spill my drink or at least yell, "Yuck, I'm not eating this crap."

We can't continue staring at each other over an expanse of linen, crystal and candlelight forever.

Here goes: "So? How was your day?"

Donald: "Terrible."

Me, with real concern: "What happened?"

Donald: "Nothing. The usual pricks."

The usual pricks? No, Donald must be mistaken; the usual pricks work in the parking lot at Dingwall. I launch into a tirade about the guys who ticketed me twice last week when I was only five minutes late for the meter, and they saw me coming. Somehow this cheers Donald up.

By dessert, Donald has warmed up past monosyllabic communication and, changing the topic, utters a complete sentence: "I bought a new TV today."

Me, swallowing hard: "What?"

"It's huge. The definition is unbelievable and it has the fastest re-fresh rate on the market."

"But we don't need another gigantic television. I thought we agreed to repaint the front porch ..."

"You agreed we were repainting the front porch."

I am suddenly furious. Donald is going out buying himself new toys as if nothing's wrong. "When do I ever get to agree with you on anything anyway? You're hardly ever home."

Donald's jaw goes rigid. "What do you want me to do? Quit my job?"

"Stop saying that. Of course I don't want you to quit your job. You could start by talking to me once in a while."

Donald leans back in his chair and folds his arms across his chest. "Here I am. What do you want to talk about?"

"Forget the porch. Maybe we need to figure out why we aren't getting along. I think we need to get into counseling."

"Forget it. I'm not going to talk to some ooogie-woogie whackjob about our personal business."

A vision of Lindsay swarms into my head. "Then maybe you would prefer to talk about our problems with a lawyer?"

"If that's what you want, fine by me."

Donald grabs for his suit jacket. I snatch up my purse. Neither of us speaks all the way home. Upon arrival home, Donald stamps upstairs and slams the door on his way into the spare room.

CHAPTER 8

Bona Fides

Bona Fides: In personnel recovery, the use of verbal or visual communication by individuals who are unknown to one another, to establish their authenticity, sincerity, honesty, and truthfulness. See also evasion; recovery; recovery operations.—Department of Defense Dictionary of Military and Associated Terms

Monday morning, 3 a.m., I fall into bed, exhausted, essay at last completed. My eyes won't close. I mash the pillow about, get up and take some aspirin, then lie back down. What's wrong? Should I run another spellcheck on my essay, due today? How do I check that it makes sense? My neck feels like a tangle of ropes. Nope. There's something more going on here. Maybe it's because my car needs new tires? Without a regular paycheck, my bank account is emptying rapidly. Is that it? Tires and money and my poetry essay? All things I can handle. What else is wrong? Thunder rumbles in the distance. Ah.

My mind sets the way-back machine to the early days after my deployment to Afghanistan. Sleep and normalcy were impossible after months of brutal heat, rumbling in convoys up and down steeply winding rock-strewn roads. Every so often, we stopped to wait for an All Clear, passed around cheap Pakistani cigarettes in the shade of the trucks with the bab-bap-bap sound of mortar fire in the distance, the smell of burning phosphorus in our noses. Afterwards, all too often,

I saw the blood-soaked uniforms piled up for cleaning in the supply depot. Everywhere I saw dusty faces, always the dusty faces. Back at home, Serenity, barely 4 years old, clung to me constantly, for fear I might disappear again. My ex, a veteran himself, drank himself to sleep every night and punched holes in the walls. I asked the dentist for a mouth-guard to keep me from grinding my teeth. I chewed several packs of gum every day. Then I asked for a divorce.

A few months after my divorce, I met Donald. A few more months went by, and he started staying late every weekend night, slipping away before Serenity woke up. One night, I had one of my episodes in the middle of the night: *boom, boom, boom, the ground shakes beneath me. An RPG blast. That was close, really close. Serenity needs her blue blanket. We have to bug out but I've lost it somewhere, I can't find it. I scrabble around in the dark. It must be in my kit bag. Where's my barracks box? I have to find it. There's sand and razor wire everywhere. Here's the blanket but it is torn and dirty, tangled up in all the wire. My throat is raw, there's that smell of burning phosphorus, the insurgents are here. It's time to go. I choke, my throat fills with sharp grit, as my weapon sinks into the sand, disappears. I fall on my knees in the sand to dig. Without my weapon, I can't protect my baby girl. I dig and dig. My hands come up empty, the sand pours away between my fingers. I cry out her name. Serenity.*

A pair of strong arms circled my waist and held me tight. A calm voice whispered into my ear, "It's just a little thunder, it's okay, you're safe, it's okay." I cried, "No, no, you don't understand. Please, help me, I don't know where Serenity is and I have to find her, she's lost in the desert."

"No, Serenity is fine, she's asleep in her room, and you're at home, you're safe with me. At home."

He scooped me gently from the bed and set me on my feet. Taking me by the hand, he led me down the hall to Serenity's room. "She's right in there. Go see for yourself."

In the faint glow of the nightlight, Serenity's face was soft with sleep, her chubby little hands clutching her blue blanket to her cheek. I dropped to my knees beside the bed and watched her breathe.

Serenity's eyes opened and she immediately wrapped her arms around my neck. "Mommy, you stay with me."

I glanced back at Donald hesitating by the door. I didn't know what to do. Donald whispered, "I'll go. She needs you."

"Please don't go," I said. "Stay with us." I picked Serenity up and carried her back to my room, and we snuggled in with her. It felt just right, nestled between Serenity and Donald, the three of us together, safe and warm. With my arms wrapped around Serenity, and Donald's arms wrapped around us, we slept, a family.

In the morning, I woke up, alone in the bed. I found Serenity downstairs, seated at the breakfast table, eating pancakes decorated with chocolate chip smiley faces. Donald, shaved and dressed for the day, kissed me good morning and handed me a cup of coffee, fixed just the way I like it.

Now he's slumbering in the next room. I can hear him snoring through the wall. So near but so far. We're still barely talking since our dinner out. I don't know if he called his lawyer or if he was just posturing.

All he ever worries about is his career. I wonder what he dreams about? Lindsay, maybe? The ropes in my neck loop into a tight noose.

My list of worries just got much too long. Time to stop obsessing and get some sleep. Tomorrow I have to get up earlier than usual to get the kids ready for their day camp. As the Jeep is going in for brake realigning today, I'll have to ask Donald to help. He can drive the kids to camp while I can take the bus. I find my earplugs in the bedside drawer and close my eyes tight to wait for a sleepy feeling which fails to arrive.

At the beginning of class, I hand in my essay. Michael quickly launches into a long lecture on critical theories addressing the linguistics of visionary imagery vis-à-vis the inherent abstractions within pre-postmodern syntactical structure. Or something like that. After an hour of verbal gymnastics, he pauses to ask if anyone has questions. One student wants to know if early modern ambiguous linguistic theory will be on the midterm. Michael laughs and says, "Maybe, maybe not."

He goes back to lecturing on Ezra Pound and imagism. I want to lay my head on my arms and take a nap.

Finally, class is over and we are free to go. It's baking hot out here. I sleepily trudge around the parking lot until I am practically dripping with sweat. Where on earth did I park the Jeep?

Michael pulls up alongside me in his car, and rolls down his window. "Everything okay?"

Suddenly, I remember about the brakes. "Fine. I'm, uh, looking for the bus stop."

"It's back that way." Oh God, I hope he didn't see me zigzagging around the lot, stupidly searching for the Jeep.

"Can I give you a lift?"

"Yes, that would be awesome." As I run around to the passenger side, I swipe the perspiration from my face with the back of my hand.

Michael tosses his briefcase from the passenger seat into the back seat on top of a huge jumble of books and boxes. "Sorry. Research papers. For my doctoral dissertation," he says, as I climb in.

More books are scattered on the floor of the passenger seat. I pick them up and hold them carefully on my lap, relishing the blast of cold air from Michael's air conditioning.

"You can toss those books in the back with the rest."

There's a silence as he winds his way from the parking lot and eases into the traffic lanes outside the campus gates. Sitting next to me in the cool car, Michael smells nice, a mixture of leather and citrus, the same aftershave he wore the day he rescued me from the roadside on his motorcycle. I remember leaning into the curves with him and gripping the bike with my thighs. I feel a blush of warmth coming straight up from my core heater. No air conditioning in the world can help me now.

Michael finally speaks up. "So, what other courses are you taking at Dingwall?"

"Financial Management and Organizational Behavior. I'm a business major. Your course is my liberal arts elective."

"What did you do before?"

"I was a Consultant for Wifi-Robes. Before that I was in the army for seven years."

Michael's eyes widen. Either he's impressed or he thinks I'm crazy. "The army? Why did you join the army?"

"Everyone asks me that. Most people say they joined up because of the challenge. I just didn't have a better plan when I finished high school. Mostly it was because of my Dad. He encouraged me. And it seemed like a good idea at the time."

"And was it? A good idea?"

"I don't regret it. Everyone talks about doing their time, you know, like it's prison, but I've never met anyone who truly regretted it in the end."

"Except maybe the ones who don't make it home."

"Yeah, maybe some of them. And some of the ones who get hurt."

Michael snaps his head to stare at me. "Some?"

Judging by Michael's reaction, I can tell he doesn't get it. Civilians rarely do. Maybe that's why veterans don't talk about their experiences much. Even if you get hurt, it was a choice you made and you don't regret it. On the contrary, you feel a sense of pride.

Softly, I say, "It's hard to describe. You get caught up in the life and the army becomes like family. You're part of a team, and you believe in what you are doing. It's about fighting for freedom right? I know that sounds corny but it's true. It's a totally different way of life. I mean, you do get to see the world." I laugh and add, "But not necessarily a part of the world you'd want to see."

Michael gives me a quizzical look.

"I did a tour in Afghanistan."

"Ah."

"The Middle East is beautiful but you can't go out walking around. Because of the mines. Most of the time it was a ton of hard work. I was a supply tech. We slept in plywood huts and ate a lot of bad pizza in the mess hall. I had a daughter at home. At the end of my deployment, my time was up. So, I got out."

"So what's next? After you get your degree?"

"I don't know yet. I was thinking maybe I'd start my own business. Or become a self-made billionaire. Whichever comes first."

Michael laughs, showing a set of attractive crinkles around his eyes. "What are you going to do after you get your doctorate? Go for tenure track?"

"I guess that would be next." Michael looks less than excited by the thought.

"If you could do anything you wanted, what would you do?

He gets a faraway look in his eyes. Then he says, "Travel. Sail around the world, maybe. What about you?"

Briefly I picture myself splashing into the sunset on gold-tipped waves, and hoisting the jib sail with a handsome sailor who has attractive crinkles around his eyes. "I agree. I think I'd go sailing too."

As we near home, Michael points out his street. Oh. My. I had no idea we lived so close together. So close I could easily ride my bike over to his house. I wonder if Michael owns a bicycle? We might bump into each other while pedaling in that quiet part of the park near the river. "Mind if I turn up the AC?" I yelp.

When Michael pulls in to the driveway, he says, "We live so close we could carpool." He turns his head to look at me. "Are you taking the second half of my course in the fall? Modern American Poetry II? It's for advanced students. I think you'd enjoy it."

I'm disarmed by a pair of deep brown eyes. "Sure. That sounds great," I manage to say, weakly, while gathering up my bag and books. "Thanks for the ride."

Oh no. Why did I say that? If I find a job, I won't be coming back in the fall. Now if I return, I'll have to write another poetry essay next term. Feeling wobbly, I try not to trip over my feet as I climb out of his car.

I have to take a written midterm exam in poetry class today. Michael isn't exactly making this course into a sweet summer breeze. But the good news is today marks the midpoint of the term. I have one more essay and one more in-class final exam left to write and I'm free. I walk into class chewing my lip with anxiety. Who cares about midterms? Michael wants to carpool with me.

I find a seat and try to focus on the exam questions. The thing is, do I want to return to school for the fall term? And, if so, do I want to carpool with Michael? The thought makes me twitch all over. I'd have to be on time without fail, and keep the Jeep clear of banana peels and dog snot. And I'd have to stop putting on my lipstick and mascara at red lights.

At the end of class, Michael hands back my essay. He makes no mention of any ride-sharing plan. I feel deflated but only until I see that Michael has granted me a B+. A scrawled note at the bottom of my paper is especially gratifying: *Pauline, I found this essay interesting and insightful. Keep up the fine effort.—M.*

To celebrate the halfway mark, everyone is meeting at the Dingy Cup for pizza and beers. Inside the pub, it's standing room only and we crowd around a long table out on the patio. There's a live band playing rock covers and the music is so loud the umbrellas are reverberating. One of the female students asks Michael to dance and suddenly half our table is up dancing. I sit back in my seat and observe. Michael is a good dancer.

A couple of guys from the next table begin to arm wrestle for beers. One shouts above the din, "Any of you ladies want to try?"

Total amateurs.

I used to be a crook at arm wrestling. When your Dad was a Master Sergeant you learn tricks like the Tippy Tap Top Roll and the Skyfinger Grip. Dad even gave me a hand gripper for Christmas one year so I could develop my finger strength.

"I'll try. But you have to beat me within 20 seconds or I win."

Guys always fall for this. I move over to their table, wedge in tight, and set my right foot forward. If you can achieve body position and leverage, you don't need to be as strong as your opponent.

Dad taught me how to set my wrist correctly, wrap the thumb, and move quickly to get high on your opponent's hand. A good finger squeeze technique will cramp your opponent's wrist strength. Throw your back and shoulders into the game, make eye contact and the contest will soon be over.

Within no time, I have won three beers. I look up and realize Michael is looking on.

Then it's game over. I can feel Michael's eyes on my failing grip as I'm taken down by a skinny kid who actually knows what he's doing. Skinny Kid has my wrist and arm open in seconds, and I'm pinned. I push one of the beers across the table toward him, and offer the extra one to Michael.

We sip as we watch Skinny Kid win a few more beers in quick succession. Then Michael sets his glass down on the table, and says, "Would you like to dance?"

I would.

We weave our way to the crowded floor. As we begin to dance, pushed close together in the crush of people, I think of how fun it would be to be pinned by Michael.

The pub crowd is thinning. Most of our group left over an hour ago but a few stragglers hung on to share a platter of nachos. When the last two students get up to leave, Michael says to me, "I'm going to grab a coffee. Want one too?"

Good idea. We find a spot to sit inside the pub. While Michael goes up to the bar to order, I check my pocket for my car keys and phone. I should be getting home. I've downed a little too much beer. I better call a cab.

We happen to be seated at the same cozy table Michael and I shared the last time, when we talked about books. Oh, what's the rush? Serenity is babysitting for me tonight as Donald is working late. I call home and Serenity answers. While we chat, Michael returns with our coffees and sits in the chair opposite me.

"Thanks," I mime, pointing to the coffee.

I tell Serenity I'll be home soon and put the phone back in my pocket.

"I was checking in with my kids."

Michael looks perplexed.

"My oldest is still up cause she's a teenager."

"How many kids have you got?"

"Three."

We dig into bag and wallet to exchange the photos. Michael admits that his son, Nick, is a handful. Carmen, his wife, took Nick to the doctor recently, and he upped his Ritalin. Michael shakes his head, and leans on his elbows over his mug, staring into his coffee as if he's hoping to see an answer bobbing there. "I don't know if that's the best approach."

He remains silent for a moment and glances up at me. "How long have you been married?"

"Ten years."

Michael looks confused. "But, you have a teenager?"

"I had a starter marriage."

"Ah. Now you have a second chance," he says in a faraway voice. "Are you happy now?"

Michael has caught me off guard. I don't know what to say. So much for second chances? Do I tell the truth? That my husband is never home anymore and I think he might be having an affair? Possibly right at this moment?

Before I can open my mouth to answer, Michael cuts me off. "I didn't mean to put you on the spot."

"How long have you been married?"

"Ten years."

Michael looks worried. I cock my head. He takes a deep breath, lets it out slowly and says, "My wife is … constantly exhausted. She works 12-hour days and sometimes weekends. She collapsed in her office a couple of weeks ago and had to be rushed to the hospital. The doctor said it's stress."

"What does she do?"

"Investment banking."

"My husband is a financial planner. It's the times, Michael. Everyone in that business is stressed."

"Yeah, I guess. But not everyone who is stressed runs out and buys $15,000 worth of Prada luggage."

I'm warming to Michael's wife. She obviously has excellent taste, and she certainly knows a good investment when she sees one.

Michael continues. "It's her money. But she won't ever use the luggage. She's too afraid the airlines will lose it. Why bother?"

I keep my own counsel on this. The airlines lose everything. No sensible woman lets Prada out of her sight. I wonder if she has any Ferragamo belts? How can I wrangle a tour of her closets?

As if he can read my mind, Michael adds, "There's no room left in any of our closets."

Of course all she needs is a better system of organization, a little professional help. A good wardrobe editor could set her straight in a flash.

Michael looks uncomfortable as if he's thinking he shouldn't be sharing this with me, a student he hardly knows.

I nod my head in sympathy. "Hey, it's okay. Don't worry about it. All marriages have their ups and downs."

Michael's face suggests that there are a lot of downs right now and few ups.

"Carmen and I will have to work through this I guess." He drains his coffee. "Want to share a cab home?"

I catch myself humming as I empty the dishwasher of breakfast dishes and refill it with supper dishes. Last night was so much fun. Michael asked me to dance twice. And I can't help but wonder ... is it possible Michael likes me?

What am I thinking? I'm delusional. He likes all his students. He's married. Okay, he asked me to dance two times but then he danced with all the females from class. Who's counting? Everyone was dancing.

I close the dishwasher door and lean on the counter. Suddenly my good cheer vanishes and I want to lie on the couch. The thrill of my brief dances with Michael last night rushes through me: I thought the beer caused me to want to lock my legs around his waist. What's this? Good grief. I have developed a crush on Michael. I better not sign up for his advanced poetry course this fall after all. No more classes with Michael would be for the best. I wouldn't want to allow a baby crush to balloon out of proportion. A little time will let the air out of any puffy attraction.

I check my phone again. Donald isn't home yet. I haven't seen him since yesterday morning. Last night he missed the last train and grabbed a hotel room. He said he ran into late meetings. Serenity said he came home this morning and went right out again.

I texted him three times in the past hour to remind him I have a hockey game. No response. I'm about to try again when he pulls in the driveway. Bibienne pulls in behind him.

As he squeezes past me in the hall, I notice he smells like he's fresh out of the shower. "I went to the gym. I had a squash game," he says when he sees my unsmiling face.

"Never mind."

George is lying across my hockey bag. I shove him off and shoulder my equipment. Donald says, "What? Are you mad at me? Is this about last night?"

I shoulder my gear and reach for the door knob. "Don't worry about it. I have to go, I have a game."

"I was working late. That's it."

"Whatever."

George starts barking and whining as I yank open the door. "Oh yeah, I forgot. Could you please feed George? I don't know where Serenity is."

Donald looks at me as if to say when do I ever know where she is but thinks better of his timing.

I race out the door, stuff my equipment into the back of Bibienne's van and jump in.

"What's up? You seem pissed."

"Nothing."

"Come on."

"Donald. He didn't make it home last night. Again."

"Are you still doing separate bedrooms?

I nod yes.

"Just how separated are you guys? Is Donald dating?"

"Not as far as I know. He won't talk to me."

"What does your gut tell you?"

"Yesterday I went to a website that says the top sign that your husband is having an affair is that you're having to ask the question."

"Then you just proved it. You're asking the question. Donald is having an affair. How long are you going to obsess about this? What are you going to do?"

"Don't I need proof first, before I call a lawyer?"

"Proof helps. But if you don't trust him anymore, you don't trust him, am I right?"

I'm thinking about Michael and me. Together. Drinking late night coffees at the Dingy Cup.

The thing I don't say to Bibienne is: I don't trust me anymore.

After the game, Bibi and I head over to the Puck Stop Lounge with the team.

At the bar, Mackie pulls out her wallet and motions me to put mine away. "That was sick," she says to me, with a huge grin. "You owned that winger, Parril."

I don't tell Mackie that it's because I have a new technique. Every time an opposing player got a piece of the puck, I pictured Donald playing squash with Lindsay.

CHAPTER 9

Adversary

Adversary: A party acknowledged as potentially hostile to a friendly party and against which the use of force may be envisaged.—Department of Defense Dictionary of Military and Associated Terms

Holy crap. George escaped from the back yard one too many times and now the Morriston's poodle is the proud Mom to a litter of seven pups. This morning Lewis's lawyer served us with notice that we're being sued for $25,000 for loss of breeding opportunity, veterinary services including examinations, tests, inoculations, whelping fees, etc. I'll have to make Donald sit down in the living room when I show him this so when he grabs for his chest, he can expire in the comfort of his favorite armchair.

For once, Donald arrives home from work early. He comes into the kitchen, where I'm rinsing lettuce leaves in the sink, and drapes his suit jacket over the back of a chair. I hand him the notice. He scans it, crumples it and tosses it into the garbage can.

"You don't think he'll follow through?"

"Nope. He's just posturing." Donald sits on the kitchen chair watching me spin the leaves in the salad spinner.

"You're home early."

"Yeah, I felt like getting out of there. Do you want some help?"

What's this? Donald's offering to help me make dinner? I wave my hand at the fridge. "Sure. You could chop some ginger for the dressing."

He rummages in the spice drawer and holds up a small jar. "Is this what you wanted?"

"You can't chop powdered ginger. The fresh ginger is in the top crisper."

Donald crouches down to dig through the drawers at the bottom of the fridge. "Do you have anything going on Saturday?"

"Don't think so."

"It's the annual company barbecue. Would you like to come?"

Now I need to grab for my chest. Go out to a company barbecue with Donald? Will Lindsay be there? Probably. I set the salad spinner down on the counter feeling like my head was spinning.

"Why?"

"I just thought you and the kids might like to go."

Donald shoves his arm blindly toward the back of the fridge and a bottle of soy sauce tips forward. I leap to catch it before it falls to the floor. "I said the ginger is in the *top* crisper."

He yanks open the crisper drawer and fishes out the ginger root while I stare at the back of his head. Slowly I say, "I thought we were separated. That means I don't have to go out to your company shindigs. If you want to take the kids, go ahead."

He whirls at me with steely eyes. "Just thought I'd ask. You don't have to come."

He whips the ginger root at the sink, hard, and snatches up his suit jacket.

"Hang on." I say. "Wait a minute. I don't think you 'just thought you'd ask me' at all. You want me to play the wife. So you'll look good in front of the CEO. You don't get to have it both ways, you know."

He rushes out of the house. I hear his car lurch out of the driveway.

I stalk into the living room to sit in the wingback chair. The couch is strewn with Olympia's coloring books and crayons. Getting up, I gather all the books into a pile on the coffee table. I crawl around on the floor on my hands and knees to gather up stray crayons. I hate this old carpet. All of a sudden I hate the whole room. Everything needs to be redone, especially the ugly pesto-colored wallpaper, leftover from the previous owners.

The paper is lifting in places beside the fireplace. I finger the curling paper edge. Seizing the edge firmly, I tear off a long length, leaving a jagged white strip of bare wall. No turning back now. I rip off another piece.

Within twenty minutes, the walls are shredded, and my fingernails are torn and bleeding. In many places, the paper stuck fast. I need buckets of water, drop sheets, scraping tools.

I need to follow through. Yes. I need to change everything.

Bibienne has volunteered to help me shop for wallpaper. On the way to the mall, she asks, "How's it going with you and Donald?"

"He isn't around much lately. We just go our separate ways as much as possible and try to be civil with each other."

I don't mention our fight over the company picnic. Donald took the kids, and I stayed home to finish stripping the wallpaper. Since he moved into the spare room, he gets up at 5 a.m. and leaves hurriedly before anyone is out of bed. Most days he works past dinnertime, comes home and flops in front of the television with a sandwich. Now we communicate mostly by text and email to negotiate who does what with household chores and who is on deck with the kids. Basically he takes his turns with the kid's baths and bedtime, cuts the grass and takes out the garbage, and I do everything else."

"Do you have a separation agreement?"

"Donald says we don't need a legal separation agreement to be separated. Anyway you cut it, the arrangement is still clunky."

I glance down at my ring finger. When I stripped the walls, just before dunking my hands into the bucket of warm water, I removed my wedding rings and tucked them in my jewelry box for safekeeping. I forgot to put them back on. Now I'm not sure I want to.

"What do the kids think?"

"Serenity thinks we're idiots. Jack and Olympia are clueless. I mean, it's not like we're screaming and throwing plates or anything like that."

"That's trendy nowadays. Being separated under one roof."

"Donald's not trendy. He's too busy running his career to file for a divorce. Plus, he's worried about the optics. It's the family guys who get promotions in the financial sector. Divorced guys look too unstable. Plus in our own financial sector, we can't afford two roofs. And then there're the kids. Neither of us wants to rock that boat. It seems easier to just co-exist."

"Do you want a divorce?"

I sigh. "I don't know. Donald and I agreed to wait until I've finished my term at Dingwall and I find another job. Then we'll figure out the next step."

I'm tempted to tell her about Michael. As I prepare to open my mouth again, Bibienne says, "One of my clients almost divorced her husband over toothpaste scum."

"Huh?"

"The guy never rinsed his toothbrush. He'd stick his brush back in the cup all covered with gunk. She asked him to stop and he couldn't be bothered. Finally she decided he didn't care about her needs. She asked for a divorce."

"Just because he wouldn't rinse his toothbrush?"

"Not just because. Think about it. It didn't bother him. So it wasn't important. But it bothered her. She had to look at his gross sticky saliva running down his toothbrush handle every day and decided it was all too much to bear. Plus he left his whiskers in the sink."

"Ewww."

We sit in silence and digest this for a moment.

"So then they got a divorce?"

"She kicked him out of the ensuite. He built himself a bathroom of his own in the basement."

"So now she has a bathroom all to herself?"

"You got it." Bibienne stares ahead into traffic. I know what she's thinking. Get out the blueprints and floor plans. There's got to be a way to get a bathroom of one's own.

I jump out of bed at 5:30 and run out to the driveway to catch Donald, before he has a chance to get out the door to work. I have an urgent face-to-face request.

It rained last night. Donald is gingerly picking up orange peels and a mess of soggy newspapers that are strewn all across the front lawn. Looks like a neighborhood dog—most likely our very own neighborhood dog, George—raided the garbage cans again last night. Before Donald put the garbage out I texted him to suggest he wait until morning as all too often we wake up to a mess. He ignored me.

I struggle to keep from snorting and rolling my eyes to the sky, where fat drops of rain drain down from a mountain of grey clouds.

Donald glares at me. "What do you want?"

"I want to spend the weekend at Mom's house. Alone. I need to catch up on my courses. I'm behind."

Nestled in my purse are the keys to my mother's house. She asked me to check on the house and water the plants while she's off pretending to be Julia Roberts. Donald's eyes shift over to land on Jasper who is sniffing at George's bottom as he poops out a large brown mound on the grass beside me.

"Don't worry. I'll take the dogs with me. Serenity said she'd help out here."

The benefit of Serenity's helping hand doesn't add much to my case but I'm grasping here. And, of course, there's the unspoken part: with me gone, Donald can't stay over in the city tonight.

"Do whatever you want." Donald turns away and bends down to pick up an onion bag.

Mom's bed is magical, all pillow topped and feathered and fluffed. How does she ever get up in the morning? The house is a wonderland of silence: no sounds of Jack and Olympia quarrelling, Donald yelling at them to pipe down, and Serenity and Shae attempting to drown everyone out with what sounds like a test-punk-rap-fist-fusion meltdown. The setting is ideal for studying, and I certainly intend to get cracking on that right away … right after I borrow one of Mom's terry cloth robes and slip out to the hot tub.

In Mom's closet, I'm taken aback to find a wealth of lingerie from Victoria's Secret, all lace and underwires, frills and satin bows, in a rainbow of colors. It's more of a riddle to explain the presence of a red-and-black lacy bra with peek-a-boo cutouts and matching crotch-less panties. Trying them on, I find they're a perfect fit. Surely I'm not the same size as my mother? I paw through mounds of silky nothings frantically. If I don't find an ugly, shapeless, moth-eaten granny gown soon, I'm going to need some powerful mood benders.

Who needs a robe? I'll run for it. The hot tub is out in the screened porch. I slip on Mom's pink Victoria's Secret movie starlet heels and dash across the porch to submerge myself in steaming hot water.

Bliss. I relax deeper into the water and close my eyes. Michael floats in on the mist, reciting poetry. I like the way he sits on the edge of his desk while he reads out loud to the class, his lean legs stretched in front of him, his long fingers gently pressing the spine of the book in his hands.

I could use a long-fingered spinal pressing right about now. There are a variety of nozzles in this tub, including a pulsating jet that of-fers real possibilities. Well, why not? Spreading my legs, I advance toward the spray. Trouble is, the jets aren't strategically positioned. The smooth sides of the tub keep me at bay.

Despite many attempts to take the tub firmly in hand, I can't quite shimmy into the sweet spot. Tremendous flexibility, like that of a tree frog, is required for a touchdown. I should never have quit that yoga class.

With a tendon-stretching shove that will cowboy my gait for days, I manage to pinch in close enough. I close my eyes. Hot mist envelops us as Michael tosses aside the book of poems to recite me instead.

Turns out, Michael is worthy of all the jets.

Afterwards, I step from the tub slowly, so as to stay in the present moment of utter relaxation. Every pore on my body is wide open, pumping out loads of toxins and stress. My skin will be amazing for weeks.

I pile my books on Mom's dining room table and try to study, but my thoughts keep drifting back to Michael: What was it about the way he glanced at me last week, over the top edge of a book of poetry, while he read out loud to the class?

I have to stop thinking about that man.

Holy smokes. The baby crush has turned into a monster crush. It makes no sense. His disarming brown—or are they green?—well, so what—his dreamy blue eyes bob in front of the page when I try to read.

Help me, I'm drowning. I can't wait to see him again.

I am such an idiot: I stepped through the classroom door today and, instead of ecstatic leaping toward me as if we were in a field of daisies, Michael acted perfectly normal. Of course.

What in the world did I expect? Now I can see, with the sickening thump of a reality check, that to him, I'm merely a student he sees once a week. Of course he has no feelings toward me. From now on, Michael is banned from my thoughts.

CHAPTER 10

Classified Information

Classified Information: Official information that has been determined to require, in the interests of national security, protection against unauthorized disclosure and which has been so designated.—Department of Defense Dictionary of Military and Associated Terms

I twisted and turned restlessly all night. The result is a nasty kink in my neck. I can barely move my head. I tiptoe, wincing, to the bathroom and rifle the medicine cabinet for muscle relaxers and painkillers. I take two of each while wondering why I am such a wreck today?

As if I don't already know the answer. It's because I have the house all to myself on a Saturday. Serenity and Shae have gone off to a Queer Arts Film Festival and it's Donald's weekend to look after Jack and Olympia. He's taking them to the Museum of Science in the city.

And, yesterday, Michael offered to meet with students at the Dingy Cup to help us prepare for finals. When I was the only one to sign up for extra help, he said, "Carpool?"

I said, "Why drive all the way to the university?"

Now Michael is coming here, to the house. What if I make a fool of myself? What if Michael were to fall on his knees before me and declare his passion? What would I do? What if I happened to be wearing my sexy navy sweater with the zippered front? Or, better yet, the blue chambray dress with the pearl buttons that go all the way down? Best sleepless night I've ever had.

Despite the debilitating kink in my neck, I help Donald pack up the kids for their excursion. As they troop out the door, my stomach does a little flip flop. Should I have mentioned my study plan to Donald? Am I futzing with the rules by inviting Michael here, into the private recesses of Donald's own scruffy castle? But, this is innocent, right? I've no plan to actually seduce Michael. My intentions are honorable: to enlist academic assistance from my teacher. Guilt is for actual wrongdoers. I've done nothing wrong. Michael will help me prepare for the exam. Then he'll go home. End of story. This will be nothing but a friendly cram session.

Thoughts of friendly cramming with Michael are causing a racing pulse, shaky hands, and lightheadedness. I spy a pack of Serenity's smokes lying on the kitchen counter. A little nicotine might help. One cigarette won't kill me. Maybe I'll have just one puff, to take the edge off. It's not like I'm going back to smoking again.

It's cool and damp out this morning. Pulling on my windbreaker, I step out onto the back deck to light up. With one deep inhale, the top of my head lifts off. All the jitters and guilty feelings float away on the exhale. I might as well enjoy a few more puffs.

I hear the sound of a loud motor coming from the driveway. Sounds like Donald's car needs a new muffler. I'll never hear the end of it if he catches me smoking. Panicking, I stub out my cigarette, and hide the butt in my windbreaker pocket.

I race back inside to assume an innocent pose with my textbook. The doorbell rings. Wait a sec—Donald wouldn't be ringing the doorbell. What the …? Oh my God, it must be Michael. Jumping up, I hurry to the door and invite him in with racing pulse, shaky hands, and lightheadedness.

Michael steps over the threshold with his motorcycle helmet under his arm, saying, "I'm early, hope that's okay. Were you on your way out?"

What? Right. I'm still wearing my jacket. Confused, I bob my head, yes, yes, and no, no, like a deranged bobblehead doll.

Michael shrugs off his leather coat. I take off my own jacket feeling that removing any article of clothing in front of Michael is too suggestive and, possibly, slightly indecent. A shortage of hangers means I have to hang our jackets wrapped together on one in the hall closet: I'm enraptured at the sight of his jacket hugging mine.

Michael examines the bookshelves in the living room while I make the coffee and lay mugs of cream and sugar on the coffee table. I sit on the edge of the wingback chair. "I guess we could start with reviewing notes and then move onto sample exam questions," I stammer to the back of Michael's head.

Michael turns from the bookshelves, and glances at me with that look again. The room is becoming unbearably hot and cold at the same time. With any luck, he won't notice my red, flushed face. To avoid eye contact, I bend my head down over my books and flip through my binder, pretending to be searching for pertinent study notes. He says nothing, and turns back to the bookshelves. The silence in the room makes the rustle of the turning pages excruciatingly loud.

He lingers in the poetry corner for a long time, leafing through the odd volume. Then he asks, "Who are your favorite poets?"

"Yeats, I guess. Mary Oliver. Robert Pinsky. And the lyrical poets, Bob Dylan and Leonard Cohen."

"Leonard Cohen? Interesting. He's one of my favorites too."

In a flash, half the afternoon has passed by in conversation about poetry, novels, movies, restaurants, food, and travel. Amazing. For the past hour now, I've been sitting beside Michael, cross-legged on the floor, our backs leaning against the couch, one thrilled knee twitching against his.

Michael is telling me all about his work-study term in India, back in the days when he was still an undergraduate; he spent a year traveling, writing poetry, and reading the mystic poets. Michael's been studying meditation for years. He has his own guru and everything. He's even writing a dissertation on mysticism.

"I've always wanted to go to India and learn how to meditate."

"Really? It's easy. You don't need to go to an ashram. I can show you how, right here."

Michael sits up straighter. "You can try the half lotus position, like this. Set your hands comfortably on your knees, like this."

I set my hands palms up on my knees in the position of openness to the forces of the universe. Michael nods, that's it.

"You can either close your eyes or half-gaze at a spot on the floor in front of you. Now try to clear the mind and focus on the breath. Don't try to force it or anything, just breathe and feel the air as it moves in and out of your chest."

I can't help but focus on the fact that if I were to accidentally shift my hand over two inches, my fingertips would be brushing against Michael's thigh. Thinking about touching Michael causes my neck to kink up more. Michael looks at me and says, "Try to relax your muscles. You seem tense."

Me? Tense? No, not at all. Tense? No, not me.

"I'm fine. I have a sore neck. I probably slept on it wrong, that's all."

Michael reaches over and places his hand on the back of my neck and squeezes. "Your neck muscles are in knots on the right side. Do you want me to try some Abhyanga? It's an Ayurvedic massage technique I studied in India."

With the touch of his fingers, a surge of electricity bolts down my spine and burns holes through the soles of my feet. My eyes zoom in and out of focus, so I close them. My heart is racing. Is it wrong to be alone with a captivating man who is running his fingers up and down the nape of my neck? Probably.

Okay, first I need to get a grip. This is just a friendly massage. And it's from India, a very spiritual place. Bibienne recently showed me how to do similar massage techniques. No serious line of propriety is crossed. Leaning forward, I tuck my chin onto my chest to offer Michael better access to my neck. I wonder if offering to remove my blouse to facilitate the massage might be interpreted as sending out signals. What am I thinking? Maybe it's high time I say thanks, and put a stop to this.

I open my mouth to speak but no words come out, a good thing, as I would probably start moaning uncontrollably: "Give me the Mumbai Woody Massage, baby."

Abhyanga is phenomenal: all my soreness has magically vanished, but Michael says I'm still in knots and, slipping behind me, proceeds to vibrate my shoulders.

The shoulder vibrating produces incredible tingly reactions in all zones. Michael's warm breath tickles my cheek as he leans closer and gently brushes my hair aside to whisper in my ear, "Would you like me to do your back too? I can work your doshas and marmas, the pressure points, that can release stuck energy."

My doshas and marmas start screaming yes, yes, yes!

Something tells me that perhaps Michael is sending out signals. At a critical time like this I had always thought that I would probably balk. I ought to balk. I ought to at least consider balking. To facilitate the back massage, it would be helpful if I stretched out on the floor. I dive for the carpet, landing face down, panting slightly and getting dog hairs on my tongue and up my nose in the process.

Michael places his hands on my back, and begins a lovely stroking motion but I'm distracted by the mouthful of dog hair. I attempt to spit the hairs out, surreptitiously.

Abruptly, Michael removes his hands. I snap my head around and stare as Michael stands up slowly and sighs. "I better go."

I jump up from the floor. "Why?"

Michael rubs his forehead. "This is wrong. All I can think about is kissing you. I should go."

I step close enough to smell his citrus aftershave. I place my hands on his shoulders. Then I tilt my chin up and offer him my lips.

A wonderful, long, standing-up kiss ensues. A voice shouts from the front parlor of my head, *What do you think you're doing?*

I yank the parlor curtains closed, and urge the voice to go out in the yard: *Get some fresh air, why don't ya? This is private business here.*

My lips want Michael's lips, and they want them now.

Stop. Married. Wrong. The voice commands me to cut it out, now.

It's a kiss. No big deal. I can handle it, okay? I reply.

I shove the voice outside, firmly, and lock the door as my knees turn to mush. I better do something before they buckle out from under me.

It's too late. So long, knees. The wonderful, long, standing-up kiss has somehow turned into a wonderful, long, lying down, rolling-around-beneath-the-coffee-table kiss. The parlor is in danger of becoming a boudoir. Good thing that busybody voice is outside. Wait, no, it's running all around the perimeter of the house peeking in the windows, yelling and rapping its knuckles on the panes.

My lips scream: *Hey everybody, why don't you all shut up, relax and enjoy the ride?* Okay. Michael's mouth is soft like a poem, like a sonnet, like free verse, like rhyming couplets, like … the voice slides back in the front door. *What NOW?* Lips and I scream.

What if Donald were to walk in on this charming little scene?

Meh. I can explain. It's only an ayurvedic massage. And you're just trying to rule me with fear.

You should be afraid when you play vengeful games like this.

Revenge? Is that what you think this is about?

Lips chime in to yell: *No fear, no fear! This kiss is an act of courage and rebellion! Rise up! Besides, this guy's lips are dynamite. They really know what they're doing.*

Voice and I stand back as Lips take charge of the rebel forces. That's all we needed, a little leadership. Where were we? Oh yes, rhyming couplets.

Voice begins to whine again: *Don't you think this floor is uncomfortable?*

It'll do. Go back outside, I say.

The carpet smells like smoke.

Fine. I'll rent a steam cleaner, tomorrow, just shut up.

Maybe it's time to buy a new carpet? How about that Faded French Vanilla Merlot color? It's fabulous.

Go away. I know what you're doing. You're just trying to distract me with domestic stuff.

The voice goes silent as Michael slides his hands further underneath my blouse. Better yet, he's deploying an exciting nuzzling tongue technique across the side of my neck just below my ear. I can't recall Bibienne ever doing a nuzzling tongue when she massaged my back.

My ears ring as if a siren is sounding off inside my head. My eyes are stinging. Michael abruptly stops running his hands up my back. Lips, the voice, and I are all about to protest when we realize the siren sound is the smoke alarm going off in the hall.

I open my eyes. The air is filled with smoke. I glance down below—I've heard of things like this but never before believed it possible. Wait a minute … holy smokes, my kitten isn't on fire. My house is! Snatching myself up from the carpet, I scramble to the hall to see thick plumes of blue smoke and fiery balls rocketing out of the closet, down the hall and into the kitchen where they explode into hundreds of brilliantly colored stars and streaks.

Grabbing my phone, I duck my head, and run outside with Michael, while calling the fire department. A throng of neighborhood residents and passers-by scramble to watch the pyrotechnic display. Every few seconds another explosive round of crackers or out-of-control pinwheels comes careening out the side door, making the crowd shout "ooh" and "ahh" appreciatively. The unpredictable rockets slow the progress of the volunteer firefighters as they run more hoses and foam. They manage to extinguish the fire, which the Fire Chief pronounces to have begun somehow in my hall closet where, by the way, a large number of fireworks were improperly stored; fortunately they were able to contain the fire. I tell the Fire Chief I'm mystified as to how the fire could've been started.

I'm lucky to have a home left according to the Chief. Not to mention that I should also be thankful for the safe deliverance of all my cherished household pets now furiously barking and hissing and squabbling in the back seat of the Jeep. The closet side of my house is shredded as is, I fear, my newborn relationship with Michael given the pained expression on his face as he inspected the charred remains of his leather coat before heading home. As he climbed onto his motorcycle, he handed me his card saying, "Here's my number. Send me a text tonight. Just so I know you're okay."

I step back in the house to find everything dripping wet. The walls are black and the floors, ruined. Serenity's smokes are still lying on the kitchen counter. Perhaps some nicotine will soothe away the tension.

As I draw a smoke out of the pack, I remember the butt hastily shoved in my jacket pocket earlier—but I won't volunteer this clue to anyone, especially to the insurance adjuster who has been called and is on his way over here along with Donald. I go back outside to stand beside the car in the driveway, and light up quickly, closing my eyes and sucking deeply, another pea-brained mistake as Donald pulls in at the same moment.

We meet with the adjuster who says the smoke and water damage extends throughout much of the house; however, he promises to send in a crew and compensate for all affected areas. I'm doubtful, unless there's a deductible for the memory of Michael's hand brushing my neck, the most affected area of all.

Serenity came home from the arts festival without Shae. Apparently Shae shook her sugar a little too close to a belly dance instructor. Serenity locked herself in her bedroom and now she refuses to come out. I volunteered to move back into the house, explaining to Donald that support and supervision of Serenity is essential. Meanwhile, he and the kids are staying at a local motel. This is pure bliss: even Jasper and the cats are safely kenneled out of harm's way while a team of fire-cleaning specialists work their magic. Not only that but the insurance payout means Faded French Vanilla Merlot shag carpeting.

I should try to burn my house down more often.

Second thoughts are as persistent as the smell of smoke in the house. What might've happened if not for the fire? While emptying drawers and closets of reeking clothing for the cleaners, everything comes clear: Saturday's study date with Michael was a close call. I better not let my guard down again.

After all, the state of my underwear is truly shocking. A review of my dresser drawers reveal that my entire supply of bras is in tatters and most are at least a cup size too small. I have to avoid all possibility of further close encounters with Michael until I've had an opportunity to replace my greying and shabby stock of bras and panties.

After class today, Michael, unsmiling, suggested we grab a coffee in the Dingy Cup. At last: a chance to talk to him since the afternoon of our fateful smoking hot kiss. We automatically head for "our" table in the back and sit facing one another.

"Sorry about your jacket," I venture. "But the insurance is going to…"

"Forget the jacket. I can't stop thinking about what happened last weekend. I was way out of line. I apologize. It will never happen again. I'm going to find someone to take over teaching the class."

"Michael, you don't have to apologize. I'm as much to blame. Please don't give up your course. You love teaching poetry. I'll drop the class."

Michael leans back in his seat and folds his arms against my idea. "No. That's not fair. It's too late for you to drop out anyway. You'd have to take an academic penalty."

I prop my chin on my hand to think. What to do? Then I wonder: why do we need to do anything? This is between Michael and me. We can straighten up and march on.

I lift my chin and square my forearms on the table. "Then how about we act like mature adults, forget what happened, and move on? It's only a few weeks till the course is over. Let's just say Saturday afternoon never happened."

"I don't know."

"We can start now. There's nothing going on here, we're just two friends having a coffee, okay?"

Michael stares into his mug, and shakes his head. I lean toward him and tilt my head, "Is it okay to be friends? I can go now if you want me to."

"Yes. No, I mean, don't go. Having coffee and being friends on campus, it's not a big deal. And I could use a friend to talk to right now."

"What's the matter?"

"I just found out Carmen's been taking Nick's Ritalin."

"Are you sure?"

"I confronted her last night. She confessed. It all makes sense now. She knows she's too thin but she won't eat, just drinks coffee all day. Then she stays up all night working. We haven't had sex for months."

I do a quick mental calculation. Who has been in a sexless marriage the longest? Donald started sleeping in the spare room weeks ago, but I can't even remember the last time we had sex before that, so it's been months for us too.

"What are you going to do?"

"I don't know. She needs help. But she doesn't think it's a big deal."

I make the mistake of placing my hand on Michael's forearm in a comforting gesture. Of course, I might as well have dragged him under the table and licked his nipples clean off. The unintentional side effect of hand contact causes our eyes to lock. His eyes are saying, "Okay, I just told you I haven't had sex in six months, right? Your hand is making this very hard for me … don't move a muscle."

My eyes are saying, "Help. My hand has fallen on your arm and it can't get up."

CHAPTER 11

Warning Order

Warning Order: A preliminary notice of an order or action that is to follow. —*Department of Defense Dictionary of Military and Associated Terms*

The frickin' cleaners have worked so rapidly and efficiently that the house is once again fit to receive Donald and the kids. They troop in marveling at the gleaming walls and floors. "It's fantastic, isn't it?"

Donald nods but says nothing. The house has never looked so immaculate. He looks away quickly but I'm sure I spotted tears in his eyes.

In the living room, Donald glances down at the new carpet. "Orange? Isn't that kind of seventies?"

"It's not orange. It's Faded French Vanilla Merlot."

"Okay, then. It's … different."

"You don't like it."

"I didn't say that. Maybe it's the curtains. Pink and orange don't go together."

"The drapes aren't pink. They're terracotta."

"Only if terracotta is the same color as that stuff you take for diarrhea."

Serenity's cat, Scratches, comes into the room and rubs up against my leg, purring. Isn't that sweet? She missed me. Then Donald and I watch as she discovers the carpet and buries her claws deep into the shag.

"Out," I cry.

Wait. One annoying pet is missing. "Donald, did you forget to pick up Jasper at the kennel?"

"Not exactly. I thought maybe we could keep him there till your Mom gets back. It's a first-rate kennel with a vet and everything."

"I agree. Excellent idea."

I'm overjoyed with Donald's arrangements. Shae is gone along with George: that means no dogs in the house! Oh my! I'm in danger of falling back in love with my clever husband.

"For what they charge, Jasper better be fine. Uh, we don't have to say anything to your Mom?"

"Cross my heart."

Donald picks up his bag and says, "Where would you like me to put this?"

"What do you mean?"

"Oh, come on. How long are you going to keep this nonsense up?"

My cheeks grow hot. "Nonsense? That's all our issues are to you? An inconvenient passing phase and all you have to do is wait it out?"

Donald's jaw clenches with rage. "You know what? Never mind. I'm done with waiting. Forget I asked, okay?"

I'm still not speaking to Donald but it looks like Serenity and Shae, at least, patched things up last night. Serenity's bedroom door is firmly closed with a leather tie draped over the doorknob. There's been no actual visual of Shae yet but the sight of her pickup truck parked back in the driveway and George Bush parked back on my bed with wet, muddy paws, is enough confirmation for me.

It's not always possible to keep up a campaign of not speaking. When Donald walked in from work tonight I had to know: "The vet called today. He wants to know when you're planning to pick up the cremains."

"The cremains?"

"Yes, from Jasper."

"Jasper is dead?"

"Yes—the vet said you told them to have him put to sleep."

Donald's face balls up in a huge grimace and then he face-palms himself several times, so hard I can hear slapping sounds. "I told those idiots I'd like to have the dog put down, not for them to actually do it."

"My mother is going to flip."

"Shhhhhiiiittt."

"When you go to pick up the ashes, maybe you could take the new television back so we can pay off the vet bill."

Mom's on the phone. She's relaxing in her suite and wants to speak to Jasper: "Put the phone up to his widdle ear so I can tell him how much I miss my sweet widdle poopy-pup."

At least the loss of Jasper has brought Donald and me back together a little, if only to the point of talking cordially again. Donald and I decided to put off telling Mom about Jasper for now. Why ruin her vacation? Covering the receiver with my hand, I hand the phone to Donald. "Hey poopy-pup, come over here and pant for my mother." I hold the phone up to Donald's ear while Donald pretends to slobber on the receiver. Best part of my day.

CHAPTER 12

R&R

R&R: The withdrawal of individuals from combat or duty in a combat area for short periods of rest and recuperation.—Department of Defense Dictionary of Military and Associated Terms

Michael just texted me some promo on a spoken word event he's emceeing at the Dingy tonight. He added a personal message: *Hope you can make it.* He posted the invitation on the class board too, so it's innocent, not like a date or anything. I have to say no because I have a hockey game. Immediately I get another text: *What about after the game?*

I text him back to explain: after the game Mackie is throwing a party for the whole team at her house. The theme is Hawaiian Cruise. Bibienne and I are hard at work in her basement making coconut shell bras.

Bibienne finishes adjusting the leather straps on her creation and looks up at me as I sample the crantinis once again before putting the jug back in the freezer: "Go easy on the vodka, we have a game tonight, remember?"

My bra is ready to try on. I tuck the girls into their shells in front of the mirror and admire the results. Those Hawaiian lovelies sure know what they're doing. Nothing beats a coconut shell for providing trustworthy support and cleavage.

The Devilicious are the toughest team in the loop but we squashed them for once, winning the game 1–0 mostly thanks to Bibienne, who rocked her net tonight. Decker, that rotten pest of a dirty left-winger, took it out on Mackie who is now sitting in a corner nursing a rum drink and a groin pull.

Michael just texted me again, wondering how my party is going. Too bad he can't see me in my Hawaiian outfit. I bet Michael would love the coconut bra. And now we're texting each other right? Why not share? I snap a selfie with my phone and flip it over to him.

Nothing gets past Bibienne. "Who're you sending that to?"

"Facebook," I say and immediately regret it. Now I have to post this stupid pic.

It's tempting to tell Bibi about Michael. But I know she'll only tell me to go easy on the vodka.

Mom just got home, and is on the phone asking for Jasper. She's wondering why Donald sent her a giant arrangement of flowers. That coward. Guess it's up to me to break the news to her gently. "Mom, when you're talking to Dad, do you sense anyone else there with him?"

While sitting in Financial Management class, I get a text from Bibienne: "Whup ass time!"

Tonight's the night. The season finale: it's ours to win or lose. The whole team has been texting pregame trash twitters every few minutes, all day long. "The Devilicious are dead meat." "The Furies are coming." "I can't wait to wipe their boats!" Game on.

I play better when I have extra carbs laid on. As I hand out plates of spaghetti, Donald comes in the door from work and spies my hockey bag on the hall bench. "You have a game tonight?"

"It's only been on the calendar for weeks."

He sighs heavily, glances at his watch and gives me his distressed face. "I have to go back to the office tonight."

"Are you kidding me? It's your night to watch the kids. Serenity just took off somewhere."

"I know, but they're all going insane in there with that pension disaster thing. I'm sick of it."

"But we agreed: tonight is my night out and I can't miss this game."

Jack breaks in. "Daddy, can we go see Mom play hockey? Please?"

Donald looks at Jack and his expression relaxes. "Sure. Why not?"

In the dressing room, Coach is getting worried. "Listen up everyone. This isn't going to be a grudge match. I don't want anyone getting hurt."

Coach is wrong. This most definitely is a grudge match. Mackie is looking for blood tonight after being handed her ass in our last game with the Devilicious. They hate us because they think we hate them for being younger than us. We don't exactly hate them, but those college girls are total posers. They think they're so tough.

Mackie tightens her skate laces with a vicious tug. "Don't worry Coach. We won't get hurt. We're putting all the hurt on the baby pukes."

One of the forwards looks up from shaping a huge tape ball on the butt end of her stick. "Yeah, they're going to be puking their baby food all over the ice."

Everyone guffaws. Coach sighs. "I'm warning you all. Don't let them suck you into the penalty box. That especially means you, Mackie."

Mackie chirps back immediately: "Okay. No sucking allowed."

Ferris holds up her stick. "Except for their goalie. She can suck on this."

As we straggle out onto the ice, the Devilicious are circling their end. They show off by flicking pucks high at the glass and performing a complicated choreography of fancy warm-up exercises. Meanwhile their goalie flops around in her net with her feet dancing above her ears and her legs splitting wide sideways across the crease.

Our goalie is late. "Where the hell is Bibi?" everyone is saying. Where's our captain, Mackie? Shouldn't she be jacking us through our warm-up moves? There she is, slapping puck missiles from the blue line, smiling and nodding, *See you real soon* at the Devilicious goalie while staring down the defense line. Mackie has the best hockey glare in town. After ten years of playing, I've seen all the tricks. It's mostly a mind game. Outsmart the opposition. Mind your position. Play a clean and sober defense.

Wait. OMG. I've just spotted Michael in the stands. Of all nights to pick to come see one of my games, he had to pick this night. I speed up to show off. Scanning the seats, I spot the kids and Donald, seated several rows below Michael. They're waving at me and yelling, "Go Mom," as I glide past. I do a fancy stop, carving an ice rooster with my blades, and wave back at them with my stick. Michael waves too.

Mackie skates past and checks me with her shoulder, knocking me off balance, "Why are you standing around? Move your arse, Parril."

Bibi arrives in the nick of time. She inspects her net and the puck is dropped. The fight is on within a few plays as the Devilicious quickly get steamed with Ferris for crowding their goalie. Mackie whispers to me between whistles, "Keep Decker over there out of the crease. She's trying to rattle the Bib."

I know the one: the ratty left-winger, the one who handed Mackie the groin pull. Decker and Bibi have been ramping it up all summer. No one can unnerve the Bib, but the pest keeps on trying. "No problem. Decker is toast," I cry as the puck is dropped in our zone.

The Devilicious captain knocks it into the corner and races in after it. I fly straight down the boards after her, elbows poised and at the ready. Mackie is cruising in on my wing.

They don't call me Elbows for nothing. That's because I know how to make it all look unintentional, innocent, an accident. Their captain soon goes down with the puck somewhere underneath her. Not my fault, she tripped over her own feet. As Mackie and I dig for the puck, I can hear Decker piling in on us from behind. She's screaming, "Get off the ice, cougar tits. You're going to get yourself hurt."

That's it. I've had it with that kid and her endless chirping all season long. You do what you have to do. I spin around fast. Decker's grin is wrapped tight around her mouthguard. Bracing myself to take the hit, an instant later her stick slams into my chest and I crumple backwards on top of the captain who takes the opportunity to start punching at my helmet.

A whistle blows, hard. The ref pulls me up by the front of my jersey and drags me off the captain who is swearing like a hardrock miner. The ref looks cross. Good, I hope both of them get a penalty. But the ref hangs onto my arm and points me toward the box. An elbowing penalty? What? You call that an elbow? "Come on, ref. She cross-checked me," In protest, I pound my stick on the ice. "COME ON."

The ref shakes her head warningly and checks the back of my jersey for my number before showing me off the ice. There goes my penalty-free season. As I slump into the box, the whole bench starts screaming insults at Decker and the Devilicious's captain who are cackling in triumph and high fiving with their goalie. I look up into the stands to see Donald hand Olympia his camera so she can snap a few pics of Mom in the box.

Mackie is chest to chest with the ref, screaming. The ref dumps her into the box beside me. Up in the stands Shae and Serenity are on their feet whistling and shouting. They showed up at the end of the second period. Donald stayed anyway. He is grinning. Even Jack looks impressed. I can't read the expression on Michael's face. He's sitting too far back.

Because of Mackie and me, the Devilicious now have a two-woman advantage. Bibienne is soon whirling around in the net. Decker is getting more brazen by the second, jabbing at Bibi with her stick every time the ref looks away. Decker then turns and backs tight into the crease to wait for a pass. Bibi shoves her back out of the crease a couple of times and finally jabs her stick into the unprotected back-stretch of Decker's calf. Decker flops down, moaning and clutching her leg, like the big faker she is, while Bibi stands there shrugging and grinning. The ref blows the whistle and Decker is helped off the ice, her limp large and heavily embellished. Ferris joins us in the box to serve out Bibi's slashing penalty.

After one scrimmage, where no one can see what's happening as there are so many enemy shirts charging our net, the whistle blows and Bibi is lying facedown on the ice. Where's the puck? Slowly she gets up, takes off her catcher, reaches into her bra and scoops out the puck. The crowd goes wild.

Mackie is fuming beside me, planning a bloodbath. "You take the high road, and I'll take the low," she shrieks as the penalty clock ticks to zero. She throws her legs over the boards and lands, feet splayed wide, like a furious wildcat off a rocky ledge.

A cool move, the leap over the boards. I try to follow suit but wind up tangled up in my stick and I plunge over the boards instead, belly flopping onto the ice with a sickening ouff, looking, no doubt, more like a dead possum plopping out of a tree than a wild anything. A titter runs through the crowd as I cross the ice, winded and limping, to the bench.

Everyone is grumbling that the ref's cousin plays for the Devilicious. Coach says, "Don't give her any excuses then." We all watch as Chainsaw, miraculously limp-free, hooks Mackie's skate and Mackie goes down. Ferris skates past the ref, lips a-flapping. Seconds later the whistle blows. Ferris is back in the box with a penalty for mouthing off the ref.

Coach sends me back in. We kill off the penalty, Mackie scores a shorthanded goal and rolls out her rub-it-in dance all around their net. As we face off, I make sucking noises at Decker, while pretending to put the thumb of my glove in my mouth. The puck drops and Ferris slaps it into their zone and we all tear after it. Mackie gets there first. Decker plows her into the boards from behind.

Mackie loses her mind. She jumps up, throws her gloves off and tackles Decker. Decker tosses her gloves, grabs Mackie by the front of the jersey with one hand and chainsaws her with her other fist. The whistle blows. An angry Devilicious player skates past me and hooks my skate, sending me sprawling on the ice. Quickly, I jump up to settle the score. Ferris leaps in to help me.

After all the sticks and gloves are cleared from the ice, Mackie and Decker have been exiled to the dressing room. The rest of us get warnings. Back on the bench, Coach reams us out until, subdued, we hang our heads in shame. The game ends in a tie. No one wins.

By the time I shuffle out of the dressing room, Michael is nowhere to be seen. Shae claps me on the back. She wants to join the Furies. "That was kick-ass," she keeps saying over and over.

Donald is waiting in the lobby. He grins at me. "When did you turn into such a dirty player?"

"I'm not a dirty player. No more than anyone else."

Donald raises his elbows and flaps them in the air.

"Shut up."

One more weekend left to hit the books and I'm done with all my courses. As I stare out the window of the den, the phone on my desk rings. I hope it isn't Mom. She calls me every day to talk about whether she should stay with Ted or go back to Brian. I pick up at the same time as Serenity. It's Shae.

Before I can hang up my end, Serenity shrieks straight into my ear: "Stop calling me, bitch. And I'm keeping George Bush."

Serenity has been in a complete snit all morning as Shae stormed out last night yelling, "Don't be such a whiny vagina." Those two are constantly fighting and reconciling. Shae will probably be back in time for supper.

I close the door to the den but I can still hear Serenity screaming at the receiver in the kitchen. Soon Jack starts in, whining at Serenity to get off the landline already. Olympia is yelling at them to shut up because she can't hear the television. Donald is, of course, long gone to his office, far from the keening and crying of his offspring. Tonight he's going out with friends. Who knows who or where? I won't wait up.

I hear cupboard doors slam, more shouting, and then a crash and a thud. Abandoning my textbook, I head to the kitchen to mediate the uproar. Jack is lying on the floor, howling, and Serenity is standing over him, arms akimbo.

"What was that crashing sound? What's going on?"

"Jack threw the popcorn maker at me."

"Serenity hurt my toe."

"He tried to kick me and hit the cupboard instead."

I glance at the cupboard door. There's a large crack running down the middle of the panel. Jack says, "It's okay, it didn't break."

Serenity storms out of the house. While I make sandwiches for lunch, Jack hangs around to discuss lizards. He wants an iguana. Apparently life isn't worth living without a lizard companion.

"Rather than hassling me for an iguana, how about inviting a friend over to play?" Just in time, I stop myself from saying, "Maybe that one who looks like an iguana?"

I go back to the den. Jack promptly calls three buddies and Olympia, two, before I catch on. I confiscate the phone and put an end to the free for all, but it's too late to cancel the impending invasion by neighborhood kids: their ecstatic parents are, no doubt, in blistering fast transit by now.

It isn't long before Jack and three friends are hunkered down in front of the television with video games, cans of soda pop, and a large bag of mini chocolate bars. I step into the room as Jack flips a candy wrapper aside and says to his friends, "You can throw them on the floor, my Mom will pick them up."

"Pick up that mess," I say, "and go play down in the rec room." This was a bad directive as they soon commence a musical interlude using Donald's ancient amp, an electric guitar, keyboard, and my bongos.

Back in the den, I attempt to put the finishing touches on my final poetry essay about Emily Dickenson, due tomorrow. Essay writing has become tinged with eroticism. Knowing that Michael will be reading my naked prose makes my fingers tingle as they type. I want to drape myself across the page, and let his eyes advance slowly across my silky sentences, stripping off all my punctuation and splitting my infinitives. I want to use words like squeeze, tickle, and press, and I want to end up quivering in a puddle of soft consonants, ooo's, and aaaa's, after arching my vowels under his poetic gaze.

This is going to be a long night.

CHAPTER 13

Go No-Go

Go No-Go: The condition or state of operability of a component or system: "go," functioning properly; or "no-go," not functioning properly. Alternatively, a critical point at which a decision to proceed or not must be made.—Department of Defense Dictionary of Military and Associated Terms

With classes done, final essays handed in, and exams written, I no longer know what to do with myself. I sit at the kitchen table and re-check my agenda: nothing but a blank page. It's a glorious late August morning: warm, dry and, I can't help but think, picture perfect for a picnic lunch or a bicycle ride with Michael. Trouble is, I decided to let Jack and Olympia stay home with me today to take a break from day camp.

Serenity comes into the kitchen in her pajamas, and slumps into the chair across from me. Her eyes are red and puffy.

"Do you want some tea? Are you hungry? Here, I'll make you some honey toast." Jumping up, I slip two slices of bread into the toaster.

Serenity sniffs and shrugs. Shae and Serenity's latest reconciliation ended with a bang late last night when Shae gunned it out of the driveway in her truck, backfiring as always. Shae's toolbox has disappeared from the corner beside the door. George is lying under the kitchen table with his head tucked between his paws.

Serenity sees my glance at George and sniffs again. "Don't worry. Shae says she'll come back later and collect George."

Oh no. I was kind of getting used to having George around. "I'm sorry honey," I say and pat Serenity's shoulder.

Unfortunately, my mood isn't much better. What if I blew my finals? Guess I need to start looking for work again. Or register for more classes. I can't decide. Or maybe I should hang the wallpaper today. The rolls I bought weeks ago are tucked behind the couch. I pull one out to examine it. Donald's eyes bugged right out when he saw the receipt. I'd return the rolls except now the living room walls are stripped bare. If we end up splitting up we'll probably have to sell the house. I'll have to stage the living room. Guess I'll hang the wallpaper today and hang myself out to dry on the job market tomorrow. Or, since it's a nice day out, a better plan would be to weed the flowerbeds, neglected all summer long.

I throw on my clothes and am about to go in search of my gardening gloves when my phone beeps. It's a text from Michael! *What are you doing today? I'm at the park with Nick.*

Forget the wallpaper, forget the flowerbeds. I'm going to the park with Jack and Olympia.

Soon Michael and I are relaxing under a shady tree in the park with two tall iced cappuccinos. What extraordinary good luck—I waxed my legs last night, and I'm wearing my sexy gardening shorts. As Jack, Olympia, and Nick are occupied on the jungle gym, Michael is free to tease me by twirling grass across my silky smooth shins. After a while, he whispers in my ear that he's glad he can no longer be fired from his job for imagining me naked. "When can I see you alone?" he asks.

Michael has a suggestion—perhaps we might wish to go for a ride on his motorcycle, say, tomorrow? Tomorrow is Friday. What do I have on?

"Perfect. I already have Serenity lined up to babysit. I have a job interview downtown. Maybe we could meet after lunch?"

"What's the job?"

"The company sells electrical equipment. They need someone to head up the size #2 rubber resisters. If I am good I can move up to thermal capacitators and they might even send me to the national convention on semi-conductors in Omaha next year.

Michael makes a face. "That sounds awful."

What else can I do? There's one good part: I can justify a pre-interview haircut appointment at that fabulous new salon in town that Bibienne keeps raving about. And now, after the interview, I'm going out with Michael!

I direct the kids to clear away the breakfast dishes while I get dressed and go over my plan. First, the salon appointment. I can go straight from there to my interview. Then, meet with Michael. I wonder if I can get away with a casual Friday outfit for a Friday interview? Well, why not? I couldn't care less about this job anyway. It's bound to be a pathetic joke like all the rest; why do I even bother?

Checking my watch, I see that I'm running out of racetrack to get to my hair appointment on time. Arggh. I can't find my favorite lipstick. I rummage through the bathroom cabinets and vanity drawers while ignoring the sounds of a loud argument in the kitchen: Jack and Olympia are fighting over who should clear the last glass from the table. I hear a glass shatter, then a brief silence, and then a fresh eruption over whose fault it was.

"Jack, I hate you, you shittybutthead."

"Don't say 'shittybutthead.' Mom, Lumpy's saying swear words again."

I run downstairs to break up the fight and clear away the broken glass. Jamming the shards into the overflowing pail, I attempt to tie off the garbage bag at which one of the shards rips through the plastic and jabs straight into my wrist.

Jack and Olympia stop fighting to watch their mother trying not to faint at the sight of blood spurting all over the cuff of her favorite casual day blouse. Shit, shit, shit. Now I'll have to find something else to wear. Oh God, the blood is going everywhere. Except to my legs. I better lean over the sink. I wonder how long it takes to bleed to death? Need doctor. Now.

I feel woozy: maybe it's too late for the doctor? How many klutzes like me slash their wrists by accident and in so doing deprive their heirs of the pots of insurance money? No underwriter could doubt my motivation given my crumbling house, joblessness, roving husband, etc. "Shit, shit, shit."

"Mommy, don't say 'shit,'" says Olympia.

"Olympia said 'shit,'" says Jack. "Put her in a timeout."

"Never mind that. Jack, where's Serenity?"

"I dunno. I think she went out."

Wrapping my wrist in towels, I leave Jack in charge of Olympia and drive myself to the ER.

I'm in agony. Four stitches were required to close my wrist wound. I'm now incapable of lifting heavy objects like dishcloths and cupfuls of laundry soap and the like.

The job interview was a complete disaster. My hair was a rat's nest because of missing the salon appointment, and I was hours late because of lineups at the hospital ER where, when my turn came around the nurse, knitting her brows over my slashed wrist, called in a social worker, who wanted to ask me if I have enough support at home and if I have ever thought about getting help, and then she put her hand on my shoulder and said that the next time I feel like giving up, I need to tell myself that I can hold off for just one more day, hour, minute—whatever I can manage.

After, I flew home to change out of my blood-soaked outfit. I could find nothing else interview-worthy to wear but my winter-weight wool suit, the skirt-half of which I located under the cat in a heap on the floor at the back of my closet.

I was the last applicant to be interviewed. While waiting my turn I, very regretfully, texted my apologies to Michael, picked the cat hair from my skirt with my good hand and told myself to try to hold off for at least one more hour.

Then I had to face down a forbidding panel of seven interviewers. Seven. For me. I'll be wanting a cushy job in upper management in my next life, yes, please, and thank you very much. Everyone looked knowingly at the bulky cotton dressing on my wrist while I, slowly boiling to mush in my winter-weight suit, used it to mop my red, dripping face. When they asked me about my salary expectations I lost my head, and snortily told them of course I expected a salary, and a damn good one too.

After the interview debacle, Donald received the news with a concerned shrug and then smirked. "Most people slash their wrists *after* having a bad day."

Damn. Damn. Damn. Last week's flummoxed job interview has produced a serious offer. They're giving me a couple of weeks to think it over. It's a sweet deal with a fat pay scale, decent benefits plan and possible occasional travel. I picture myself touching up my nail polish and relaxing on a comfy hotel room bed while coolly parenting long distance over the phone like those neatly tucked in business women on television ads: I'd work for free if they'd guarantee the travel. Jack hopes I'll go for it since he wants a wave pool for his birthday.

I describe the job offer to Donald when he arrives home from work. He shrugs and says, "It's a solid company. And a good benefits package. Are you going to take it?"

"I guess I should."

"You don't sound very excited."

I shrug. What does he want me to say? That I'm dying to go into rubber resistor sales?

"What do you really want to do?"

"I'd like to finish my degree this fall. If I go full time, I'll be done by Christmas."

"Fine. Finish your degree then."

"But what about us? I mean, the sooner I go back to work, the sooner we can move on. What do you want me to do?"

I've got him cornered. Our eyes meet. His turn slate grey and angry. "Do whatever you want. I don't care."

Then he storms off to the den and shuts the door.

I sit in the wingchair to think. Is Donald angry because he wants me to take the job so he can be free of me? If he wants out so badly, why is he urging me to finish my degree? Does he even know what he wants?

Do I know what I want? Working means never having a minute to myself again. Back to cranky bosses and office politics. Back to terrible overhead lighting that gives me headaches and makes my skin look pasty.

Going back to work means making a final decision about Donald and me.

Going back to school this fall means staying seated on my comfortable wingchair-shaped fence, taking time to think.

Going back to school means coffee dates with Michael at the Dingy. Well, shouldn't I finish what I've started?

CHAPTER 14

Command Post Exercise

Command Post Exercise: an exercise in which the forces are simulated, involving the commander, the staff, and communications within and between headquarters.—Department of Defense Dictionary of Military and Associated Terms

If only George would stop barking at every tiny little thing, the house would be quiet and peaceful tonight. This morning Donald flew off to Calgary with the Doubles prospecting team—a team that includes good old Lindsay—to assess possibilities for a new Canadian branch. Yesterday I put Serenity on a bus to go visit her Dad for a few days, and Olympia and Jack are both at friends' houses for sleepovers. Cool.

I pour myself a glass of wine and lie on the couch with my laptop. Michael is online. I message him: *I'm alone. I have the house all to myself.*

Almost immediately, my cell phone rings. Furious, George leaps off the couch to bark at the door, his fur rising in a sharp ridge across his back. Jumping up, I grab his collar and try to shush him while answering: it's Michael.

"What's all that barking about?"

"George thinks he's a tough dog. He's making me nervous; there've been a lot of break-ins in the neighborhood recently. I wish you were here."

"I wish I could be there too. Carmen's gone out but I've got Nick tonight."

"Oh."

"He's asleep, though. We can talk. Hang on a sec."

A minute later he comes back on the phone. "I want to share something with you," he says. "It's a poem I wrote."

The poem is about a couple. They're paddling together across a pretty hidden lake. The woman reclines, trails the tips of her fingers in the water and then runs them across her throat letting the droplets trickle down.

Michael pauses to say, "Go ahead, trail your fingers in the water too."

"My fingers are already dripping."

I like where this is going. Michael sure knows how to make a woman want to get naked in a canoe.

I don't think Michael actually used the word throbbing but that's what everything in the lake is doing. Frogs dart their long licking tongues in a frenzy of tasting, touching, and teasing while dragonflies flirt around stands of cattails. The man continues paddling across the lake with slow intention and purpose. He dips his big, thick, sopping wet oar, plunging it, deeper, harder as the cattails sway, undulate and moan, and the rippling waves swell.

By the end of the poem, I've sunk to the carpet, throbbing too, all hot and sloppy with desire.

"Now you have to come over and mop me off the floor."

"You know I'd love to."

Michael wishes me a good night. Oh well. Maybe there's a good show on. I scan the channels while George patrols the perimeter. At the back door he stops to growl deep in his throat; this time I, too, hear a noise: a muffled thump on the back deck. What could it be? A cat? A skunk? A raccoon? A ruthless, throat-slashing woman-raping killer?

It's just the cat. After double-checking all the door locks, I turn off my phone and lie down on the couch with the television remote. George jumps onto the couch with me and settles down, his huge bony head resting on my feet. I'm glad Shae didn't come back to get him after all. Serenity says she took off up north to plant trees. For good.

I'm fast asleep when George suddenly flies off the couch to hurl himself at the front door in a barking frenzy. This time he refuses to shut up. Peeking through my blinds I see, parked in front of my house, a police cruiser with all of its lights flashing. Two officers are ushering a man into the back seat. Stepping out onto the porch, I spy Lewis standing on his front lawn, arms folded across his chest.

"What's going on?" I say to Lewis.

"That sneaky SOB was sitting in his car with the lights off, right over there in front of your house. Casing out the neighborhood."

As the cruiser pulls away from the curb, I spot Michael's car parked across the street.

I hurry down to the station, aim my voice into the microphone in front of a plate glass window and explain the situation to the officer in charge. The OC turns to his computer, types in my name, address, and phone number and points me at a chair in a long hallway.

I sit and stare at a rack of pamphlets with titles like *So You've Been Charged With An Offense* while hoping the officer didn't smell wine on my breath. It's been hours since I had a sip but that's enough to pretty a picture up nicely. My hair is uncombed and there's cat hair on my sweater from lolling around on the carpet pretending I'm a water nymph. Yes, I am the real deal of a reliable witness, sitting in a police station in the middle of the night with stringy hair and booze on my breath. In fact, I might well be harmful to Michael's case.

An hour passes. An angry-looking woman shows up to collect her son, picked up earlier for underage drinking. The kid is still unsteady on his feet and the woman hauls him away, her eyes beveled with cut-glass ire.

I go back to watching the officer in charge ruffle through papers on his desk. He refuses to make eye contact with me. Every time the phone rings he yawns, stretches, and answers in a bored voice.

More time passes. Finally Michael emerges and the officer buzzes him out to the hall. Michael isn't smiling.

"I'm free to go," he says to the wall above my head.

"Do you want a ride home?"

"It's probably better if I grab a cab."

He turns and heads for the door with a rapid stride. I follow him outside onto the stairs where he lights a cigarette and takes a deep drag. As an afterthought he offers me a puff but I shake my head, no. I wait but he doesn't say anything. Instead, he intently watches the smoke trails as he blows them, one after another, straight up to the night sky. There is the faintest tinge of dawn on the horizon.

I can't stand it anymore. "What happened?"

"I was sitting in my car trying to text you when those bozos showed up and dragged me down here. They said there was a robbery in the neighborhood earlier tonight, and I fit the description of the guy. I've been discharged as a case of unfounded arrest."

"That's a relief."

Michael doesn't look relieved. He looks like the angry mother.

"There's an incident report with my name on it in their files. Forever. *Forever.* It says suspected robber. In block lettering."

"The file is closed now. And those files are confidential."

Michael's voice goes wry and incredulous, and he says, as if to himself, "I've never been a person of interest before." And shakes his head, sadly.

Then he looks at me as if he's reflecting on the progress of his life since he met me. I feel like that edgy girl who gets everyone else to smoke in the schoolyard.

He turns his head away. His jaw tightens and he says, "They wouldn't let me see what else they wrote on the file."

"I'm sure it's okay. Try not to worry."

Michael takes another deep drag off his cigarette.

"Carmen came home just after we talked. I told her I was going out to a spoken word thing. I should've been home hours ago. I guess it's the great big dog house for me."

He yanks out his phone and checks the screen. "They wouldn't even give me my one call."

A taxicab pulls up to the curb. I watch him climb into the back seat and lean forward to give the driver his address. *Just after the park, the big doghouse on the left.* Before closing the cab door, he leans out slightly and says, distractedly, "I'll call you. Wait, maybe you should call me. I don't know."

"Take care," I offer as the window goes up. He slumps back in the seat and the cab pulls away.

CHAPTER 15

CONPLAN

CONPLAN: In the context of joint operation planning, level 3 planning detail, an operation plan in an abbreviated format that may require considerable expansion or alteration to convert it into a complete operation plan or operation order.—Department of Defense Dictionary of Military and Associated Terms

"I have news." Donald rolls in the door, off his flight from Calgary, wearing an intense expression on his face. "Doubles is offering me a sweet deal. They need a top gun out in Calgary to set up the new branch office. Eight months out west and I'll get a promotion. They're promising me a directorship. And a big increase plus living expenses."

Calgary? Calgary is way out west. And way up north in Canada where it's bitterly cold. The west is full of cows. They have stampedes up there. And gas and oil wells all over the place. And snow. Lots of snow. My mind races on past a vision of an endless line of oilrigs propped in snowbanks to a string of questions: does Donald want us to move west with him? And what about Lindsay? Lindsay is up for a directorship, too. And she's been with Doubles longer. She's next in line. What are they doing with her?

As if reading my mind, Donald says, "Lindsay Bambraugh is working on the international development portfolio a lot these days. She's not that interested in staying in New England."

These days, decision-making discussions between Donald and me are all too often as intricate and choreographed as a rare bird-mating dance on a late-night wildlife documentary. Donald hasn't spoken to me this solicitously in months. He really wants this promotion.

I begin with a show of ruffled feathers: "You want to move to Canada? For eight months? What about the kids?"

Donald opens his beak slightly as he realizes that I'm deftly serving the first volley of the Mating Dance Game of Convincing Me to Stay Home With the Kids While He Flits About Freely Out West (leaving me to my own free-flitting agenda). Your move, Donald.

"I can't see all of us going. I don't know how that will work out for the kids' schooling," he frowns, as if Jack and Olympia might be irreparably harmed by the sight of a Calgarian classroom, no doubt a cheap thin prefab, listing precariously under the harsh prairie winds. Of course, Jack and Olympia are being schooled in a crumbling building that saw the Kennedy administration come and go, but what of that?

I frown and nod too, and then adopt a look of innocent thoughtfulness. "We'd have to rent the house. I don't know what sort of people might want to rent a house for only eight months though."

We pause to shiver at the thought of our basement becoming the hub of a grow-op or a terrorist cell or, worse, a frat boy hangout.

It's critical to be the one to come up with the last objection so the other one will have to offer up the alternative arrangement. We furrow our brows as we try to think of more compelling objections. Donald isn't giving in too quickly.

"And then there's Serenity," he says.

"Yes, Serenity. And of course there's work, what will I do for work?" I add, cleverly ignoring the part that I'm unemployed and doing absolutely nothing.

Donald gives in first. He squints at me and pops the question:

"Do you think you would be up to holding down the fort here at home?"

Eight months on my own with the kids here at home. And Donald might never come back. The pain. Eight months on my own with Michael. The pleasure. Oh my.

Donald tucks his wings under and cocks his head as he waits for my reaction while I tilt my head upwards in a thoughtful angle. He adds, "It will also give us time to think."

"Yes. We do need time to think."

It's as easy as two birds falling off a wire.

"As far as marital policy goes, do you think I should be letting Donald run wild and free in Canada for the next eight months?" I ask Bibienne as I stretch my arms up over my head and lean back further in my chaise lounge.

There's nothing better than relaxing in Bibienne's backyard drinking pink lemonade spiked with vodka and watching the kids filling the pool with grass. Bernie hates grass in his pool but he isn't here and Bibienne just waves at them benignly once in a while. As long as they don't bother us and don't get grass in her drink, they can do whatever they want.

Bibienne says, "Marital policy? I don't get it. I thought you two were splitting up?"

"Call it a trial separation."

Bibienne shrugs. "If he keeps sending back the child support, it would work for me."

I stare down at my toenails. Ugh. Time to book a pedicure.

"He's going to send support payments right?"

"Yeah, yeah, yeah."

I wish I could tell Bibienne about Michael but I'm afraid she'll disapprove. He's the reason I'm cool with the Calgary plan. I'm not so cool with the thought that Lindsay is, perhaps, a key player in this whole arrangement and, if so, this clearly means she's winning in the Donald department. If that's the case, am I willing to forfeit?

"You think you can handle everything on your own?"

"Plenty of women do."

"Not without a decent cleaning service, they don't. Better get some help."

"Good plan."

Which is about all the planning I've done so far.

My final Grade Report has arrived in my inbox. I scan the marks: B+ in Modern American Poetry. No more, no less, than deserved. I scored top marks in drumming, and Donald will never believe that I aced both Financial Management and Organizational Behavior.

Funny, but I haven't heard from Michael for days now, ever since he got picked up by the cops. Is he angry with me? Or is he finished with me? Is it possible Michael is one of those serial profs who take advantage of female students? Was I nothing but the freshman flavor of the year?

Should I go back to school or work? I have the weekend to decide: if it's school, next Tuesday will my first day back at Dingwall. Do I withdraw and go into rubber resistors? With all the stress, this morning I got on the scales to find I've gained five pounds in two weeks. I need to take action. But what should I do? Take the job offer or finish my degree? But how can I return to Dingwall while Michael is roving the campus, preying on innocent female hearts? How can I diet when everyone knows diets don't work?

A dark pit of gloom opens wide across my solar plexus. I'm sorely in need of some energy work but the last time my chakras were exposed to healing influences, I ran out and spent $200 on recordings of the kind of music you would hear if you were stuck in an elevator in the middle of a forest.

I'd even call Mom to confide in her, but she's back with Brian and they've gone off to Vegas for a wedding-free honeymoon. She's got herself a fancy new camera so she can upload daily snaps to her blog. I can see from today's pic that she's bought herself a snazzy outfit. Camel toes visits the Hoover Dam. Brian is beaming with pride. He's a good guy. I'm happy that she's happy.

Of course, I'm unhappy that I'm unhappy. The best thing to do is find a quiet place to be alone, think, clear my head. I grab my keys, drive to the Clearview Conservation Park and lurch off down a hiking trail.

I press on down the path until I'm panting and out of breath. Slowing down into a steady pace, I begin to notice birdsong and the sound of the wind rustling the leaves of the trees. I reach the pond lookout where I stand in silence and watch dragonflies darting over the water. The peaceful scene reminds me of the day I first met Michael, when he showed me the Great Blue Heron. I remember holding on to him, tightly, on the back of his motorcycle as we leaned through the curves together on a sunlit ribbon of a back road.

Why do I need Michael to show me the Great Blue Herons of the world? Do I need men in my life at all? Now there's a thought. Without men balling up my life, I can walk my own path and open my mind to the majesties of the natural world, unencumbered. Clearly it's time I loosen myself from the sucking mud of relationships. Yes. From now on, I walk alone but free. Invigorated with strength from my newly forged inner direction, I continue walking at a brisk pace along the path.

Walking alone is lonely.

I yank my phone out of my pocket. That's it. I have to know. Now. I text Michael: "I need to talk to you."

Within minutes, I receive a text back from Michael: "Meet me at the Dingy."

Half an hour later, we are tucked into our corner. Michael holds my hand underneath the table and stares into my eyes. He seems to have forgotten the incident report. I won't remind him.

"Why didn't you call me?"

"I needed time. To think. I went up to the cottage."

"You have a cottage?"

"Up in Vermont. It's basic. It's just a cabin beside a lake. I wished you were there the whole time."

"I would've liked to have been there."

He looks at me as if he's in a confessional. "You didn't call me. I thought you were upset."

"What?"

"For showing up at your house like that."

"Why would I be upset? Besides, I did try to call you at work. I left a voice mail. And you didn't answer your cell."

"There's no cell access at the cottage. And I told you my office is closed for the last week of summer."

Right again. Where are my brains?

"You don't listen, do you?"

He says this teasingly as if this is one of my most endearing qualities and he'd like to kiss me all over because I'm so adorably cute. I can't help but think of how Donald says I don't listen but in a much different tone of voice.

Then Michael leans in and says, "I'm going back up to the cottage. This weekend. Will you come with me?"

"Yes."

I drive home slowly, park my car in the driveway and hesitate before going into the house. I stare at my hands, still clutching the steering wheel. What am I doing? Did I just agree to a weekend alone with Michael?

My phone rings: maybe Michael is having second thoughts too?

It's Mackie, home from a weeklong training exercise.

"How was it?"

"Terrible. I need the name of that lawyer you had when you got your divorce. You did alright out of that."

"You think? Half of nothing is still nothing."

"You got custody of Serenity."

True.

"What's going on?"

"Look, I don't want to talk about this over the phone. Can we have a girls' night out? Meet me at the Legion."

Mackie picks a booth directly across from the bar. She orders wings and a pitcher of beer, and starts downing glassfuls at an impressive rate. I sip from my glass and look around the room. Two guys made of granite ripples are standing by the bar, eyeing us. They couldn't be more than 25 years old. I avert my eyes quickly.

"Drink up girl. You're letting the team down."

Mackie says this to me while batting her eyes at the guys by the bar.

"Why do you want my lawyer's number? What happened with you and Thad?"

She digs in her bag and pulls out a tube of lip gloss. "The usual crap. I went on an exercise. He got busy."

"Are those false eyelashes?"

"Yep." She dabs her lips with the gloss, and then trails her fingertips across her cleavage. The two guys at the bar visibly startle. If they were in uniform, now's the moment they would straighten their ties.

Mackie leans in to me. "Those guys? Both vets. The cute one with the mustache? He's going on his third tour soon. I saw him first."

"Cut it out, Mac," I hiss. "This girls' night out isn't going to be like back in the day."

"Why not?"

"You know why not."

"God, how long have you been married? Don't tell me you don't, you know, take the long way home, once in a while?"

I take a gulp of beer.

"No."

"So you and Donald are still in lurrve?" She bugs out her eyes and sticks out her tongue.

I make a face and shrug my shoulders. "I don't know anymore."

"Spill."

"Spill what?"

"I know that look. Don't be lyin' to me now. What's going on?"

I take another gulp of beer.

Guess it's time to cut the crap. I give her the whole scoop on Donald and Lindsay, and Donald moving to Calgary. Then I tell her about Michael, knowing that my secret is safe. Mackie knows stuff about national security that would curl Mustache's sideburns up over his ears. I know stuff too. Tradition. Respect. Honor. It's the army way.

Mackie is so in.

"Okay," she says, passing me a napkin and fishing a pen from her bag. "Remember your basic mission planning. First—what's your mission?"

I write down: bivouac in the field (cottage) overnight with friendly troops (Michael) while remaining undiscovered and unsuspected by the enemy.

"What's your terrain like?"

"Secure. Michael has a cottage in Vermont."

"Acknowledged. Troops?"

"Troops?"

"Basic mission planning. You have to define your troops, remember? Obviously you and Michael are the friendlies."

"You know, in some countries we could be beheaded for having a conversation like this."

"God bless America." Mackie raises her glass. "What are your primary objectives?"

The usual military objective is to engage and kill, or at least capture the enemy; however, in this case, Mackie and I feel it's advisable to simply disperse the enemy during the period of operations. Top-drawer tactical planners call this calculated approach Hi Diddle Diddle, Up the Middle.

Mackie continues. "I would say your primary objective is horizontal envelopment between friendly troops."

I make a note: horizontal envelopment. Sounds good. I can't wait for the envelopment to begin.

"Of course you'll need a Diversion Plan for the unfriendly troops. And a detailed Plan of Engagement."

"That's what I was thinking. I'm going to need a lot more napkins."

Next morning I pull a thick wad of napkins out of my purse. Once Mackie and I had the Basic Mission Planning in place, it was simple to prepare a five-pronged Plan of Engagement. Michael and I will deploy in a surprise retreat maneuver and bunker down in the field of operations. Therefore we have code named the Plan of Engagement *Over the Moon*. My operative code name is Dish, and Michael is Spoon.

To set the first prong in place, I waylay Donald in the kitchen: "I've signed up for a hockey skills weekend." I pause, and then toss in the kicker, "It's this weekend." I add, with a straight face, "I need to practice my stick handling."

He receives this bogus intelligence with barely concealed fury.

"This weekend?" He juts out his chin. "You didn't write it on the calendar."

"I only just heard about it. A whole bunch of women on the team are going. It's in Rochester. New York."

This is actually true. Ferris and Coach are going and if I weren't signing on for Michael, I'd be headed for Rochester too.

Donald blinks and runs his hand across his forehead as if he's experiencing the light flashes that signal the onset of a migraine but that might be because Jack has turned the television volume up to a million in the family room. Donald stomps down the hall, pokes his head into the family room and bellows at Jack, "Turn that down."

I follow him down the hall. "Why are you angry? What's the big deal? You don't have any plans for the weekend. And you've gone on two missions already this spring. I'd like some time away before you leave for Calgary."

"Missions?"

"Um, you know, weekends." I quickly throw in a snappy salute. "Sir, yes, sir." I grin, showing my teeth, to let him know I'm making a little joke.

Donald gives me an odd look.

Then he says, "You seem to be under a lot of stress lately. I guess it's okay with me. Go. Have fun."

D-Day: I wake up at 5 a.m. and can't get back to sleep. Propped up on my pillow, I stare out the window until the first hint of sunrise tinges the horizon. Down the hall, someone is showering, probably Donald getting ready for work.

Back in the early days, we would rise before dawn to shower together, before the kids woke up. We found ways to connect when it wasn't easy. What happened that we stopped doing that? Did our lives become too fast, too frantic?

It's not too late to call Michael and cancel.

Dressing quickly, I go downstairs to make coffee. When Donald comes down, I offer him a cup.

"No," he says, checking his watch. "No time. I'm going into the city today." Then he hurries out the door, closing it firmly behind him without saying goodbye. In the silence of the kitchen, I sit and watch the sun rise all the way to the top of the cherry tree in the back yard.

I wake the kids up and drive them to school. Slowly, I head back to the house to pack my overnight bag and tuck it, along with my hockey gear, into the trunk of the Jeep, feeling as if I'm floating outside my body. It's not too late to call Michael and cancel, but instead, I float back into the house, jump into the shower stall and, closing my eyes, lift my face to the steaming hot water.

CHAPTER 16

Mission

Mission: The task, together with the purpose, that clearly indicates the action to be taken and the reason therefore.—Department of Defense Dictionary of Military and Associated Terms

I call Michael on his cell. "Flight Plan is operational. ETA ontime ring location, 1300 hours."

"1300 hours. What time is that really?"

"1 p.m."

There's a silence. God. Civilians.

"I'll meet you at the donut place at 1 p.m."

"Right."

"I hope you remembered to bring the battle jackets."

"The what?"

"Battle Jackets. Condoms."

"Yes. I mean, check. Uh, I know you're having fun and all, but can we quit with the military terminology now?"

The Flight Plan is faultlessly executed, and we soon arrive at the cottage. I explore the waterfront while Michael waves the key with a grin and opens the cottage to air. Sitting on the sandy beach, I hug my knees and stare across the lake. The breeze coming across the water feels too chilly for early September.

My brain goes haywire and produces crazy visions: the image of Donald toiling in his office, and then Jack and Olympia and Serenity bent over their lessons at school—well, perhaps that's going a bit far—especially as Serenity is probably, at this moment, speeding her way to the nearest women's festival—but still, what about all the good, hardworking teachers tending to the education and well-being of my younger children? What about the cadre of support workers, principal administrators, social workers, librarians, secretaries, Indeed, all of society is involved when one thinks about it: fire fighters, police officers, doctors, nurses, farmers and so on, all of them trusting that I, too, will be conscientiously engaged in an honest day's work, in some way, great or small, working for the betterment of society, for a finer future for all our children. Meanwhile, I am racing headlong into the arms of a man, a man who isn't my lawfully wedded husband—a husband to whom I promised fidelity, honesty, love, and commitment. Maybe Donald broke his promises but does that make it okay for me to break mine?

I hear Michael's footstep behind me and freeze: I will tell him quickly and get it over with: I can't go through with this underhanded business after all.

Michael kneels beside me and, as I open my mouth to deliver the news—be brave my darling—he reaches out his hand and gently brushes a strand of hair from my cheek.

"Hi Dish," breathes Michael into my ear.

"Hi Spoon!"

I wake up to the smell of coffee brewing. From the loft where I'm lying, I can see Michael downstairs in the galley kitchen opening and shutting cabinets. Sitting up, I spy a sheet of birch bark lying on the pillow next to mine. On it, Michael has drawn a series of pictures of a man embracing a woman. The man is sprouting wings on his back. I feel a pair of wings sprout on my heart. I'm lifted to the ceiling where I swoop in circles around the room.

Michael comes in with steaming mugs and a bowl of strawberries. We sit naked and cross-legged, facing one another, sipping and smiling and dropping berries into each other's mouths. Because it was chilly last night, we gathered up every pillow and blanket in the cottage and piled them into the loft. Now we have a lovely warm nest. I never want this to end.

Michael is staring into my eyes and I stare back into his.

"You have flecks of gold in your irises," Michael says, softly.

"I can't believe this is happening."

"Me neither."

"I've never done anything like this before."

"Me neither."

Michael looks relieved when I say this.

I sit up straighter. "What, you think I do this sort of thing regularly?"

"No. But you seem so comfortable with ... this."

"I'm comfortable with you."

He smiles.

"But I know what you mean."

"Donald and Carmen?"

"Donald and Carmen."

"What are we going to do?"

"I don't know."

"We'll figure something out."

"Tomorrow."

"Next week."

We fall into silence for a moment.

Michael reaches around me with his arms, pulls my hips toward him and leans in closer to me. My hips, plus everything in between, burst into flames.

Michael says, "C'mon. Let's take the canoe out for a paddle. I know of an island with a sweet lookout point."

It's long past time to part company. But we do, with promises and lingering kisses before settling into our cars. As I drive along the highway, my mind keeps returning to this romantic detail and that: how we deflowered the lookout point twice and then canoed back to the cottage and napped all afternoon, arms and legs entwined with our heads at the foot of the bed because that's where we happened to be when we fell asleep. And how we skinny dipped at midnight, and then humped around on the beach like young otters in heat. And how Michael kept saying, with wide eyes: "Let's do it again."

He even kissed me while I was peeing on the toilet, which proves he loves me.

What would it be like to be with Michael all the time? I guess the first thing is I'd have to ask Donald for a divorce. Then we'd have to break it to the kids. And then we'd have to divide up all our stuff and sell the house. Moving, even under peaceful conditions, is ridiculously stressful. Moving because of a split up must be way, way up there on the scale. And Donald probably wouldn't lift a finger. The thought of sorting and packing the clutter in the basement makes my shoulders head straight for my ears.

Plus Michael mentioned his mother a couple of times. That's an ominous sign. I'd have to break in a third mother-in-law, despite the fact that my first two ex-mothers-in-law are still around to purse their lips over every move I make. If only Michael were an orphan.

I can see the back of Michael's head in the car ahead of me. Come to think of it, Michael paid a lot of attention to my nipples. What do they call those kinds of guys?

Mama's boys.

My nipples tingle at the thought of Michael nibbling on them. I already want to go back to the cottage. What am I going to do? What would Bibienne do?

How I would love to call her and talk it all over. But, despite the fact that Bibienne is my best friend, I can't grant her the security clearance. Loose lips sink ships and I've already created a potential leak in the form of Mackie.

I was supposed to call her. She made me promise to give her a thorough debriefing. I dial. "It was amazing. Michael is amazing. Best weekend of my life."

"So now what? Are you going to ask Donald for a divorce?"

"Geez, Mac. Let's not get too hasty."

"What's the hitch? I thought you said 'best weekend of your life'?"

"Yes, but I don't know. I need time to think. Michael's mother is still living you know."

I can actually hear Mackie shuddering through the phone.

"Well then, what's your re-entry plan?"

Good question.

First, I better try to stop thinking about Michael. Donald might notice if I'm glowing from head to foot—it's too dangerous to roll into the house all white hot and steaming like a stream of molten lava. It's even more dangerous to think about Donald though.

Donald.

My mind's eye pastes up unwelcome visions. Donald with a sad face. Donald with an angry face. A long corridor, dimly lit. Donald in a suit being pulled by a hand on his tie into a room. A door squeaks open and bangs shut again. Lindsay tiptoes by in a short silk teddy. Michael scurries across the hall at the far end. Michael's wife, Carmen, is lurking here somewhere.

Or was Lindsay only my imagination? Did I just slam the door on my marriage? This isn't a French farce. What now?

One thing's certain. I've stepped over a threshold and there's no backing out now. I have to see this through. But now is not the time to make major decisions. I need time to think. And right now, the part I want to think about is the fact that Michael is the most romantic lover on the planet.

He even wrote a poem about us while I was sleeping. All about how two people can be drawn together like two incomplete chemistry sets, melding element to element to create a whole and perfect mix. My gold completes his gold, his silver completes mine. His iron is penetrating deep into my cobalt. I'm like a rare earth magnet in the periodic table of love. Or something like that.

Donald never wrote a poem about us. But then, he has some sterling qualities too. He can make me laugh like no one else can. He's smart. Handsome. A good listener. And we made gold together: Jack and Olympia. Plus there's that throw-down factor. Donald has so much throw-down that women like Lindsay can smell it. And then they chase him.

If Donald let her catch him, we are even. If she caught him.

But what if he's innocent?

And the bigger question: if he's guilty, what's the point of turning the situation into an entrenched war game of getting even? Basic training says there's an enemy out there, so you shoot to kill, ask questions later. It's like I've pulled the pin from a hand grenade and I can't decide what to do with it.

I switch on the radio. Maybe there's a good talk show on. Anything. Even the news. Better find out what the rest of the world has been doing all weekend. It's hard to stop thinking though. The big news flash for me is that I've been a bad, bad girl.

I can hardly blame my behavior on the army, my chemistry teacher, or that all too often I forget to take my calcium supplements. I'm a tarnished woman.

But. There's plenty of time to beat myself up later. For now I'm still enjoying the glow of mixing all my elemental properties with Michael's. Feelings of guilt and remorse could scotch everything. I won't permit it, not while I'm still enjoying the basking away part. I'm sure I can repent later, although memories of this weekend could keep me in a bask-like pose for the next seven hundred years.

Pulling into the driveway, I spy Donald standing at the top of a ladder, which is propped up against the house. The bottom of the ladder is planted squarely in my dahlias. Donald has a saw in his hand. He's busy carving away at a gaping hole in the siding at the peak of the roof. I can smell smoke. "Hi," I say. "Is something burning?"

Donald stops sawing at the hole for a minute, glances down and sees me. "Probably the hotdogs. Would you mind going and checking the barbecue? I asked Serenity to keep an eye on things but …

oh, I guess I should ask you, how was your weekend? A successful mission was it?"

I stare up at him. Was that the tiniest hint of sarcasm in his voice? He's the one perched on a ladder but I'm the unbalanced one about to topple to the ground. I rub the back of my neck where there might actually be a hickey in full bloom. I suppose I can say my neck guard was rubbing me a little hard there.

"Not bad. But what's going on here? What's that in your hand?"

"The red squirrels are back." He holds a bundle of rags aloft. "And this is a smoke bomb."

"But that didn't work the last time."

"But this one is better. Bernie gave me the good stuff. It'll work." Donald stares into the hole with the eyes of a madman. "Little bastards," he's muttering as he shoves his anti-squirrel kit into the hole. A grin is spreading across his face.

"Be careful."

I don't want to watch the show. It occurs to me as I walk toward the door that I may not have to pack any boxes after all because Donald is probably about to burn the house down. As I reach for the doorknob, all I can think is that I have quite the choice: it's fairly evenly divided between a Mama's boy and a crazy man.

Throwing open the door, I'm greeted by Jack and Olympia. "Mom! Mom! Lewis said we can keep them!"

Tumbling across the living room floor to meet me are eight ecstatic puppies that look remarkably like George Bush. All barking.

CHAPTER 17

Threat Warning

Threat Warning: The urgent communication and acknowledgement of time-critical information essential for the preservation of life and/or vital resources.—Department of Defense Dictionary of Military and Associated Terms

Monday morning and I'm still sizzling. It's even dangerous to take a shower as the hot water pouring down my hips and thighs makes me think of Michael. Everything makes me think of Michael.

Downstairs, the sight of the mess the puppies made in their makeshift cardboard pen overnight fails to distract my thoughts. Even the puppy poo mounds all over make me think of Michael and his lovely warm brown eyes. While scooping up soggy newspapers into a garbage bag, and handing out fresh bowls of water and chow, my mind keeps spinning through the details of my weekend.

My belly button itches. Despite two showers since I got home, I still have sand tamped in all my crevices from playing slick otters in heat on the beach. A deep excavation of my navel is arrested by the sight of a pup squirming its fat form over the side of the pen. I block him with my foot and plop him back in with his littermates. The pup looks up at me, barks, and tries to climb back out again, while the rest of the pups nose around. It's only a matter of time until the rest are over the wall too. On today's agenda is to either find homes for them or devise a better way to corral them. Jack slips down from eating his breakfast at the counter and comes over to stand beside me.

"Please, can't we keep one?" he says picking up the smart-aleckey one who figured out how to escape. "His name is Rocket."

"Na-ah," shrieks Olympia, leaping down from her stool. "We're keeping this one." She grabs another wriggling body from the fray. "Her name is Holly Berry."

Jack and Olympia love the puppies; they want to keep all of them.

"Don't give them names. We can't keep any of them. They need good homes with responsible, caring owners and quiet, patient handling."

We can't provide anything like that.

Jack sets Rocket down outside the pen. Rocket sniffs at the floor and squats. I scoop him back up, mid-squirt and tuck him back into the pen.

"What are you two still doing here anyway; you're going to be late for school. Put Holly Berry down. Go." I say. "Wait, where's Serenity. Is she up yet?"

"Don't know," they shout as they grab their lunches and backpacks and race out the door.

Serenity's bed is empty. She must've set out for school early today. Maybe she's finally pulling it together? How wonderful that would be if it were true. But I can't help but feel that it'll be a miracle if she stays in school this term let alone attend classes on time.

The phone rings a minute later. It's Mackie. I know she wants another debriefing. "Is the coast clear? Can you talk?" she asks breathlessly.

"Yes. No one's home."

"So? What're you going to do?"

"Cut the lawn maybe. Hey, would you like a puppy?"

"Don't try to change the subject. What're you going to do?"

"I don't know yet."

"Do you think Donald suspects?"

"Hope not."

"When are you going to see Michael again?"

"Wednesday morning. We're meeting for coffee."

"Mom! You said I could borrow your car on Wednesday morning."

I whirl around to see Serenity bent over the pen, her long blonde hair swinging across her face as she plays with the pups. Where did she come from? She's still wearing her pajama bottoms and her favorite nightshirt. She must've slept in the basement rec room in front of the television again. More importantly though: how long has she been in the room listening?

"Mac, I gotta go."

I face my eldest, born of my starter marriage to a sergeant from an infantry unit. Which, if you know anything about army guys, says it all. She inherited his wide dove eyes, the mow 'em down flat approach and his forward operating base attitude.

"When did I say you could borrow my car? Last time you ran it bone dry."

"Did not. It was empty when you loaned it to me." She puts her hands on her hips. "I'll give you $20 of my own scrilla to cover the gas then."

"Where did you get $20?"

"From Donald. For babysitting on the weekend. Saturday night."

Odd. Donald never mentioned to me that he went out while I was away over the weekend. Of course he never tells me anything about where he's going these days.

"Donald went out Saturday night? Where?"

"I don't know. What about the car? Can I have it?"

"I need my car Wednesday morning."

"Why? Who are you meeting for coffee?"

"A friend. From school. Why do you need to know?"

Serenity glares at me. I better be careful. She also inherited my mother's ability to read minds. A wormhole begins to form in my forehead as Serenity bores her eyes straight into my brain to suck out all my secrets like a Jack Russell Terrier skinning down a hole after a ferret. Fortunately the phone rings, saving me.

It's Mom. If she worms into my forehead, I'm done for. She lives miles away but she still knows more about what's going on at my house than I do some days.

"Pauline," she says, "I've been thinking about your financial situation lately and I've decided to give you some of the proceeds from your father's estate. He's appalled to see how you're living these days."

I sure as hell hope Dad can't see me from his gunnery station up in heaven. If he knew what I was up to lately, he'd load my butt full of shrapnel in a barrage of artillery fire from above.

"Cut it out, Mom. Dad's dead. He can't see anything. And what do you mean how I'm living these days?"

"Your house for starters. It's practically … ruined."

She's right about that. Donald and the red squirrels made a mess of the siding at the top of the house, and George has been chewing on the bottom half. He's still prone to digging holes in the back yard. And now we have his eight fat pups.

I don't want to accept money from Mom. However, Donald says Mom's loaded with cash plus she has a diversified raft of stocks, bonds, options, annuities, the works. On the other hand, she already gave me the Caddy, and Serenity, Jack, and Olympia have all his medals, mugs, plaques, sashes, and swords.

Of course, unless I find a job, I can't afford to keep the Caddy anymore. It's been parked in the garage for months. Mom says, "I want to help you kids get back on your feet. You told me you were thinking of starting a business. Have you given any more thought to that?"

I had forgotten all about that plan. Suddenly, thanks to Mom, I know what I'm going to do. I'm going to go into business for myself. Screw rubber resistors and screw going back to school. This is a sign. And with this thought, the tight feeling across the back of my shoulders loosens, and my feet suddenly feel light as if I have sprouted fluttering golden wings from my scapulas.

"Thank you, thank you, thank you, for saving me from the National Semi-Conductor Convention. I love you forever. But let's set it up as a loan. I'll pay you back. With interest."

"We'll talk about it. Your father says we would've lost half our savings in the recession if it weren't for Donald. Your Dad wants to help you kids now. Do I hear barking? Did you take one of your neighbor's puppies?"

"Yes. I mean no. We have the puppies here. Lewis dropped them off yesterday. He says they're our responsibility since George is the father."

"It's a good thing you're having that dog neutered."

"I am?"

"Aren't you?"

"I ... well ... okay, yes, I'll make an appointment with the vet today."

At last, I manage to escape all barking puppies, my first-born, my mother and my best old army buddy by going outside and firing up the lawn mower. I can use this time to think about what kind of business I want to start with the loan from Mom. Cutting the grass makes me think of Michael: the powerful hum of the motor is vibrating through every fiber of my being. The prospect of a becoming a powerful business mogul barely captures my attention when I'm imagining that the mower is Michael and I'm a lush lawn submitting to his powerful blades.

By lunchtime, all lusty thoughts are rudely swept aside when my imagination serves up the elephant that has been firmly locked out of the room. The door splinters down and in roars the pachyderm of my forsaken principles, brandishing a rifle in its curled trunk. Donald enters astride, in full silk regalia, looking every bit the imperial sultan, and he looks pissed. His hand rests lightly on the hilt of his jeweled sword and his dark eyes flash down at me.

"Pauline, what have you been up to?"

"I might ask that same question of you, m'Lord."

Donald crosses his arms. "I admit to nothing."

But I can hear a sound like an emissary from the lickable lips of Lindsay Bambraugh outside the door. Her mirth enters the room on a warmish breeze that spreads through the air like an elephant fart.

All I can think to do is buy myself an elephant gun and a peasant style dress with an easy-rip bodice.

I wake up in the middle of the night, in a dead panic. Bolting into the den, I close the door and scan the calendar. I check the dates once, then twice, count, and then recount the days. Thirteen days have passed since my last period. My calculations quickly confirm: Days Nine, Ten and Eleven of my cycle were Michael Days. I might be in big trouble. Heaven knows, it's possible to ovulate super early in one's cycle. Otherwise, I wouldn't have been blessed with Olympia.

No wonder our weekend was so luscious—ovulation time is always my most horny time of the month too—my ovaries were no doubt spitting out eggs like a carp. Mother Nature is no fool. But—she wouldn't be so cruel—would she?

After all, we were careful to use protection every time. Except for that one incomplete touchdown in the shower, but surely nothing could come of that. After all, Donald and I have practiced withdrawal for years. In more ways than one.

It's time to get my tubes tied. Hope it's not too late.

Arghh. For days I've been obsessed with the appalling thought that I could be pregnant. I better stifle this negativity: after all, there's no way to know for sure until I actually miss my period, which isn't due for at least another week. No more agonizing. I won't allow my fears to ruin my coffee date with Michael this afternoon. It's a beautiful September day outside, so warm and sunny there's no need to bring a jacket or, hopefully, underwear.

I arrive at the Dingy Cup at the same time as Michael: we are so in sync. We sit in our usual corner for a few minutes staring at each other across the table. Awkward. Michael interlaces his fingers behind his head. He stretches his long legs out under the table and leans back in his chair. I glance around the room. The place is crowded with noisy freshmen, excited about their first day of classes. I feel a bit out of place now that I've decided not to return to school. Michael seems a bit disappointed, too, when I explain about my plan to start a new business. "What kind of business?" he asks.

"Dunno yet. Did you want to order a coffee or something?"

"No."

Michael leans forward. "Let's get out of here. It's too nice out to stay inside. Do you want to go for a ride?"

Of course.

We head out to the countryside. The road is familiar and I lean into the curves with him, my cheek pressed to his back and my hands tucked into his jacket pockets. When we come to a stone bridge over a narrow river, Michael pulls over and removes his helmet.

"This is where we saw that Great Blue Heron last spring," he said pointing down the embankment.

I nod. I'm touched that Michael remembers this small detail from that day back in May when he rescued me from the side of the road. We didn't even know each other's names then.

We descend to the riverside and walk until we find a quiet spot around a small bend. We spread a picnic blanket on the grassy banks and flop down to relax. Michael opens his saddlebag, which is stuffed with baguettes, Brie, grapes, pomegranate juice, and a bottle of cold champagne. The pomegranate cocktails look delicious but I remember my maybe-delicate condition in time to occasionally tip the glass into the grass behind Michael's back. Just in case.

Soon Michael leans me back onto the blanket with that look in his eye, and delivers a lengthy kiss. I can taste the champagne on his lips. Without taking his lips off mine, Michael fumbles for a condom and manages to drop it into the sand.

"Oh no. That was the last one," he says trying to brush off the dirt.

"Don't worry about it," I say. "I'm safe right now anyway."

Well, why not? I'm totally done for already.

Another sleepless night. Am I pregnant or not? I can't wait another minute let alone a whole week to find out. Nowadays, test kits are sensitive enough to pick up a pregnancy even before missing a period. Yesterday, I sneaked into a drugstore way across town to buy a home test kit. I spent half an hour examining my choices: would I prefer to see a heart shaped icon turn pink or watch a blue dot form in the navel of a teddy-bear? Why can't they design one that shows a dead duck shape or a red line forming across the image of a carefree skipping-along woman?

I finally selected a simple looking kit with two complete tests in case the first trial gets botched or is inconclusive.

At dawn I tiptoe toward the bathroom to perform the secret test. The instructions say it's best to use a morning urine sample when the pregnancy hormone, HCG (human chorionic gonadotrophin—try saying that fast first thing in the morning with a smile on your face), is at its highest concentration.

As I reach the bathroom door, Serenity emerges from her bedroom at the other end of the hall. Her face twists with irritation. I tell her I'm in a hurry, so go use the bathroom downstairs, please. Serenity glowers at me, and retreats back into her bedroom. What is a teenager doing up at this hour anyway? A rueful thought strikes me that it's been almost eighteen years since I've been permitted to go into a bathroom first without enduring someone's baleful looks. Please, please, may the test results show that I'm not about to a sign on for another eighteen.

I retrieve the test kit, cunningly concealed within a large box of premium name-brand tampons. I was planning to treat myself this month. At least there's no chance the tampons will spoil. Serenity can always use them up. Lucky her, being a lesbian. Certainly she'll never face the specter of an unwanted pregnancy. Her children, if she ever decides to have any, will be coaxed to conception with the aid of a turkey baster no doubt. I wish I were an unfettered lesbian at this moment. It's possibly too late to change over now.

The stupid test kit must have been designed by a man. I don't want to pee on a stick. It's much easier for men to perform peeing-on-stick maneuvers. Where's the woman-friendly pregnancy test kit? They could at least put in a few grocery coupons and a chocolate bar to eat while waiting for the result.

An alternate method is to pee in a cup, then dip the stick. But Serenity is bound to take over the bathroom if I go off in search of a cup. I can't risk it. Besides, I have to pee now. I seize Donald's tooth-brush cup, and rinse it out.

Olympia is now twisting the door handle and scrabbling at the door.

"I gotta poo now."

"Hang on," I yell. I check my watch. In five short minutes I could be toast.

Olympia is now frantic, and howling, "The poo is coming out."

I better let her in. I stuff the whole assembly into the cabinet be-hind the plumbing under the sink and stash the remaining test kit back in the tampon box.

I open the door to admit Olympia. Fine. I'll go downstairs and plug in the coffee maker. Two minutes later, I race back upstairs only to find Olympia is out of bathroom and Serenity is now in.

I rap on the door again. "Hurry up in there."

Jack appears beside me, and starts frantically hammering on the door too.

Serenity yells, "Hold on, I'll be done in a sec."

Since Jack is making such a fuss to go next, I might as well go back downstairs for my mug of coffee. Next pregnancy scare, I will use the downstairs toilet.

Ten minutes later, I race upstairs to the bathroom only to find the door locked again. Behind the door, I can hear familiar sounds of splashing, rumbling and snorting, like a bull walrus is rolling around in our tub. Damn that Donald; my whole future is hanging by a thread in there and he's lolling in the bath. I can't stand this waiting any longer. How do I get him out?

"Donald? I need ... a tampon." I congratulate myself on such quick and clever thinking.

"Hold on, I'll grab you one," he shouts back through the door.

Stupid, stupid, stupid. Whatever possessed me to say that? The extra test kit is hidden in the tampon box.

I feel faint as I listen to the sounds of Donald rifling through the cabinets. Soon, he bellows out, "Where on earth do you keep them?" The door opens, Donald emerges, wrapped in a towel and muttering, "Never mind, I'm done anyway."

For the first time ever, I give thanks for his useless male can't-find-things genes.

I hurry into the bathroom, lock the door, crouch down and grope about for the test, which is still hidden from prying eyes in the dark recesses behind the sink plumbing at the back of the cabinet. Got it. I stand up and look at the result. The room spins. My heart flumps around in my chest. It's blue. Oh no. My knees go weak. I sit on the edge of the bathtub with my head spinning while I attempt to line up my brain cells and make them walk in a straight line.

Wait a minute. I seize the box to reread the instructions. Blue means negative. Phew.

As I tuck the test kit back in the tampon box, I can't help but think what it might be like to carry Michael's child. I have a sudden vision of myself reclining in a meadow, wearing a floaty dress while Michael trails daisy chains reverently across my bump and looks into my eyes adoringly. Glow, glow, glow.

Bernie has outdone himself this year for his birthday party. He shows us a homemade pinwheel consisting of a large bicycle wheel with rockets and sparklers wired to the spokes. It's a pyro's dream nailed through the axle to a tree in his backyard.

"One fuse to rule them all," Bernie says as he points out the way all the ignition wires are connected.

"You even made your own mortar casings and gunpowder?" Donald fingers the wires, his eyes ringed with admiration. He's acting like a big kid, begging to be the one to light the fuse.

Bibienne pulls me aside to whisper, "Are you guys back together? You seem to be getting along."

"No. We're still separated. Since Donald is leaving for Calgary soon, he took some vacation time. We're trying to do stuff together, as a family, for the sake of the kids. And we both wanted to come over and wish Bernie a happy birthday."

Bibienne looks doubtful.

"I know. It's weird. We don't talk much. We both seem to be waiting for the other to make the first move."

I can't bring myself to tell her about making my move with Michael, the weirdest part of all.

As soon as it gets dark enough, we all stand back to watch as the pinwheel, flinging green and gold sparks in a ten foot arc, reaches speeds of at least 80 miles an hour before it spins off the tree and goes careening into the bushes.

"Stupidest hobby ever. It's a wonder my children survive him," Bibienne says, shaking her head and ushering the kids back into the house. The men remain in the yard sipping their beers, eyes glittering in the darkness, reminiscing about last year's strobe rocket launch.

Bibi wants to show me the set of tarot cards she's been designing. They're arranged in neat rows across her drafting table. "I started this project just for fun. Bernie threw up a website for me and I'm getting tons of hits. I've got dozens of orders already. The deck isn't even completed yet," she says. "I may even have to take a leave from the clinic to finish. I'm still working on the minor arcana of the coins, but the wands, swords, and cups are finished."

I pick up the Queen of Cups card with a small pang, remembering the reading from last spring when she turned up. The good woman card: she was supposed to be me. Bibi peers over my shoulder.

"This card is one of my favorites," she says. "You know, I kept thinking of you when I drew her. See? She even looks like you."

I stare at the image. The queen is smiling but her eyes look sad.

"I drew her standing on a stone bridge to show her tendency to be caught between two opposing shores. Water means change. There's a river flowing under her feet and she needs to get across safely. She has a cup in her hands and she has to carry her burden carefully so she won't spill what's inside."

I set the queen card back down beside the Knight of Cups. I remember now, I got that card too. The man of poetry, romance, and passion. Michael. Funny how accurate the card reading turned out to be. Or maybe the cards are whatever we think they are.

I wake up at 3 a.m., my insides hollowing out with fear. Could it be I'm pregnant after all? Maybe I took the pregnancy test too early? In my head, I count the days again. To be sure of the results, I probably should wait a few more days before I test again.

I can't get back to sleep for worrying. If pregnant, I will have to give birth once again. Serenity dragged her elbows along my spine during labor. Olympia's head got stuck halfway down and the forceps halfway up. Jack tried to come out sideways. All three of them left me teetering on an inflatable ring for days afterwards. I lie awake, lemur-eyed in the dark. While waiting in vain for sleep, I have to get up to pee no less than three times. And so it begins.

I head downstairs to make a pot of coffee and, while waiting for it to brew, I'm hit with another horrific realization: coffee contains caffeine, which is verboten to expectant mothers. Ditto for meds and liquor. I can't even have an aspirin. Which I will likely need soon since I just spied my next-door neighbor Lewis coming up the walk. I open the door.

"This is for you," Lewis says as he hands me an envelope.

Inside the envelope is a letter outlining a number of items regarding our property that are in need of our urgent attention. There's also a newspaper clipping on lawn care.

"Lewis, we cut the grass yesterday."

"Ah, yes, but you cut it too short. You're encouraging the weeds that way."

Donald appears behind me and says, "Our lawn length is none of your business. What's in that envelope?"

I hand Donald the newspaper clipping. Lewis stabs his gnarly forefinger at it, "See? It says here that the blade should never be cut shorter than 3 inches. You took it down to less than 2 inches."

"You measured our grass again? Keep off my lawn."

While they start into bickering, I look at the list. Among the usual complaints about our peeling porch, too many dandelions, and George's barking, a critical issue is the presence of a couple of bird's nests in our back yard. Apparently the neighborhood is overrun with starlings and robins and this is a serious matter for the gardeners who want to guard their worm populations. Not to mention the outrage of early morning birdsong and a few incidents involving bird poop and unprotected heads on decks.

There's no way I'm scuppering any bird's nests. And it's too bad, but the peeling porch will have to wait. I've got other plans. Over breakfast, I share them with Donald: "I've been looking into starting a small business. My Mom is going to loan me the money."

He snaps his head up from his newspaper and bulges his eyes out at me: "Like what?"

"I don't know, maybe a flower shop. Or antiques."

"I thought you wanted to finish your degree?"

"I do. But isn't this better? I only have three more credits left to do; I can finish them at night school."

Donald lays his paper on the table as if his arms have been drained of all their blood. "But you don't know a thing about retail. Maybe you should take a marketing course at Dingwall first."

"I can learn as I go. The small business center downtown has a lending library and free seminars. I'd like to head down there today, actually."

Whoa, where did that last bit come from? Evidently, my strategic fudging skills have advanced considerably since I met Michael. Last night Donald asked me to go to the zoo with him and the kids today. I'm desperate for a good excuse to get out of it. After all, I volunteered to go on Olympia's school zoo trip just last June. Why should I have to go on another excursion to the zoo again, so soon? Donald's the one who needs to spend quality time with the kids before he leaves town. Besides, it's his turn to be run ragged through the Lion Pit and the Monkey House.

An odd thing has happened. I woke up early this morning, and couldn't get back to sleep due to my imagination producing the sensation of little kicks already. I slipped into the bathroom to do the retest.

This time I was prepared with a clean glass to collect my morning urine but the extra test has mysteriously vanished. I've racked my brains to think what I might have done with it. Maybe one of the kids has found it, played with it.

I checked Jack and Olympia's bedrooms, but no luck. What could've happened to it?

After breakfast, on a sudden wild-blue-sky hunch, I confront Serenity re the missing test.

Serenity presses her lips together in a scowl. "I found it in the tampon box." She bites on her baby fingernail. "I missed my period."

"And?"

I'm Pauline Peacock. In the conservatory. With a rope.

It's time for an emergency visit to the doctor for Serenity and me. Serenity has all the symptoms: sore, tender nipples, constant nausea, fatigue, and cravings. I have all the symptoms of a nervous breakdown: sore tender feelings, constant irritation, and a craving to pulverize my eldest daughter.

The doctor immediately sends us to the lab for blood tests; she wants us both to come back tomorrow as she'll have our results by then, our paps are overdue and she wants to go over birth control options with Serenity. The doctor's raised eyebrows clearly suggested she thinks I ought to sit in on a little egg-meets-sperm lecture too. Serenity, with a look of fury, rolls her eyes around as if this kind of thing has nothing to do with her.

On the way home in the car, I decide it's time for a talk about the birds and the bees; in this case, I'm the one who is confused and naive:

"How is this possible? I thought you were … uh …"

"The word is 'lesbian' Mom. And, yes, I'm one of those."

"I know, I know, but explain to me the part about how … ?"

"I was trying to get back at Shae I guess. She hates wishy-washy dykes."

"So you think getting pregnant is a punishment for Shae?"

"I didn't plan on the pregnant part. I just got slightly too high on the revenge trip with Jude."

"Jude?"

"Don't worry. He's really nice. Gay, thank god."

I'm back in the doctor's office with Serenity. The doctor says she'll go over my results first.

Thank you, thank you. The doctor says my test came back negative. My missed period was probably due to stress. Or perimenopause. The doctor explains, all cheerfully, that periods can become erratic as women approach real menopause, which is a gradual transitional period of four to fifteen years. During that time I may experience one or all of the following: vaginal itching and dryness, mood swings, hot and/or cold flashes, erratic cycles, heart palpitations, joint pain, weight gain, thinning of hair and bones. My spirits sag at the thought of turning into a hairless, bedridden old crone. Pregnancy is sounding better all the time.

Still, I'm relieved that I'm not pregnant. My relief lasts about 13 seconds as the doctor clears her throat, turns to her keyboard and pulls up the lab results from Serenity's file. Serenity's definitely going to need a full physical examination and prenatal vitamins.

On the way home Serenity wants to go shopping for maternity clothes.

"Not today," I say. My eyes are misting over so much I can barely drive, let alone navigate a shopping mall.

"Why do you keep putting on the windshield wipers, Mom? It's not raining."

Because I'm fighting back tears, that's why. I'm so confused. I'm going to be a grandmother. A grandmother! I'm only 37. It's going to take a lot more than a wiper blade to smooth away these tears.

Whatever will Michael think? He's doing a granny? Maybe we should go shopping. I may be much closer than I thought to incontinence pads.

Serenity will have to make do with her wardrobe as it is, for now. It would be cruel to show her what's in store for her anyway. Ugly smocks and huge bras. Stretchy pink tops with bouncing bunnies and arrows pointing at the bulge. I hate to tell her but the skater stores don't carry anything in panel pants.

We arrive home and, as I enter the house, my ears are assaulted by an awful screeching noise coming from the den. I poke my head in to see Donald, red-faced, blowing into a saxophone.

"Look what I got," he yells upon seeing me. "It's a vintage Selmer. Check it out—it's engraved and has mother-of-pearl touch points and the Zagar mouthpiece and everything." He blasts off a loud honk and says, "It's amazing how much I still remember."

Donald can't sit still when he takes a vacation. He's been shopping online all week, buying all kinds of toys. Last week he found a coffee bean roaster and yesterday he ordered a giant trampoline.

At least he's relaxing and enjoying himself. I can't possibly prick his bubble by imparting Serenity's news right now.

Serenity's been on the phone talking nonstop to her friends ever since the doctor's visit, two days ago now. You'd think her positive result was a full scholarship to Harvard or the equivalent. Instead of being upset, she's delighted. Her dyke friends are all thrilled too. Not many baby showers happen in that circle. They've all pledged pregnancy and labor support, free babysitting, one girl has already lined up a crib and high chair; this baby will be a group project like they did together in high school but "way better." Jude is coming over tomorrow to meet us. He says he wants joint custody. I wonder if he'd like to take on a puppy or two as well?

Serenity's condition has given me an evil blinding headache. Wish it were a deafening headache as I just spied Donald walking by, heading for the den again with his saxophone. Despite all the clear evidence—for starters, Serenity has been lying around on the living room couch for days on end with two sets of headphones, one for her head and one clamped around her belly—Donald still hasn't caught on. He never will. I realized that the day I went into labor with Jack and Donald actually thought we could use the short term parking at the hospital.

I poke my head into the living room first where Serenity is painting her toenails a bright blue.

"Do you want to tell Donald or shall I share your news with him myself?"

"I already told Dad so it's cool with me if you tell Donald," she says.

"What did your father say?"

"He was being a real jerk. I think he was drunk. He kept laughing and saying that kids are a self-inflicted wound. He asked how you are. He was laughing so much I couldn't hear what he was saying after that so I hung up on him."

Now I can't wait to phone up my ex and tell him he's going to be a grandfather. Bet that detail hasn't occurred to him yet. One last laugh coming right up.

But first I have to tell Donald that he's going to be a step-grandfather. Too late. I hear the first blaring sounds coming from the den. Maybe I'll wait and shout it out when he's practicing somersaults on his trampoline.

Enter Jude. Stage left. Jude just clinched an audition with Queer Park Productions.

Jude has long silky hair and huge brown eyes fringed with gorgeous lashes. I can totally see why Serenity made a gay pride exception in his case. He's a darling. I wanted to sit him on my lap and play butterfly lashes with him. I couldn't though because I was too busy shoveling pizzas out onto the patio table. Of course Serenity neglected to mention that she was throwing a party so all her friends could meet all of Jude's friends.

Bibienne came over with a six-pack of vodka coolers and we stood in the kitchen sipping and looking through the window at Jude sitting out on the deck, his long legs propped up on the deck rail. After a few minutes, she looked at me as if she wanted to say something but was thinking better of it.

"He's 20 so we're allowed to be cougars," I said.

All she could say was, "Mmmm, lanky."

We've never had so much fun at a party: Jude & Company have solved all our troubles including problem skin and hair style while the girls climbed up on the roof with flashlights and fixed the leak.

Bibienne cracked open her third cooler and, after tossing half of it down her throat, finally said, "See? These kids are yet another reminder of just how useless our husbands are."

After I went to bed, the kids stayed on to run around the neighborhood playing tag until 3 a.m. Meanwhile Donald missed the whole thing because he went fishing with Bernie.

The best part is that all the pups are taken, adopted by Serenity's friends.

Shae is back. She heard the news and rushed back from Maine to see Serenity. She's been up north fighting forest fires since the big breakup. Serenity was transported with delight to see her. Now Shae the Lumberjack is bonding with Donald over the Red Sox while drinking beer on the living room couch with her steeltoed boots hiked up on my coffee table. How do you like that, sports fans?

The blinds are closed and the television screen is so dusty I don't know how Donald and Shae can watch the ballgame. Chip bags and soda cans litter the floor around them.

Maybe I'm not pregnant after all but my disgusting house cries out for a woman with a serious nesting urge. I call everyone into the kitchen to make an announcement: "I'm delighted to see you're all enjoying a relaxing weekend. However, I regret to inform you that there's no maid service at this resort. Everyone has to do their share. Therefore, I want one hour of solid effort from each of you. Jack can vacuum, Olympia dust, Serenity and Shae wash windows, I'll do the bathrooms and, Donald, you could start with changing the burnt out bulbs in the ceiling fixture in the kitchen."

Olympia needs to know how to dust. I can explain:

"First, take everything off the top of the piano, wipe off all the dust, and then put everything back."

Olympia looks puzzled. I have to show her how. I spend twenty minutes demonstrating the procedure to Olympia and then I tell her to go dust the TV. I look around: there are no vacuuming sounds, and Serenity and Shae have disappeared. Donald is teetering on a kitchen chair grimacing at a broken bulb stuck in the light fixture, a box of light bulbs tucked under his arm.

"Stupid thing broke when I tried to twist it out," he grumbles.

Where's Jack? I find him behind the shed in the back yard playing with his army action figures. I reel him back inside to commence his vacuuming. As I go by, I spy Serenity and Shae washing Shae's truck in the driveway.

"What about my windows?"

"Later."

Olympia's sidetracked too: she stopped to watch TV while dusting.

"You're supposed to be helping," I say as I switch off the set. "Go dust the bookshelves in the den. Now."

From the kitchen, I hear the sound of several light bulbs shattering on the kitchen floor, then Donald cursing. Jack walks by hauling the vacuum cleaner, I tell him he might as well start in the kitchen. I will start on the bathrooms now.

The upstairs bathroom is a disaster. Seizing a can of cleansing powder, I shake it liberally over all surfaces. I begin polishing the sink with a rag and notice my new silver earrings, a gift from Michael, lying beside the sink, I better put them away before … one earring flies from my wet fingers straight down the drain. I spend the next half hour with a bucket and wrench, cleaning out the trap under the sink, and finally retrieve my earring, which is now coated in slimy brown gunk.

As I stick my head back under the sink to restore the plumbing, the lights go out. I bonk my head in an effort to stand up. I smell smoke. Something's burning. I run down to the kitchen to find the power shut off, the vacuum cleaner abandoned, glass shards still all over the floor and burnt electrical wires hanging from a blackened ceiling.

"The damn thing shorted out when I tried to remove the busted bulb." Donald drops what's left of the ceiling fixture into a cardboard box. "I have to go to the store and buy a new one."

My shining hour is up: Shae's truck is gone, Jack is nowhere to be seen, my kitchen is destroyed and, in the den, every book has been removed from the bookshelves and several hundred are now piled up helter skelter in the middle of the room.

"I'm finished dusting the shelves," says Olympia. "Can I go now?"

"Go," I say wearily as I survey the mess. A copy of *What Americans Think* is on top of the pile. Curious, I scan the contents. Am I normal? Or way beyond the pale?

Interesting. According to the book, only 12% of Americans are having or have had an affair while married to their current partner. Guess that means I am some kind of bad. I would've thought the numbers were much higher. What's the matter with us? If you believe Jilly Cooper or any other informed British writer, the Brits are way ahead of us in this kind of thing. At least half, probably more, have recently been or are currently messing around. All the fault of the royals no doubt, who have more like a 95% rate of adultery going on.

Maybe the truth is that Americans are big fat liars. After all, if some Nosy-Parker-Pollster called me up this minute and demanded to know, have you had or are you currently having an affair? I would, naturally, lie.

No doubt Mr. Nosy calls at the supper hour when the spouse is in the room listening. Who is going to own up under those circumstances?

Snapping the volume shut, I set to the task of picking up the
heaped jumble of books. Might as well organize the collection properly for once. But how? By genre? By author? By Library of Congress
number? By spine color?

Between Donald and me, we own a gazillion books. They've been
all mixed together ever since we shared our first shelf. If we split up,
it will be a devil to sort out the yours, mine, and no-longer-ours. My
misting eyes fall upon the giant dictionary resting on its own little
table. A prize indeed. It belonged to Donald, originally. How will I
ever gain custody of that worthy tome without a damn good lawyer?
I fell in love with Donald because of that thing. That man had the
biggest dictionary I'd ever seen.

Michael has a respectable dictionary, too. But is it truly compa-
rable to Donald's?

CHAPTER 18

Operationally Ready

Operationally Ready: A unit, ship, or weapon system capable of performing the missions or functions for which organized or designed.—Department of Defense Dictionary of Military and Associated Terms

A week of unfounded eating for two plus another couple weeks of emotional eating on Serenity's behalf, and I'm well on the way toward a brand new set of stretch marks. I set my alarm extra-early so I can fit in my exercise plan. If I run for 30 minutes at the first streak of dawn every morning, I will be in tip-top shape for single parenting when Donald is gone to Calgary only a couple of days from now. Plus, of course, my toned runner's ass will make Michael pant for it.

Dawn is a perfect time for running. Jogging past Bibienne's house, I wonder if she's even out of bed yet. Probably not, lazy girl. Most of the homes on my street look quiet and sleepy. These people are sleeping their lives away. What a waste. Meanwhile, here I am, my body moving cleanly, my lungs expanding in the fresh air, the steady beat of my footfalls, one, two, one, two, my head opening to the rush of adrenaline as I get into the zone. Gorgeous.

I'm sure Michael would be impressed if he were to see me. I'm wearing my short-shorts and I have George with me. He loves the running plan too, and is being a well-behaved dog for once by running nicely and evenly beside me on his leash.

We hit the park where we let it out. Two men pass me on the path and I earn a view of their running shorts. They've been making outstanding progress on their glute components. How come I've never caught on to the running scene before? I try to keep up with the gluteus twins but it's no use. They're out of sight in no time and my lungs are on fire with the effort.

I stop to check my cool new runner's watch that features a built-in heart rate monitor. My heart rate must be powered up now since I can barely breathe and certainly wouldn't be able to carry on a conversation. According to all the running magazines, I'm overexerting myself if I'm breathless or can't talk during my workout.

According to the monitor, however, I am lying on the couch eating cupcakes. This can't be. I'm not even close to target. How do you raise your heart rate to the target zone while still being able to breathe and hold a conversation? Maybe the monitor thingy is broken. I'll do five more minutes in the cupcake zone and then I'm heading home.

As I jog into the driveway, I see that one of the kids left a bicycle lying on the asphalt behind Donald's car. Good thing I discovered this in time as Donald would no doubt back over it without even noticing.

The garage door is locked. Tying George to the garage door handle, I walk the bicycle around to the side door, let myself in and flip the light switch. No wonder Jack left his bike in the driveway. The garage is a giant tilting mess. The Caddy, covered with a tarp, takes up more than half the space. There's an open paint can on the workbench, which reminds me that the bathroom is way overdue for a fresh coat of paint. Painting might actually be a good idea for this week as I have nothing much planned and the kids are back to school.

Ramping up the mental checklist, I poke around in the corners looking for the paint trays, brushes, and drop sheets. There must be fifteen cans of old paint here. I should go through all of this clutter and toss the stuff that's no longer usable. There are loads of mysterious substances in cans and bottles lurking in every corner. I better add a run to the toxic waste disposal to today's to-do list. I have to get started on baby-proofing this dump sometime. Serenity's kid is bound to be a real handful.

That reminds me: there's a sweet old cradle stored up in the rafters. I could haul it down and clean it up, give it fresh coat of paint while I'm wielding the brushes. It's dark and gloomy up there though. Brown recluse territory. Black widows. Daddy long-legs.

Some sunlight will help keep the spiders at bay. I flick the switch to the garage door opener. Where's the ladder? I turn around just in time to see George's leash, still attached to the garage door handle, drawing upwards.

In two bounds, I reach the dog and attempt to disconnect the leash from his collar. The clip is being pulled tighter and tighter by the steadily rising door. So is his collar. Quickly, I heave George to the height of my waist, while still attempting to disconnect the clip with one hand. As the door continues to rise, I have to hoist the dog ever higher, to my shoulders and then my head to keep him safe. The door finally reaches its zenith and the whir of the motor dies away. My nose is now at the level of George's privates. They're wet. With any luck, that's morning dew. George is able to breathe as long as I hold him aloft with his testicles pressed against my cheek. He weighs a ton. I need both of my aching arms to keep him tucked up high in the air. Reaching up one hand to pull the door down again is out of the question. If I let go of him, he'll be in big trouble. All I can do is stand there with a dog drooling all over my head and my nose full of smelly wet fur until someone comes along to rescue us.

The first person along is, of course, Lewis. I know because I can hear his distinctive chuckling sneer. I don't even have to be able to see him to know he's standing at the end of my driveway with his hands on his hips, debating whether or not to help me. He hates George and me enough to walk away but his sense of decency finally kicks in. He undoes George's collar and I drop the dog from my burning arms.

"Thank you very much, Lewis," I say with all due sincerity.

He grunts at me and stalks away.

I go back in the house where I find Donald sitting with his coffee at the kitchen table, one eye on the stock market ticker tape scrolling across his iPad and the other scanning the morning paper. Obviously he walked past that bicycle to get to his sports news.

Donald snorts. "You have grass bits in your hair."

"So when, exactly, do you leave for Calgary?" I ask.

Running every morning is getting in the way of sleeping in. And, since I just heard on the news that French women don't exercise, I guess I don't have to either. But they do drink beaucoup de water. Therefore I'm starting my water-drinking project today.

Twelve bottles will be sluiced down my throat every day from now on. I figure I need to down one every 80 minutes starting at 7 a.m. Since I got up late this morning, I'm already behind so I have to drink two at once to catch up. Best to guzzle it down like a college boy.

I still need my morning coffee. My stomach is gurgling. Surely this gets easier.

Donald is freaking out. "The shuttle leaves in 20 minutes."

"You don't have to yell, I'm coming."

I need to pee but I better hurry. He's going to Calgary for a few days to hunt for an apartment and do some fact-finding for the new job. He'll come home again for two weeks and then he'll be gone again, for the duration.

I run out to the car and hop behind the wheel. Perfect. The trip to the shuttle gives me a chance to update him on Serenity. As soon as we turn onto the highway, I seize my opportunity: "Donald, I have something to tell you."

Donald is pecking away at his phone.

"Hmmm?"

"Serenity's pregnant."

No answer.

"I'm thinking about selling the house on eBay while you're in Calgary."

"Uh huh."

"Donald!"

He startles. "What was that about the house?"

"You might as well stick April 20th in your phone."

"April 20th?"

"Serenity's due date."

I have Donald's undivided attention now.

"But I … How?"

I explain about Jude and the revenge trip. Donald might be going into hypertensive shock. He's all red in the face and his neck veins are bulging. He whips his phone, hard, onto the console. "Oh, I get it. She's playing a game! It's like a little racing game! Will she get her high school diploma first or a baby?"

"You don't have to be so sarcastic."

"Shit, she's only 16 years old."

"She'll be 17 in a few weeks."

"Oh, well, it's all good then."

"Don't talk to me like that. I wish I hadn't said anything."

"Talk to you like what? What in the world did you expect me to say?"

"Something supportive, maybe?"

Donald throws his hands in the air. "Give me a minute here while I think of something."

This isn't going well. I mean, the water drinking is getting to me. I've got to go. Now. I pull into a Dunkin' Donuts and sprint across the parking lot.

Back in the car I pass Donald a large coffee and a box of Munchkins. I wheel back onto the road and watch Donald out of the corner of my eye. He's sipping his coffee in silence and staring straight ahead at the traffic. I crack the lid of my own coffee and gulp some down. I check my watch and realize it's past time for another bottle. No matter what, I have to drink if I want the benefits of exceptional hydration. Those French women must have camel bladders. The traffic is heavy today; the flight is, hopefully, running late, too.

It isn't. The shuttle has pushed off and there won't be another one for hours. Donald opens his palms skyward.

"Now what?"

"Don't panic. I'll drive you to Logan."

By the time we hit the highway I have to pee again.

Donald speaks again, this time with a softer voice. He wants to know what Serenity is planning to do. Is she keeping the baby? Who is going to raise the baby? What about Jude? What about support?

"Yes," I tell Donald, "Serenity is going to keep her baby."

Beyond that, I wish I knew. But I know one thing for sure: I certainly don't want to change any more diapers. Ten to twelve diapers a day times three kids times an average of two and a half years in diapers each, means I've changed roughly 30,000 smelly diapers, at least half of them cloth, for crying out loud. Which means I've washed something in the neighborhood of 15,000 diapers. That's 700 wash-loads all faithfully performed in the interest of befriending the environment. No wonder my machine is making that weird cranking sound.

I wonder if Serenity will be crunchy enough to want to wring a poo-smeared square of pre-folded cotton in the toilet with her bare hands several times a day? I doubt it. Knowing her, she will use her crushing powers of guilt-induction to corner me into doing it. I should buy one of those hand-saver ducks this time out. Bibienne had one. It hung by her toilet for years. I wonder if she still has it?

It's high time to change the subject. I have a plan that I keep meaning to mention to Donald.

"I know what I want to do with the money from my Mom."

Donald slides his eyes sideways at me. He's afraid to make solid eye contact. Last week's plan to open a cafe and roast my own free trade coffee beans didn't exactly impress him. "People like to drink coffee in the morning," he pointed out. "You don't, er, manage well in the morning, remember?"

Too true. For a few days I toyed with the thought that maybe it could be an Irish Coffee kind of place, leaning to evening hours and spoken word events and cool jazz musicians playing in the corner. Trouble is, all day breakfast joints are the only economically feasible restaurants in America. I can't stand bacon and I have expensive leftist leanings on fresh-squeezed juice and free-range eggs. So now I have decided that I want to open my own bookstore.

"Brick Books is up for sale," I say with energy and enthusiasm.

"What?"

the perils of pauline   **157**

"That cute little bookstore downtown. You know, that one that used be a curio shop, and then when it became a bookstore, the owners couldn't afford a new sign? They just changed Bric-a-Brac into Brick Books."

"I thought it was a junk store with a crappy sign."

"No, Donald, it's been a bookstore for years. Everyone knows that. That old sign is part of its charm."

Donald's features are frozen with doubt so I go on to explain that Brick Books is a darling little store, full of wonderful new and used books and Jennifer, the owner, is always having visiting authors and special events and she even has a sweet little coffee bar.

"Nobody ever goes in there," he gasps. Donald looks even more horrified at this than with Serenity's news.

It's true that ever since the big box discount place and the chain bookstore in the mall opened, the store's been having trouble. But Jennifer says the right person could get it going again and even make a decent living. "Someone with a little energy and enthusiasm," she said, adding that it's time for her to move on to something new. "I've always wanted to try running an all-day breakfast place," she added.

The highway is backed up at the airport turn-off. I'm desperate. I can't wait to find a restroom. I'm curling my toes up inside my shoes. The urge is unbelievably strong. Every bump in the road is torture. I undo the top button of my jeans and try to breathe only at the top of my lungs.

Thank god, there's the sign for Departures. The traffic has come to a full stop. A police cruiser races by us on the shoulder, sirens blaring. Probably an accident ahead. This can't be happening. I can't wait. I can't wait. The terminal is just around the corner but at this rate we'll never get there. I can't wait. I can't. Several more minutes pass and we aren't moving at all. Throwing the Jeep into park and grabbing my purse, I leap out and yell to Donald to deal with parking and meet me at the baggage counter. I can get there faster on foot.

I jog along the side of the road while all the drivers and passengers idling across three lanes of backed-up traffic watch me go by. A plane takes off low overhead and I can feel all eyes on the ground and up in the air staring at me as I step up the pace. My bladder is about to explode in front of an entire international assembly. I round the corner only to find a longer line-up of cars and I realize the terminal is still a fair distance off. Now I can see the difficulty: there's construction ahead and a guy with a stop sign is holding back the line so a crane can drop some girders. Where there's construction, there has to be a Porta-Potty. Sure enough, I can see one: it's just a short dash beyond a couple of trailers and across a parking lot full of tractors. I have to climb over a few concrete barriers and side-step rolls of wire and other construction debris. A man in a yellow hard hat is yelling at me.

Apparently I'm in a restricted zone. I point across the lot at the Porta-Potty and make pleading hand gestures. And I run.

I leap inside and secure the latch while trying not to think about the fact that none of the hundreds of construction workers who use this facility ever bother to wash their hands after handling their dankest parts. As I yank down my jeans I wonder: how will I ever get out without touching that latch again?

I can see that more than one man has already missed the hole and ruined the seat. A few weeks ago, Shae explained to me how to pee standing up at a urinal. She said all the women in Texas learn to do this at an early age. Apparently any worthy cowgirl can aim her stream through her open zipper and accomplish the task without a dribble or drip. It's all got to do with proper manipulation of the labia with the fingers positioned in a tight V and then emptying with force. I was planning to practice the trick in the shower but never got around to it yet.

Since I remain uninitiated in the Texan Finger-Assist Method, I have no choice but to hover over the hole while clutching my purse against my chest.

There's no toilet paper. I hate that wet feeling. I squirm back into my jeans. Standing up, I can see a trail of dribbles and drips across the legs of my jeans. These are the unhappy consequences of neglecting my kegels.

I emerge from the Porta-Potty blinking in the sunlight and gasping for fresh air. Airport security is waiting for me. He's a young guy; I can handle him.

"I realize I'm out of bounds here, but you see I was ..."

The guard opens the rear door of a vehicle that has a whirring flashing light on the top.

"Get in," he says without a hint of sympathy.

"Look, I don't think this is necessary."

"I said GET. IN."

As I climb into the back of the security guard's vehicle, all I can think is that my right hand touched that latch. Twice. My nose itches but I can't scratch it with my right hand. I hope they let detainees wash their hands. Maybe the guard has some hand sanitizer. I lean forward and tap on the partition.

"Excuse me. Where are you taking me? I need to get to International Departures to meet my husband. He has a ticket to Calgary. Canada. He works for Double's Group Financial. He's going on a business trip. Take me there and I can prove it."

Silence.

"This is crazy. You're making such a big deal. What's your name? I'm going to be filing a complaint if you don't let me go this second. I'm calling my husband. I have a right to make one phone call."

I puff out my chest and play my best card: "Did you even look at my ID? I am a United States veteran."

"Put that phone away, Ma'am."

"Why?"

"I said put it away."

"Fine. Do you have any hand sanitizer?"

An hour later, after a detour through the underground security halls of the airport where menacing photos of known and suspected terrorists are pasted on the walls, the security guy escorts me to the doors of the Departures terminal. Apparently my hand gestures to the man with the yellow hard hat were regarded as a potential terrorist communication. What with the homeland team being distracted by my Porta-Potty plotting, no doubt some real perp has slipped right through their fingers. Donald's plane is probably about to be hijacked because of me.

I race to the check-in desk. The agent informs me that Donald's plane pushed off a few minutes ago.

"Are you Pauline Parril? Your husband left this for you." She hands me an envelope with my name on it. Inside I find the car keys and a scrawled note:

Pauline: I'll call you as soon as I get to Calgary. Donald. PS. Try not to worry about Serenity. We'll get her through this.

We'll get her through this. *We'll* get her through this. *We?* Are we still a we? I'm so confused.

One thing's certain. And I gasp with the revelation as it drops with a plop deep into my consciousness: Serenity is pregnant and I am going to be a grandmother. For real.

I can do this. I know I can. I want to raise my fist a la Scarlet O'Hara and shout (except I'm standing in the middle of Terminal Three): As God is my witness, I am going to be a good grandmother! I am going to be a fantastic grandmother. And Donald will be a reasonably competent grandfather. We know all kinds of stuff about raising kids. It took us awhile to figure it all out but we could survive as grandparents, I'm sure of it. We still have our teeth and hair so we won't be too scary looking at any rate.

I remain all misty-eyed until I realize my magnificent grandfather-to-be husband hasn't mentioned where he parked the car. I'm shaking my fist at the sky again. Dammit, Donald, there are six levels of parking here.

The car turns out to be on level five at the far end. By the time I unlock the door, I'm parched with the heat and dust. My water bottles are all empty. I still haven't had a chance to cleanse my hands.

I can't go back into the terminal to find a bathroom with that security guy hanging around me. I'll stop somewhere on the way home. If I don't get going, I'll be late picking the kids up. The security guy follows me all the way to the on-ramp, and then spins away back to the terminal after making a quick u-turn.

I wonder if my photo was secretly captured and is already hanging on that wall with all the others? Every one of them had black caterpillars for eyebrows and unruly facial hair. Even the women. I quickly glance into the rearview mirror: have I plucked my eyebrows lately? What about those darkish hairs I found growing above my lip the other day? Did I

get them all with my tweezers? I wouldn't want to be displayed with un-
kempt eyebrows and a scraggly mustache. Maybe it's time for a proper
waxing. I could book an appointment for tomorrow morning. I could get
a little Brazilian job while I'm at it and surprise Michael.

Oh no!—Michael! I was supposed to call him this morning. Snatching up my cell, I turn it on and check my messages. There are five,
all from Michael. He wants to say good morning darling, where am I,
what I am doing, why am I not answering messages, and am I okay?

I text him back one word: Brazil! A little mystery for him to figure
out. By the time I see him, I will be shaking my maracas at him and
offering him a little salsa dip.

The trial week without Donald is almost over. I've barely noticed he's
gone. Of course, the kids have been in school all week, and Serenity
and Shae disappeared off on a road trip for a few days. I've had the
house to myself and I've put it to good use.

Michael came over three times. I drew the line at romping in the
conjugal bed but that didn't stop us from having a go in the shower,
the den, and the basement rec room.

Michael wanted to come back today but I begged off. Too much
sex is too much sex. My Brazilian wax job is used up. Not to mention that the waxing has caused an itchy, spreading rash. I'm going
to apply some calamine lotion and give it a rest.

Plus I'm getting a little paranoid about getting caught. Someone
knocked on the side door while we were in the basement yesterday
and then we heard the squeak of a door hinge. It was Bibienne; I
heard her voice calling for me. We tried to be quiet, but Michael kept
tickling me and making me giggle. After a moment, I heard the door
snap shut. Rather abruptly I thought.

Michael's sneakers were on the mat beside the door. Bibienne
won't blow my cover but still. Maybe I've gone too far.

Of course, every time I get to feeling on the wrong side of the
law I remember that Lindsay is off on this little Calgary junket with
Donald. Not that I can pin anything on the two of them, but what if

he isn't having an affair with Lindsay? I won't think about it. It's early days after all. Every time the guilt rises, Michael slaps it back down with a grin and a well-aimed nuzzle.

I won't let any of this bother me today. Everyone comes trooping back tomorrow and I have one last glorious day to myself. I'm using it to research my bookstore-buying plan. Donald isn't crazy about the idea but he says if that's what I want, I should at least take the time to research it. And prepare a business plan. So Jennifer and I are having a business lunch.

"Donald!" I cry as soon as he gets off the airport shuttle. "Guess what? You're looking at the new owner of Brick Books! I can't believe my luck! Jennifer is letting me take over the business with just a tiny down payment. She's going to teach me the ropes and I can start next week."

Donald heaves his suitcase into the trunk and turns to stare at me. "You don't know a thing about book retailing."

"But I love books! Isn't that all I need? Passion?"

Donald climbs into the passenger seat and leans his head against the headrest, closing his eyes. I jump into the driver's seat.

"Tell me about Calgary. How was your trip?"

Donald opens his eyes again and lifts his head off the headrest. "Great. But there's a load of work to be done and they want me back on site as soon as possible. The field manager is up to his armpits."

"How soon?"

"Monday?"

That's soon. I sag in my seat. For once in my life I can't think of anything to say. Weird thing is, I feel like I'm going to miss Donald. Like I don't know if I can handle the whole hot dog cart without him. Like maybe this is the end. Like it's finally final. And maybe I don't want it to be.

Donald glances at my face. "If you need me to postpone I can."

"I'll be alright."

Donald spent most of the weekend packing for Calgary. His bags are stuffed and his closet is empty.

Neither of us have much to say as I take him back to the shuttle. I wonder what Donald is thinking? For once, he isn't absorbed with his Blackberry. He stares ahead into the traffic.

Is he thinking what I'm thinking? Is this the end?

Is his chest as tight as mine?

As we pull into the parking lot, I spy Lindsay climbing out of a cab. She's smartly dressed with a short skirt and spikey heels.

"Lindsay is going out to Calgary with you again?"

"She's the project manager." Donald's eyes meet mine but I can't read his expression. Is it deliberately neutral and composed?

"What? Is something wrong?"

"I thought you were the project manager. You told me Lindsay wasn't part of this arrangement."

"We are both project managers. It's complicated. I thought I told you Doubles decided to … Look, I have a plane to catch. Can we talk about this later?"

"Whatever."

He transfers his bags to the shuttle, and turns to say goodbye. What do we do here? Shake hands? Suddenly he has me in his arms, hugging me. It's been a long time since I pressed my cheek into the familiar crook of his shoulder. Donald kisses the top of my head and holds me rather tightly. Eyes burning, I pull away from his embrace. I refuse to cry in front of him, and I sure as hell won't cry in front of Lindsay.

As he climbs aboard, he glances back at me, and waves a quick wave. I can't decide if his expression is rueful, guilty or sad. Then he disappears onto the shuttle.

With Lindsay.

Maybe I do want it to be the end.

"The word torrid springs to mind."

I whirl my head around to see Bibienne standing inside the back door. She has a large bowl of garden tomatoes in her hands and her Mona Lisa smile on her face.

"Oh God. Is it that obvious?"

"I've known you since forever," she says handing me the bowl and settling into the wingchair in the living room.

"Nice tomatoes. Wow, they're still warm."

"Big sneakers. I'm thinking size 15?"

"I was going to tell you, honestly."

"No worries."

"So that was you at the door the other day?"

Bibienne cocks her head at me. "Uh huh."

"Don't uh huh me. I'm not a kid. I know all about that uh huh trick."

"Uh huh."

"Fine. His name is Michael and I met him at Dingwall. He's my Modern American Poetry prof. I mean he was my prof. Nothing happened until after. He's one of the most beautiful and sexy men I've ever met. He thinks I'm beautiful and sexy. And he's only a 14."

Bibienne lifts one eyebrow. "That's it?"

"That's it."

Bibienne stares me down. "What about Donald?"

"He's a 12. Regular."

Bibienne snorts. "So it's out with the old, in with the new?"

"Not exactly. The old has gone out west to live. And Lindsay is out there with him."

"You found out for sure Donald is with her? Like, they're together?"

"No, not for sure. This isn't about revenge anyway. It's about me."

"Hey, it's okay. Just be careful."

"Thanks for the lovely tomatoes."

"I have plenty more if you want them. Stupid Bernie went gaga and planted a million billion plants." She lets out a sigh. "Size 14 huh?"

"We're talking extra wide."

"Ouch ouch baby," she says. She's smiling but I can see a touch of the old green sap rising in her eyes.

Despite her jealous pique, I know my secret is safe with Bibi. Her lips are glued shut. After all, she once bragged to me that Bernie practically wears clown shoes.

CHAPTER 19

Homeland Defense

Homeland Defense: The protection of United States sovereignty, territory, domestic population, and critical defense infrastructure against external threats and aggression or other threats as directed by the President.
—*Department of Defense Dictionary of Military and Associated Terms*

I'm all pumped up. Today's my first day working at the bookstore under Jennifer's guidance. I've just jumped into the shower and lathered my head with my new peppermint shampoo, designed to invigorate the scalp, when I hear Jack downstairs screaming, "Daddy." Throwing my bathrobe around me, I run downstairs leaving a trail of peppermint foam blobs to find Jack in the downstairs bathroom, still screaming his head off. I crack open the door and call in, "What's the matter? Why are you screaming for Daddy?"

"I need toilet paper."

"Daddy is in Canada, remember?" My scalp is starting to invigorate in a most unpleasant fashion.

"I need toilet paper."

"There's some on the shelf beside you."

"No there isn't."

"Look up higher." I need to rinse my hair before my scalp burns off.

"Oh yeah."

Yesterday at dinner Olympia asked me where Donald was. A week ago, before he left, Donald and I called a major family conference and explained the situation in detail. "Daddy is going to work in a city far away. For a long time. Any questions?"

They said, "Nope. Can we go now?"

I jump back in the shower to rinse the peppermint shampoo out of my hair hoping the stinging will subside soon.

I waylay the kids at the breakfast table. "Hey, you two. I need you both to try to grasp the fact that Daddy has gone out west to work. He'll be coming back home but not for a long time."

I think.

"How long?" asks Olympia.

"Many, many sleeps. But he'll come home and visit us."

She holds up her hand and spreads out her fingers. "More than 5 sleeps?"

Yes, I nod. Olympia bursts into tears. "I miss Daddy."

I kneel beside her chair and take her dear little hands in mine. "Oh, honey, I know. Daddy misses you too. But you can call him on the phone every day. And you can write him letters too."

Olympia's face brightens up. "Can I have a kitten then?"

"A kitten?"

"Yeah, because I miss Daddy so much and the kitten will help me feel better."

Jack yells, "No fair. If Olympia gets a kitten then I want an iguana."

"We aren't getting any new pets. We already have a dog, two cats and a fish."

They start bickering with each other over which kind of new pet we will be getting. I have to yell over their raised voices to get their attention: "No, we aren't getting an iguana or a kitten."

Jack scowls. "Can I have a turtle then?"

"Mommy, Jack is squeezing my arm."

"Jack, let go of her arm. Both of you, go get ready for school. Now. I have to start at the store this morning and I can't be late."

Jack releases Olympia's arm to ask, "What store?"

When I arrive at the store at 8:15, Jennifer shakes her head at me. "You'll need to get here well before 7 to set up for the morning coffee crowd." She hands me a stack of catalogs. "When you have a chance you need to look through these. The Christmas order should be in by the end of the week. But don't worry, I'll help you with that." Then she points at a knee-deep pile of books on the floor: "First I'll show you how to do returns."

Three hours later I'm still sitting at a desk with books piled up around my ears searching through endless packing slips, and crossing off titles as they go into a box postmarked for return to one publisher or another. I pause to read the dust jacket of a novel by someone I've never heard of. I would love to stop and read a few pages but my stomach is growling and I need to fill at least two more boxes before I can knock off for lunch. I'll add the title to my list.

"You must read so many wonderful books," I say to Jennifer as she grabs a yogurt from the fridge.

"Me? I wish. I don't have much time for reading," she replies with a shrug. "Or eating." She cracks open the yogurt container hurriedly as she turns back to the phone.

Jennifer is buried, too. Yesterday's delivery still needs to be entered on the computer and shelved. She's been on and off the phone all morning arguing with a distributor who invoiced her for 32 copies of a book on model trains she never ordered.

"Good thing the store has been so quiet this morning. We'd never get it all done," I say when she pauses by my table to check my progress.

Jennifer winces, saying, "A slow morning is never a good thing."

In the afternoon, business picks up. Whenever a customer comes through the door, Jennifer stops shelving. "Sorry, it's not out in softcover yet," I hear her apologizing to a woman who is tsk-tsking over the price of the latest crime thriller. Half an hour later, the woman leaves without buying anything, after saying, "I'm sure Bookmonster has it."

As the door closes behind her, Jennifer says, "I hate Bookmonster."

An elderly woman with a cane comes bustling through the door. "I'll get this one," I mouth to Jennifer who is back on the phone again to the distributor and I turn with a bright welcoming smile to my very first customer. "May I help you?"

She wants the latest novel by someone named Brenda. "The last name begins with a 'T,'" she says. She can't remember the title of the book. I turn to the computer to run a search on Brenda's. "No, that's not it," she keeps saying as I call out names. I try several spelling variations but still no hits. "Wait, the name is Barbara." I type in more queries. The woman is jingling her car keys with impatience. "It has a blue cover."

Jennifer interrupts us. "Are you thinking of Deanna Gabson's latest novel?" She produces a volume with a large breasted woman on a cover with lots of red. A man with no shirt and a loosened kilt is lying across a bearskin rug in the background. The woman brightens. "Yes, that's the one! Do you have it in large print?"

"I can order it in," Jennifer offers as the phone begins ringing again.

"Never mind. Bookmonster probably has it," the old woman says as she stomps out the door.

Jennifer leans over and whispers, "Deanna Gabson writes nothing but smut. That old lady comes in here every week looking for the dirtiest novels I can lay my hands on. She only comes here 'cause her daughter-in-law works at Bookmonster."

I must look completely dumbfounded as Jennifer adds, as she turns away to answer the phone again, "You have no idea, do you?"

A full week as a Brick Books trainee, and I'm stumbling with exhaustion. I make it to after-school care in the nick of time to pick up the kids. Jack says, "How come we're always the last ones to be picked up?"

"Sorry, guys, I was held up at the store again."

"Did you remember to bring me the Gobstopper book?"

Too late, I remember a blurty promise. Now I get why the cobbler's kids are shoeless. No wonder. I can't afford to buy the kids so much as a comic given the poor receipts from this week. Sales were dead slow. We will all be shoeless if I don't figure out the bookselling business quickly. I'm tempted to stop at Bookmonster and grab them something slashed in the discounted section.

I hustle over to the nearest drive-through lane and tell them to order whatever they want. I'm not hungry even though I haven't eaten all day. My mouth feels like it's stuffed with paper. The smell of books sticks in my hair and nostrils. I used to love the smell of a bookstore. Now the smell gives me a headache.

My phone beeps at me. I haven't had time to check my messages all day. It's a text message from Michael. *U and me tonite?*

I want to answer: *Forget it, chum. It's Friday night and I'm going home to crawl into a hot bath.*

Michael is overjoyed that Donald has gone to Calgary. He's been a bit of a nuisance all week. He knows I'm desperate to get up to speed at the store but he still keeps bugging me. He wants to come over to the house all the time now but I told him we still have to be discreet. I ignore the text. I will meet him for coffee next week for sure.

The phone beeps again. Another message from Michael: *need to talk to u asap.*

Sigh. I text back: *My house. Deck. 10 p.m.*

After supper, I read bedtime stories until Jack drifts off to sleep but Olympia remains owl eyed. She agrees to turn out the light right after *Days With Frog and Toad*. I turn to the first story in the book, called *Tomorrow*.

"Toad woke up. 'Drat!' he said. 'This house is a mess. I have so much work to do.'"

Ha! Toad should see my messy house. Someone spilled a puddle of shampoo on the bathroom floor a couple of days ago and didn't bother to wipe it up. There's a ripe smell emanating from Jack's closet and last night I caught Bitesalot sleeping in my basket of clean folded laundry so now my folding is all covered with cat hair and possibly fleas and worms as he's overdue for his flea and worm pills. I'll have to rewash that load which reminds me: the washing machine quit this morning halfway through the wash cycle and now there's a full load of darks still sitting in filthy cold water in the machine. First thing in the morning I better call someone to come look at the pump.

Olympia pokes me. "You stopped reading," she complains.

Right.

"'Blah,' said Toad. 'I feel down in the dumps.' 'Why?' asked Frog. 'I am thinking about tomorrow,' said Toad. 'I am thinking about all of the many things I will have to do.'"

No kidding. I know exactly how Toad feels. Tomorrow I have to meet with Kevin, the pushiest sales rep in the business according to Jennifer who, by the way, is only going to be able to help me out for a few more days. Then I will be on my own. After Kevin I have to interview for replacement sales staff as Jennifer's right hand, Dwayne, is leaving to go travel around Europe. Then I need to meet with the bookkeeper and get up to speed on payroll and taxes. I haven't finished my book returns yet and the storefront window display still needs to be revamped with an autumnal look. Olympia jabs me with her elbow deep in my ribs, shrieking: "Mommy! You stopped reading again."

Right.

"'Yes,' said Frog, 'tomorrow will be a very hard day for you.'"

I know. Poor old Toad. Tears are forming in my eyes.

Olympia says, "Did you put Squish in the freezer, Mommy?"

Squish? In the freezer?

"My fish." Olympia jabs me again.

Right. All her pet fish in the past year have been called Squish. Her latest Squish was found floating this morning. I couldn't flush him down the toilet in front of Olympia. I stuck the body in the freezer as I didn't have time to deal with a backyard burial. There's a backlog of dead goldfish stacked in a baggie in there now ever since the first Squish died in January. I better remember to inter the lot of them properly before the snow flies again. Meanwhile Olympia wants a new Squish. I pledge a visit to the pet store tomorrow and kiss her goodnight. Meanwhile my Squish is probably waiting for me on the back deck. I would like to put another Squish on ice right about now.

At last Olympia drops off to sleep. And, sure enough, I find Michael sitting in the dark on the deck, leaning forward with hunched shoulders, legs straddling the deck recliner. Smoking. His lighter is lying beside him so I pick it up and use it to light the tiki torches by the steps. "Hey," he says. "Come here."

"What's wrong?" I ask, sitting on the chair in front of him. In the flickering light I can see his face looks drawn, haggard. It looks like he hasn't shaved today. "Oh my God, Michael, you look terrible."
He shakes his head. "I feel terrible."
"Why? What happened? Is it your thesis? Didn't your advisor like it?"
"I haven't submitted it yet."
"Wasn't it due last week?"
"I'm still working on it."
Michael leans back and clasps his hands behind his head. His eyes are shiny in the dark. "Let's not talk about that now. I have something to tell you."
"What?"
"Carmen and I are filing for a divorce."
"Blah," said Toad.
Michael continues: "I moved into an apartment at Dingwall today."
"No wonder you look so exhausted." I reach out and brush the stubble on his cheeks with my fingertips.
Michael takes my hand and holds it against his cheek. He peers into my face. "You look pretty exhausted yourself."
"I am," I admit. "But never mind; I'm worried about you."
Michael touches my lips with his finger and whispers, "Shhhh." He lies back on the lounge chair pulling me down on top of him. I stuff my face into his chest while he rubs the back of my neck. We're taking a chance nuzzling on the back deck like this but Jack and Olympia are asleep in bed, and Serenity and Shae have gone out.
Soon Michael's nuzzles turn into a long and urgent kiss. It would be too risky to make love out here on the deck but, as long as we keep our clothes on, we can visit with each other. Michael puts his hand up under my t-shirt and starts comparing my nipples to tight little rosebuds. "One lick," he says.
I suppose I could let him have one lick. I lift my shirt and Michael undoes my bra. Might as well take it off. I tuck the bra under the lounger seat cushion and slip my shirt back on leaving it strategically raised for rosebud maintenance.
"Why not take off your underwear the same way?"

I slip out of my shorts, remove my underwear and then slip the shorts back on. I sit back on his lap. Michael immediately parks his hand down the front of my shorts and continues nipping at my rosebuds. After a minute he pulls me back down on top of him.

"Shhhh, Michael, you're making the lounger squeak."

"Could we be discreet underneath the trampoline?"

The trampoline is tucked in the darkest corner of the yard, beside the fence. We'd be well concealed. But, before I can summon a response, I hear a car pulling into the driveway. Serenity and Shae must be home. They are early for a Friday night. I forgot: now that Serenity is pregnant, she gets tired easily and goes to bed early. I look at Michael in a panic. How will I explain the presence of a male stranger who is chatting with me in the dark on the back deck?

The approaching voices grow louder as the pair enters the house through the side door. There's no time to douse the torches. They've spotted us. And out they come staring with curiosity at Michael.

"This is Michael, a friend from Dingwall. He's a doctoral candidate." I make my introduction with the most casual of airs, as if all married women have attractive doctoral candidates reclining on their back porches at 10 p.m. Serenity shoots me the stinkeye. *Say it ain't so, Ma.* To avoid further eye contact, I lower my gaze. I am a rotten mother. On the way to the floor, my eyes light onto Serenity's waistline. I think I can detect a thickening. She's starting to show. Correction. I am a rotten grandmother.

CHAPTER 20

Taboo Frequencies

TABOO Frequencies: Any friendly frequency of such importance that it must never be deliberately jammed or interfered with by friendly forces including international distress, safety, and controller frequencies.—Department of Defense Dictionary of Military and Associated Terms

Serenity sleeps in until noon every day which is a good way of avoiding any chance of morning sickness, at least in the morning hours, and usually by the time I get home, she can be found sprawled across the couch, watching TV and complaining that it's too hot/cold/rainy to go anywhere. She's barefoot and pregnant but not in the kitchen sense of starting dinner or anything helpful like that. I have to hand it to Shae who got all ambitious last week and landed a job with the city. She's up at dawn every day now, off to cut grass and tend to city park maintenance.

I enter the room, set down my briefcase, and scoop up a few snack wrappers and chip bags that are scattered around the room. "What's your plan for the rest of the fall?"

"I dunno."

"What happened to back to school?"

"High school sucks. I only need a couple more credits to graduate so I'm going to do them at the adult education center."

"That sounds good. Are you registered yet?"

"No."

"Maybe you could take a parenting class."

"Nah, I don't need to. I saw a kid being born on Youtube last week."

"I meant parenting, not birthing. You know, how to look after a baby."

Serenity picks up the remote control and changes the channel. "Don't stress on me. I got it all under control, aiight?"

It's my last day running the store with Jennifer's guidance. Tonight we are having an open house with a ribbon cutting ceremony plus free cake and sparkling wine for our guests. Michael says Carmen is letting him see Nick tonight but if he has time he'll drop by the store later. I haven't seen him since the night on the deck. He's been busy moving into the Dingwall grad residence, which is just as well since I've been scrambling all week at the store.

Jennifer and I are busy setting up a table with coffee cups, wine glasses, and paper plates when there's a commotion at the door. A man is attempting to heave a shopping cart full of cardboard boxes across the threshold. "A self-publisher," Jennifer whispers as he bashes the cart into the front table display. "Irish," she adds as if this explains everything.

"Morning ladies."

It's late afternoon but Jennifer gives me a warning look. "Garth, this is Pauline. She's our new owner." To me she adds, "Ghostly Garth is one of our local authors. We carry some of his books."

"And I have a brand new one." He hands me a book with a lurid cover done in silver, black, and white with red embossed lettering in a blood-dripping font.

Jennifer pulls a notebook out of the drawer. "I'll take 5 copies. The usual consignment rate, huh?" She starts writing down her terms. Clearly she wants to hurry this transaction along.

Ghostly Garth turns to me: "Did you know that this building is haunted?"

I glance at Jennifer over Garth's shoulder. She rolls her eyes.

From one of the boxes, Garth produces a radio, twists the dials and hangs it around his neck. "I've been researching the paranormal for the past thirty years and, I can tell you, there's a poltergeist in this room at this moment."

Jennifer stops writing to watch Garth as he holds out his hands, palms down, flutters his eyelids and begins to pace. There's a lot of static emitting from the radio and Garth taps it, looks back at me knowingly and stumbles into a display table. Jennifer runs to catch a book before it topples onto the floor. "As you can see, Garth is our expert on ghosts. Watch your step there, G."

Garth waves his hands palms down over the top of the filing cabinet. He shivers with vehemence. "Ah, you see, right here, this spot is very charged. It's icy cold in fact."

Jennifer crosses her arms. "There's an air conditioning vent above you. It's a draft."

Garth paces a few more steps and stops again, one foot hovering in mid-step. He says, almost to himself, "Oh yes, definitely. Right here." Then he turns and cocks his head at me: "Have you ever seen an orb? Like a wee spot of light, usually pale green or bluish green? They float around at eye level. You only usually see them out of the corner of your eye."

I've seen spots in front of my eyes because of this joint but, no, I assure him, I haven't seen any wholehog orbs lately. He looks so disappointed I add, "I've only been working here for a few weeks."

He hands me his card. Jennifer then demonstrates her considerable skills in removing Irish authors from the store but not before he spots the poster advertising our party tonight. "I'll bring ye some of me wife's tatties."

As soon as he leaves she says, "I forgot to mention the local authors. Most of them are fine, really polite, and easy to work with, but you need to watch out for the fluffers."

"Fluffers?"

"Fluffers like to rearrange the shelves so their book stands out more. Face out, or front and center in the window if they can get away with it. It's not usually a big deal, but once I had a guy set up an entire end aisle display when I was busy with another customer."

"Sneaky."

"You have no idea."

I wish she would stop saying that.

A big crowd of people has turned out for my launch party. The local paper even sent a reporter with his camera. Jennifer and I pose for the ribbon cutting in front of the store. Ghostly Garth insists on being in the picture with his new book.

We all troop inside and cut the cake while Bibienne and Bernie circulate with trays of champagne cocktails.

"Amazing how they all come out of the woodwork for free booze," says Jennifer as she tops up her glass from a bottle stashed under her counter.

I watch her swallow the contents of her glass in one gulp and reach for the bottle again. "You certainly managed to build up a loyal fan base."

"Yup. And some of them can even read."

Then she stands up, a little unsteadily, to read from a prepared speech. According to Jennifer, I am the town's shining gateway to literacy, a stalwart torchbearer for freedom of speech, and a bulwark against the evil of corporate monopolies that threaten the small independents everywhere with extinction.

She throws aside her notes and, picking up a cocktail from Bernie's tray, cries, "I propose a toashht to Pauline. Those suits at Bookshmashers can try but they'll never smush the life out of Brick Books. Pauline! Gawd, you're like a maverick, ya know, the last real bookseller, jusht one of the last good ones left in this crazy world."

After tipping most of the champagne in her glass into her mouth, she grabs my wrist with her free hand and raises my arm up to the sky like a prizefighter. Then the cocktails run out and everyone heads for the exit.

Serenity and Shae offer to take Jack and Olympia home to bed while Mom and Bibienne help clear away most of the party mess— with assistance from Ghostly Garth who singlehandedly delivers his own paper plate and napkin to the garbage bin and then hangs around to fluff a half dozen of his titles into the bestseller section. It's almost 11 p.m. when I finally lock the door behind everyone. I don't know what happened to Michael but it doesn't matter as I'm elated: for the first time, I'm alone in my very own store.

I return Garth's books to the local author shelf and pass the vacuum over a scattering of cake crumbs. Under the counter I find half a bottle of champagne that Jennifer somehow missed. I'm parched so I pour a glass and sip while tidying the booktable at the front entrance. I turn off the front lights, turn the sign on the door to "Closed," stand in the middle of the store, and look around: at last it's mine. All mine.

My glass is empty. I ought to toast the store so I pour a refill.

"To success," I say out loud, raising my glass and then taking a big snort to prove I mean it. This is good stuff. I love looking around this room at all the pretty, pretty books. This store is going to be fierce; I just know it. I'm sure I made the right move buying Jennifer out. Donald will see. The world will always welcome a good bookstore. "To Brick Books!" I take another snort.

I don't want to go home yet. I want to go dancing. I'm wearing my new 16-String dress, which has a complicated arrangement of long strings that tie the dress around my curves and is guaranteed to make Michael try to undo me. The night is still young to get undone. Maybe Michael will still show up. I take a peek out the front window. The street is dark and deserted. I check my watch. It's coming on midnight. I guess he isn't coming. I'm getting tipsy. I better call a cab. But first I will call Michael. Yes, I will pour another slug and call him.

On the first ring, it goes straight to his voicemail. I hang up. Why did he turn his phone off? I need to think of a good message to leave. I should give him a piece of my mind. When he wants something from me, I have to jump and be quick about it. Then, when I want something, what do I get? Squat.

Maybe I should call Donald instead. Come to think of it, I didn't hear a word from him either. A big night for me, and not one freaking word from my own husband. I heard from almost everyone I know tonight except Donald. And Michael.

I wonder what time it is in Canada? My head is fuzzy. I can't remember if they're ahead or behind, and by how many hours? I have lots of reference books here; I could look it up. Or I could call Donald and ask him. That's what I'll do. There's still a little wine left here; I'll finish off the bottle and call Donald. I dial the number and he picks up on the first ring.

"Hello, Donald." For some reason, I accent his name heavily.

"Pauline?"

"Yes, it's Pauline. Your wife. Remember me? Pauline?"

"Yes, we talked this afternoon. Have you been drinking?"

"I'm toasting the store. You should come on over. Join the party. But you can't 'cause you're in Canada. Far away. Wayyy, far away. So what time is it there? I jusht wanted to find out what time it is in Canada. What are you doing tonight anyway? Is Lindsay there? You know what, I wanna talk to that bitch."

"Lindsay's not here. She's at her apartment. Pauline, are you feeling alright?"

"I'm fantashtic. I jusht bought a bookstore you know."

"I know. How did the launch party go?"

"It was great; you should've been here. 'Cause you know what? I'm a maverick. But now I have to go pee." I hang up. Wait. I should call him back. I still don't know what time it is in Canada. But first I better go pee.

I stand up and the room tilts. I sit back down. I will try to call Michael again. No answer again so this time I leave him a message: "Michael, where are you? I had a party tonight and you didn't come. You're a complete shit and I have to go pee now."

I make my way to the staff bathroom at the back of the store. I'm dizzy and I have to grope the wall to find the switch for the overhead light. I flick the switch only to hear the bulb ping out. I have to leave the door open to see. The bathroom is tiny. It's hard to manage in here even when sober. I tug my panty hose down to my knees, which effectively locks them together. Some of the longer strings on the back of the dress fall into the toilet. I gather the skirt section and all the wayward strings up around my waist, and sit down quickly so no bit gets away from me.

Funny, the spot I'm sitting in has flashed over with an icy coldness and an eerie feeling comes over me like there's someone outside the door hiding in the shadows watching me pee.

I stand up and flush. A few of the strings have jumped back in the bowl. I yank them back quickly before my whole dress is sucked down into the pipes. The old plumbing bangs and thumps, but the noise is louder and lasts longer than usual. My hands are shaky; it's hard to tuck all the strings back the way they were especially since they're dripping wet.

I hear a thump from the back of the store. Did I remember to lock the back door? Did someone slip in while I was on the toilet?

"Garth?"

I step out of the bathroom and peer into the shadowy corners. Nothing. Maybe it's Michael come at last?

"Hello? Is that you, Michael?"

Nothing. A flare of light behind me causes a horde of shadows to shuttle across the wall. My heart flubs a beat. Oh, it's okay. Just headlights going by. My heart is still flubbing though, and that's when I hear a floorboard creak in the office, and one of the deepest, blackest shadows wavers ever so slightly. Without the aid of any headlights at all.

Someone—or something—is lurking at the back of the store.

"I can hear you back there. Come out now before I call the police." I use my parade square holler. I know a thing or two about hand-to-hand urban combat and I know all the words to Goodnight Saigon, too, and this butthead is going to get it.

Nothing. I call again, "I mean it, come out right now, I'm dialing."

I edge toward the phone while listening carefully. Nothing. All I can hear is the sound of water running somewhere. And then a loud knocking. Only the pipes in the basement. I should call a plumber instead of the police.

I pick up the receiver and then think better of it. Maybe my ears are playing tricks on me. This is an old building, I'm tired and it's just kind of creepy being here alone. Problem is I still have to call a cab and I can't leave without my purse, which is in the back office. What if someone is hiding back there?

I have a weapon. I pick up the vacuum cleaner and, holding the wand in an aggressive, head-bashing manner, haul it to the back. I use the wand to flip on the overhead light switch. Empty.

I pull open the closet door. There's no one standing there wielding a Bowie knife. The overhead light makes a crackling noise and goes out, leaving me in the clammy darkness. I feel my way along the wall to the light switch but the bulb is gone. Very strange.

Then I hear a noise, this time it's coming from the basement. I hear footsteps and then a kind of a rattling noise, like chains. I'm dead afraid to go out back. Ghostly Garth was right. This place is haunted. I'm likely dealing with the ghost of the pawnbroker who, come to think if it, died of a heart attack in this shop, maybe even on the spot I'm standing on now. No one found him for two days.

Or maybe the pawnbroker saw the ghost and that's what stopped his heart. Which makes at least two ghosts. The pawnbroker ghost is likely pissed that he was left to molder for two days. The other ghost probably is stuck here because he has souls to suck and hasn't met his quota. The place is obviously jam-packed with unhappy spirits. I could be next to join them. Jennifer never breathed a word of this problem to me.

Jennifer is still alive and kicking which makes me feel better until it occurs to me that insanity might be one of the curses. She was acting pretty crazy tonight.

I've got to get out of here now. I'm selling this bloody business tomorrow, to heck with being a maverick. Now I know why Jennifer said I was brave. Crazy and brave, she said. Brave my ass. Crazy for sure. I grab my keys and prepare to run for it.

There's no way I'm going out the back door now which is at the end of a short but creepy length of hallway. The hallway passes the stairs that lead to the slithery blackness of the basement where murdered wraiths and disembodied demonic souls are no doubt lurking.

I speed toward the front, careening down the side aisle past the travel section. I crash straight into the book spinner in the middle of the aisle, where we dragged it out of the way when we set up the refreshments table. It topples over, books spill out everywhere, and I fall on top of it. I try to stand up but some of the strings and my foot are tangled in the spinner. I yank hard on the strings to free them and step forward with my free foot onto a pile of paperbacks, landing in an open scissor split back on the floor again. My foot is still trapped by the spinner so I pull hard. My shoe comes off and I hear a ripping noise, probably a string off my dress. I crawl as fast as I can through the spillage of books toward the door, which seems to recede into the distance.

Go, go, go, get out. My legs feel all gloopy. At last I reach the front door. I can barely unlock it what with my shaking hands and I leap across the threshold, straight into the bulk of a dark shape with arms that wrap around me and hold me fast. I scream.

It's Michael. He peers into my face anxiously. "Are you okay? You look like you've just seen a ghost."

"Oh my God, you have no idea. There's something, it's like a presence in the bathroom. I heard these rattling noises coming from the back and the lights went out and there was a cold spot and ..."

"I was at the back door a minute ago. I came to the front at first, but I saw a light at the back. I thought you were back there so I went around but the door was locked so I came back around here and, wow, you're all sweaty. Mmmm. I like that."

"You scared the crap out of me. And you like the weirdest things."

"You're missing a shoe."

I bend over all the way and inspect my feet. "You're right!"

Michael grabs a few of my dress strings and pulls me upright as if I were a marionette. "And you're ... happy."

"I'm glad you're here." I pull Michael in to the shadows of the door and give him a kiss. "Come on in and join the party," I whisper in his ear.

Michael licks his lips. "You taste like blueberries and champagne."

I stuff my nose inside Michael's shirt and smell his chest. "You smell like popcorn." I start undoing his shirt buttons. "I want popcorn. Mmmm. With lots of melted butter."

"How many glasses have you had?"

"Jusht a few."

"I'm sorry I missed your party. I took Nick to see a movie and then I brought him back to Carmen. I thought I'd have time to get back here for some of it but …"

"Thash alright. Oopsh, your buttons don't work."

"Wait, don't yank them off like that. We better go inside."

Brick Books has been well and truly launched. After Michael helped me find my shoe, he picked up all the spilled books and spread a tablecloth on the floor at the back of the store. And then he untied all my strings slow-like and we had a picnic. No strings attached. And then I threw up.

Best bookstore launch party ever.

CHAPTER 21

Minefield

Minefield: In land warfare, an area of ground containing mines emplaced with or without a pattern.—Department of Defense Dictionary of Military and Associated Terms

I hate Tuesday mornings in the store. That's when Johnny Rotten comes in to trash the kid's section. Mommy Rotten pretty much ignores the brat while she thumbs through the magazine racks while saying, "Don't touch anything." Meanwhile J.R. tosses all the picture books on the floor and smudges the covers with his sticky sproggy fingers. Today he spun the book turner so fast the books flipped like Frisbees across the room. Several books whapped him in the face, triggering a screaming tantrum. Mommy Rotten finally hauled him out of the store but not before complaining that my spinner is clearly unstable and I should do something about it. As I stoop to pick the mess up, Dwayne waves the phone at me.

I signal Dwayne to watch the front and slip into the back room. It's Michael.

"What time do you want me to pick you up?"

Uh oh. I forgot. I promised to have lunch with him today.

"I don't know if I can get away. I'm swamped. I did four interviews this morning, and not one of the applicants has actually read anything since high school. One of them has no car so she wants me to give her a ride or pay her extra for cab fare. There was only one who seemed okay. Until she blessed me. She held her hand over my head and mumbled something about banishing Satan."

"You need a break. I'll pick you up in half an hour."

I weakly say yes and hang up. I feel like laying my head down to close my eyes, just for a few minutes, but my desk is piled high with folders and catalogues. I pick up a pen to sign a stack of checks left for me by the bookkeeper. It's payday. For everyone else but me that is.

A few minutes later, Serenity and Jude step through the door. Huge smiles. "Look," says Serenity as she hands me a photo, "an ultrasound picture of the baby. The technician says I'm exactly 14 weeks along and the heartbeat is perfect. Isn't she cute?"

I can see fuzzy grey head and torso shapes with some indistinct blobby elongations that are most likely the arms and legs.

"Adorable." I give Serenity a hug. "But what about that bit sticking up there? Unless that's a high heel or a lipstick, I think you might be having a boy."

Jude grins even more broadly at this. "That's what I said. The technician thought it might be a boy too. I think he looks like Johnny Depp."

Serenity scowls, takes the photo from my hand and tucks it in her bag. "It's a girl. I know it. And Shae thinks so too."

"Where is Shae?"

"She had to go back to work. She said to tell you that she's going to bring you a new bench this afternoon to replace that old crappy one."

Man, I love that Shae found that job with the City Works Department. The pothole in the sidewalk has been repaired, two planters of fall flowers appeared last week and now a new bench for outside my store!

"Mom, did you know there's a woman walking around outside in front of the store drawing crosses in the air and telling everyone who goes by that the eye of Lucifer is upon you?"

"I wouldn't give her a job."

Jude and Serenity exchange glances. "Hang on. We'll get rid of her for you."

Two minutes later, they march back in. "All gone," says Jude, brushing off his hands.

Impressive. And then, all in a rush, a brilliant trumpets-blaring, why-didn't-I-think-of-that-before idea floods my brain: "Would you two like to work here at the store for me?

Miraculously they look at each other, smile and nod their heads, yes. Before they can change their minds, I yell, "Excellent! I need you to start today. Immediately."

I run into the bathroom and run a sniff check. I smell like a musk ox. Removing my panties and grabbing the rose scented air freshener, I spray the air and wave them around. I add a squirt into the air between my thighs and do a little swishy hips motion for good measure. I haven't shaved my legs in two weeks. You can't have everything. I'm all prickly, but rose-scented and more than ready for lunch.

Turns out, *I* was lunch. I feel completely deflowered. Mowed down even. Michael says he likes my legs all prickly. He kept running his hands up and down my shins saying the hair felt soft and sleek. I kept my arms down though, so he couldn't pat the pelts in my armpits.

Even better, I returned to the store to find that Jude had tidied up the entire YA section and Dwayne says Serenity's a whizz on the cash register already.

"What a week," I say to Michael as he ushers me in to his apartment at the residence. We set down my bags of laundry in the vestibule. Since my washing machine is still busted, I told Michael that I would only have dinner with him if he lets me use the residence washing machines.

He leads me out to his tiny kitchen and starts tossing the salad while I sit on a counter stool.

"Jack almost got suspended yesterday," I moan, "and Olympia is mad 'cause she's needed new indoor shoes for school for weeks. I told her I'll go shopping with her tomorrow. If it weren't for Jude and Serenity I don't know how I would've survived."

Michael holds up a bottle of red wine. "This should help."

He stabs the cork out of the bottle with a penknife because he hasn't got a corkscrew. Or glasses. He pours the wine into two plastic mugs left by the last tenant.

I take a hefty swig. "The store is crazy. There're all kinds of people coming in the door all day long but hardly anyone is in the market for books. An old lady came in today looking for a can of tomato soup. I pointed out the grocery store across the street and she wanted to know why the hell they went and moved it over there."

Michael says, in a soothing voice, "Try to forget about work. It's all in the past now. Relax and be present in the moment."

"It's hard to relax. You know, today I had to counsel a man about his parenting problems. He came in for a book on how to control teenagers. Then he asked me for my advice. That's pretty funny when you think about it. Everyone thinks a bookstore owner has read every single book in the store, twice, and that we know everything about everything."

I take another sip of wine. Michael's right. I should try to relax but all I can think about is the fall returns and finishing the paperwork on my overdue sales tax. Meanwhile Michael has been sweet enough to make me dinner with candles and everything. Or maybe I should say candles and … nothing. We will have to eat on paper plates as Michael hasn't had a chance to buy any kitchen stuff and his wife refuses to give him so much as an eggcup.

While Michael sets the garlic bread under the broiler, I wander over and peek out the window. Michael has no curtains yet either. But who needs curtains way up on the sixth floor of the grad residence? I'm staring across a short span at a huge windowless concrete wall, the view compliments of the newest student residence on campus. Good job, Dingwall.

There are books and papers piled everywhere in the living room, and the sound of someone down the hall strumming a guitar and the cork bits in the wine make me feel like I'm a college girl again.

After dinner, Michael helps me lug all my baskets and supplies into the basement laundry room, which is, thankfully, deserted. I have all the machines to myself. I begin dumping clothes and soap into machines and sliding coins into the slots. Michael watches me from the doorway. Our eyes meet over the top of an agitating washer.

"Haven't I seen you here before?" Leaning against the frame, he runs his eyes up and down my body in an obvious fashion.

Oh, I get it. We're playing strangers in a laundromat. "Maybe." I bend low over my basket, showing my cleavage. Peering up at him through blond curls and thick lashes I say, "What's your name?"

Turns out, he's Arthur Miller and I'm Marilyn Monroe.

Another lunch date at the residence and I'm all caught up on my laundry.

After lunch, as I approach the store, I hear music cranked so loud it makes my eardrums bulge. Must be those kids who run the skateboard store down near the crosswalk. Someone from the BIA better warn them to cut it out; they're driving away business. As I get closer, I see the door of the book shop is propped open. The racket is coming from my store.

Across the street, the guy who runs the pita place is melting down: he's yelling something I can't hear because of the noise, and waving his fist in the air.

This isn't shopping music, unless you are looking for brass knuckles or a Rambo knife. What is Serenity thinking?

I run straight to the sound system at the back of the store to poke at the "off" button. Where is Serenity, anyway? I turn my stern gaze toward the front counter. A tall, twiggy girl is behind the counter, leaning over, arms folded, like an auto parts guy. She cocks her head at me, and says, "Can I help you?"

I can barely see her eyes under the fringe of colored, uneven strands of hair.

"Who are you?"

"Who wants to know?"

"Me. I'm the owner of this store." My eyes light on a pickle jar sitting beside the cash register. I pick it up and read the childish handwriting: 'Wendy's Tips.' "You must be Wendy."

"You're the Momsie!" She leaps around the counter with such enthusiasm, I have to take a step back. "Serenity had an appointment. Guess what? I sold three books. The store got totally cray cray for a while there. I didn't know how the cash register works so I, you know." She points at a small pile of bills and change on the counter. "Serenity said she'd train me when she gets back. But I figured it out on my own. A total moron could run your store, but most are computerized now. Maybe you should check it out. I had a job last summer at the dollar store and I got, like, mad skilled at it. You know, you count everything up, two items, two bucks, ten items, ten bucks. You could get that system going here and simplify. One price, one book, you should try that. I have, like, soooo many ideas. I wrote some of the coolest ones down." She hands me a piece of paper and flashes me a grin. "This place is gonna be so-o-o-o amazing."

Wendy spends half the afternoon chatting on her cell. Every time I walk by her, I hear snippets of her side of the conversation, which consists mostly of, "Just sayin'. I'm not sayin' … know what I'm sayin'?"

As soon as Serenity comes back, I call her into the back office and gesture toward the front where Wendy is busy sending out tweets from her Twitter account with the store computer.

"I'm the one who makes the hiring decisions. Know what I'm sayin'?"

"Ewww, Mom, don't talk like that. It's just wrong."

"Don't try to change the subject."

"I had to give her a job. Her Dad is in jail for, like, armed robbery or something like that, and her Mom is a total crack addict. Give her a break."

"I don't know. I need a reliable person and she's a bit flakey you know? Like, the gun show is always on, even when no one's watching."

"When she takes her meds she's fine. Give her a chance. She's super smart. Like a genius."

I'm unconvinced but I have to admit she'll be unbeatable when it comes to shelving books because she can reach the top shelves without stretching.

But the best thing about having Wendy working for me is that my hiring days are over for now. Between Serenity, Wendy, and Jude, I can go do laundry whenever I want.

Having three employees also means I can get caught up on all kinds of backsliding. Within the space of two days I have everyone humming along with a detailed schedule posted on the office wall and everything. Here's my chance to zip over to the bank to make a payment on my overdraft.

"These fines are hurting your business," the accounts manager warns me.

"I have it all under control," I tell her. "The overdraft will be cleared by the end of next week."

… I hope. My overdraft is even larger than expected. Once Mom gives me the final installment, I can pay it off. I'll call her tonight. Maybe the check is ready.

When I get back to the store, all is quiet. Too quiet. Where's Wendy? I scheduled her for a full day today. There's no one around except a lone shopper who, when she sees me step behind the counter, asks me what I'm doing.

"I'm the owner. May I help you find something?"

"No. Your salesgirl had to step out for a bite to eat. She asked me to keep an eye on the store."

When my open-mouthed, blank-eyed stare goes on a little too long she adds, in an accusing tone, "She said she hadn't had anything to eat for a couple of days."

What is she talking about? I haven't had breakfast yet while Wendy helped herself to two chocolate chip muffins from the coffee bar this morning. No point arguing with a customer though.

The woman glares at me. "You were supposed to be back ten minutes ago." Her lips compress into a thin line.

"I got held up."

Her lips disappear completely.

"Thanks for helping out," I add, helplessly.

The woman tucks her purse under her arm. She looks at me as if she wants to take off her loafer and smack me across the cheek with it. "I have to get back to work now." She marches toward the door and then turns and says, "Oh yes, your mother called. She wants you to call her back on her cell. It's an emergency."

Then she's gone. Too late, I wonder if I should've offered her a free book or a coupon or maybe a handful of gummy worms from Wendy's candy stash under the counter?

That's it. Wendy has got go. Where is Serenity? And Jude? All three of them were here when I left.

First I have to call Mom. She sounds frantic: "I'm trapped inside my car."

"Oh my God, have you been in an accident?"

"No, of course not." She sounds indignant. "I'm in my driveway. I was going to book club and now I'm going to be late. It's raining. The car stalled and the doors all locked themselves and I can't get out."

"Isn't there a manual lock? Like a latch or lever or something like that? Look on the door. You have to find it and press on it."

"I tried the manual lock already. It won't budge. It's stuck I tell you. You don't understand. There's something wrong with the electrical system. I need you to come let me out."

I can't drop everything and go over there right now. "Did you try the back doors?"

"You want me to climb over the seats to try the back doors?"

"Yes."

"I can't do that. I'm wearing a skirt."

"So?"

"Someone could see me."

"If someone can see you then you could wave at them to come let you out."

"There's no one around."

How has my mother lived so long without getting murdered by her only daughter?

"Isn't there anyone else you can call? Brian maybe?"

"Brian isn't answering his phone. I'm hardly going to call anyone else either. It'll get out. They'll blab it all over. This kind of gossip spreads like wildfire." Her voice rises to a sarcastic singsong: "I can just hear them now: Wee hee, Marion got locked in her own car." She pauses to take a breath. "Don't even suggest I call 911. For God's sake, I don't need police and fire trucks and a big scene on the street. They'll put my name in the paper. This is a narrow town you know."

Maybe I could call 911 myself. She'll get over it eventually.

"I know what you're thinking and don't you dare. If you call 911 you can forget about the last installment I was planning to give you."

By the time I roll across Narrow Town, I find Brian in the driveway with his head stuffed under the hood of the car. He's replacing the battery and checking the wiring. "Your mother is inside, resting," he says, in a cheery voice.

I storm into the house. Mom is sitting in the living room reading a book. "Why didn't you at least text me to let me know Brian got you out?"

"I hate texting. Takes forever to tap out a message."

Before I can complain that I had to rearrange my whole day to get away, she hands me a check.

First item of business this morning, I call Serenity into the office.

"Chill out, Mom. Nothing happened."

"Chill out? Nothing happened? Wendy left a customer in charge of the store. Then when I needed her most she never came back. I had to close the store yesterday to go rescue your grandmother. I have to let Wendy go. Or I should say, you have to let her go."

"I can't. You don't get it, Mom. She was hungry. She hadn't eaten for two days. Besides, I gave her two weeks advance on her pay so if you fire her now, you'll probably never get it back."

What? No wonder my overdraft is so high. "You cut her a check without my approval? When did you do that?"

"I dunno. A couple of days ago. You were gone out to the Laundromat or something. Wendy was behind on her rent and the food bank can't give her any more groceries until next week."

"How can she afford a phone then? She never puts it down. She's texting and tweeting and facebooking all day long."

Serenity's eyes go all wide. Give up a cell? That's so harsh.

"Fine, but you have to explain to her that she can't leave the store unattended ever again. Ever again, got it? She needs to pay attention to the schedule. No more texting except on her scheduled breaks. And for God's sake make her stop leaning over the counter like she's a gas station attendant."

CHAPTER 22

Check Fire

Check Fire: In artillery, mortar, and naval gunfire support, a command to cause a temporary halt in firing.—Department of Defense Dictionary of Military and Associated Terms

Ghostly Garth just stepped through the door with a tin of pumpkin muffins reminding me that Thanksgiving is only a few short weeks away. Business is picking up and I'm finally starting to adjust to the ebb and flow in the store. We have our regulars, a few avid reader types, and the a.m. crew who filter in for coffee and newspapers. There's Ghostly Garth and there's Yard, the delusional street guy who thinks he's a bike courier (Yard is short for Yard Sale because of a spectacular wipeout when he left a spray of pedals, chains, and water bottles across someone's front lawn). When he comes in to pick up his deliveries, bike helmet stuffed up into his armpit, Wendy gives him a coffee, a muffin, and a few dog-eared envelopes wrapped with a rubber band to deliver to the florist at the other end of town. The florist, who is in on the game, gives him some change and sends him on to the dry cleaner who passes him back over town to the print shop. The printer eventually dispatches him back to us. The run generally takes all day or longer, since Yard's bike is patchy and prone to flat tires, so it works.

"Pay attention," Garth commands, holding up a radio-like contraption. "This is known as a tri-axial EMF meter. It's very sensitive to magnetic flux densities."

I look up from scanning shelves for a few missing books that are listed as in stock. Garth twists the knobs. Nothing happens. Too bad his contraption can't locate my lost inventory.

"Wait a minute." He begins searching through his bags.

I pluck a diet book out of the magazine racks and return the wanderer to its proper place. A minute later I hear a loud whump. I turn to find my most expensive coffee table book flipped open and upside-down on the floor. Garth stands nearby, his ample hip inches from my book display table. He lifts his arms in a show of surprise.

"Did you see that? Unbelievable. That book flew off the table all by itself!" He shakes his head as if overcome with astonishment. "Poltergeists often throw things. They are so strong they can even toss a person out of bed."

I'd like to thump Garth on the head for hip-chucking my book off the table but he makes up for it with regular deliveries of too-delicious homemade treats made by his wife. Garth's wife should consider becoming an author herself, of a recipe book on how to make incredibly scrumptious baked goods.

"It should be working properly now," announces Garth after a few more adjustments. "This is the most active building in town. The readings in this room are usually off the clock. I'll show you."

Serenity pops the lid off the muffin tin, and we each grab one while carefully standing back to watch Garth's demonstration. He twists another dial, and the machine immediately begins to emit an excruciating, high-pitched nails-on-blackboard shrieking sound. Serenity drops her muffin and leaps at the machine.

"Turn it off!" she screams.

Garth grapples with all the knobs to no avail while two customers browsing in the bestseller section hold their hands over their ears.

"Garth, take that thing out of here," I yell as I beat a retreat to the storeroom.

I stand behind the door and rub my forehead. The change in weather plus Garth being Garth is giving me a headache. A few minutes after I settle down to work, Serenity pokes her head into the storeroom office to say the school principal is on the line. With trepidation, I pick up the phone. What did Jack do now?

"I have Olympia here in my office. She's having a rough day," the principal says. "According to the teacher on yard duty, Olympia punched a boy in the Peace Garden and knocked him over. His arm is showing some bruising."

I withhold a cheer—no rotten boy messes with my girl—as the principal goes on.

"Olympia says the boy threw an earth worm at her. The boy says he was only pretending to throw it. She put the worm on his desk. We have the worm here."

I don't know what to say. I'm wondering why she has the worm on her desk. Is the worm okay? Am I supposed to ask about the worm's well-being?

"We feel Olympia is exhibiting bullying behaviors. Board policy requires a two-day suspension for this sort of thing. Both children are banned from using the Peace Garden for the rest of the term."

That's good news for the worms I guess.

"Has Olympia ever had a pediatric assessment?" the Principal asks.

"No. She's usually very healthy."

"I meant developmental behavior screening. Perhaps it would be a good idea," continues the Principal. "Olympia's teacher says Olympia is having difficulties listening and following classroom rules."

The Principal is waiting for a response from me regarding Olympia's lack of proper playground etiquette. I refrain from sharing my nostalgia for the golden age of xlacker attackers and Skip-it trippers. I'm thinking all the fun toys have been taken away and all the kids have left to work with is their fists.

"I'll call Olympia's doctor today and ask for a referral," I proffer.

"Olympia's suspension begins immediately," the Principal says, and hangs up.

What am I going to do? I can't bring Olympia to work with me. She'll drive me bananas. Serenity has a prenatal appointment tomorrow, and Jude is in rehearsals so neither of them can cover the store, and I have no backup sitter arrangements. I hate to leave Wendy in charge. She and

Yard seem to have become an item lately. Whenever he comes in the store, lately two or three times a day, she loses all her ability to work. I have to conjure up some proper help. After all, it was less than a week ago Mom had me drop everything to rescue her from her car. Now it's me with an emergency. She owes me one. I call her. "Would you be willing to watch Olympia, please? I have to be in the store tomorrow."

"I can't, I have life drawing class."

"Can't you skip it for one day?"

"You don't understand, Pauline. I'm the model."

I call Michael. All he can offer is: "Far too many kids are on Ritalin these days."

Apparently Michael watched a special on TV recently and he knows all about Attention Deficit Hyperactivity Disorder. He should know. There's only one kid I know who is wilder than Jack and that's Michael's son.

"I have to go now but whatever you do, don't put Olympia on drugs," he warns me.

I go online to run a search. There's plenty of information available including a self-test for adult ADHD. Adult ADHD? Symptoms range from "a tendency to be easily distracted" to "chronic lateness" to "frequently feeling tired." I run through the whole list, checking off many of the items and press the submit button. According to the test, I have "a strong tendency toward ADHD."

I study the list of symptoms again. A prisoner of the moment. Chronically late or chronically in a hurry. Often have piles of stuff. Easily overwhelmed by tasks of daily living. Mood swings. Sense of impending doom. I have all that and more. What a relief.

I print out the list and, locking up a few minutes early, race over to Bibienne's. "Look—I have Adult ADHD."

She peers at the list for a moment and then tosses it on the kitchen table. "I don't know any women with kids who don't have all those symptoms. Piles of stuff? Chronically late? Come on. Stop worrying. I'll make you a drink."

"Fine." But I remain unconvinced. Two of the biggies are relational difficulties and a frequent search for high stimulation. Maybe a blast of Ritalin is what I need to overcome my troubles with Donald and Michael.

Giving up dairy is highly recommended for persons suffering from ADHD. I poured all the cow milk in the house down the drain (ugh, cow's mucus) and replaced that toxic waste with healthy rice milk, which comes in four flavors: chocolate, strawberry, vanilla, and plain. At dinner, I offer a glass of the vanilla rice milk to Olympia, who allows but one tiny bud on the tip of her tongue to make contact with the liquid. Immediately, she spits it out and wipes furiously at the entire surface of her tongue with her fingernails.

"I don't like it," she screams. "It tastes like puke."

"Wait," I say, "Puke isn't one of the flavors. Here, try the chocolate one. I'm sure you'll like it." I add a white rice milk lie: "All kids like chocolate rice milk."

"No, they don't," she screams. "I don't want it. I hate rice milk."

I pour a glass and demonstrate intense enjoyment of rice milk by slurping and making a large milk mustache. Olympia is right: the vanilla one is kind of pukey.

I just spent an hour making a mushy looking soup with fifteen kinds of vegetables. There's every color of vegetable except yellow, as all yellow vegetables and fruits are verboten. Bananas are acceptable as long as you don't allow the yellow of the peel to touch the white part of the banana.

Olympia hates the ADHD diet with a passion. I offer her a bowl of soup.

"I'm not hungry. Can we have pizza?" she asks.

"No. Pizza is a very unhealthy choice."

Serenity and Shae choose this exact moment to traipse in the door with a pizza. It smells yummy even though it has congealed cow's mucus smeared all over its surface. The tomato sauce probably came from a can—disgusting—and the pepperoni is nothing less than discs of toxic sludge. The mushrooms are, I'm sure, the mold-bearing kind, but I don't recall a prohibition against onions—and pizza has no soy products, which are expressly forbidden. Therefore, based on the fact that the pizza is loaded with delicious onions, and the fact that we're observing the rule on soy, I think we should go ahead and enjoy. Olympia picks all the onions and green peppers off, and eats three pieces.

I'm about to rustle her upstairs for her bath when the phone rings. It's Donald. He grabbed a cab from the airport shuttle and he's on his way home. I wasn't expecting him until tomorrow. Olympia shrieks and runs to pin up the Welcome Home banner she made while serving out her suspension and driving me to distraction at the store this week. A few minutes later Donald walks through the door wearing a black cowboy hat and the biggest silver belt buckle I've ever seen. The white-cotton-shirt-and-jeans look is actually kind of Butch Cassidy hot. Jack and Olympia race to greet him. "Daddy! Daddy!" they scream.

"Howdy, partner," he says to Jack while scooping Olympia into the air and up onto his shoulders. With Olympia still perched on his shoulders he crouches down to bear hug Jack and then fishes into a bag, producing Calgary Flames jerseys and candy bouquets. The kids crawl all over him, shrieking with excitement. I step back to watch this splendid family scene. Donald should go away for long absences more often.

After a few minutes he looks up from tussling with the kids and, catching my eye, tips his hat and winks. He stands up, popping the hat on Olympia's head and comes over to greet me with a kiss. On the cheek. "You look great," he says.

Donald smells different. Good different. A new kind of aftershave, I guess.

Olympia wants Donald to read her a bedtime story. He picks up his bags by the door, and our eyes meet.

Awkward. Do I want to invite Donald back into the bedroom? That would be wrong on so many levels. Does he even want an invitation? Who makes the first move? King to Queen, or Queen to King? Is there an opening advantage? This feels more like the endgame. What are the rules to this stupid game anyway?

"I'll put these in the spare room on my way up."

I nod. King checks Queen in another stalemate.

On Monday morning I drive Donald back to the airport shuttle. We stop at the bookstore on the way. As Donald climbs out of the car, he winces at the sight of my wooden store sign, which I can't bring myself to replace. It's hanging precariously above the door, crooked and peeling and full of fabulous faded-glory character. "The Pita Gnat is constantly complaining about the sign, but he can stuff it."

"The Pita Gnat?"

"See that short guy standing over there? That guy who's staring at us? He hangs around in his entrance all day. I don't know how he gets any work done. All the business owners hate him because his food is terrible and he's rude to everyone." I wave across the road. Pita Gnat wheels back into his shop and slams his door.

"I see what you mean."

We go inside. Jude is chatting up a customer while Serenity is wiping down the espresso machine. She picks up a coffee scoop. "How about Ethiopian Mochacinos? Fair trade, of course."

While we wait for our coffees, we stroll about the store. I straighten a book on the front table. "There's lots left to do but it's coming along, don't you think?"

Donald nods. "Absolutely."

I reward him with my best smile.

An hour later, as I watch the shuttle pull away, I think how the Calgary Plan could prove to be a real lifesaver for my sunken marriage. We were carefully cordial all weekend. Friendly even. No one brought up tough questions about marriage, separation, or divorce. Donald even complimented me on my business plan. Every husband should be sent to live thousands of miles away when things get rough. When they come home for a visit, it's handsome smiles and pretty compliments, aftershave and big buckles, and best of all, they will even fix the broken washing machine without being asked.

CHAPTER 23

MIA

MIA: Missing in action.—*Department of Defense Dictionary of Military and Associated Terms*

The house is lovely and quiet at 6 a.m., on a Sunday—the perfect lineup for meditating. Michael is always pestering me to learn to still the mind. He claims he can sit with zero thoughts in his head for 30 minutes at a stretch. That doesn't impress me much. Any man can do that. I've seen Donald suppress all brain activity for hours when he's watching sports on TV. Once in a while a stray thought will cross his mind urging him to get up and grab a bag of peanuts and a cold one. Otherwise, nothing.

For women with children, stopping the mind is more of a challenge. If we shush for five minutes, the house will be on fire and the children thigh deep in the forbidden creek by the time we return from the stillness.

I sit up in a straight-backed lotus position and rest my hands in the open mudra position on my lap. As I rise, George, sleeping at the foot of my bed, wakes up and stretches.

"No George, go back to sleep, not time to get up yet."

George jumps off the end of the bed and limps over to the bedroom door and scratches the frame. He wants to go out. If I let him outside he'll probably start barking at the red squirrels eating breakfast at the bird feeder.

"Shhhh, George, go lie down." George lies down beside the door with a huffy sigh and stuffs his head between his paws to watch me.

Breathe in gently, let those stomach muscles relax, don't think about how big this makes the belly, breathe out slowly, stop thinking about the belly. I better lay off on the post-game brewskies in the locker room this season. Maybe I don't have time for hockey this year anyway. I've missed the last four practices. This week is going to be a busy week. Tuesday night Michael wants me come out to the spoken word event he's organizing at the Dingy Cup. Oh yes, and book club is on Wednesday night. And why is George limping anyway? Maybe he needs his nails clipped?

My mind divides evenly into three parallel tracks and, as I consider the fact of book club, I also contemplate the fact that I haven't arranged the sitter yet for Tuesday night, and when was the last time George got his nails clipped? I can't call the sitter now, so I better jot it down on my to-do list. Where is my to-do list? An optional fourth track opens up. I didn't want to join the book club, but Jennifer says it's essential promotion. I better call the dog groomer today and book George in. Is Tuesday night when the sitter has her violin lessons? It's the biggest book club in town and they always order their books through us. If I quit the book club, we might lose the business. I better remember to schedule the sitter for Friday night and read at least the first two chapters of the book club book before Tuesday. Wait, Bibi said her sitter can watch Jack and Olympia on Friday night and Shae can take George to the groomer because it is her dog after all and maybe I should just read that book on how to pretend you've read a book already.

What's down for Thursday night? Do I need a sitter for that night too? What should I wear to Michael's spoken word event? My poet-friendly jacket with the cool buckles is at the cleaners and … oops. I've let my mind go off the breath.

I don't like following the breath anyway. So boring. Maybe I'd be better off with using a mantra. I could try the OM mantra, which, according to Michael, is supposed to bring a balancing and centering quality to daily life. He says OM is the primordial word that most closely resembles the universal breath and has the power to connect me to the vast substratum of the universe.

A substratum sounds like a layer of dirt to me. If we're talking dirt, I'm already pretty well connected here at home. Obviously those monks who make this stuff up get out way more than me: for sure they never had to vacuum under the refrigerator. Maybe women should say GOO instead of OM.

At this point, I have to go downstairs and retrieve my mind as it has gone off to rest in contemplation of the thick layer of eternal grease that is slabbed in under the stove. Stop it, I shout inwardly. Be still.

Inhale deep silence. On exhalation, think: OMmmmmm. Inhale deep silence. Exhale: OMmmmmm. The OM word sounds like M-o-m. Which makes sense. The universal vibration is creative, maternal. It is both the gentle sigh and wolf howl of the Great Mother. The thought immediately unbalances me as I remember that my Mom, my personal Great Wolfy Mother, is coming over for dinner tonight, and I haven't passed the vacuum for weeks. Forget GOO and OM, time to deal with TO-DO.

I'm down in the basement throwing in a load of laundry when I hear Mom's chirrupy voice coming in the door upstairs: "Hellooooo! Helloooooo! Jack, help me with these bags. Watch this one, now, that's my wine. You can take this one, it's a vegetable dip; better go put it in the fridge. Hello, Olympia dear, I brought you kids some treats."

I hurry upstairs to greet her.

"Pauline, what's the matter with George? He's limping."

"His toenails need clipping."

"Look. He's scratching. You know, he might have the Red Mange. If I were you I would take him straight to the vet. If you let Mange get out of control, it can cover the whole dog. The hair all falls out eventually and the skin turns red. It never goes away, and it can transfer to humans. You better tie him up outside."

For the rest of the evening, that's all she can talk about. That and Barack Obama. She's got a big thing for him. "There's an article about him in The Oprah Magazine," she says while I'm stuffing the chicken.

She fishes the magazine out of her handbag and shows me his picture. "He's so handsome. He's like the son I never had."

Things are getting easier now that I have Jude and Serenity helping in the store, but I'm still a wreck by 9 p.m. each night. That's usually when Donald calls to say goodnight to the kids. Tonight, Olympia's gone for a sleepover birthday party and Jack is gone to a show with his friends.

Donald is in a chatty mood. "Head office came out today. They're really happy how everything is coming along. We'll be able to launch on deadline."

"Congratulations."

I sit on the edge of the bed as he describes his day in detail. The bestseller Bibienne raved about rests on the bedstand. Picking it up, I stroke the spine. The book and my fluffiest pillow are calling.

"How was your day?" Donald suddenly asks.

I tell him how Serenity has turned out to be a wonder worker: "She even straightened out that Johnny Rotten kid. He's flat out terrified of her."

There's a beep on the line. Who could be calling so late?

"Hang on," I say, "I have another call, and I'm afraid it might be a problem with Olympia at the sleepover."

I switch over. Uh oh. The caller is Michael. "I finished my dissertation! I have a bottle of champagne with your name on it. Is it cool if I come over for a while?"

I feel a draining sensation in my shoulders like someone pulled a plug from the back of my neck. I'm so tired I could sleep for a week. "Can I call you back? I have Donald on the other line," I confess.

A long silence ensues. Michael speaks first. "You know, maybe it's time for you to decide what you really want."

"Please don't be mad. This isn't a good time. I have to go."

"Wait, wait, hold on. I know … I'm not being fair. I'm sorry. I shouldn't pressure you. I just wanted to tell you my news."

"I'm sorry too. I mean, wow, your dissertation is done? That's awesome."

"It's a load off my mind. Now all I can think about is you. I bought you a present the other day you know. It's got five speeds. The sales guy said it's the taser of vibrators."

Really? Mmm, taser tingles. I can feel them already. But Donald is on the other line. Tingling with impatience no doubt.

"Be right back," I say to Michael.

"Hey," I say to Donald, trying to think of a way to wrap this up quick.

"Is everything okay at the sleepover?"

"Yes, I ..." Another beep on the line. This time it's at Donald's end.

"Can you wait a minute? I need to take this call," he says.

Who is he so anxious to talk to at this time of night? Lindsay? I quickly tap back to Michael.

"So where were we?"

Michael is exactly where a girl might want him to be. I'm being tasered before I know it. I can't believe how charged up a person can get talking about high voltage and direct currents. Michael has such a way with words. The taser has turned into a long-range wireless electro-shock projectile and for some reason the thought of such a device is the most erotic thing I've ever imagined. I'm transfixed by the suggestion that one is coming for me right now when another beep comes on the line, and I remember about Donald. I use the Olympia excuse on Michael this time.

Michael says, "Hold that thought and call me back."

I tap back over and Donald apologizes, "I lost you there."

"That's nice. I mean, that's okay."

"You sound out of breath."

"Do I?"

All I can think about is cattle prods. As I end the conversation and hang up the phone, George's collar jingles. He's leaning against my leg, vigorously scratching his ear with his back paw.

George has been scratching a lot lately. Maybe Mom is right. Maybe he does have the Red Mange. My head feels itchy and there was a lot of hair in my brush this morning. Oh no.

Forget Michael and his cattle prod. This is an emergency. I run to the computer and google "Red Mange." 2,600,000 sites. Millions of people are all up on this issue, yet I never heard of this problem before Mom told me about it.

I click on a site. Ewww. Red Mange is a revolting skin disease caused by tiny mites. George is lying on my bare feet. I yank my feet away from him. He's probably crammed with the creepy, crawly creatures. There's even a YouTube video. I feel nauseated at the sight of numerous wiggling legs and a worm-like head that features an oversized gobbling mouth-like apparatus. Mom's right—although cases are rare, the Red Mange can spread to humans. I click on a photo spread of a poor woman who contracted it. She has ugly red lesions all over her face, picked up from her Irish Setter. It was months before she was able to kick the infestation.

Funny. I have an itchy pimple on the back of my neck. And I can't stop scratching my chin, especially in one spot where I've found a small scab. Or a lesion.

There may well be a rapidly exploding population of mangy mites boring holes all over my head right now. Soon all my hair will fall out, my scalp will turn red, and my face will be covered with unsightly lesions. It's all my fault for not listening to my mother and being a poor manager. Through a disastrous confluence of ignorance and neglect, I've let the Red Mange rage out of control through my household. First thing in the morning, I'm going straight to the doctor and George is going to be quarantined at the vet. I better not mention this development to Serenity. The remedy involves dunkings in a toxic bath of insecticides and antibiotics. Unfortunately, she'll have to put up with her mites and lesions until after the baby is born.

Google is addicting. One horrible mite leads to the next: apparently everyone has eyelash mites, which live and mate and die in the follicles of the eyelashes. According to this site, if I were to pull out an eyelash and place it under a microscope I would probably see one. Or more. The mature adults and maybe even some of the teens have pulled the curtains and are humping away furiously, in my follicles, at this moment. And, as far as I can tell, nobody is doing a thing about this.

I can't resist taking a peek at the house dust mite. It is related to the arachnid. In other words, my pillow is, apparently, chock full of spiders which are busily defecating and urinating in my pristine, sleepy-time fibers all night long right under my nose. That's it. Tomorrow I'm treating everyone to a new pillow with impermeable covers.

From here it would be a short hop to search for information on human parasites and lice. Not a good idea since, because of Google, before I hit the sack tonight I will need to swab the entire house, change my sheets, swathe my pillow and mattress with plastic wrap, dip the dog in insecticide and pull out all my eyelashes.

Saturday morning: within minutes of opening the store, a rash of kids come piling through the door for Story Time With Serenity. Johnny Rotten runs straight up to Serenity and dares her to guess what's inside his backpack.

"A severed hand?"

"Nope."

"Your baby brother?"

"I don't have a baby brother."

"Good thing," says Serenity. "What've you got?"

Johnny unzips the bag, pulls out a plastic margarine tub and pops the lid: "He's my new pet."

"No, no, no, whatever it is, don't let it out," I shriek.

"No worries." Serenity shrugs. "It's only a caterpillar." All the Story Hour kids crowd around Johnny to poke the caterpillar.

"Don't squeeze it," says Serenity. "If you squeeze it, the insides come out and it won't work anymore." Then she adds, "I think we should read *The Very Hungry Caterpillar* today." All the kids shout their approval.

I go into my office to work on my quarterly taxes. I don't mind the kids nor the taxes as I'm very excited. Michael is taking me out to dinner tonight at the coolest new restaurant in town. Everyone is talking about this place and Bibienne says it's impossible to get a Saturday night reservation.

We're taking a chance dining in public but I'm sick of hanging out at the student residence; it feels weird and sophomoric, like everyone knows what we're up to. I've taken to wearing my hoodie and pulling it up around my head and pretending to be all east side as I go in, hands in my pockets, head down and shuffling. Tonight I will lose the hoodie and give him everything he wants.

I meet Michael at the residence and we drive to the restaurant. The waiter delivers tall glasses of cold Chablis to go with our starter, the gingered apple and fennel soup. For my main I've chosen the Salmon Tagine while Michael orders the Green Tomato Penne. Funny, I haven't seen Michael eat meat for months.

"Did you quit eating meat?"

"Yes. Last summer. I told you that months ago."

"Oh probably. I guess you did. I forgot."

"You don't hear half the stuff I tell you."

"Maybe you haven't noticed but I have a lot on my plate these days."

"No kidding. You need to slow down. Maybe you could go on a silent retreat and meditate."

"A silent retreat? That sounds like fun. Sign me up right now 'cause I've got all kinds of time. Come on Michael, I have to look after the store, the house, the kids, all by myself. My mother calls me every day because she can't figure out how to work her television remote or her debit card or even unlock her own car. I'm up to my neck in paperwork. How can I possibly drop everything to go on a retreat?"

"You don't need to drop anything. Just … never mind about the retreat. You don't have to go on a retreat. Just be present in the moment with whatever you're doing. Pay attention and listen when someone is talking to you."

"Fine. Next time a customer yells at me because the book they wanted is out of print, I'll try that."

"See? Your egoic mind is creating all this unnecessary anger."

"My egoic mind? What about your egoic mind which is always judging me and telling me that I need to listen to everything you say extremely carefully and take detailed notes because there might be a test later?"

Michael sets down his spoon. "I don't get the feeling that you're into this anymore."

A flood of contrition washes through me. "I'm sorry. I am into this. I was looking forward to tonight. I don't want to have a fight with you."

"But you are fighting me." Michael shakes his head and looks away. I can tell his egoic mind is feeling pretty snarky.

The service is horribly slow around here. While waiting for the main course, I try slipping off my shoe and running my foot up the side of his leg while waggling my eyebrows, a trick that usually has him sucking my toes in seconds, but no dice. He pulls his leg away and leans back in his chair.

The Salmon Tagine is dry and the gingered apple soup has provided me with a splash of ginger-flavored heartburn. We drive back to the residence in silence. As we pull into the parking lot I can't take it anymore. Michael has gone off into a silent retreat huff and I don't have my hoodie. "Just drop me beside my car, Michael."

He throws his car into reverse without a word.

As soon as I get home, I remember Olympia wanted me to sew a badge on her Brownie sash. It's eleven p.m. but I need to ride the range a little longer. I pull out the sewing kit and thread a needle. The phone rings. It's Donald.

I tuck the phone under my ear and attempt to untangle a knot in the thread. "You're calling too late. The kids have already gone to bed."

"Sorry. My meetings went over. You sound tired. Is everything okay?"

"Do you want the entire list or just the broad strokes? For starters, Jack's teacher called me today and he's on the war path again."

I tell Donald how Jack and Olympia have joined forces as a kind of tag team of wayward behavior at school so I get to have a nice chat with one of their teachers or the principal almost every day. All Donald says is, "Hmm."

"Ouch. God, I just stabbed myself."

"What?"

"With a sewing needle." I pop my bleeding thumb in my mouth and keep talking: "Then there's George. The course of antibiotics is finished and I've soaked that dog's paw to death but he's still limping.

Intermittently, of course. Never in front of the vet. Dr. Loewen thinks George has extra sensitive footpads. Now George is supposed to wear leather booties whenever he goes outside. The booties cost a fortune and he hates them."

Donald says hmm.

"And the bathtub faucet is leaking again. I can't remember the name of that plumber who we called last time. Do you?"

"Beats me."

I stab my thumb again in exactly the same place. "Ouch!" I can feel myself losing it. "Beats me? Hmm? Is that all you can say to me? I'm drowning here and you're being totally useless."

There's a long intercontinental silence where we glare at each other across the 49th parallel and then Donald says, "What do you want? You want me to fix the plumbing? Fine, I'll book a flight right now, this minute, and come home and fix the plumbing."

"I didn't say ... look, you know what? Next time I'm going to tell Jack's teacher to call you at work."

"Fine. I would be happy to talk to her."

"Him."

"Him?"

"Yes, him, Jack's teacher is a man. You don't even know his name, do you?"

"I know his name: it's Morton, right? I forgot for a second there. Give me a break. What's the school phone number? I'll call him to-morrow."

"See? That's my point. I know the school number by heart and you, of course, don't. That just goes to show ... Wait a minute, I dropped something." I set down the receiver and crawl under the table to retrieve my spool of thread. And bonk my head.

This is so not working for me. Tomorrow I need to go out and buy a headset, so next time Donald and I can have a more convenient, hands-free argument.

Serenity's cat has crapped in the basement again, underneath the laundry sink where it's dark, cramped and slimy. I crouch down on my hands and knees to peer into the corner where, no doubt, a rabid spider with 360 degree vision is guarding its lair. The sight of three separate mounds of cat poo brings out the arsenic-and-old-lace urges in me. Maybe it's the cat's time? She already had a grey muzzle, failing vision and highly unpredictable kidneys when Serenity rescued her from a shelter over two years ago. As I close my fist over the paper-towel-draped squishy mounds, I'm warming to my end game.

I go upstairs to find Serenity. She's lying on her bed reading *What to Expect When You're Expecting*, the book propped neatly against her bump. Obviously Serenity isn't expecting to have to pitch in on any household chores now that she's in such an advanced delicate condition. She's only five months along. Holy hell. When I was nine months along with Serenity, I was still squeezing into my combats and shuffling into the detachment every day.

I cross my arms and wait for Serenity to pry her nose out of the book. She glances up and scowls at me.

"Your cat pooped in the basement again."

She points at the book. "Toxoplasmosis. It's a disease that pregnant women can get from cat shit. I can't go near it."

She's right of course. This is the same excuse I used on Donald to get out of changing the cat litter during my pregnancies with Jack and Olympia. It even worked on him while I was breastfeeding.

"What about washing the dishes then? There's no prohibitions in your book against doing dishes is there?"

"Those dishes downstairs aren't mine." She points to a heap of crusty plates and glasses littering the floor at the end of her bed. "Those are mine." She pauses, but before I have a chance to open my mouth she adds, "I'll do them later, aight?"

"I've been cleaning up after Scratches every day for a long time now. I think you could either help out some more or something's gonna give. I can't do everything around here you know."

At this moment, Shae comes into the room. Serenity smiles win-
ningly, stretches her legs out and wriggles her feet. Shae plops on
the end of the bed, lovingly places Serenity's left foot in her lap and
begins to massage her instep. Serenity grabs a bottle of lavender oil
from her bedstand and hands it to Shae who uncorks it expertly.

Serenity points at her book again. "You know, it says here that
raspberry leaf tea is good for the uterus."

Shae runs her oiled hand up Serenity's shin and Serenity closes
her eyes. The room shrinks.

I back away but not before overhearing Serenity giggle and Shae
saying something about how soft pregnancy makes a woman's skin.

When did Donald ever rub my pregnant feet with essential oils,
brew me a cup of raspberry leaf tea and admire my pregnant shins?
When's the last time I had a foot rub or any kind of rub for that matter? I wonder if Michael is still mad at me? I could try texting him, a
safe way to test the water. I run downstairs and sit on the couch with
my phone. *I wish you could come over and rub my shins tonight.* I sit back
to wait for a response.

Scratches leaps up onto my lap. She expects me to pet her. Her
ears are charming in their delicate soft prettiness. "Are you my little
kissyface cat? Yes, you are. Oh, yes you are." She purrs, loudly, and
stretches up her chin for a tickle.

I'm a pushover.

Michael's text message comes back swiftly. "Your shins, my place?"

By the time I get over to his apartment Michael has ignited a big
mess of violet tealights. From the door of the apartment he has made
a path of candlelight leading into the bedroom, which he has trans-
formed into a shelter of erotic delight complete with essential oils,
red silk sheets and sandalwood incense.

I remove my coat and push one of the candles on the desk away
from the blinds. "We better be careful not to burn down the residence."

Michael takes my coat and kisses the nape of my neck. "You're
going to be burning very soon. Think of me as your personal sex guru."

He picks up a book from the coffee table. "I got this book on tantric sex. It's all about achieving heightened intimacy. Using these techniques, we can connect on the deepest levels, mentally, physically, and spiritually." Michael holds the book up with both hands, like he's delivering a report. The cover has a picture of a radiant couple, both emitting waves of rainbow light from all their chakras. He adds, "With practice, tantric sex can give you an orgasm that can last 10 to 15 minutes."

"Let me see that."

I flip through the pages, pausing to examine some of the hand-drawn illustrations. The tantric men all sport alarmingly large *lingams* and the women appear serene and unafraid for their *yonis*.

Michael points out that, for beginners, concentrating on the simpler basic positions should do the tantric trick. He's keen to start with the Yab-Yum position and, after half an hour or so, move on to Scissors, and then Dancing, then Cow, then Shiva, then Shakti and maybe some Kneeling too. A half hour for each is about right.

I do the sex math in my head. "That's three and a half hours. I have to get up early."

"Maybe we can cut it back to 20 minutes for each then."

I check my watch. "It's getting late. How about 10 minutes?"

"15?"

I run another calculation in my head. "Oh alright."

Tantric sex is awesome. The idea is to move the energy around the body. I did well as, about seven minutes in, my ear lobes grew hot. As soon as we changed over to Scissors, the energy all plunged down to Michael's pointiest part, real quick and then it was a fast clippity clip to the finish line.

I'm hooked. Next time I want to check out the chapter on the ananga ranga. Whatever it is, it sounds incredibly sexy.

Michael suggests that I might want to work on my PC (Pubo-coccygeus) muscle exercises so I can become more proficient at the Vadavaka, a gripping technique. Tightening the pelvic floor area is an excellent way to enhance the flow of the life force, called prana. Right. This sounds like old school kegels to me. Mom is always at me about doing my kegels too; now Michael is jumping on the bandwagon.

"I'll exercise my PC's at work all day long," I promise.

"That's a good idea. When you're standing at the cash register—hey, why not every time you sell a book, think of me and do some squeezes."

He's seriously deranged. Most of the time I'd rather squeeze the customers' necks.

As I put on my coat, Michael hands me a CD. "I bought you something. To help you with stress," he said. "And to apologize for what happened at the restaurant."

At home, I set my alarm and slide into bed. I have to get up early but the sleepy feeling won't come. An hour ticks by. Maybe Michael's CD will help.

I slip the CD into my disc player and put on a pair of headphones. The program consists of a short intro from a guy speaking in a soft, soothing monotone telling me to sit up straight and meditate right followed by a chime to signal the start. Then 10 minutes of total silence and three chimes to signal the end. There's also a 20-minute, a 30-minute and a one-hour meditation, all beginning and ending with chimes. In other words, Michael forked over $20 for a mostly blank CD.

I call Michael first thing this morning to say thanks for the gift. Then I make the mistake of saying, "Ha, ha. I bought a big batch of blank CDs the other day, which is sort of like having the whole meditation boxed set."

His voice sounds terse. "I can't talk now. I'll call you later."

At lunch I phone Michael back again. "I'm sorry about that joke I made about the CDs. I love my present. Seriously. I should do more meditation."

"No worries. You don't have to apologize. If you don't enjoy meditation, that's alright."

"I want to. It helps me to relax. I can see the benefits for sure. In fact, that thing you said about going on a silent retreat? The other night at the restaurant? I've been thinking about it and you're right. A silent retreat would be good for me. My life is crazy. I need to make space for me."

At this Michael gets excited. "Excellent. I'm going on a retreat next weekend. If you can get away, I can probably get you in. I'll talk to the guru."

What have I done?

Preparing for my stress-reducing silent retreat weekend is building an anxiety bomb inside me. I may have to take Monday off work to decompress from this experience. I've never been on a silent retreat and I don't know what to bring. Possibly duct tape or an extra sock to stuff in my mouth would be a good idea, as shutting up for two whole days might be impossible without a gag.

I'm also wondering if I should pack in my pajamas or lingerie. Each person gets their own room. Maybe Michael and I can arrange a little hush hush visiting in the night?

I have to be on the road by 4 p.m. so I rush out at lunch to the grocery store to stock up for the weekend. We are out of everything. I wheel my cart up and down the aisles looking for the peanut butter. Crunchy or smooth? I can never remember which one the kids won't eat. I put two jars of each type in the cart as lately Serenity has developed some pregnancy cravings: all she will eat is white bread with peanut butter and mini-marshmallows.

Every time Olympia sees her downing a marshmallow sandwich, she flips out and wants one too. It's hard to shop for kids who are engaged in a tag team of food dislikes: Jack hates onions, potatoes, and spinach; Serenity hates peas, asparagus, and yams; and Olympia hates everything else in the vegetable world. There is no meal they will all eat readily except for mini marshmallow sandwiches. Since Serenity is in charge for the weekend I better buy several bags. Shae can cook a mean roast so I toss in short ribs and a bag of carrots. You never know.

I am driving, so I pick up Michael and we head out. It's a four hour trip to the ashram so we can at least talk on the way and get it all out of our systems.

First thing, Michael falls asleep. I drive along in silence. It's good practice, I suppose.

After a while, I feel sleepy. I poke Michael and tell him he has to take over the wheel. We switch places and, as I lay my head back on the headrest, Michael asks, "Did you get a chance to read over the guidelines?"

I rummage for the retreat information in my tote bag. The guidelines are clear: *Upon entry to the retreat grounds, please refrain from talking at any and all times. Reading, writing, journaling, or use of the telephone is disquieting and may be a barrier to your stillness practice. Following these recommendations carefully and mindfully will allow you to be in community with others in a supportive, respectful way.*

"What if there's an emergency?"

"In that case they will inform us."

"What if I get sick? Or what if I need something. Like toilet paper?"

"If it's necessary, you can write a note to the retreat organizer. And it's a shared bathroom. Don't worry. There will be lots of toilet paper."

"That's good to know. But what if I'm at dinner and I want someone to pass the salt?"

"Do you really need the salt?" Michael looks at me intently. "You realize you can't talk at all for the whole weekend. No please, no thank you, no pass the salt."

"It sounds like you don't think I can do this."

Michael looks back at the road. "I didn't say that. It's … difficult the first time. No communication means just that: no communication. That includes hand gestures or any other type of body language. Even eye contact is discouraged."

Fine. My eyeballs will remain fixed on the floor all weekend. I won't say this to Michael but this sounds like a reverse staring contest. I was always good at those as a kid.

Michael glances at me and then he actually reads my mind: "Don't think of it as a contest. It's about clearing your mind. It's surprising what you might hear if you stop talking long enough to listen to your inner voice."

My inner voice is yammering: "I'll show you, Michael. I can own them at this New Age shutting up competition."

As promised by the posted schedule, a bonging sound awakes me. I check my watch: 5:00 a.m. Why does spirituality have to start so early? Everywhere I go, there's a hot-wired insomniac running the show. It's tempting to close my eyes again for a few more minutes. Too bad the bong alarm system doesn't have a snooze button. I better throw off the covers now before I fall back to sleep. We are starting with a silent yoga session in the main hall.

In the communal women's bathroom, I wait my turn for the shower while staring at the floor. I check the stall for toilet paper before I go in. I remain in the moment as I brush my teeth, thoroughly enjoying the sensation of the mint toothpaste and the sound of the water trickling from the taps. For this moment, there's nothing else but the breath and a section of dental floss around my fingers. Turns out anyone can be a Zen master while picking at her teeth.

My silent sun salutation is slow to rise this morning. I jackknife my hips into downward dog as everyone else lightly hops forward into a forward fold. I make it to forward fold at the same time everyone else rises for mountain pose. It's all because I can't see the leader at the front of the room. I decide to copy the girl beside me. Big mistake. Evidently she's made of liquid steel. She moves effortlessly through the poses. Her full cobra is a powerful statement and when she shifts into downward dog her long blonde braid curls around her shoulders attractively. My cobra wants to slither under a rock and, during downward dog, my unsecured hair flips in front of my eyes and into my mouth. Michael is behind us. I wonder if he's noticing how the braid girl can tuck her knees neatly behind her ears during plow posture?

After yoga, we go into the meditation hall for our first session before breaking for breakfast. The yoga has woken up my stomach.

Within minutes of sitting, my stomach starts to growl. I tell it to go back to sleep, but it doesn't want to. My brain, however, does. I keep drifting off only to jerk awake as my head rebounds off one shoulder or the other.

I startle to the sound of a bong and realize I've been sound asleep with my chin resting on my chest. As I stand up, trying to rub the crick out of the back of my neck, it strikes me that I've probably been snoring. I turn to ask Michael. It hits me now: There's no talking.

Luckily the breakfast is buffet style and I've no need to ask anyone to pass me the salt. I follow Michael to a table and sit beside him. Michael shifts his chair to make room for me. By shifting his chair an inch, he might as well have yelled good morning. I keep my eyes focused on my plate. The sound of chewing is amplified. It has dawned on me that I have a bad habit of scraping my plate with my utensils. This is very illuminating.

After a short break we go back to the main hall for the next session of meditation. This time I resolve to stay awake. I choose a cushion beside Michael and sit.

And sit. And sit and sit and sit until the muscles in my upper back and shoulders are burning. My butt is sore. My right foot is going to sleep. I wiggle my toes surreptitiously and clench and unclench my thigh muscles only to feel the painful tingling spreading into my calf. I try shifting, ever so slightly, the position of the leg. This helps for about a minute and then the tingling resumes but now it's in my knee and the toes on my left foot are feeling weird.

I'm supposed to be stilling my mind but all I can think about is my throbbing legs. What will happen if I don't move my legs? If the blood is prevented from circulating, could I get a blood clot? I should've chosen to sit on one of the benches at the back of the room. I twitch each leg an inch and continue wiggling, clenching, and unclenching my butt muscles to force the blood down to my toes. I can't stretch the leg straight out in front of me or I will poke braid girl in the butt.

Braid girl has remained wigglefree and clenchless for 30 minutes now. Her thick blonde braid falls straight down her back complementing her ramrod straight spine. I feel a stab of jealousy. The thick braid, the perfect posture, the cute yoga pants that show off her tiny waist. This girl won't ever have to ripple her butt cheeks to prevent a deep vein thrombosis or sit on any loser's bench at the back. She probably sits motionless for hours every morning in a forest glade surrounded by small, adoring birds and animals who follow her home afterwards to sing and dance while they do her laundry. Then she eats apples and chia seeds for lunch while standing on her head.

To shift my attention from my screaming muscles, I make up a mantra for myself: shut the fuck up, don't think, shut the fuck up, don't think. Very soothing actually. The meditation session finally ends and I have to wait for my blood flow to return before I can stand. I rub my legs vigorously to regain the circulation. One of the retreat organizers approaches me and quietly suggests I try the bench for meditation next time. I've been busted. Meanwhile Michael left in a hurry. I wonder if he's mad at me for being so wiggly during meditation?

Once I manage to get the circulation restored in my legs, everyone drifts back in to the room and sits down for a lecture from the leader, Guru Greg. I shuffle to a spot on the bench. A woman with hoop earrings plunks down beside me, muttering. "Thank God I'm not the only one stuck back here." I smile back at the whispering woman. I'm about to undertone something back to her when I see Michael glancing around to see where I went. I spit the smile from my lips as fast as I can and lower my gaze to the floor knowing I've been busted once again and it isn't even lunchtime yet.

Now I get why Michael is so into this stuff. Guru Greg should be a standup comic he's so funny. Laughing soundlessly makes me wet the bench. Greg praised all the beginners in the room. He made a special point of praising those of us who have chosen to sit on the bench saying we are honest and likely know ourselves better than those who strive in distracted discomfort on their cushions. We beginners are more open minded too as we haven't had a chance to become rigid in our practice. He chuckled and said spirituality has nothing to do with a fancy physical pose but has everything to do with the pose inside the head. One can sit still for hours while the mind gallops.

Then he launches into a discussion of something he calls the unwordable word: "What is behind a word? What is behind the world? Try to move beyond the word. Move beyond the world of form. Don't get lost in translation from formless to form. Unword the world."

At first my mind gallops around the concept. Unword the world? The unwordable word? What does it all mean? What is that? When I look at the world from behind the world of form, problems are an illusion. All my worries dissolve into the mist of unwordable words. I get it now. My worries only exist inside my head. In reality, my worries are insignificant, meaningless. Michael's guru says we should unword the world.

I can do that.

I mean, so what if Serenity is having a baby? Babies are lovely. Brand new beings of unwordable light. We have to welcome them into the world of form.

And so what if the bookstore is running in the red? It is what it is. A bookstore full of books made of … insignificant words. It will either work or it won't. Hardly the end of the world.

And so what if Donald is in Calgary? So what if he's having an affair with another woman? So what if I can't decide what to do about Michael? These are only problems if I make them so.

I love sitting here on this bench in this tranquil space. I love everyone in this room now, even braid girl. She's beautiful, a wondrous rainbow being. I want to hug her. Michael's guru is fantastic. I can't wait to share these revelations with Michael. I want to lie with him tonight and share unwordable words. The silence has spoken to me.

For the rest of the day, I drift in euphoria. In the afternoon, which turns out to be a mild day for late November, I take a walk around the grounds and revel in the silence of the unwordable forest. I stare at the gnarly bark on the trees and, pulling off my mitten, I reach out and finger the brown roughness. I am touching a tree! For maybe the first time in my life! I have an urge to hug the tree but there are people around so I slip my hand back into my mitten and pat the tree in a loving sort of way.

I can't wait for bedtime when I plan to slip into Michael's room and share my bodily form with his on the broad plateau of silence. I want to spend the night wrapped up in his arms and then open up and feel his form press in wordless concord into mine.

As soon as the last bing-bong of lights out peals, I slipper down the hall and tap on Michael's door. He cracks open the door. I have nothing on but a blanket and a smile. He still has his clothes on. And a frown.

I step into the room and close the door behind me. "I know I shouldn't speak but I have to tell you how extraordinary this weekend has been for me. The unwordable word says it all. I had a huge revelation. I think I've reached a sort of turning point in my life."

Michael heaves an unsilent sigh. He refuses to speak to me but his irritated expression clearly says, "Can't this wait until the drive home?"

The form on form plan dissolves. I feel silly standing here naked under my blanket. I back out of the room and close the door extra quietly.

I return to my room feeling like a kid being sent to sit in a timeout. My bed feels cold and I'm shivering. I get up and put on socks and a hoodie. Why does Michael have to be so stuffy about this?

For the rest of the weekend it should be easy to maintain complete silence. Because I'm seriously pissed off.

I ignore the 5 a.m. bing-bong, the 6 a.m. bing-bong and the 7 a.m. bing-bong. In between bing-bongs, the only sound is the occasional rattle of my window frame from a gust of wintry wind. My cot is warm and cozy. My pillow is cool on my cheek. Now this is the kind of silent retreat I can get behind. I would stay tucked in bed except that it's a long haul to lunchtime if I miss out on breakfast. I dress quickly and rush to table where I keep my eyes fastened on my plate and concentrate on mastication and swallowing.

Morning meditation on the bench slips by as my thoughts drift lazily through my mind. In the afternoon I peruse the notice board. There's a sign-up sheet for a private interview with Greg so I add my name.

When my appointment time comes, I go and sit on a chair in his office. Greg is standing beside the window staring outside with a thoughtful expression. He turns to look at me, smiles, and waves me over to sit on a cushion. Quickly I take up my position. I rest my palms on my knees and then wonder if they should be in my lap. Do I keep my eyes lowered or what? Do I speak? I wish I had asked Michael about the proper procedure for private interviews.

Greg chuckles. "You're taking this very seriously." Then he reaches out and pats me on the head.

It's the nicest feeling to be patted on the head by a little, bald, mirthful monk.

Greg spends the next few minutes arranging himself on his cushion and adjusting his sash. He scratches the back of his shoulder. "I've had trouble with eczema for years. I can't get rid of it."

Why is he telling me about his skin problems?

We sit in silence for another long minute while Greg scratches his other shoulder, and readjusts his sash. "Very itchy. Yes. Some things we can't change. Whatever it is, better to accept it."

"How do I do that?"

"With patience."

Yeah, right, patience.

"You have doubts. This is fine. Doubts, they come and go. All things come and go. Try to let go of all these attachments Let go of these doubts. Let go and watch. This is the way to wisdom."

Now my shoulder feels itchy. I leave, scratching thoughtfully.

On the way home, Michael says he feels breached: "I'm not mad. I'm disappointed. I'd hoped you would stick this out."

"Aren't you being a bit rigid?"

"It's my fault. I encouraged you to come. Maybe you weren't ready for a silent retreat."

"Oh, I get it now. You're better than me. So much more spiritual and ready."

"No. You made a vow and then you ignored it. It was important to me to keep silence but you ignored that, too."

"I was excited about the lecture. Why is it such a big deal?"

"No big deal. It is what it is."

It is what it is. Ah. The nicey-nice zen way of dismissing someone. He might as well have said, "Fuck off." But he's right. And, yet, I'm right too. We are both right. He's so inflexible he can't see both points of view. I am so flexible, I could argue both sides. So flexible, I can't keep my vows.

Vows. I look down at my hand, at my empty ring finger. Ever since I stripped the wallpaper, my wedding rings have remained abandoned in my jewelry box. My walls remain unpapered. My marriage remains bare and abandoned too. Now I am ripping at my relationship with Michael. Is it because I am afraid of making a commitment? I wrench my eyes away to stare out the window.

For the rest of the way home, we have unwordable words. As in, we aren't speaking to each other anymore.

CHAPTER 24

Decision Point

Decision Point: A point in space and time when the commander or staff anticipates making a key decision concerning a specific course of action.
—Department of Defense Dictionary of Military and Associated Terms

Donald is on the phone to wish us all a Happy Thanksgiving. "Sorry, I couldn't make it home. It's nuts here, with the opening coming up next week. And I might as well warn you now, I don't have much time off at Christmas."

"What do you mean?"

"I can get a flight home on the 24th but I have to fly back on the 26th as I have to meet with the lawyers on the 27th and 28th. I can get a couple days off for New Year's and that's about it."

"You have major meetings scheduled between Christmas and New Year's?"

"Out of my hands; the dates were set up by head office. It's all the lawyers had available, and if we don't take them, we have to push everything off until the New Year, which I would love to do but the finals have to be signed off by December 31 or we're snookered at tax time. They're bending over backwards for us."

I can't think of a thing to say. I can feel my jaw tightening and my cheeks getting hot.

Donald says, after a minute, "I wish it wasn't like this. I wanted to come home for Christmas."

"You mean to say you're not coming at all? The kids are going to be very disappointed."

"I could if you want me to. For the two days. If I can even get the flights booked now. It might be hard to get a flip on Christmas Eve though and it'll be expensive. Do you think it's worth it for just two days?"

"What do you want to do?"

"Fine, then, I'll book the flights. I'll be happy to do that." His voice sounds tense rather than happy.

"Forget it, Donald, you're right, it's not worth it. Too much money and too much stress. We'll manage."

"I'm sorry, really I am."

"Look, I've gotta go. We'll talk later."

I hang up and clasp my hands under my chin. What the hell was that? We'll manage? Not sure how but I will have to now. Thanksgiving is here, and I still haven't done a speck of Christmas shopping. Maybe this is a good thing. Having Donald home for Christmas creates more stress. This way I won't have to buy him any presents.

I should send him a lump of coal. Hell. Maybe I should just fly out there and deliver it in person.

Then I get an idea. A very good, very bad, and very twisted idea. Maybe we could all fly out there and surprise-visit him? The kids and me. We've never been to Calgary.

Or. Maybe just me. I can move much faster alone. We need time to talk, face to face. We have to make a decision. Better to work it out without the kids.

I could go for New Year's Eve. Donald's meetings will be over so he should be in sharp trim by then. The kids will be so submerged in candy and Santa swag they won't even notice me gone. I could ask Mom to come stay with them for a few days. Maybe she'll even come spend Christmas with us this year. Last year I invited her but she refused even though it was our first Christmas without Dad. She said she wanted to sing with her choir on Christmas Day. I guess she thought having Christmas at our house would make it final, like

Dad's really gone. It's easier for me; I can imagine him at home with Mom, setting up the tree and hanging the star, crookedly, as always. I pick up the phone to call her.

Why does the busiest shopping season of the year have to be held during the winter when an arctic squall accompanies every visitor into the bookstore? As a result, I have a miserable cold. Nonetheless this morning I was forced to crawl from my warm duvet and lumber outside to scrape ice off the windshield of the car, so I could open the coffee bar on time. Donald always scraped the ice off my car when he did his own. These early morning Saturdays are a solid bummer compared to my pre-store weekend mornings where all I had to do was leave some bananas out on the coffee table for the kids before going to bed and then listen for the TV being turned on around dawn.

The snowplow guy filled in the bottom of the driveway again. I gun the car in reverse through the drift, fishtailing onto the road. I'll tackle the driveway later when I get home. Of course I won't be home until well after dark.

Jennifer said the top rule of bookselling is extra long hours during the run-up to Christmas. Recently she dropped in to the store to re-warn me: "If you don't bury your nuts now, you'll be sunk." And today is the ugliest of long days: a December Saturday. People are increasingly frantic to finish their shopping and all proprieties of manners have been trampled into the ankle-deep slush of the sidewalks outside.

As I approach the store I'm relieved to see that Ghostly Garth is nowhere to be seen. Garth has taken to showing up to help me open in the mornings. I would love a whole day without Garth or Johnny Rotten dropping by to talk about poltergeists or tear apart the children's section. I'm beginning to loathe most of my customers. Like the lady who always shows up on a full moon to stroke the spines of the books. She always breaks down in huge sobs in the romance section. Or the scary man last week who, upon being told his book order wasn't in yet, shouted as he stormed out of the store, "That pisses me off."

Now all Jude has to do to crack Serenity up—usually when she's serving a touchy customer—is stand behind the customer in Serenity's line of sight and sign his pitch-perfect Crazy Man impression by pounding the air with his fist and mouth-yelling, "That pisses me off." At the threshold I see that someone has thrown up all over my Holly Berries planter—the vomit is no doubt compliments of one of last night's holiday revelers from the pub three doors down. It's frozen solid in mid-drip from the red berries and I knock a few pukesicles off with my mitten. Someone obviously consumed a few too many beers plus a chicken pita. Looks like the ranch dressing. Serves them right for buying anything from the Pita Gnat across the street.

As I switch on the register, Shae bashes open the door. "Did you see the puke?" she yells. "Disgusting. Why does everybody always get the ranch dressing?"

In the middle of a selling scrum, Michael texts to remind me of our lunch date. Oops. I forgot. I hate to blow him off just when we have managed to patch things up from the silent retreat over a series of apologetic emails. Now he wants to see me. But Yard is here dressed as a reedy Santa Claus, definitely a Nightmare Before Christmas version; Wendy is handing out treat bags; and Johnny Rotten has three or four candy canes in various stages of meltdown in each fist. I have to get that child out of the store before the oncoming blood sugar shockwave. Plus Serenity looks pale, like she needs to sit down and rest. Her bump seems to get bigger by the minute.

It's nuts in here. I'm completely swamped, I text to Michael in between hand signals to let Jude know that a lineup is forming at the register. *I'm going to grab something to-go at the pub.*

Ten minutes later, my favorite book rep, Kevin, wanders into the store. I also forgot I agreed to meet with him today. "I'm starved," I say to him, "How about a sandwich in the pub and we can go over the catalogs while we eat?"

In Hollywood movies, everyone knows this is a stupid and ill-fated move. I'm obviously starring, because Michael shows up as we sit down with our pints and hot beef dips. I might as well have had a Pita Gnat Special with ranch dressing. His look of betrayal and pain makes my stomach grind. I excuse myself from Kevin and hurry over to Michael. He's standing at the checkout picking up a takeout order for one. He turns to me, unsmiling.

"Michael, it's a business lunch. That guy is a sales rep. I forgot to—"

"You don't have to explain anything to me."

"I know, but I didn't want you to think I'm lying to you."

"No. You would never do that." Michael's voice is clipped.

Our eyes meet. Me? Lie?

As Michael turns away and heads for the door, my thoroughly deceived husband appears in the scene, figuratively of course. He's the cuckold leaping like a lord in the tight white leotards. Or is he the sneaky fellow with the long twirly mustache? Or the hot cowboy in the leather chaps? Central casting keeps changing things up on me. So, which is he? All I know is, in my next big Hollywood role, I want to be the good guy.

After lunch, I return to the store to find Serenity and Jude standing shoulder to shoulder at the cash register. They're grinning and making faces behind the back of a woman dressed entirely, from head to foot, in red and green. Even her purse and boots match.

Jude slides a pink sticky note over to Serenity. On it he has written, "She could use more green." Serenity snorts and bends over the note to add her reply.

"Woman in trench coat at 4 o'clock: WTF is up with that hair?"

I always have to warn them about passing notes. If the customers only knew. There's a drawer under the counter overflowing with color-coded stickies. Pink for fashion violations. Orange for weirdos. If they totally hate a customer they yank out the yellow pad. A yellow slip that says "skanky biatch" is currently on top of the pile. It went to the lady who came in yesterday looking for a travel guide to Costa Rica. She held up her wristwatch and said to Serenity: "You have four minutes."

Mid-afternoon, there's a lull: here's a chance to meet Michael for a quick coffee. Why not? Wendy and Jude are handling things. I can tell Serenity I have to go do some shopping.

Michael agrees to meet me at the Dingy. Trouble is, my cold has settled throughout my sinuses, and I have to keep wiping my nose so it doesn't drip into my latte.

"I'm sorry about the way I acted in the pub. I felt uncomfortable seeing you in the corner having lunch with that guy," Michael says.

"I told you already, he's a sales rep. That's it." I tilt my head and look earnestly into his eyes.

"I know." Michael leans forward. "Do you have time to come back to the res with me? I want to make love to you."

My ear lobes start tingling but I should get back to the store. The yellow stickies are really piling up and a last minute order is due to arrive. I don't want Serenity lifting boxes of books. Jude has to go to an audition and Shae is going for a road test for her Class D license. If she passes, she could be clearing the town's streets of snow as early as next week. Then she'll probably be making more money than me.

Michael's lip pouts out slightly. I don't want to get into yet another tiff so I reluctantly say yes. Wendy is at the store; she can lift the boxes. Serenity can go home and rest, order in some pizza for Jack and Olympia.

Michael immediately wants to know if my hockey gear is in the trunk of the car. He doesn't have to explain. I know that deep down he has been fantasizing about me dressed in naught but a hockey jersey and maybe a pair of high heels. Men just have a thing about doing it with a woman wearing a good set of knee pads. It's all Janet Jones Gretzsky's fault for posing in Sports Illustrated with her little blonde braids and gartered hockey socks. The idea is intriguing though. I suppose the pads will protect my patellas if we do it doggy style.

We drag the hockey bag up to his place and I slip into the bathroom to don my gear. I figure it will be more fun for him if I put on all the equipment; that'll make the strip tease last longer. I strap on the Jill and pull on the body armour, socks and jersey. My hockey equipment doesn't smell so fresh. I hope Michael won't notice.

At the last minute I decide to leave off the helmet for fear of helmet hair. And the mouth guard doesn't exactly say kiss me.

I'm not sure if he wants the skates or not. Janet had the skates. And I like the thought of skates in bed. There's something deeply kinky about dangerously sharp blades on waving feet. I could take his ears off if I get too carried away. I lace up and stand to survey myself in the mirror. This settles it. Male fetishes are plain weird. All I need is a mullet and I will look exactly like Wayne Gretzky.

Because of the shoulder pads, I have to turn sideways to get through the narrow door. Michael is waiting for me at the end of the hall. My nose starts running faster than ever as I clump toward him in the skates. I try to wipe it on my hockey glove. Michael blinks at me a couple of times and then he makes a half-snort, half-laugh sound through his nose.

"You didn't need to put everything on."

"I didn't."

Michael grins. "Holy shit, your head looks … so tiny. And you have no neck."

"It's the shoulder pads, you jerk," I say as I whirl back into the bathroom. "Forget it, this was a dumbass idea."

I smack the door shut, lock it and yank at the skate laces in a fury. Right away, Michael taps on the door. "Please come out. You're right—it was a dumb idea. My dumb idea."

"Go away."

I peel all the equipment off and shove it back into the bag. Then I fill the tub with hot water. Climbing in, I prop my legs up on the wall and, as I watch the steam rise into the air, my aching sinuses begin to unclog. Lovely. Michael can stew in his own smelly locker room fantasy juices for a while.

I let him stew for a long time before I emerge, dressed in my jeans and t-shirt again, sinuses nicely clear and a towel wrapped around my wet hair. Michael is sitting in a chair reading a book. He immediately jumps up and, taking my hand, leads me into the bedroom. There's a wooden tray with a pot of tea and a plate of chocolate cookies laid on the bed. And a bowl of oranges. I know what he means by the tea and oranges. They're from "Suzanne", his favorite love poem, by Leonard Cohen. They mean love and beauty and sadness and longing. I forgive him.

I sit cross-legged on the bed sipping my tea and peeling oranges. Michael drapes himself across the bed in front of me and watches me chew. "I love watching you. Even the way you eat oranges is sexy."

I lean in close and treat him to a citrus kiss. Michael sits up, takes the teacup from my hands and gently pushes me back against the pillows. He's all quiet, tender, and sweet, and afterwards we lie on our sides facing each other and do the stare into each other's eyes thing that is always the best part with Michael.

Michael's face turns serious. "Suzanne was married to someone else you know, when Cohen wrote that poem about her."

"Does that really matter now?"

"No. But I think it made him want her more. She was so unavailable to him."

"I'm here now, aren't I?"

"I want you to ask Donald for a divorce."

There it is.

"I know."

Less than a week to go before Christmas and the race is on: I unlock the doors extra early, instruct Serenity to start the coffee machines and Jude to open the till, then I speed to my office at the back of the store hoping no customer will pounce on me. The phone on my desk is blinking and there's a raft of emails, including one from Michael that I will have to save for later. Last night, I kissed Michael goodbye and hurried away with a promise to give him an answer soon. I don't know when I will get a chance to think though.

Minutes later, Serenity pokes her head into the room and extends her arm: in her hand is a large mug of coffee. I leap straight for it. "Thank you, thank you, thank you. Where is Wendy?"

"On the way. She stopped to try to help Yard fix his bike chain again."

"How does he ever pedal that wreck through the snow anyway?"

"Dunno. He wipes out a lot. Wendy's afraid he's going to get hit by a car one of these days."

I start sorting through the tower of paperwork on and beside my desk. It looks like there's more paper in my piles of paperwork than in the books out on the shelves. In one pile I find Jack's Christmas wish list: his top entry is a the new *Twisted Hilt* video game but every store clerk in town says they've been sold out of those for weeks. Then they usually chortle at me: *Good luck with that one, Mom.* I stayed up until 2 a.m. last night, scouring the Internet and making last minute rush orders. Four hours' sleep and it was a race back to the store to work on the rest of the town's blinking wish list all day long.

I know what's on top of Michael's list: a final decision from me. This item is way out of Santa's league. One thing's for sure: I'm perched at the top of Santa's naughty list so I better watch my step or I might get pulped with sticks by some gang of stern punishing elves in a back alley.

No matter what, I always seem to be on the naughty list. I'm a bad boss. I haven't organized Christmas presents for the store staff yet or even treated them to a party. I am a bad mother. I haven't conjured up a Magician's Kit. I am a bad wife and a bad daughter. And I am a bad mistress: I didn't tell Michael I am going to Calgary for New Year's. I lay my head on the desk. Bad, bad, bad and nothing I can do about it.

Wait. There is one thing I can do. Jumping up from my chair, I grab my purse and coat. As I pass the cash register, I snatch up a handful of tens and twenties and stuff them in a red and green striped stocking from the window display. Shoving the stocking into my coat pocket, I yell, "Serenity, I have to go out."

I stop at the florist, the dry cleaner's and the print shop. The printer says I better drop by Bonnie's Café. Bonnie sends me to the hardware store. Everyone knows Yard and wants to contribute. It doesn't take long to fill my stocking with cash. My last stop is the local bike shop. "I want a decent quality street bike. With saddlebags and winter tires and, you know, the works. For a tall guy."

The bike shop guy nods and points at a red hybrid, "I know what Yard would like. He's in here all the time looking around. I'm throwing in a top-of-the-line gelfoam saddle for free."

Best bit of fun I've had all year.

Christmas Eve: I'm so burnt out. And very, very ticked. Everyone took off around noon leaving me to fend off the last minute shoppers all by myself. Serenity said she had to finish her Christmas shopping, Jude begged off with a headache, and Wendy didn't show up at all. Shae must be at work although we haven't had snow for days.

I tried to close the store at noon but customers kept arriving in a steady stream. Many of them were hoping to snag one of Serenity's specialty pre-stuffed stockings: the one for baby comes with powder and lotion, board books and waterproof bath books, and the one for Mom is filled with bath soaps, scented tealights, chocolates and a couple of the season's hot reads. Once the word got around town, all the stockings sold out quickly including all of the Haunted Stockings she made up to please Garth.

This final week before Christmas has been crazy. I haven't had a minute to myself. I bought a tree last week but it remains frozen on the front porch awaiting its decorations in vain. The presents for under the tree are still under my bed, and the baking is on my to-do list.

Donald obviously had some extra time on his hands as a huge gift-filled box from him arrived last night by overnight courier. Serenity stacked all the pretty packages in the corner of the living room, and warned us to keep our paws off them until Christmas morning. I can't wait to open my gifts, which are a confection of tissue and gold stickers. Obviously Calgarian shoppers have way better gift-wrapping services than we do. I'm feeling terribly bitter now. Of course one of my gifts came in a tiny jewelry-box-sized package. Bless those new-money oil patch barons.

Of course, this all reminds me that I haven't managed to wrap a single gift yet.

Last night on the phone I prevaricated, "It's been so crazy, I didn't get over to the post office yet."

"Don't worry. I don't expect you to get me anything. You're doing everything at home. I know you have no time."

Now I feel terrible. The truth is I haven't even shopped for him yet. My plan was to bring him something when I surprise him on New Year's Eve.

At 4:00 p.m. I look outside. It's starting to snow, which is good news as the crowds will thin now.

Finally at 4:20, I usher the last customer outside, lock the door, turn the sign to closed, and duck down to hide behind the counter as I count the day's receipts. Within minutes I hear knocking. I risk a peek. It's Michael. I run to let him in.

We sit in the office and look at each other in silence. We haven't seen each other since our tea and oranges afternoon. Michael still doesn't know I'm planning to go to Calgary for New Year's. I'm tempted to forget to mention it at all. I hate to see him pout. He's right about one thing though. I have to make up my mind.

It's difficult. Funny but I never realized that I would miss Donald as much as I do.

"I have to go soon but I wanted to give you this." Michael hands me a red and gold box with a dragon motif on the lid.

"I didn't think you celebrated Christmas anymore."

"I don't. But I wanted to surprise you."

I lift the lid. Nestled in soft rice paper is a beautiful copper bowl finely etched with symbols around the rim.

"It's a Tibetan singing bowl."

"Thank you. It's lovely." I run my finger over a conch shell, a knot and a wheel.

"Those are the Eight Auspicious Signs of the Ashtamangala." He points at a symbol of two intertwined fish. "The fish represent fearlessness as they swim without danger of drowning in samsara, or suffering."

"I didn't get you anything."

"I don't expect anything."

My pretty Buddhist bowl is overflowing with guilt. I'm afraid I'm about to drown in an ocean of samsara. "Michael, there's something I need to tell you."

As expected, the samsara response comes quickly. I'm up to my neck in samsara. Once I finish confessing my plan, Michael shakes his head and stands up to leave.

"Wait Michael, please try to understand. I can't explain why I'm going to Calgary to see Donald but I need to go. I don't understand it myself. I'm not ready to walk away from my marriage yet."

"Yet? Do you think you will, ever? Do you even have a marriage?"

I put my hand on his. "I don't know anymore. I just need a little more time."

Michael pulls away. "I can't do this anymore. You have to decide."

"I know."

Michael tugs his coat on. "I have to go now."

He walks away down the street without looking back.

I sit in my office, turning the empty bowl on the desk in front of me, the eight auspicious symbols endlessly circling the rim. The lotus flower symbol is etched on the bottom of the bowl as well as on the rim. Michael said lotus flowers represent purity. The lotus is pure because it floats on the water above it all, free from desire and attachment. It is the symbol of letting go.

There should be a ninth symbol, special for me and my type of situation: the suffering waffle, representing the eternal sticky entrapment of pure wishy-washyness.

As I drive home, the singing bowl tucked back in its dragon box on the seat beside me, a wave of fatigue washes over me. I have to make and serve dinner, slam-decorate the tree, tuck the kids in bed and read them an abridged version of The Night Before Christmas.

I'll be up well past midnight wrapping presents. I don't even have a dinner plan. Usually I make homemade pesto pasta and Caesar salad on Christmas Eve: everyone loves this long-standing family tradition but I'm not sure if I have any basil cubes or pine nuts in the freezer. Donald always took care of the salad. Will the kids notice if I skip the ritual this year and heat up a frozen pizza? I'm such a joke. *Tenacity. Mental toughness. Shoulder your arms, soldier.* I pull the car over and sit with my forehead on the steering wheel for a few minutes. Then I walk around the car taking big gulps of air and dab at my temples with a mittenful of snow.

Stepping through the kitchen door, my nose fills with the scents of ginger, pine boughs, warm butter, and garlic. My mother and Shae are standing in front of the counter rolling out cookie dough. Am I hallucinating? Shae is wearing an apron, one of Mom's aprons, the one with the kittens.

I peek over her shoulder. "What kind are you making?"

"Gingerbread. My Mom always made gingerbread people and horses and stars and things on Christmas Eve and we hung them on the tree."

I give her a little hug. Shae's Mom died when Shae was only 14 years old.

"I like the apron. It suits you."

Shae grins at me. "Shut up. Go look in the living room."

Mom and Shae follow me in and everyone jumps up and yells, "Merry Christmas, Mom."

Now I know why everyone deserted me in the store this afternoon. They've been busy. The Christmas tree is all set up and decorated.

Serenity crouches down beside the tree to rearrange a teetering pile of wrapped gifts. I see one bearing a tag that says "To Mom," from Jack and Olympia. As I bend over to pick it up, Serenity sets her hand on my arm. "Better not shake that one."

"This box better not come with breathing holes." I glance over at Jack who is giggling.

"No, it's breakable that's all."

Looking up I see our Christmas star from home, the one Dad always hung, presiding over all. Mom must have brought it with her. As always, it's tilting precariously, but it's perfect. I stuff the lump in my throat back down.

"Do you like it?"

"I love it. Thanks, guys."

I'm still wearing my boots and coat, and the gift box per Merriam Webster from Michael is still tucked under one arm. I bend down to slip the red and gold box under the branches. My temples start pounding again so I rub them hard. My mother looks at the box and then at me, opens her mouth to say something, and then closes it again. "We made pesto pasta for dinner. Come and eat."

CHAPTER 25

Reconnaissance

Reconnaissance: A mission undertaken to obtain, by visual observation or other detection methods, information about the activities and resources of an enemy or adversary, or to secure data concerning the meteorological, hydrographic, or geographic characteristics of a particular area.
—Department of Defense Dictionary of Military and Associated Terms

I can't believe how much work it is to go out of town for a few days. For one thing, I have to prepare the house for Mom. Meaning I have to hide the evidence of all things Michael. I don't know why I'm taking a risk keeping a secret cache of damning photos, notes, and lovers' mementos, but I can't bring myself to burn the goods. The explosive collection is, of course, carefully squirreled away in a box in the darkest corner of my bedroom closet with a pile of purses and shoe boxes heaped on top. No one will ever notice it here. No one except Mom that is.

I heave the box out of the closet and, against my better judgment, lift the lid. On top is a batch of photos taken at the cottage that Michael printed. I flip through the shots and cringe at the one where I'm leaping and dancing through long grass, arms raised, pretending to be a sylph: one boob is swinging straight up, nipple pointing at the sky while the other is zooming off in the opposite direction toward my armpit.

I love Michael's pencil drawings the best. There's a smiling naked couple that looks remarkably like us walking together, hand in hand, down a sidewalk; the woman is looking back over her shoulder and smiling. In another drawing, another naked couple who looks like us is lying together under an apple tree and, in a third favorite, is a series of frames depicting the man embracing the woman: each successive frame shows him sprouting wings on his back.

There's a thick file folder containing printouts of six months' worth of our emails: Michael loved to write to me at length about books and music and movies. There are the poems on sheets of birch bark that he wrote during our weekend at the cottage and a collection of handwritten quotes and notes on exquisite cards. I pick one up. It says, "I want too much when I'm with you. Longingly, achingly, M."

What a mess I've made of things. I feel like running to Michael right now and wrapping my arms around him. But I know I can't do that. Michael was firm: I have to be sure. That's a no-holds-barred, all-or-nothing step that I can't take yet. Or ever.

Because deep down, I'm suspecting a box of heat-of-the-night love letters isn't going to be enough. Morning always comes with dull grey laundry, and the box will grow dusty in the back of a closet as we tear each other apart in the glare of the day.

Meanwhile, what if someone finds this box? I should burn the whole works but I can't bring myself to do it, yet. I have to leave my car at the Shuttle Park. The box can go in the trunk. First-rate security all for $5 a day.

Checking my watch, I realize I've wasted an hour mooning over my Michael stuff. I have to leave for the airport in an hour. That's loads of time. Anyone who has ever been in uniform is capable of bugging out from anywhere to anywhere in less than 5 minutes.

Oh crap. Unless their mother shows up early to "help" that is. Downstairs I hear Jack yelling, "Mom! Grandma's here."

Dammit. She wasn't due for another half an hour. Now I have to somehow try to sneak the box past her to stash it in the trunk. Tucking the box under the bed, I hurry downstairs to greet her.

I show her the sitter notes: phone numbers, health cards, where to find stuff, the usual. I hand her two bottles. "Here's Jack's and

Olympia's chewable vitamins. The prenatal ones are for Serenity of
course. Make sure they brush their teeth before bed. That's about it."

Then I show her George's paw kit: "There's his paw wax which
needs to be rubbed on the pads every morning and here's a bottle
of liquid glucosamine—he gets two capfuls twice a day. And his vitamins and nail file. There's plenty of dog food—it's stored here in
the cupboard, and he can have some of these anti-inflammatory dog
treats that Dr. Loewen is trying him on, they have all the omega
fatty acids in them. His booties and leash are over here in the basket
beside by the door; get Olympia to show you the way to tie them
on so George can't get them off. Never leave the booties on once he
comes in or he'll chew them off. Those stupid boots cost more than
my leather coat. Oh, and don't forget to rinse his feet off if he does
manage to sneak out. There's a dip bucket and towels under the sink.
Mom, are you listening to me?"

"Yes, dear, I'll give the children their vitamins. Are you sure
George doesn't still have the Red Mange? Look, he's scratching."

"He never had the Red Mange. The vet thinks he has an allergy so
be sure to give him his antihistamines." I point to them in the cabinet
above the sink. "He likes it if you wrap the pill in cheese or bacon."

Mom presses her lips together in a way that means George will be
lucky if he gets a fresh kick up his itchy ass once in a while.

Then I run back upstairs to pack. I upend the contents of the
Michael box into a second, smaller suitcase and zip it closed. I'm a
genius of course. Now I can waltz right past my mother carrying all
the evidence for safe deposit in the trunk of my car.

Minutes after I plop the trunk lid down with a self-satisfied smirk,
my plan springs a leak. Mom wants to use my car while I'm away. Her
brakes need servicing. She'll drop me at the shuttle.

Looks like I'm taking the evidence to Calgary with me.

At the airport check-in, the ticket agent apologizes: I'm being bumped.
No explanation why, but the next flight doesn't push off for hours,
and then I'll have to wait for several hours more in Chicago for my

connecting flight, which means I won't arrive in Calgary until well after midnight. I don't want to greet the New Year in a skin-drying pressurized cabin while trying to steady my drink across the potholes of the polar jet stream.

I have to get on that plane. I get an idea thanks to Bibienne who knows a million ways to wiggle her way into business class. I will have to tell a little white lie but the slate wipes clean at midnight, right? All's fair in love, war, and holiday travel.

I limp over to the ticket agent and in a whispery voice I say, "I'm afraid I'm going to have to ask you to try to get me back on this flight. I have serious medical conditions. My cardiologist says it's okay to travel but I shouldn't get too tired." I rest my hand over my heart and moan softly to emphasize the situation. "A long delay could be too hard on me."

The ticket agent stares at me for a moment and sighs, "Alright then, please go sit down and I'll see what I can do."

I walk, slowly, slowly, back to my seat, favoring both legs because I can't remember which leg I used to limp over to the desk in the first place. From the corner of my eye I can see the agent talking to her supervisor and then they both look over at me. I try to make my face look as pinched and wan as possible.

A few minutes later the agent comes over pushing a wheelchair. "Good news. I've got you back on." She pats my shoulder. "We'll help board you. Don't you worry about a thing."

Best little white lie ever. The ticket agent arranged for an aide to help me with my carry-on and I got boarded first. In business class! If this plane goes down before I get a chance to atone for this duplicity, I'm going straight to the blackest greasiest oil pans of hell.

Trouble is the attendant who wheeled me aboard is the one now offering me a free beverage from the drinks cart. Can people with heart conditions drink alcohol? I better not push my luck. I'm forced to choose an orange juice without the vodka.

Calgary International is madness but de-boarding is a snap. The attendant wheels me straight over to the carousel and we watch for my suitcases. I tell the attendant that it's always a cinch to spot my bags as they are cherry red and wasn't I clever to choose a color that is easy to spot?

Where's my luggage? The carousel turns and turns but no cherry red bags appear. All the plain luggage is soon plucked off the carousel leaving an empty turning track. How quickly the karma wheel diverts my progress and spins me into the alleyways.

The baggage claims agent leans way over the counter and explains, in a loud measured voice—as if she thinks maybe the wheelchair means I'm slow in the head—that my bags are still in Boston. Or maybe they went to Atlanta? She assures me they will be located and couriered to me, by the latest, tomorrow night. She wants an estimate of the value of the contents of the bags. Clothes and sundries: $900. Bag of incriminating lover's notes: priceless.

The agent also needs an address and phone number. I give her Donald's info and ask the attendant to take me to the cab stop. Finally I'm settled in the back seat of a cab. I haven't had a chance to call Donald yet. He's sure going to be surprised to see me. I smile to myself as I dig in my purse for my phone. When I talked to him yesterday he had no plan for New Year's; he was going to order in some grub, watch TV and turn in early. Poor guy. He said all those last minute meetings nearly killed him. I was planning to wait and call him from the lobby of his apartment building but now I think I should give him a little more warning. He might want to pick up the place before I step through the door. But maybe not too much warning in case Lindsay is there with him. Not, of course, that I ever had any thought of trying to smoke Donald out of hiding with my little surprise visit. That would be wrong and pathetic.

As I dial his number, my heart is tripping around in my chest. How strange. I'm feeling nervous about seeing my husband. I use my free hand to grope in my bag for my lip gloss and comb.

Donald answers, sounding upbeat. He sounds so close which, of course, he is.

"Hi Donald, guess what? I have a surprise for you! I'm here."

"Here? You're in Banff?"

"Banff? No, I'm in Calgary."

"You're in Calgary?" Donald sounds distressed.

"Yes, I'm in a cab, this minute, on my way to your apartment!"

"Oh no."

"What's the matter?"

"I'm in Banff."

I am certainly not going to drive all the way to Banff in a junker. I make my way to the car lot and locate my ride. It's licorice black and pretty, pretty. Just looking at this sweet set of wheels makes me feel like the woman in me just had her hair backcombed, her eyelashes curled and her skirt hiked up from behind by the hired hand. Her panties are pink and frilly and wet.

The woman in me is planning to put that man of hers in a world of hurt when she gets to Banff. Donald explained that the Banff thing was a last minute change of plans. "Everyone" decided to take off for a couple days of recreation in the mountains. "Someone" has a condo that sleeps eight. "No reason you can't join us," said Donald. "If you set out now, you can make it here well before midnight."

I drive out of Calgary straight into a blizzard. By the time I reach Canmore I have whiteout blisters on my fingers and sore shoulders from stuffing them into my ears. I follow a couple of Freightliners into a truck stop for a coffee break. The waitress at the counter says with these conditions there's no way I'll make it all the way to Banff before midnight; the highway will soon be closed.

I've never welcomed in a new year in a truck stop before. With the sun rising in my rearview mirror, I drive into the mountains. Truck stop coffee plus the solid rock rise ahead throws a sober shudder into my New Year's morning. One little rockslide and I'll be screaming down into one of the chasms that decorate the shoulder of the twisting road, only a hollow heartbeat away from my hubcaps.

I locate the right mountain and the right condo and Donald greets me with a chummy hug at the door. He introduces me to Todd from the office and Todd's girlfriend Tina. They're sitting at the kitchen table drinking coffee and chatting with Lindsay. Donald is dressed but Todd is still in a robe over his boxers and Lindsay and Tina are both barefoot and clad in skimpy silky pajama bottoms and tiny spaghetti strapped tops. Maybe it's too much truck stop coffee but it feels like I'm crashing a cozy foursome.

Donald points his arm at the mountains in the window. "You missed Rob and Scott; they went off to kill themselves on the double black diamonds."

"Who are Rob and Scott?"

"The IT guys. I told you about them before didn't I?"

Right. Rob and Scott. Donald talks about those guys all the time, usually in an envious tone; they're two of the most single and whacked guys on the planet. They spend all their spare time jumping out of airplanes, rappelling down mountainsides and sneaking out of hotel rooms in the middle of the night. I tell them about my lost luggage.

Lindsay says, "I'd loan you some things but nothing of mine would fit you."

I turn to Donald. "I need to take a shower and a nap."

A few hours later I wake up and check my watch. It's the middle of the afternoon. Pulling on my jeans and blouse, I go out to find Donald sitting on the couch in the living room, tablet on his lap. The condo is deserted. Donald rises immediately, "Coffee?"

"No, thanks." I sit in an armchair. "This feels so awkward. I shouldn't have come."

"No, I'm glad you came. Surprised. But glad."

"Really? I don't know, Donald, but this whole setup feels a bit too much like a private pajama party."

Donald stiffens for a moment and then throws up his hands in a gesture of surrender. He says, in a soft voice, "It's not what you think it is. Honest. I have my own room, all by myself."

"I think I had better go home. Today."

"No, please, I want you to stay."

"Really?"

"Really."

Donald sounds so earnest that I have to believe him. "I came because I wanted to have some time together without the kids and everything. So we can talk."

"I want that too."

I don't know what to say next, where to start. Donald looks uncomfortable.

"Let's not do it now. I'm still tired. And I have no clothes. Not even a toothbrush. Can we go shopping?"

At dinner in a pub, over a giant platter of suicide wings and deep fried pickles, Rob asks me if I know how to ski.

I did, once upon a time. But I've had two pints, and Lindsay is listening so I toss my head and say I go skiing all time. Every day. All year round.

"Have you tried blading?"

"Sure. Blading is great." I haven't got the foggiest what blading is. Lindsay pipes up: "Awesome. Tomorrow we should go on a few runs together."

"Love to."

Alrighty then. Blading lessons. First thing in the morning.

Might as well coat me in batter and dip me in boiling oil because now I am in a deep fried pickle.

After a night of cartwheeling over sheer cliff drops in my sleep, I stumble into the ski rental and ask the guy at the desk to hook me up with a set of boots and blades.

He lays two little strips of wood on the counter in front of me. So what was I worried about? Blades are nothing but dinky little baby skis. I put on my boots and go outside to sit on a bench to wait for my instructor. Donald waits around to keep me company until I shoo him away. "I'm fine here, you go ahead and catch up with Rob and Scott." He eagerly hurries away to the lifts.

I love blading. I don't know how to fix the blades to my boots yet, but sitting here on the bench with the clean mountain air ionizing my skin is like a religious experience. My spirits rise even higher when a mountain man strides up to me and asks if I am Pauline. Ooh! Hello! I've been assigned to Paul Bunyan, the biggest, hottest instructor in the whole Rockies. The guy could chop down trees with that grin. Better yet, I seem to be his sole student. He kneels down beneath me and shows me how to adjust the bindings. With those shoulders, he could haul an unsuspecting woman deep into the forest.

"Before we go to the lifts, we have to wait for one more student." I look around as he says, "There she is."

Of course it's Lindsay.

I hate blading.

The dinky baby skis are unstable little planks of terror. "Blades are the bomb for stunt skiing," says Paul Bunyan. "You can do cartwheels on them."

We scale the side of a cliff and he demonstrates a few basic twists and turns. The tricky part appears to be stopping. Lindsay goes first and slides toward him, only to fall giggling at his feet. He helps her up and she holds on to him a little too long.

The slope below me looks like a straight shot to becoming an undone jellyroll at the bottom. I watch a couple of four-year-old ski ninjas whoosh by, snow roosters rising in their wake. Biting my lip, I push off, only to go sideways and then backwards before I manage to turn around the right way and fall flat on my face. Look ma, no brains.

Paul Bunyan drags us to the top of the hill again and again. My butt is munched from landing on it so many times. Then he says we're ready to go higher up the mountain where we can "catch some big air off the cliff drops."

Lindsay is determined to ride the chairlift with Bunyan. I couldn't care less. I've just noticed that his arms are way too long for his body and his high-pitched voice is getting right up my red frozen nose.

At the last second, Bunyan steps out of the lineup to chat with one of the female lift operators, and I end up riding with Lindsay. As we ascend I can't think of a thing to say. The one theme I'd like to raise is hardly appropriate: so, Twinkie, are you sleeping with my husband or what? What would Bibienne do? She'd shove Lindsay off the lift, that's what.

I picture Lindsay in a crumpled heap on the hill below, and my chapped lips feel prickly and tight as they curl into a secret smirk.

I can't wait to get off this lift. Halfway up the hill, the lift stops.

We sit swinging our legs and shrugging our shoulders at each other. Lindsay turns around and waves to Bunyan who is several chairs back talking to a girl beside him. He doesn't wave back. The wind is shredding my cheeks off, and I'm worried maybe I'll be too stiff to dismount by the time we get to the top.

Lindsay exclaims and points below. Donald is skiing by with Rob and Scott. We wave and shout until Rob looks up. He signals to Donald who looks up too, promptly loses his balance, and almost wipes out. Ha! Yes, Donald. Look at me, sitting on a chairlift with your girlfriend.

I wave at Donald and then turn to address Lindsay, all chummy like. "I love your ski jacket. Where'd you get it?"

"I was going to ask you the same thing. I love your jacket."

Donald stands on the hill below us. He waves and we wave back. Then he skis away in a hurry. Ten minutes later, the lift lurches forward again. Lindsay pulls a tube of lip gloss from her pocket, dabs it on and hands it to me. Then she checks her watch. "I'm starved. What do you say we ditch Bladeboy and go get some food? There's a lodge up top."

The lodge overlooks the mountains. We choose a table beside a panoramic window and stare out over the endless horizon of postcard peaks, blue sky, and treetops below. Lindsay orders first. "I'll have a glass of the house red and a grilled steak sandwich." Then she turns to me. "Or, if you want, we could split a carafe?"

The house red is so civilized we order a second carafe. I'm glad I'm taking the time to get to know Lindsay. Beyond the blonde hair extensions, she's funny and earthy. She tells me all about how she grew up in a series of foreign boarding schools and got herself kicked out of a bunch of them for skipping classes, smoking, and going AWOL. Meanwhile her father built his empire and her mother skipped off to Florida with her girlfriends with all their hairdressers in tow. Lindsay had to learn how to take care of herself.

And she's excellent at it. So what's wrong with that?

"I need to learn how to take better care of myself," I say as I drain my glass.

"Then you should start with your skin. Look at what the cold air has done to your cheeks. They're all red and chapped."

"So are yours."

Lindsay pulls out her phone and books us in for an afternoon facial. "God. We have to get off this mountain. Are you as wrecked as I am? Is it possible to take the chairlift back down?"

"Good question."

"I have to go to the powder room." Lindsay stands up and wobbles. "Hey, look who's here."

Donald looks as if he has been running a race, his face is red and he's panting slightly. "There you are."

"Hi ya bud." Lindsay gives him a giant bear hug. "I'll be right back. Sit down and relax. Talk to your beautiful wife a while."

Donald glances down at the empty carafes on the table and then leans in to plant a quick kiss on my cheek. "Looks like you two are having a nice time together."

"For sure. Actually we're about to head out. We made appointments for facials."

"I'll ski down with you."

"You don't have to. Why not stay here and enjoy the afternoon with Rob and Scott? Have you guys had lunch yet?"

Donald shakes his head and frowns.

"What's the matter?"

"Nothing. Everything's fine. I didn't think you liked Lindsay."

"Now that I've gotten to know her, she's not a bad person. She's fun." I can even sort of understand why Donald is attracted to her. Then, feeling a tad sly, I add, "And she's really easy to talk to."

The sunbeams are bouncing around in the fresh powder as we step out of the lodge and Lindsay and I look at each other with why-nots gleaming in our eyes. By the time I slide to the bottom of the hill, I'm a born stuntwoman, puffing out my chest proudly as I sashay through the corn and leap small moguls with a single bound. For my big finish, I edge into a show-stopping halt at the bottom, spraying out a respectable rooster. Lindsay has got the hang of her blades too. She skids up to me on one leg in a cowboy'd stance, like she's climbing onto a horse, one leg stuck out sideways on purpose and we give each other high-fisted props as we hand in all the equipment.

What is it about a spa that can make women form unflinching bonds of steadfast devotion? Lindsay and I practically hold hands as we approach the white-coated receptionist. We bend our heads together over the menu of services: page after page of manicures, pedicures, facials, body scrubs, and every kind of primping, rubbing, wrapping, waxing, and plucking procedure a woman could desire. We bow our heads reverently in front of the vast wall racks laden with bottles and tubes and glass pots packed with the rarest muds and salts of the earth, all precisely formulated with extractions of rare herbs and decoctions of roots, and fragranced with delicate infusions of wildflowers from distant alpine meadows and succulents watered by antelopes on the broad plains of Africa. An attendant hands me a package containing thoughtful little Ayurvedic relaxation slippers. We pass through the first threshold to the inner sanctum, where I spy heaped baskets of immaculate fluffy towels.

In the dressing room, we slip out of our weary street clothes. I step into my shower cubicle and an attendant briskly scrubs my back with a loofah using French milled soap specially chosen for my skin type. Mountain spring water, alternating cold, hot, and tepid, bathes every inch of me from nozzles positioned all over the walls and ceiling. Next, we loll in the steam chamber, and then soak in the bubbling hot tub as we await the main event. Finally, our scrubbed and anointed nakedness is enveloped in the softest of robes, and we are led away for the treatments we have chosen.

Lindsay is going for the Himalayan Salt Scrub while I've added the Seaweed Massage to my Steaming Clay Facial (featuring Extracts of 1000 year old Lichen scraped off Precambrian Quartz Crystals, only found in the primest locations of the arctic).

My therapist, Roberto, slathers me with oil and seaweed paste and then slides his muscular, practiced hands all over my body, smoothing away the soreness and transforming me into a greasy green blob of bliss. When he's done, another therapist comes to coat my face and neck with hot mud.

Afterwards Lindsay and I recline on chaise lounges, all steamed, mudded, rubbed, tubbed, exfoliated and defoliated, sipping flutes of Sparkling Elderflower water, sighing and loving being silky-faced women of the sisterhood.

"I don't ever want to leave," I say while admiring my flawless manicure.

"Me neither." Lindsay looks over at me. "When do you have to go home?"

"Day after tomorrow."

"So soon?"

"I have the kids and work. It took a lot of wrangling to get a few days out here."

"I thought you'd want to spend a few more days in Calgary, you know, do a little house hunting."

"House hunting? We're not moving to Calgary."

Lindsay is quiet for a minute. My mind begins to refoliate.

"Why would we move to Calgary? I thought Donald's assignment was finishing in a couple of months?"

"Yes it is. But Donald can stay on here if he likes; I mean there's always the option now that the branch is established."

"Donald never mentioned that to me."

"I guess that means he isn't interested. I wouldn't worry about it."

"I'm not worried."

Lindsay sits up to inspect her pedicure. "What do you think of this color? I wasn't sure if I should go with the green or the peach."

"Why are you trying to change the subject?"

"Perhaps I spoke out of turn. Donald loves Calgary. I know how he feels, that's all."

"I like that you know how he feels and I don't."

"We work together and we're friends. He's alone out here. Sometimes we talk about things."

As she leans over her toenails, her towel slips down and I notice she has a tramp stamp arcing across her butt crack. I've never seen such intricate handwork. I can make out intertwined flowers, a pair of eagles and the words: *carpe diem*. I can't help but wonder if Donald has ever had a chance to examine her ink too. My head fills with a picture of Donald reading her ass as he takes up the rear guard.

If I had a shotgun in my hands right now, her flowery ass-gulls would be cratered with buckshot.

"Maybe you could fill me in on a few more of my husband's thoughts and feelings?"

Lindsay jumps up from her chaise and clamps her hands on her hips. "I think it's time to go."

Seize the day indeed. Before I can stop myself, the words tumble out: "Are you and Donald having an affair?"

She looks at me straight on, woman to woman, eyeball to eyeball: "I never have love affairs with co-workers, Pauline. Your husband is a good guy. He loves you. Let it go."

As I slip back into my clothes, I mull over her statements. Donald's a good guy. Donald loves me. Donald never slept with Lindsay.

Wait a minute: Lindsay didn't say she never slept with him, she only said she doesn't have *love* affairs with co-workers. And why would she admit anything to me, anyway? She's blowing butterflies out of her ass again. I don't know what to believe anymore. But, even if that last one is a lie, two out of three ain't bad. And after all, in that whole equation, there's one more critical factor: Pauline slept with Michael.

At the front desk, I pull out my wallet. The receptionist says, "Your bill has already been settled, Ms. Parril. Ms. Bambraugh took care of everything. She left this for you." She hands me a folded piece of paper.

Pauline: I have a date tonight and I'm running late. I called a cab for you but it's also a nice walk back to the chalet if you prefer. I had soooo much fun with you today. It was awesome to have the chance to get to know you. L.

I stare down at the familiar handwriting, sprinkled with those dumb little circles over the 'i's, and I remember the time I found a business card, many moons ago, under my bed, before Michael, before I got into this whole sticky mess. I remember word for word what it said: *Thanks for lunch. Let's do it again soon. L xo.*

Donald never mentioned that lunch. Which is odd because he always liked to recount his stomach's wanderings of the day.

I stuff the paper in my pocket, and push through the doors back out onto the street. I give the cab driver a generous tip and send him away. A walk in the cold air will help to clear my head.

Donald's a good guy. Donald loves me. He sent me a diamond pendant for Christmas. On Christmas morning we skyped Donald into the living room so he could watch the kids open their presents. When they were all done, I opened the little blue velvet box. I feigned excitement as Serenity fastened the clasp. I'm not really a diamonds kind of girl. Diamonds make me think of foreign mines filled with black-lunged miners sweating away in the dark and having to eat coal dust sandwiches from tin pails. Donald knows that. Or at least he should've known it. Offscreen, I tossed the box aside. Mom picked up the box, read the certificate and said, "These are Canadian diamonds."

I snatched up the certificate and, sure enough, Donald had gone out of his way to find guilt-free Canadian diamonds from a decent mine with happy miners who have pensions and a dental plan. Of course it is a fine thing to be dripping with diamonds mined by guys with good teeth.

In all the chaos, I didn't get around to buying a Christmas present for Donald. The guilt floods in. I'm the rotten egg. I better grab something from one of the shops on the way. I scurry along the sidewalk looking in all the windows. A scarf? A jacket? Leather gloves? The stores are closing and I have only a few minutes left to choose something that doesn't look like I grabbed it at the last minute. I run into a men's shop.

The cashier is counting her receipts and shooting me irritated looks. I paw through a display of wallets. I select a nice one and head to the counter, elated that I've skinned under the wire with my gift.

I glance at the price tag—and stop short in the middle of the aisle. Mr. Frugal Man will think I'm out of my melon for wasting so much dough on a wildly overpriced wallet. I better not mention it.

The cashier is tapping her pencil on the counter. My head clears. Donald doesn't want a wallet. He doesn't expect anything. He's not like that. He's just glad I'm here. I should've known.

I put the wallet back and walk out of the store. I know what I'm giving Donald for Christmas: me, just me, wearing nothing but my glowing spa skin and a diamond pendant.

CHAPTER 26

Deception Story

Deception Story: A scenario that outlines the friendly actions that will be portrayed to cause the deception target to adopt the desired perception.
—Department of Defense Dictionary of Military and Associated Terms

"I have a surprise for you," Donald says after he pays for our meal at the legendary Full Angus, Calgary's most exclusive prime rib restaurant. "But we have to hurry and catch a cab."

"Sure," I murmur. I'm busy free falling through a serotonin rush from the richest chocolate mousse I've ever tasted, and I'm still shimmering from last night. Donald loved his Christmas present: he threw it down on the bed and ravished it all night long.

After breakfast we said goodbye to Todd, Tina, Rob and Scott, and drove back to Calgary. Lindsay was nowhere to be seen. Donald showed me around the branch offices, and then announced that he wanted to buy me a dressy outfit so he could whirl me around for a night on the town. Thank God the airline lost my luggage. I now possess a lusty little skirt and the perfect blouse and heels to go with.

Donald pulls back my brass-studded leather chair and helps me with my coat. He sure knows how to be suave and urbane for a night on the town. He even knew the chef. And, as it turns out, western chefs know their beef. My hips will know their beef, too, unless I stand down from all this holiday eating.

A few minutes later, the cabbie drops us on the sidewalk in front of the Calgary Tower. Donald swoops his arm up to point at the flame burning at the top. "It has a 360° observation deck with a glass floor. It's the best way to view the city at night. So? Are you ready for your private tour?"

"Donald, this is incredible! How did you manage to arrange it?"

"Our chief accountant out here plays golf with the guy who owns this place. He said anytime I wanted to come up ..."

After a quick ID check at the front desk, we are in the elevator ascending at high speed. I step forward to check my hair in the mirror and spy Donald watching me from behind. I stick out my tongue at him and he flashes me his Scotsman's grin, reminding me why I fell in love with him back in the day. He's always had the rogue charm of a highlander about him. Tonight he's looking very much like William Wallace in his best wool kilt with the Prince Charlie jacket and three-button vest. He knows I love it when he pulls out all the Scottish stops. I feel his hands steal onto my hips and he pulls me closer to him so I can feel his Gaelic sap rising. I nudge my rump back and forth a few times to show my appreciation for the compliment. A blush mounts my cheeks, on both ends. Donald is getting me a bit ... warm. The elevator guy studiously looks the other way as we sway together with the motion of the lift until the doors glide open at the top of the tower. The elevator guy steps back to let us pass and, tipping his cap, disappears as the doors slide closed, leaving us alone in the darkness on the observation deck.

Donald takes my hand and leads me around the deck so I can view the entire skyline. Stepping gingerly onto the glass catwalk, I'm mesmerized by the feeling of being suspended in mid-air.

It's magical. The sky is clear and I can see mountains and prairies and the whole city of Calgary twinkling like a brilliant diamond at my feet. Even from high above the ground I can feel the surging pulse of the place. Everywhere you go here, there are energetic people filled with purpose. They're busy making deals, going places and making their way in a new frontier. This city is so youthful and exciting; it makes me want to take over a conglomerate or file an injunction or at least go shopping at Aritzia.

Donald wraps his arms around me from behind. His kilt is bulging. He leans his head forward and breathes into my ear while running his hands up to my breasts and squeezing them greedily: "How would you like to join the Calgary Tower Club?"

Oh. That's why he wore his kilt tonight.

"What? Here? No. No! You're nuts. What's with you men and the whole let's get frisky in public places thing?"

I look down below my feet to the traffic far below us. "The whole city could be watching."

"The city will be jealous. C'mon, you know you want to." Donald has his hand under my skirt and is tugging my panties down. He has a point here. I'm wearing a skirt. And high heels. Isn't that the whole notion behind skirts and high heels?

Silently, I step out of my panties and drop them on the catwalk.

My CT club card is issued in about a minute and a half. Sometimes fast is good. My butt cheeks nearly froze off while he had his fun. I smooth my skirt back down and rub my buttocks to get some circulation going again while Donald leans on the window sill, huffing—the air is thin up here. He could be getting too old to play mile-high games.

This public places thing could spark revitalization for Donald and me. If I were game for the club plan, he'd follow me to the ends of the earth. I'm thinking Burj Dubai. I'm thinking Space Needle. The Golden Gate Bridge. Oooh—The Kremlin! I'm thinking my red leather skirt teamed with a black leather jacket would be perfect for Lenin's Mausoleum.

Donald leans in closer to kiss me on the lips and stare into my eyes with a limpid gaze of gratitude. "What are you thinking about?"

"Moscow. Now that's a city. We should go there some time. Or San Francisco."

"What about Calgary? How do you like Calgary?"

"I love the energy here. It's crazy, all the building and development and activity going on everywhere, there's so much potential."

"Do you think you'd ever like to live here?"

"Live here? In Calgary?"

"Yeah?"

"I don't know. I've never thought about it." A fissure of suspicion opens and my stomach sinks as if the glass floor dropped out from under me. "Why do you ask?"

Donald squints his eyes and scratches the back of his neck. "I've been offered a directorship here."

"What about the deal where they promised you a directorship at home, after you finished up with things here?"

"That was never a firm deal. We were tossing around the ideas. They're offering me Calgary."

"You didn't tell me it wasn't a firm deal."

"Didn't I?"

I can feel my face growing hot. Donald is a big fat liar. "No you didn't. You said Calgary was a temporary position. And now you tell me all this time you've been thinking about staying in Canada permanently?"

"I've been thinking about it, yes, but if you don't want to come out here, I'm prepared to come back. But I'd have to go back to my old job, at least until something opens up in the New England region."

By the look on his face, I can tell Donald would rather dig his eyeballs out with a fork and eat them with ketchup than go back to his old job. I don't like this game. It's a standoff where one of us has to give up a sizable chunk of territory. My territory includes our children, our home, the bookstore, my Mom, my friends, and New England: everything I'm familiar with. His territory means he gets to pursue his career. It always boils down to this in the end: his career. It's more important than me, the kids or anything else in Donald's life.

"I don't think you're prepared to come home at all. I think you want to stay out here in the worst way."

Donald turns his head away from me and stares out toward the Saddledome. No man can do that without a look of utter pathos and longing. I look down at the traffic crawling through the city center under my feet. I can hear horns honking way up here above the ground. Calgary is nothing but men in silly black hats racing around in sports cars, clawing and scratching at each other's throats to get

the biggest deal. I don't like being asked to make this choice. If I say
no, he gets to pout forever. If I say yes, I get cowpats, tumbleweeds,
and cold beer signs on every corner.

"So what about Lindsay? What are they doing with her?"

"I don't know. Lindsay is still looking after things out here. She's
spending most of her time running the international development portfolio these days. They could still offer her the New England directorship."

"I thought you said she wasn't interested."

"She hasn't decided yet."

For a long moment I stand there, thinking. My first thought is
that it is terribly ironic that my marriage is resting in Lindsay's hands.
Then I realize it is in Donald's hands, far more than Lindsay's. He
doesn't have to wait for Lindsay to decide what she wants. If he wants
to come home, he will. But he wants the promotion. He wants me to
drop my whole life and move to Canada. But what about Serenity,
Jack, and Olympia? And Mom? And Shae and Jude? And Bibienne
and Bernie and Mackie and Furious Ferris and, what the hell, Wendy,
Yard, Johnny Rotten, and Ghostly Garth?

What am I saying? My marriage is in my own hands. I want to
open my palms and turn them upside down.

"No." I take a deep breath. "You don't have the right to hold this
job offer over my head. You say you're prepared to come home? You
make it sound like you're prepared to serve out your sentence. If
that's the case, forget it. You have to decide what you want. But you
don't get to come back and make me feel miserable because you don't
want to be there. If you come home, come home because you want to
be with me, and the kids. If you decide to stay, you're on your own.
Because I will never, ever live here."

Donald's jaw tightens and his eyes point straight at me like pistols
at high noon. Calgary is truly the new frontier for both of us.

Donald drops me at the airport first thing in the morning. We are
barely speaking. The jetlag kicks in before I even step on the plane
so I'm grateful for the wheelchair. I wonder how long a bogus heart

condition can lurk on a person's profile? That detail coupled with the Porta-Potty incident means I'll probably never be able to leave the country again.

I'm also wondering if my luggage will make it back east? I bet some baggage handler in Los Angeles is loading my stuff onto a transcontinental jumbo jet right this minute. One little white lie and the bad karma flings my luggage into the wild blue for eternity.

Mom is standing at the gate as I come swinging through. "Where are your bags? Didn't you have two nice red ones?"

"They're probably in Hong Kong."

I follow her to the car, sling my carry-on into the back seat, and take over the wheel. "How did everything go?"

"Very well. Serenity and Shae were a big help. You look tired."

"I am."

"So what exactly is going on between you and Donald?"

They need to put my mother in charge of locating my luggage. This woman is the find-all, see-all, know-all sage of the whole freaking universe.

"What makes you think there's something going on?"

"Nothing."

"You snooped around didn't you? You found something?"

"Now what would there be to find?" Her eyes narrow and she spins her head around to pin me. Fail. I've tipped her off. Stupid, stupid, stupid.

"Is there someone else, Pauline?"

Boy, is she cagey. Did she find a stray note tucked in a book or did I just give myself away? I never could outshuffle her in this dance as a teenager and I guess I never will.

"Donald and I had a major disconnect last night. He wants us to relocate to Calgary. I said no."

"I'm sorry, honey." She falls silent and looks out the window. "You can't blame him. Canada was his first home, after all."

"But Massachusetts is our home now. Aren't *we* his family? Besides, I don't think that's the reason. He wants a promotion. He'd go anywhere to get one."

She looks back at me. "Is that it? Or is there more to the story?"

"We haven't been good for a long time. I think he was unfaithful to me. He's never admitted it but the signs are all there."

"And what about you? And that friend of yours at the university? How serious is that?"

I heave a sigh.

"Don't give up on Donald. He's a good man."

The traffic light ahead turns red. I stop, and stare at the rear bumper of the car in front of us. Mom is Donald's biggest fan. I've always suspected that she set me up to meet him when Serenity was only 5 years old. I had moved in with my parents for a few months, to get back on my feet after the divorce. One Friday afternoon after work, I strolled into the house to see Donald, wedged tightly between Mom, Dad and Serenity at the dining room table. His crisp white shirtsleeves were rolled up to the elbows, revealing a pair of nicely-shaped forearms. All of the tips of his fingers were capped with Serenity's finger puppets. His face serious and intent, he pointed the orange giraffe at a brochure on the table. While my father leaned in the scan the brochure, Donald paused, and turned with a smile to nod the lion puppet at Serenity with the index finger on his other hand. "Roar," he said, gently.

"Roar," I said to announce my presence.

Donald looked up, startled. "I better get going," he said, glancing at his watch.

"No, I want you to stay," shrieked Serenity.

Mom set a tray on the table. "You can't go yet, I just made you a sandwich. Bill, why don't you pour Donald a beer?" She turned to face me. "Pauline, this is Donald Daley, our financial advisor."

Serenity ran over to me, grabbed my hand in her small chubby one, and determinedly dragged me across the kitchen. "Mommy, you and Donald have to hold hands," she said, trying to force my hand into his.

Without removing the puppets, Donald shook my hand with a firm grip. "I've heard a lot about you." By the time he let go of my hand, I could feel my cheeks flushing.

A horn honks behind me, breaking my reverie. The traffic light has turned green.

Mom speaks up again: "Young people these days won't shoulder through. They give up so easily. In my time, men and women had affairs too, you know. We knew better than to throw away our marriages for a fling."

I glance over at her. She's looking down at her lap.

"Your father was away on temporary duty a lot."

"You had an affair?"

She ignores me and smiles. Then she laughs out loud. "I sure knew a lot of gals who did. There were always these jokes going around. That propping up the red Tide box in the basement window is a sign your man is away on deployment and the coast is clear."

"I use liquid detergent."

"Don't be flip. I loved your father very much. But we had our ups and downs. He wasn't exactly an angel on all those deployments you know."

"So what happened to your girlfriends? The ones with the Tide boxes?"

"Some of them got divorces. Some stuck it out."

She looks out the window again and we drive along in silence. "You need to take that dog of yours to the vet. I saw his, you know, poo; it has all these grainy bits in it. He has worms. Worms are easily transmitted, especially among children who don't know how to wash their hands properly. I showed Jack and Olympia the right way while you were away."

A few minutes after I get home, the phone rings. It's Donald.

"Your bags turned up here this morning, after we left for the airport. The courier dropped them off with the concierge. He just brought them up."

"Your concierge brought them up? My bags are in your apartment? Right now?"

No, this can't be happening. Donald is now in witless possession of every x-rated love note Michael ever wrote to me. Not to mention the photo albums. I sag against the kitchen counter, heart thrashing around in my chest. If I didn't have a heart condition before this trip, I surely do now. I can feel my brain emptying as the blood backwashes out of my head and pools in my legs. With no blood left to float thoughts around my cranium, I can't think. So I start babbling: "But, but … I don't understand. I called the luggage guy yesterday and told him to redirect my bags back here."

"Obviously they made a mistake. But don't worry, I already called the airline and they're going to send the courier back to pick them up. So you should have your stuff in a couple of days. It's just as well. You left a jacket and a scarf in the hall closet. I'll stick them in one of your bags."

Oh no. No. No, no, no, no, no. Holy suitcases packed with doom, Batgirl. What on earth will I do? I can't tell him to keep his snout out of my bags or he will for sure wonder why, and look in both, out of curiosity. I can feel my intestines looping themselves into a noose formation, just in time for the hangman who is riding toward me at a full gallop. All I can say is a weak, "Thanks Donald." I have a 50/50 chance that he'll open the wrong suitcase, a 50/50 chance that I'm going to turn into a pillar of salt before the end of the day. In fact, now that my blood has stopped in its tracks, I can feel my veins crusting over already.

For the rest of the day, every time the phone rings, my intestines form another clove hitch. I have so many knots in my bowels, I'll be lucky if one grain of the single bite of fried rice I managed to swallow at dinner makes it past the first bend. As for me, by the first light of dawn, after thrashing about under the covers in sleepless turmoil all night, I've officially gone beyond the bend. Robotically,

I get up, shower, and dress for work. If he doesn't call soon, I better brace myself for a communication from his lawyer before the end of the week.

Three more days crawl by and finally Donald surfaces. His voice is unfriendly, and he only wants to talk to the kids. I can't tell if his frosty tone is due to the cold war stance we've adopted since the Battle of Calgary Tower or if his curtness represents the first shot over the bow in an all out declaration of war. Before I hand the receiver over to Jack, I tell Donald that the suitcases arrived this morning. I didn't describe how I felt as I opened the innocent bag first to find, while gasping air into my lungs for what felt like the first time in a week, the jacket and scarf neatly folded and set atop my sweaters, jeans, and brand new just-in-case silk teddy.

CHAPTER 27

Hardstand

Hardstand: A paved or stabilized area where vehicles are parked.
—Department of Defense Dictionary of Military and Associated Terms

Valentine's Day is coming up. I wouldn't have noticed except that Jude decided to recreate Amsterdam's red light district in the storefront windows complete with scarlet lamp, velvet curtains, and an empty chair. Our front book table is piled high with books on erotica and all things lusty. Meanwhile, my own boudoir is darkened and dusty.

Everywhere there are lacy reminders of the day for lovers. I jerk my shopping cart past the card section at the grocery store, which is spammed thick with pink and red heart cards. No cards are coming for me this year. Tucked away in my bedside drawer is a collection of beautiful cards from Donald. Every birthday and Valentine's Day, he always picked out the laciest, most syrupy sweet cards he could find.

Donald and I haven't spoken in weeks. I stare at the display wondering if there are any appropriate valentine's cards for absentee husbands? All the cards have honeyed messages. None say "You Can Be My Valentine, But Only If You Stop Being a Prick."

I can detect a river of lacy red bile rising in my chest. Who invented the cruelty of Valentine's Day? There's a young woman standing beside me perusing cards. I suppress the urge to warn her off by explaining the utter futility of the whole exercise. Instead I continue reading the verses in search of something friendly and benign. What do I want to say with my card? Why am I thinking of buying Donald a card in the first place? Because we've always exchanged cards? Because skipping the card feels so final?

Where's the card featuring a bouquet of red hearts with festering stab wounds? I haven't heard from Michael either, but that's no surprise. He said I had to decide. How do I decide? Do I even have a choice when it comes to Donald? Ever since New Year's we have stood but one short stomp from Splittsville. All it will take is for one or the other of us to fling the first load of divorce papers on the other's head. Who is going to make the first move?

Bibienne calls me at work: She needs an Emergency Girl's Night Out. "The Greek place. I need to have a look at some real men."

John the Greek God leads us to our favorite booth, we slip into our seats, and Bibienne clasps his hand in hers and says imploringly, "Red, please. A carafe."

"Who wants to go first?"

"I do. Bernie is such an idiot. He insisted on climbing up onto the roof yesterday to try to shovel off some of the snow and get this: he slipped and managed to fall through the skylight onto our bed. A piece of the glass punctured the waterbed so now we need a new skylight and a new bed. Him and his hippie shit 70's waterbed. He picked it up at a garage sale. True story. I've been sleeping in a garage sale bed for the past 15 years. Why do I put up with his crap? At least now we can finally buy a real mattress and box spring. I ordered one of those Swedish memory foam mattresses." Her eyes go soft and dreamy.

"I hear those are fantastic. Very expensive. I'm already jealous."

"I know. Plus the water ruined the carpeting so we have to renovate the entire bedroom. We might as well have the roof reshingled when we replace the skylight. Yesterday, I had a few inches of snow on the roof. Today, I have to sleep in the bathtub. I can't even afford to buy a lousy glass of wine."

John, who has arrived to fill our glasses, almost stops pouring. "Good thing you drink good Greek wine then. No lousy."

"That's for sure." Bibi grabs her glass, tilts it into her mouth and smiles at him. "You're so pretty."

He lays a plate of hummus dip and pita wedges on the table: "You like the dip. Is Greek. Very nice," he murmurs while looking straight down Bibienne's shirtfront. He smiles at the girls and Bibienne leans forward a little more to show them off before he minces away.

"Is Bernie alright?"

"He'll be off work for a week or two. He has whiplash. We were in the ER until 3 a.m. while they ran him through a bunch of x-rays. The stupid fool. Who gets whiplash from falling off a roof? Now I have to nurse him and he expects me to give him massages. Why does all the stupid stuff have to happen to me?"

"Believe me, I know, I know." I top up our glasses from the carafe.

"I swear if you put the divorce papers under my nose right this minute I would sign off in a flash."

"But you and Bernie are so good together. You can't split up. The rest of the human race is counting on you. If you guys can't make it …"

"Are you kidding? That man drives me insane. He always dresses like he's lost a bet. And he never listens to me. I told him to stay the hell off the roof. So what does he do? He had to go up there. He was all obsessed with the snow. He heard snow can cause roof damage. Yeah, well, now we know what really causes roof damage. Idiots."

John comes back to drop off another basket of pita bread and take our order. Every time that man looks at me, I feel like my breasts just grew another size and tumbled out of my shirt to be worshiped by his Hellenic eyes. "I'll have the moussaka."

Bibienne fluffs her hair, and orders gyros in a tone of voice that suggests she'd like to get naked on a sailboat with him and suck on his toes. He turns and walks away taking his Apollonian tush with him. Bibienne lets out a sigh. "You have no idea how much I envy you. I wish Bernie would go to Calgary for a few months. Or China. For a few years."

"You envy me? I haven't slept a minute since the bag fiasco," I say to Bibienne while dozing a pita wedge through a pile of hummus.

"How come?"

"My jacket coming home in the good bag doesn't mean I'm off the hook."

"How do you figure?"

"He still might have looked in the bad bag."

"You think he looked in the bad bag but is pretending he only looked in the good bag? Why would he do that?"

"He might be biding his time while he figures out what to do."

"Which might be?"

"It depends. Donald can be *laissez-faire* when he wants to be. Maybe he's playing it cool."

Bibi shakes her head. "*Laissez-faire*? I think you mean *savoir-faire*. And that sort of thing only happens in Paris and New York. This is New England."

"Yeah but if he and Lindsay had an affair, he could be feeling guilty."

"True. Did the bad bag look touched in any way?"

"Hard to tell but there might be a couple of missing photos. There were empty spots in the albums before but I think there are more now."

"Maybe the photos fell out."

"I might have torn up a few of the crappier shots of me."

Which reminds me: I don't remember seeing the wayward boob photo when I checked the albums. Donald could easily exact a decisive revenge by posting that puppy on the Internet.

"I'm so screwed."

Bibienne reaches across the table and lays her hand on my arm. "Seriously, what's going on with you? Have you heard anything from Michael?"

"No. We haven't talked since Christmas. He said it's up to me to call him. He wants me to decide. Him or Donald."

"Have you?"

"No. I don't think I have a choice anymore. I don't think Donald wants me to come out to Calgary. And he doesn't want to come home."

"Are you sure about that?"

"No."

"Why don't you ask him? What have you got to lose?"

I sigh.

"Wait," Bibienne says reaching into her bag. "I almost forgot to give you this." She hands me a small package wrapped in red tissue. "Happy Valentine's Day."

I tear off the wrap to find a deck of tarot cards. Bibienne's face is bright.

"You finished them." I jump up to hug her. "Congratulations."

She takes a deep breath. "I had 500 decks printed. Wish me luck."

I sit back down. Bibienne points at the top of the deck. "Look."

It's the Queen of Cups. I remember how Bibienne said she was thinking of me when she drew her. She still looks like me. She's still standing on the stone bridge holding her precious cup, trying not to spill a drop. So much water has run under her feet since the last time I saw her.

I flip through the rest of the cards, studying the images. Each card and card combination offers a million angles, interpretations, suggestions.

I pause at The Emperor. I once thought that card was Donald. Now, I'm not so sure. Maybe Donald was buried in the deck that day. Maybe we both were. Suddenly I know: There are no answers here, just questions. What is feared? What is being avoided? What is true and what is an illusion? Pretty as they are, the cards are merely paper and ink. The wisdom and insight belongs to the holder of the cards.

Bibienne smiles and says, "It's a longstanding tradition that a tarot deck should come to the owner as a gift."

"Thanks, Bib. This is a beautiful gift."

Bibienne taps the face of The Emperor with her fingernail. "Maybe it's time to lay your cards on the table."

It's late when I get home and climb the stairs for bed. I prop Bibienne's tarot deck inside my Tibetan Singing Bowl, which rests on my bedstand: the first thing I see in the morning and the last thing I see at night. It's singing its sad little song about ultimatums, commitments, and decisions.

I climb into bed and snap off the light. My eyes refuse to close. Decisions, decisions. What do I want? One thing is certain: I want sleep. I haven't slept in weeks. Either I go to the doctor tomorrow, and get a prescription for sleeping pills, or I make up my mind.

My shoulder is itchy. I scratch, remembering Guru Greg. What was it he said? *Some things we can't change. Whatever it is, better to accept it.*

Accept it. I can do that. Maybe I can't change the situation but I can change the way I respond to it.

I scratch harder, scraping my nails into the skin until it hurts. Maybe I need to do something I haven't done for a long time. Like tell the truth.

Bibienne's words come back to me: *What have you got to lose?*

What if I lay all my cards on the table? Bibi's right. If Donald and I have any chance at all, we have to start with honesty.

Sitting up, I grope for my phone on the nightstand. I text a message to Donald in the dark: *I have something to tell you.* I press send.

I had an affair. My finger hovers on the key. Send.

It's over now. Send.

What can I add to this? That I regret that I made such a mess of things? That I didn't think I would get in so deep? That I didn't think at all? That I'm sorry for hurting Donald, Michael, and myself? And the kids? That I'm sorry that I'm such a fool?

I'm sorry. Send.

I lie awake all night and check my phone for messages every ten minutes. Nothing comes back.

CHAPTER 28

Impact Area

Impact Area: An area having designated boundaries within the limits of which all ordnance will detonate or impact.—Department of Defense Dictionary of Military and Associated Terms

Exhausted, I stumble into work, resolved to turn off my cell for the morning while I tackle inventory. There's plenty to distract me today since Wednesday is Mom's Morning. Serenity's pregnancy has been a boon for sales in the baby book section lately. She's like some kind of crazy magnet for all the expectant moms in town.

The Moms all troop in, bellies bulging, and sit at the back eating apple-bran muffins, discussing the best diapering methods and perusing the dog-eared baby name finder that Serenity leaves on the counter as a free service. She set up a small crib and filled it with books to share, on a leave-a-book, take-a-book honor system. Every service agency in town comes in to drop off pamphlets on everything from breastfeeding to free growth charts. Whenever they visit, the agencies order books for their own libraries. And Serenity has turned into a fountain of useful information. She has read every baby-related book in print, and knows which lead-filled pacifiers have been recalled and where to buy the cutest booties.

Wearily, I begin shelving books. Mommy Rotten crashes through the door with JR. In a loud voice she announces, to the apple bran group, "O. M. G. I can't believe it. I'm pregnant. My doctor told me that I could get cancer from smoking and taking birth control pills at the same time. So I stopped taking the pill. Now look at me." She lifts her shirt to show a bulge and then starts pawing through the crib for her free book. JR grabs a muffin, picks all the blueberries out, and throws them on the floor.

At lunch I run to my cell and turn it on. Nothing from Donald but there's a message from Michael: "Meet me at the Dingy Cup. I need to tell you something."

I grab my coat, leaving Serenity in charge.

On the way over, I wonder what it might be. Has he gone back to his wife? Found a new lover? Is over me? All of the above?

I enter the bar and spy him at the back, sitting at our favorite table, the one where we first met to talk about books and canoodle the afternoons away. He's reading a book and doesn't see me come in. There is still something about him that melts my heart into a puddle but at this moment I know I can't keep on.

It's a deep down knowing, an unwordable word knowing. I love Michael, but we won't survive. By the time I get to the table I have my speech ready. I sit down and blurt it out straight away before I can change my mind: "I love you, Michael. But you need a woman who will adore you. You know I'm not the adoring type."

Michael nods. I put my hand on his. "I told Donald about us. I still love him, but I don't think he's coming home now. That doesn't change anything between you and me. I can't start over with you, or anyone, just now. Not with Jack and Olympia and Serenity and the baby coming. I hope you understand."

I sit back hoping Michael won't make a scene or cry or shout at me. I deserve it. I am a terrible person to be crushing his beautiful soul this way.

Instead, Michael's face breaks into a radiant smile of relief. "I'm glad you feel that way about us because I've made a decision, too. I went on a two-week silent retreat in January and something powerful happened. I came back to tell you and make all the arrangements." He pauses and looks at me as if trying to gauge my reaction.

"It's okay, go ahead, you can tell me."

"I'm going away again, this time for an extended silent retreat. At least six months."

"Six months? Why so long?"

"That's not long, relatively. There are people who go into silent retreats for years. There're even dark retreats where you spend the time in total darkness."

"So you're going to live in a cave in India?"

"No, no. No caves. I'm staying in a heated cabin. In the country. There's a small hermitage in upstate New York called the Diamond Mountain Center. It's mostly for aspirants and students. Guru Greg is going to be my teaching advisor. Carmen is okay with it. And when I get back, Nick will come live with me for six months."

"You're planning to become a monk, aren't you?"

"Not necessarily. I've always wanted to go deeper into my practice. Now's a good time for me, that's all. I've been looking for answers in all the wrong places. All those years of research, reading and studying. I thought you might be the answer. Turns out, you were an amazing question."

What does he mean, I'm an amazing question? Whatever, it sounds cool.

Michael continues. "I finally figured out that I have to look inside. I need time to do that."

Michael is going to become a monk. In a way, I've known it all along.

He grins at me. "You finally admitted it. You love me. I knew it all along."

"Shut up."

We sit in a comfortable silence for a few minutes, smiling at each other. I'm trying to picture Michael with a shaved head wearing a saffron robe. Wait, no, saffron is the Hare Krishna's thing. The Benedictines are dark brown with a rope. The Dalai Lama has an attractive red robe.

"What color is your robe going to be?"

"Robes are worn by ordained monks only."

"But if you do get ordained, what color would you get?"

"Yellow." He looks at me and sighs. "Cotton."

"Nice," I say. Even without his long curly hair, Michael is going to be a very handsome monk.

Michael leans over the table and looks into my eyes. "I think you did the right thing, telling Donald. Are you alright?"

"Thanks. Yeah, I'm okay. Well, maybe not so okay, but I'll manage. I'll just have to keep going."

"How're things going at the store?"

"I'm starting to get the hang of the book business. But I've decided I'm going to turn the shop over to Serenity eventually. It's really her store. She loves it."

"Then what are you going to do?"

"I'll still help out. With the baby and everything. Serenity is going to need a lot of extra hands. But beyond that, you know, I want to finish my degree. And then maybe grad school."

Grad school? Where did that come from? That's the first time that idea ever occurred to me. It's a good thought. "I was also thinking of starting a communist cell."

On the way home it strikes me: if Michael is going to be a monk, I wonder what I might have driven Donald to? CEO of a major corporation?

Wendy wants to host a surprise baby shower for Serenity. By host she means have it at my house. I set the date, extended the invitations, cleaned the place and supplied the food. I even birthed the guest of honor. Wendy said she "will do the rest." When she gets here. She's running late.

Meanwhile I'm Wendy-Pauline, dipping and soaring all over the house, putting clean hand towels in the bathroom, adding ice to the punch and mopping up the spill Olympia made when she sampled the punch.

Wendy's guests are due any minute, and Shae is upstairs doing her maximum to keep Serenity from coming downstairs into the living room where Jack and Olympia have been decorating. Olympia is building a diaper mountain by taping together a pile of disposables with masking tape and Jack is making balloon animals. He wanted me to make the balloon animals but I ran out of racetrack. I suggested he make balloon worms, or maybe some pregnant balloon worms.

As soon as I say this, Olympia wants to know how worms get pregnant. Jack shows her by humping a green worm and an orange worm across the living room. Charmed, Olympia grabs a yellow and red pair, and soon the living room is writhing and humping in a colorful worm balloon orgy. I'm sure this idea will go over big at the next birthday party she goes to.

Disaster strikes when Olympia's yellow balloon worm pops. She runs upstairs shrieking. I hurry after her to console her as the doorbell bongs. "Get the door, Jack," I call.

I find Olympia in Serenity's room. Serenity is wearing purple pajama bottoms tucked under her belly and a tiny Mars Volta t-shirt. Shae is drawing an elaborate graffiti design on Serenity's bump with temporary tattoo markers. She has written, "Hello my name is …" Shae hands Olympia a neon green inkpen and points at her broad canvas: "You can color in the H." Serenity giggles as the tip of the marker scribbles across her skin.

Good, solid grown-up fun could be had with those markers. Trouble is I have no one to play graffiti with me now.

I race back downstairs to find Wendy twirling around in the living room. She has sprinkled a ton of heart confetti and pink glitter over every surface, including the side tables, the chairs and the carpet. Some is floating in the punch. "It's so close to Valentine's, I decided we should do a Valentine's theme," she squeals.

Winter static is causing the confetti to stand on end and leap straight at me as I cross the floor. I must look disgruntled as I pick bits of confetti from the chip dip as she shouts, "Don't worry, confetti is easy to clean up."

Bibienne arrives carrying a cake. "There's, like, a ton of confetti all over your walkway and doorsteps."

I turn to glare at Wendy.

"I'll vacuum it up later," she cries and runs back outside to her car.

"We don't need any more confetti," I yell after her.

"What games have you got planned?" Bibienne asks me.

Games? When I was expecting Serenity, my party consisted of drinking games since my friends were all enlisted gals and a baby shower is as good an excuse as any other day. They stayed sober long enough to stick a gooey paper plate on my head. I remember drinking ginger ale and shuddering at the sight of a mountain of bonnets, receiving blankets, and tiny onesies.

I know one thing: if I stick a plate of bows on Serenity's head, she'll rip my face off.

It's too late to google shower games; the doorbell is bonging again and the guests are arriving. Mackie arrives with a bottle of champagne, and she and Bibienne and I watch from the door of the living room. A girl with braces is telling everyone that she drove over here in her dad's car as she passed her driver's license today, and she only hit the curb once. She looks about 12 years old. I'm tempted to run outside to check my car for dents.

Serenity comes downstairs and lifts up her t-shirt to show them Bump, covered with Shae's graffiti drawings of seahorses, dolphins and a spouting whale. They all squeal and pull out their phones to take pictures of Bump so they can upload them to the Internet.

"Oh God, they all look so young," says Mackie.

"That's because they're so young."

"Are you ready for this?" Bibi asks.

"What? The shower?"

Bibienne shakes her head and looks me straight in the eye.

"Oh. Right. Am I ready for my baby having a baby? I don't know. Some days I think my daughter is hopelessly immature, and completely unprepared for the world. And then other days she surprises me with how smart and resourceful she can be."

Bibienne hugs me. "It'll work out. She's a good kid. We weren't that much older when we got started, remember?"

True. I was 20 when I had Serenity. A lifetime ago. Yesterday.

None of the kids are of legal age so army-style drinking games are out of the question. But I'm more than old enough for combat, and so are Mac and Bib. We go back out to the kitchen where I pop the cork from Mackie's bottle and pour three glasses. "Chin, chin," I say. "A baby shower is as good as any other day."

The kids were all happy with soda pop and pizza, worm balloon games and hanging out. Easy peasy. In a year or so, when the baby turns one, we can run this same party formula all over again.

Serenity loved her gifts. Mom and Brian stopped over and brought over a rocking chair that Brian refinished himself, and I threw in a bassinette filled with swaddling blankets. Jude's friends all gave the cutest little girly outfits while the girls all gave toy cars and trucks.

"No dolls," Serenity warned us all in advance. "And no pink ponies."

"Are you sure you're having a girl?" asked Bibienne as she surveyed a set of pink Matchbox racecars.

"Only unless it's a boy," said Jude.

Serenity is adamant. "It's a girl. I'm craving orange juice. And I did the wedding ring test."

"But you aren't married. Maybe it doesn't count," said Wendy.

"Does too. We used Shae's silver skull ring."

"Why not just get a blood test?" asked Mackie.

Serenity shrugged dismissively. "It's a girl."

At that moment George limped into the room and everyone rang in with their opinions on George's paw.

Jude thinks it's allergies while Wendy thinks maybe George has scurvy. Wendy had scurvy when she was little but her mother used crystals and now she's cured. I was afraid to ask if she meant vitamin C, amethysts, or crack.

"Maybe it's early onset arthritis," suggested Bibienne.

"But George is barely two years old," I said.

"Osteo issues aren't unheard of in a young animal."

She went on to say that if I plug him with glucosamine now, I may be able to delay, for a couple of years anyway, the inevitable hip dysplasia that comes with arthritic pets. In other words, in a few short years, Bibienne figures I'm going to be carrying George up and down stairs, and supporting his butt when he has to pee and poo.

4 a.m. Serenity is standing beside my bed. "Mom, I feel funny."

I sit up, fast. That's new mom speak for "the baby is coming." This is only the third week of March. Serenity's due date is still a month away but I knew this baby would come early, I knew it. I have a sixth sense for this kind of thing.

I snap on the light and peer at Serenity's face, which is crimped in pain.

"A contraction?"

"No. I don't think so. I don't know. My back hurts like crazy. Wait, it's getting better now." She sighs, and sits on the end of my bed.

"And these pains in your back? How far apart are they?"

"I don't know. They started coming yesterday but now I can't sleep, it hurts too much."

"Where's Shae?"

"I paged her but she isn't answering. She's out plowing. It's snowing again."

"Did you call your midwife?"

"Wait. I have to go to the bathroom."

I run downstairs. The baby is coming! I better alert Bibienne. She said she would watch Jack and Olympia. And Jude. I better call Jude first. Wait, no, I still don't know if Serenity paged the midwife. What's her name again? Wait. First, I should call Mom. And maybe I better try to page Shae again. I wish I could call Donald. It's been a week since I texted him my messages. Nothing came back. It's over.

On the way to the phone, I peer out the window. My car is buried under a plodge of snow. A major clipper blew in last night, and the snow is still falling. I grab a broom and, throwing on my boots and coat, I run outside in my nightgown to sweep snow off the hood of the car. By the time I finish clearing the back window, the front is covered again. I should've grabbed a hat. My legs are freezing off and my hair is frozen solid. The bottom of my nightgown is stiff with snow. Nothing I can do about it though. The baby is coming.

I have to call Bibienne. Or I could run over to her house to wake her, rather than phone over and rouse her whole household.

I struggle through drifts of snow, and wade around to Bibienne's side door. I knock and then knock again, harder. No answer. The door is locked. I think my knees are getting frostbite. I thump on the door with my fist.

Lights come on and the door cracks open as far as the chain will allow.

Bernie stares out at me warily, as if I'm offering him a religious pamphlet. Bibienne and all the kids appear behind Bernie. They're all in their pajamas. The door swings wide; Bernie is clutching a baseball bat. He looks like he would like to use it, even after I tell him the baby is coming.

"Please come quickly, Bibi." I run back out into the storm. As I race down her driveway, my foot hits an icy patch. My gown flies up, and I flip backwards, crunching down hard on my spine. A sickening little twist curls up my discs.

How peaceful and quiet it is to lie in Bibienne's driveway in the middle of the night staring up into a flake-filled sky, bare buttocks pressed to the cold ground. I think I'm supposed to go phone somebody. I remember now: the midwife's name is Janice! *The baby is coming. I have to go call Janice.* I limp back to my driveway to find the car socked in under the snow mountain again.

I better hurry and get changed out of my wet gown and make my phone calls. My tailbone hurts like crazy but there's nothing I can do about it right now. I hobble up the stairs to check on Serenity. She's still in the bathroom, the door is locked and she's moaning. Loudly. I can hear splashing and thumping sounds.

"Don't tell me you're in the bathtub. Are you in the bathtub?"

In a strangled voice she finally answers, "Yes. Where were you?" "Never mind, can you unlock the door?" No response. Silence. She must be having a contraction.

"Are you all right? Have you paged the midwife?" More silence. "Serenity?"

"No," she howls. Then the moaning resumes. Another contraction. That's, like, barely ten seconds apart.

The midwife number must be listed on Serenity's phone. I run down to her room to find the phone and scan through the directory. But which entry is it? It's all coded gobbledygook. There are no entries that could make sense to anyone but Serenity. I find a j on the list and press dial. Jude answers. "Serenity's in labor. Better come now." At last I've done something right.

I run back down the hall and call through the bathroom door: "Hello? I can't figure out which one is your midwife's number." Serenity is still moaning and unable to speak. Unable to speak through a contraction: I know what that means.

It's time to panic.

Fine, I can do that.

"You have to unlock the door," I shout.

It's quiet in the bathroom. "Are you okay in there?"

The door opens and Serenity emerges, dripping wet. She attempts to wrap a bath towel around her belly and says, "What's it like when your water breaks?"

"It's wet when your water breaks." Kind of like how I feel right now. My nightgown is defrosting, and it's a real toss-up who is dripping more water on the floor.

Jack comes out of his bedroom, and steps in the puddle around Serenity and me. Now we all have wet feet. "Why are you two yelling so much? What's going on?" He glares at me. He looks exactly like Donald at this moment.

"The baby is coming. If you want to help, go back to bed."

He goes downstairs instead, making damp amniotic fluid footprints on the stairs, and turns the television on.

Serenity's face is white. I hold up the phone. "We have to call your midwife."

Serenity grabs the phone from my hand, goes into my room and curls up on my bed clutching the phone between her legs. She starts moaning again. I hope she isn't going to give birth on my prized matelassé bedspread. I kneel beside her and attempt to rub her back.

"Harder!"

"I'm pressing as hard as I can." Her phone rings between her legs. "Move your leg a tad, Serenity." I pry the phone out from between her rigid thighs and then her even more rigid fingers. It's Shae. "I paged Janice. Don't worry, I'm on the way."

Serenity grabs the phone, shoves it underneath her ear and bites her lip. Shae must be trying to coach her because she starts screaming into the phone, "Don't tell me to breathe, Shae. Fuck you, Shae, fuck you, I AM breathing. Are you kidding? It hurts!"

A minute later, the doorbell rings but Serenity gloms onto my arm and screams, "Stay with me."

A moment later, Bibienne enters the room shaking snowflakes out of her hair. "Bernie's out there shoveling your drive. But the roads look horrible. I don't think the midwife is going to be able to get through."

Just when I'm about to say, "Can this get any worse?"... the power goes out.

Where the hell is Janice? I grab the cell and scan the directory again. It has to be here. There's a B here. B is for baby. Makes sense. I dial. A sleepy voice answers. It's Wendy. I apologize for waking her. "I was trying to contact Serenity's midwife and"... the exact stupidest thing I could say. "No, wait," I shout, but it's too late. Now Wendy is on her way over to help out.

Bibienne takes over massage duty while I go in search of blankets, candles and flashlights. I have to sneak into Olympia's room to borrow her pink kid flashlight as none of the seven assorted grown-up ones in the emergency storage box have juice.

Serenity doesn't want blankets, candles or a flashlight. She wants me to massage her back again. She complains that Bibienne's hands

are too soft and warm. "I like your hands—they're all cold and bony
and that feels awesome."

I kneel back into position to rub Serenity's back. My own back
is starting to hurt bending over like this. I think my lumbar region
was shortened by a couple of vertebrae during the fall. That's bad
news for anyone who is already short-waisted. As it is, I can never
wear bolero jackets and sagging boobs are the kiss of fashion death
for women like me. This thought reminds me that I'm overdue for a
visit to the bra store.

"Mom!"

Apparently I am slacking off. I have to press harder, harder,
HARDER. I accept Bibienne's offer to rub my back while I work on
Serenity. We all feel like cheering when Shae comes in. "Janice says
she'll meet us at the hospital. We're taking the plow."

Serenity wants me to ride beside her and keep applying the coun-
terpressure. I've had no time to change, which means I'm heading
to the hospital wearing a soaking wet flannel nightdress, my hockey
jacket and boots with no socks. So what? Won't be the first time.

Halfway to the hospital Serenity turns to Shae and says, "Wait!
Turn around! We forgot the birthing bag."

Oh yes, now I remember, Serenity packed her bag last week and
set it beside the door. It contains her slippers and dressing gown plus
essential labor aids: her favorite stuffed animals, a selection of gummi
candy and chocolate bars, a magnum of Pepsi, and a sleeve of tennis
balls in case of back labor.

Shae is disgruntled. "Do you know how hard it is to turn a plow
around?"

Serenity responds with equal disgruntling: "Do you know how
hard it is to birth a baby?"

By the time we are ushered into a birthing suite, Serenity's contractions have stopped. I sit in a chair in the corner. The chair is slippery
and ergonomically designed to prevent comfort. My back is killing
me. Maybe I could ask for a little gas or something. The nurse sets up

a monitor and an IV stand as Janice listens for the baby's heartbeat. The room grows quiet as everyone focuses on the stethoscope pressing into Serenity's bump. Janice listens for a long time and, finally, says, "The heartbeat is normal. I'd like to check your cervix now."

Oh god, poor Serenity, that's the absolute worst part. I remember the doctor checking my cervix once during a particularly nasty contraction with Jack. The doctor looked like a pirate and his big hairy hand was wider than a plank. He used forceps to jam his fist up there. Then it felt like his fingers turned into five big hooks that ripped straight through my cervix. He tore me open more going in than Jack did coming out.

Janice stops poking around and says, "Your water sac is still intact. It's probably false labor. Possibly early labor. You might as well go home and rest. It could be days, even weeks, before your baby comes."

I try to rise but my back is so crippled I can't stand up straight. I bend over while holding tightly to the arms of my chair. Serenity flings aside her hospital gown and pulls her clothes back on. Together with Shae, the two take my arms and support me over to the ER so I can see a doctor. The nurse shoots me a mean look when she sees my hugely pregnant daughter helping to lower me into a wheelchair.

An x-ray and three prescriptions later, we are back in the plow, heading home. The doctor says I've pulled a few muscles; I should rest for a couple of days. Streaks of dawn light up the snow in the driveway as Shae drops us off. The power is back on. In the living room, Wendy is sprawled on the couch, asleep, and Jack and Olympia are owl-eyed in front of the TV. Bibienne helps me upstairs and I crawl into bed.

CHAPTER 29

Zone of Fire

*Zone of Fire: An area into which a designated ground unit or fire sup-
port ship delivers, or is prepared to deliver, fire support.*—Department of
Defense Dictionary of Military and Associated Terms

By mid-morning I can barely lift my head, let alone my torso. Even
frowning causes pain to ripple up and down my spine. Lying in bed
motionless, eyeballs straight and unmoving, is the only way to keep
the pain in check.

George keeps me company for a while but eventually he begins to
whine and prance back and forth in his I'm Going Straight Downstairs
to Pee on the Good Carpet If You Ignore Me dance. Finally he gives up
and heads for the stairs. I shout after him, "Jack? Olympia? Anyone?
Someone please let George out." The yelling tortures my back.

Serenity comes up to see what all the racket is about. She says
she checked her own cervix first thing this morning. "Janice was
wrong. I'm at least four centimeters and halfway effaced," she says
with an indignant lilt in her voice. Then she waddles back down to
the kitchen to make me lunch: mini-marshmallow and peanut butter
sandwiches. They taste so super-scrumptious, I think for a horrified
moment I might be pregnant.

Then I remember: it's impossible to conceive if you haven't had
any sex in what is beginning to feel like forever.

Dozing off and watching daytime television is driving me to distraction. I toss the remote aside and tilt my head back to stare at the ceiling. I'd happily trade in my wrenched spine for a week of Johnny Rotten days. Wendy opened up the store this morning while Shae and Serenity are minding Jack and Olympia. The kids have it all under control.

They have it all under control and they don't need me.

I have nothing to do but lie here with my thoughts.

I've ruined everything. Michael is gone and Donald is gone. My marriage is over. I've ruined everything.

Donald is gone. My eyes burn.

Dad's voice comes into my head: *A good soldier displays tenacity and mental toughness in stressful situations.*

I can't do this anymore. I let the tears roll. "Dad, I'm sorry. I've made a mess of everything."

I see Dad, in his full dress uniform, sitting at the end of my bed. His face is gentle. *It's true you're down but you aren't beaten, soldier. And I never said you can't cry. Soldiers do cry sometimes. It's good for the heart. My heart gave out but that's because I ate too much of your mother's good cooking. Go ahead, cry it out. That's an order.*

"Thanks, Dad."

You're welcome.

I reach for the tissue box. I'm going to need all of them. "I miss you, Daddy."

I miss you too, Kitten. When you're done with all your snuffling, you know it's time for you to clean up your act. You can start with the Caddy. Get it back on the road. After you change the oil, don't forget to buff up the chrome and scrub the whitewalls.

I lift my hand to my forehead in a salute: I promise.

CHAPTER 30

Special Cargo

Special Cargo: Cargo that requires special handling or protection, such as pyrotechnics, detonators, watches, and precision instruments.—Department of Defense Dictionary of Military and Associated Terms

Two days go by in a haze of muscle relaxers and codeine, and I'm finally able to walk without clinging to the walls and furniture.

I put the kettle on and start wiping counters and loading the dishwasher. I'm sitting at the kitchen table in my dressing gown waiting for the kettle to boil. There's a tapping at the door. It opens and in comes Donald. Just like that.

"Hi."

"Hi."

I stand up and gesture at my dressing gown. "I didn't know you were coming."

Donald has a look of concern on his face. "Serenity told me you hurt your back. Are you okay?"

"Yeah. It's much better now." I run my hand through my hair, still damp from the shower. The kettle starts whistling. "I'm making tea. Want some?"

Donald shakes his head and sits at the table.

I unplug the kettle and pour water into my mug.

"I turned down Calgary."

"You did?"

"I told them I want the directorship here. Or forget it."

"And?"

"I have to meet with the CEO this afternoon. We'll see." Donald shrugs. "So, anyway, I've been thinking."

"About?"

"About us. You and me. Our relationship."

Holy smokes. Donald said the word relationship. Without mumbling or prompting or careful steering from a couple's counselor. He has my attention now. "Our relashunship?" Now I'm the one mumbling.

"I guess it wasn't much of a relationship, was it?"

I shake my head. "No. It wasn't. Not lately anyway. Definitely more shun than ship."

I stir the teabag around in my mug with a spoon. We both watch the tea seep into the water. "Well, Donald. What do you want to do?"

Donald leans forward in his chair. "I miss us. I miss you. And I love you."

I am speechless.

"Calgary was nothing to me without you there. I wasn't being fair. I know that now. I made some huge mistakes. I am sorry. Maybe it's too late for us but I'm more than willing to try, if you are."

"You got my text messages?"

"Yes. I got them. But I already knew. Serenity told me some guy was coming over here. And I opened your suitcase. At that point I almost called a lawyer." Donald's face changes to a look of incredulousness. "What the hell was all that crap?"

"What the hell was all that crap with Lindsay?"

Donald stares at the table for a minute and then looks me directly in the eye. "I was an idiot. It's over."

"Since when?"

"Since the day I got on the plane to Calgary. That's the day I realized you were the most important person to me in the world, and that I had screwed everything up."

I sit and try to digest Donald's candor. At last. Even though I knew the truth about Lindsay, the words sear. My chest is roiling and sore and some monstrous thing inside is threatening to engulf me. I don't know whether to scream at him, throw my mug at his head, or simply accept that we've both been idiots. And try to mop up our mess. Why make a bigger mess? I take a gulp of hot tea, and then one gulp of air after another until my breathing slows down again. I think I will hold on to my mug, and hold on to Donald too. "We're going to have to talk. We have to come clean with each other. It won't be easy," I say.

"I know. Maybe we could get a counselor?"

Donald lays his forearms flat on the table and dunks his head down so he can peer up into my eyes. "Do you want to start over? Do you want me to come home?"

And now I really have to finally decide.

And it takes about half a second: "Yes. Come home."

By the time Donald returns from his meeting, Shae, Serenity, and I have slam-shifted through every sticky gear in the house and brought the place from a full reverse into a nice throaty hum. We cleaned the bathrooms, folded towels, changed all the beds and passed the vacuum. Not because Donald is home, but because Serenity is nesting. It's too bad this useful urge never kicked in before today but it's better than nothing. Shae and I are afraid she'll overdo so we raced around behind her, picking up baskets of laundry and making her sit down for a break every half hour.

We're chopping the garlic, onions and carrots for stew when Donald comes home. Olympia and Jack leap on him and then he tells them his news: "I got the promotion."

All through dinner, Donald keeps giving me his Scot's taber toss face. I know what he's thinking. I'm thinking about a taber toss too, and we work in tight accord to hustle Jack and Olympia to bed. He reads them one last story while I slip into the bathroom to brush my teeth. Forgotten on the floor are two sets of wet towels, Jack's and Olympia's. I scoop them up and run downstairs to add them to the last load in the washing machine. For once, I'm all caught up with the laundry and, with the whole house all shiny and ship-shape, I'm determined to try to stay caught up. As I pass through the living room, I straighten all the couch cushions and deliver Jack's library book to his backpack. Which leads to looking over his daily report. Wow. *Jack had a very good day* is written across the top of his behavior sheet. Then I check Olympia's backpack, which also lacks alarming notes. I wash out their lunchboxes and set them in the sink to drain. As I wipe a puddle from the counter, the phone rings. It's Mom: "So Donald is home again, how nice."

"What? How the ...? What color is the dishcloth I'm holding?"

By the time I get back upstairs, Donald is freshly showered and shaved and wearing his favorite bathrobe. I can smell aftershave. He winks at me and whistles into the bedroom. I sashay in after him, close the door, and pull the curtains across both windows, tightly. Donald reaches for me but as he does, I spy his wet towel lying on the carpet in front of the closet door.

"Wait a sec," I deke away from him and, snatching up the towel, I wave it in front of his nose. "Remind me again why I love you?"

"I've got that big fat director's bank account now, remember, Dollface?"

He flips the towel aside and grabs me, all masterfully, scooping his arms under me to throw me down, but in a gentle way, onto the bed. He leans in to kiss me and I puff up my lips in anticipation. This action is immediately interrupted by a loud rapping on the door, followed by Shae yelling, "It's time. Her water broke. See you at the hospital."

As Donald and I step through the double doors of the birthing wing, we can already hear Serenity: she's somehow yelling and swearing and moaning all at once. We hurry down the hall and three tennis balls come rolling and bouncing out through an open door. "Keep those stupid fucking balls away from me," she screams and through the door I can see Serenity pacing up and down the room. Between tears and gasps of breath she says, "Shae, my ass hurts. A lot. Call the anesthetist now. I need drugs. I need drugs."

Janice is waving a blood pressure cuff. "Serenity, listen to me. You have to calm down. I need to check your vitals first before we can give you anything."

"No!"

Serenity stops pacing, bends over, clutches her knees and bawls: "Here comes another one. Fuuuuck ...."

Shae reaches out to rub her back. Serenity screams, "Don't touch me."

Janice slips up beside Serenity and deftly wraps the cuff around her arm while donning her stethoscope. A nurse is adjusting the dials on a heart monitor machine; she has an IV pole and a tray of scissors and syringes and she looks like she means business. As soon as the contraction ends, while Serenity is still huffing, they hustle her over to the bed and get her to sit. She looks up, sees me and tries to get up. "Mom!"

"Hey, baby. I'm here."

The business-like nurse glares at us, holds up her hand and says, "Are you family?"

"That's my daughter."

"Then you better go find the change rooms and get gowned up."

By the time I get back in the room, I find Serenity leaning over the back of a chair, chewing on Shae's arm. Janice studies the screen of a handheld Doppler, which she's pressing into the side of Serenity's bump. As the contraction ends, Serenity pants for breath. "I want an epidural now," she shrieks, wild-eyed.

From the look of Shae's arm, covered in bite marks, I can tell she's in almost as much pain and may need an epidural too.

Janice looks up from the Doppler screen, smiles at me and says, "She's almost fully dilated. Baby is doing fine."

Within a minute or two, Serenity howls and bends over again. I can tell she's having a huge contraction by the way she's bearing down on Shae's arm and Shae's eyes are bulging out.

I time the contraction on my watch. It lasts almost two minutes. When it ends, Serenity clings to Shae and closes her eyes. She's swaying with exhaustion but refuses to sit or lie down. Shae holds her upright. I find a damp washcloth and dab gently at her forehead. Her hair is damp with sweat. Soon her face contorts again and she begins to moan, this time in a deep growl of pain. She hangs onto Shae's neck and lets Jude rub her back this time. Jude is careful to keep his limbs away from Serenity's teeth.

Janice crouches between Serenity's legs and, with two gloved hands, reaches up to massage Serenity's perineum.

"Those huge contractions are doing the job. Your baby's head is almost down," she says straightening up as the contraction ends. "Are you feeling an urge to push yet?"

Serenity keeps her eyes closed and shakes her head. Janice reaches into her bag and pulls out a small three-legged stool saying, "This is a birthing stool. Do you want to try it?"

Serenity opens her eyes and shouts, "No! Get that thing away from me. I don't need it. I'm going home now." She throws off the hospital gown and turns toward a chair where she has piled her clothes. Shae picks the gown up from the floor and says, "You can't go now, the baby is coming."

"I don't want to have a baby. I want to go to sleep." At this she takes a step toward the bed and then stops, a look of sheer confusion upon her face. She looks at me and opens her mouth to say something but then goes ooohhhhhhh and sinks into a deep squat. Janice snatches up the birthing chair and shoves it under her while Shae slides in close to support her from behind. Within seconds, Janice is masked, gloved, and kneeling, her head bent way down to see, her cheek grazing the floor. She continues massaging the perineum and coaching: "You can push now, but go easy Serenity. Just think, out like butter, that's it, beautiful, you're doing great."

I race from the room, down to the lounge where Donald is waiting with Jack and Olympia, watching TV: "If you guys want to see the baby being born, you better come now."

Jack and Olympia come running, slipping masks over their mouths. They both have cans of root beer in their hands. They perch on the edge of the window-sill and look on like they're watching an action-adventure movie. Without taking their eyes off Serenity, they occasionally push the masks up to sip from their cans of pop. All they need is a bowl of popcorn.

I'm holding my breath with each push. Serenity's face is screwed up into a tight ball of concentrated pain and power.

Donald catches my hand and squeezes it. I squeeze back.

We can see the baby's head bulging, wet and urgent, and Serenity gives one more primitive groan, and in one long push out comes a chubby peach with vigorously waving arms and legs. Everyone pretends not to see the girly bits and holds their breath as Janice holds the baby up for Serenity to see. "It's a girl," Serenity announces. "See, I knew it all along."

And then the chubby peach opens its tiny mouth and lets out an indignant squawk. I know what she's saying. She's saying: "Hey ya, you don't know nothing, nohow, anymore, know what I'm sayin', Mommycakes? Now go buy me a pink pony."

CHAPTER 31

Return to Base

Return to Base: An order to proceed to the point indicated by the displayed information or by verbal communication.—Department of Defense Dictionary of Military and Associated Terms

At dawn, I wake to the sound of a baby crying. For a moment I am disoriented but then I remember. Summer is only one week old and the whole household parades around under her command already. Slipping on my robe, I make my way down the hall to Serenity's bedroom and knock on the door.

Entering, I find Shae and Serenity facing each other cross-legged on the bed, Summer lying between them, red-faced, kicking her legs and howling.

"Mom, she's been up nursing, like, every hour, all night long. Now she won't go to sleep. We've changed her and held her and burped her and everything but she won't settle down. Do you think there's something wrong?"

"No. She's fine. Why not let me take her for a while? You two get some sleep."

They hand her over gratefully and, as I slip out of the room, I see the two of them slide deep under the covers and swiftly wriggle into spoon formation. I'll miss them when they move to their apartment next month.

I carry Summer downstairs. She continues screaming as I pace around the living room patting her back and murmuring to her. She squirms and writhes and finally, when I'm beginning to wonder if there's actually something wrong with her, she lets out a healthy belch and immediately settles into a quieter pattern of fussing and wriggling.

At last, Summer relaxes into my shoulder but I don't want to take her back upstairs quite yet and disturb Shae and Serenity. I can smell coffee brewing so I carry her into the kitchen where I find Donald sitting at the table reading the newspaper. Like he'd never left.

Donald looks up as I enter. "I know what's the matter with George's paw."

"Really?"

"Look at the way he's lying."

George is settled in his favorite place beside the back door, one paw tucked neatly underneath him and the other sticking straight out.

"George, come here." George gets up and slowly, painfully, limps over to Donald.

He sits and holds out his sore paw and Donald rubs it for a few minutes. George looks at Donald and then at me. Donald continues to massage his paw while George thumps his tail happily on the floor. Then, Donald tosses a scrap of toast from his plate to the other side of the kitchen, and George leaps after it, nimbly and happily, without a trace of a limp.

"See? When he lies on his paw like that, he puts it to sleep."

Unbelievable.

"Plus, I saw him hanging around under the bird feeder this morning eating bird seed. The blue jays dump out all the little stuff trying to get to the sunflower seeds. That explains the grainy bits."

"George is eating bird seed?" I shake my head and stare out at the seed-spattered snow under the feeder and a solid scattering of paw prints. "How come I never noticed him doing this?"

"You've been too busy, I guess. Want some coffee?"

I sit at the kitchen table as Donald fills my favorite mug and adds the exact right amount of milk and sugar.

Then, setting the mug on the table in front of me, he lifts Summer from my arms gently, expertly even, and I can see he's remembering back when he used to perform this delicate transfer maneuver with Jack and Olympia. Summer's eyelids flutter briefly as she burps another small burp. A little milky drool escapes from the side of her tiny lips, and is absorbed into the folds of Donald's shirt. She sighs contentedly, her buttery form nestled warm and protected in the crook of Donald's arm.

Donald smiles down at her. After a moment his tender gaze passes from Summer's face to mine. He peers into my eyes as if he's seeing them for the first time in a long time, and I fasten my eyes to his. It has been a long time. I want to live in this beautiful moment forever. "She looks just like you," he tells me, "when she burps like that."

ABOUT
THE AUTHOR

COLLETTE YVONNE is a writer, community volunteer, yoga teacher, and freelance journalist. Since graduating with honors from York University's Creative Writing Program, her short stories, blog posts, reviews, articles, and interviews have appeared in numerous publications ranging from fictional anthologies to articles in national newspapers. Her words have also been pro- duced on stage and in film. Collette lives in Ontario where she is working on perfecting her downward dog and corpse pose, and writing her next book.

Collette maintains her blog at www.colletteyvonne.ca

ACKNOWLEDGEMENTS

Many many thanks...

... To my wonderful agent, Stephany Evans, for her incredible insight, guidance, and perseverance, I am forever grateful. Thanks, also, belong to Robert Astle and Astor+Blue for taking a chance on me. Thanks to editor Jillian Ports for her excellent skills and sharp eyes. To writing group friends Joy Barber, Ellen Case, Maria Cioni, Debi Goodwin, Janet Looker, Ffion Llwd-Jones, Netta Rondinelli, Maria Coletta McLean, Bryna Wasserman, Jamie Zeppa: your critical input has been invaluable. Maria CM: you endlessly kept my spirits up and constantly reminded me where my place was—in the chair, writing. To Evangeline Moffat, who made an early draft of the manuscript much better which is exactly what a good editor is supposed to do. To writing teachers: Bruce Powe who once upon a time said I could write, I've dined out on that comment for years, and to Sarah Sheard, Elisabeth Harvor, Don Coles and Susan Swan whose wonderful writing classes gave me many critical tools to think and practice the craft. To Ottawa scribes: Agnes Cadieux, Kelly Lalonde, Jeff Secker and Caroline Wissing, thanks for making Ottawa rock for me. To the members of the Writers Community of Durham Region (WCDR) and Brian Baker, Karen Cole, Kevin Craig, Sherry Hinman, Barbara Hunt, Myrna Marcelline, Susan Statham and Heather Tucker of Works in Progress Group (WIP) for being such an incredible resource of motivation and community, and to friend Shirley Tye: thanks for knocking on my doors so many moons ago. To John Butcher, James Dewar, Frances Horibe, Jessica Outram, and Sue Lynn Reynolds: thanks for your invaluable help shaping my stories over our many wonderful summer writing retreats. To Shelley Macbeth and the staff of the best independent bookstore on the planet, Blue Heron Books of Uxbridge, for fervently supporting local writers. To Chuck Cross, another fellow traveler, who sent me poems and clippings and talked shop with me. To solid gold friends: Lucy Bondarenko for saying she will wait to read the manuscript when it is published and not before, Catherine McNeill for having a "Collette File," Jane MacIntosh who always had a encouraging word at every turn, and Linda Zernask who listened and listened and listened. To friends Deb Boyd, Ann Budway, Sherry Craighead, Loretta Harrison, Leslie Kerrivan, Helen Litt, Vera Lohse, Deborah Seager, and Mary Vincent: Thanks for wanting to know what I was writing and applauding every publishing credit along the way. Every woman needs a true blue circle like you. Special thanks go to Irene Greer for her sharp editorial eye and to Debbie Myers: Thank you for opening your cottage to us and for laughing till the tears ran down your cheeks. You have no idea how this has sustained me. To Betty Jo Hakanson who said, at a critical point in this venture, "Own the thought that you deserve to be heard." So many others helped along the way, I would be remiss not to mention Lisa Argue, Natalie Bondarenko, Brandy Ford, Cindy Revell, and Teresa Willison for their help at critical times. To my sister, Teresa Hannigan, who is quite simply the wind beneath my wings. To my parents, Paul and Sheila Argue, for simply everything. To my aunt, Donna Procher, for the guitar and all the great art supplies when I was a kid—you knew how much these things matter. To my wonderful husband, Peter McKeracher: You never once stopped believing. And to my children: Liam, Colleen, and Alex, you keep me in the real world and show me every day what love is.